W9-AYP-676

The
Snitch

Also by Robert Leuci

Fence Jumpers
Double Edge
Captain Butterfly
Odessa Beach
Doyle's Disciples

The Snitch

Robert Leuci

St. Martin's Press
New York

A THOMAS DUNNE BOOK.
An imprint of St. Martin's Press.

Design by Bryanna Millis

Library of Congress Cataloging-in-Publication Data

Leuci, Robert.
    The snitch/Robert Leuci.—1st ed.
        p.   cm.
    "A Thomas Dunne book."
    ISBN 0-312-14739-2
    I. Title.
    PS3562.E857S65 1997
    813'.54—dc20   96-34917
                                                                CIP

First Edition: March 1997

10   9   8   7   6   5   4   3   2   1

For the long-suffering Cuban people

Ballad of the Cid,
Author Unknown

He found before him
A beautiful Mooress,
Skilled at shooting
Arrows from a quiver
With a Turkish bow;
Star was what they called her
Because of her excellence
At striking with the javelin.

Acknowledgments

Help came from many directions in the writing of *The Snitch*. The wit and conversation from my Rhode Island neighbors, especially the fishermen of Galilee and Point Judith. I am particularly grateful to Captain Donny Matera of the *Hawk*, who opened my eyes to the pure joys and excitement of shark and tuna fishing; to my daughter-in-law Myra Malave Leuci for her help with Spanish phrases; to my overworked editor Ruth Cavin, who clears the muddy waters; to Nora Cavin for her tough, consummate professionalism; and for the continuing support of the inimitable Esther Newberg and the encouragement and patience of Linda Barban. Thanks to you all.

New York City
April 1979

Chapter 1

Nick Manaris was pouring coffee when the pack of them came into the office. He turned away, seeing the afternoon and night, and the couple days ahead turn to madhouse time, no time to relax, all the peacefulness of his life gone. Thoughts of the upcoming thirty-six, forty-eight hours froze his heart, but it had already been a bad day, hard on his chest all around, starting with watching Renata pack last night, with her standing in the bedroom putting her Victoria's Secrets in the suitcase, staring at him, a chunk of polar ice, trying to tell him something about her college reunion, her talking a whole lot without saying much, then on to this morning driving her to that damn nut factory, JFK Airport, with traffic backed up for fucking miles, waiting for two hours until her plane took off. Then Captain Hawks this afternoon telling him the hit could go down real soon and that he was needed and he'd have to hang loose, and now the crew coming in carrying on at decibels for the deaf, yakking and laughing, making fools of themselves, Sonny McCabe looking at Nick like what are you doing standing over there by yourself?

Nick turned away, thinking, Of all the teams I could have hooked up with. Wanting to throw on his jacket and bug out of there, feeling like he was lost, his compass gone, his chest tightening like it was wrapped in baling wire. "C'mon! C'mon!" Sonny called out. "Will you move your ass."

"I'm coming, calm down. What's the hurry?" At that moment Nick Manaris's discomfort knew no bounds.

Nick would be thirty-six in the fall, a first-grade detective assigned to the Organized Crime Control Unit. He was number two on the sergeant's list and about as ready for the next lieutenant's test as anyone could be. A man on the rise in a job he no longer loved—a job, if the truth be known, he was beginning to hate. On this day he felt as resigned to his private unhappiness as he was to the city's never-ending cycle of violence and evil and corruption. He'd had it all right, up to here.

Coming up, when Nick had determined the path of his life, he considered the fact that there was nothing worse than to live in an unbroken cycle where yesterday and tomorrow are identical to today. The prison of it. No more to learn than what you already know. To know that next year will be no different than this and tomorrow a reflection of today was a kind of tormented life that he wanted no part of. Police work offered something else, a whole lot else. Next year he would have ten years in the job. He had ten more to do and the second ten, they say, go like a shot. Remembering this, he felt a little better. Imagining himself years down the road. He saw himself at the helm of a charter fishing boat, sailing the Atlantic, fishing for shark, tuna, and marlin. Living a life quiet and alone, with a salty cottage on a bay that opened to the ocean.

Right now, though, there was this off-the-wall group he was teamed with. Big-time arrest guys, to be sure, but wackos nonetheless. A proud, sacrificing, hardworking group, but as close as you can get to outlaws themselves.

"Yo, Nick," Carl Suarez called out, "get on the stick, willya? We're having a meeting here."

Sonny McCabe and the rest of the team, there were three of them, walked through the office, strutted past the field detectives' cubicles into the captain's conference room, Nick following them. Captain Hawks stood at the conference room door, gesturing for him to hurry, nervously throwing him a high five.

Nick entered the conference room, hoping the hit that McCabe and his team were planning would fall through. He wasn't up for breaking down doors, rolling around with a bunch of bad guys.

Nick's earliest sense of himself was as a separated figure: there in the front was the world, off on the horizon as far off as you can get was he. Of average height and muscular, Nick was about twelve when his father started working him out with push-ups and sit-ups and banging the heavy bag. The habit stayed, grew to pure enjoyment. His round open face was not bad looking, even with his flat broken nose that ran a little in the cold. He had a different look that seemed to combine strength, concern, and more than a bit of slyness. Nick Manaris could not be intimidated. He was as smart as anyone, brighter than most, the son of an ex–pro fighter, and a guy who had six professional fights of his own to boot. People were not lining up to take him on head to head.

Captain Hawks sat at the head of the table, chin up, arms folded across his chest, intense, a case jacket lying open in front of him. Nick felt a sharp twinge of anxiety, this Hawks was a hummer. A flushed, middle-aged, silver-haired, slippery piece of work, he oozed trouble. The captain drove a late-model Thunderbird, wore expensive suits, and talked out of the side of his mouth like a hoodlum. The day Nick met the captain he pinned the guy bad news. He glanced at Hawks again, sighed, and asked himself, what gives you the right to judge?

Nick flashed on the first day he was assigned to the office. He'd left after a two-hour interview with Hawks, the sickening intuition that the man was a money guy, no two ways about it, eating at him. Ten years in the department, he could nail the breed in a heartbeat. A beguiling charm, and the moral convictions of a hit man. Nick couldn't figure it. Since he'd been on the job people dropped out of the sky just to make him nuts. Maybe it's me, he thought, maybe I just don't get the message, whatever the goddamn message is.

No one on the team acknowledged Nick when he came in. They sat silently, apparently lost in concentration, listening to Sonny McCabe, who was at that moment doing his song and dance. Nick studied McCabe for a second. Then he put his elbow on the table and rested his cheek in the palm of his hand. He watched Sonny McCabe talk, listening but not hearing the team's other first-grade detective bullshit. McCabe talked about this case of his like it was the French Connection, when it seemed to Nick that what McCabe really had was a bunch of half-assed Cubans and South Americans trying to connect with a crew of Mafia wanna-bes out of Brooklyn. That's all McCabe had, nothing more than that.

After a minute or two, Nick figured that maybe there was a chance in a hundred he might be wrong, maybe this team did have something here. He leaned back in his chair, convince-me style. Either way he had a bad feeling about this case, this crew, he felt like a missionary in the Amazon forest.

McCabe had their attention, everyone in the room listening as the king of bullshit bullshat. McCabe went to the blackboard and drew a flow chart, Cubans and Colombians on one side, Italians on the other, the guy doing a good job of thinking and talking on his feet. Captain Hawks saying the DA, Assistant DA Robinson was doing cartwheels over this one, expecting big things here.

Nick watched McCabe thinking, thinking, finally saying, "What does the snitch say?"

Eddie Moran, a second-grade detective and McCabe's steady partner, sat opposite Nick, rolling a cup of coffee between his palms. He said slow and easy, "Sonny's going to run him down later today."

Moran was a big balding man into wearing ten-gallon hats and cowboy boots made of some reptile's skin, jeans, a belt with a huge polished silver buckle. Moran had never been further west than Pennsylvania and looked about as country as Johnny Cash.

"The last thing the snitch told me," Sonny said, "was that the guns are on their way. Should arrive in the city tonight, tomorrow at the latest."

Captain Hawks got up from the table, went to the coffee machine and poured himself a cup, sat back down, drank half the coffee, and said, "I wanted you on this case, Nick, because, well, you know. Nothing personal, you're a good investigator and all—I mean Christ, you're a first-grader, you should be—nothing personal, but I wanted you here because of your relationship with Robinson. You and the DA been buddies for years, right? Now that's no insult, my friend, that's the truth."

Nick flipped his pen onto his pad.

Andre Robinson, Nick's Fordham law professor, was now an assistant district attorney in Queens County. Andre was deep into politics, on his way to becoming DA and one of Nick's few close friends. The man had a ton of drag with the department, connections that lined up to do him favors, all of them figuring that the dapper, handsome, black, slick piece of work could one day be mayor.

"We need you to help nail down a few warrants," Sonny said.

The captain's comment was pretty honest and Nick was not one to downplay honesty, since there was so little of it in the department these days. Nick nodded to himself, feeling vaguely humiliated.

"Andre Robinson," he said, "is a good guy. He's not going to put up with any crap. Either we have something here or we don't. It seems to me that we got plenty. So what's the problem?"

Everyone was watching him, heads bobbing in courteous confirmation. Before him sat Captain Hawks, McCabe stood at the blackboard, his partner Moran and the translators, Monserette and Suarez, sat directly across from Nick. An eager group, and in his mind Nick decided to call them Jesse James and his Four Desperados.

Hawks had put this team together at the request of McCabe and the members had all been handpicked by the first-grader. Why they had tapped him to work this case Nick had not been able to figure. At least not until this moment. His friendship with the DA, that was it. Hawks trying to maneuver him into a position to ask Andre for a favor. Quintessential slick cop bullshit and totally predictable.

Captain Hawks, McCabe, and the others sitting around the table gave Nick a case of the chokes.

"Anyway," the captain said, "considering your friendship and all, I figured we'd get a little more from the DA. I mean he'd give us a little room to operate here."

Nick looked at the captain. "What did you think the man was going to do for us?" *The man—Christ, listen to me.*

Hawks made a backhand waving gesture. "Give us the warrants that we need, that's all. We'll do the rest."

"You got the snitch, you got the bug at Los Campos, and you got observations. We shouldn't have any problem getting whatever warrants we need," Nick said.

"I'm trying to quit smoking," the captain said. "Anyone got a smoke?"

Nick said, "So who gets lucky? Who do we want warrants for?"

"Benny Matos, the Colombian guy Medina, and Tony Bellatesta," Sonny McCabe said, cocking his head, giving Nick a smile as if he could read his mind. "What we need are search warrants for Los Campos. The club itself, the office, and the basement. And another for Matos's house and car. We grab hold of the snitch later today, see what else he's got for us."

"Sounds good to me. I mean, if your guy lays it out, shouldn't be any puzzle."

"You're new here. A new man. I don't expect that you'll understand the headaches we've had with your buddy. Robinson's a pain in the ass. Let me tell ya, I've worked with the man, he's a regular ballbreaker," McCabe said.

"He's a DA," Nick said. "What do you expect from a DA? It's his job to be a ballbreaker."

Captain Hawks puffed out some air and rubbed the back of his neck.

"Look," Nick said, "I'm here, what, two months? I came on board this case three weeks ago. I'm along for the ride, there's something you want me to do, tell me, I'll do it." The frustration of his day seeping into his voice.

"See, see, we do have a problem. I'll tell ya the dilemma, you ready to hear the dilemma?" McCabe said.

There flowed from Sonny McCabe the kind of cold-blooded toughness that had everything to do with presence.

A week ago Friday this guy Cellini from narco told Nick that McCabe was a mercenary, had no use for anyone that wasn't a cop. Unless they were gangsters laying envelopes stuffed fat with cash into his hand. Nick figured it was something Cellini would know.

Nick and Sonny were both first-graders and Nick had heard the rumors, the stories about Sonny McCabe. Like he was the most corrupt cop who ever breathed. His affair, his life. This corrupt-cop business was a touchy subject for Nick. Years ago he'd thrown in the idealistic towel. Looking at McCabe standing there smartass and smiling gave Nick an unpleasant feeling of vertigo. What do I know, what don't I know? People do what they do and who am I to judge? McCabe staring at him and Nick could feel him thinking and wanted to shut him off, to shut off his own thinking too. These thoughts bringing him to a place he didn't want to be.

To Nick nothing symbolized Sonny McCabe's approach to the job more than the two dozen suits he owned. Silk, expensive, flashy. McCabe didn't fret a whole lot at what anyone thought, he was a well-connected first-grader from the old school. He knew his way around the police department like it was his college fraternity and he was the president. Like the story Nick had heard about how the chief of detectives had told one of his new inspectors, new to the detective division, at a medal day at headquarters, "You want to know about the Organized Crime Control Unit, ask McCabe, McCabe's your man."

Sonny was pushing forty, though he looked a lot younger, the guy still banging down doors and kicking ass. A big tough man in a job where there were a whole lot of big tough men. Even so, Sonny McCabe demanded and had the kind of celebrity that came to few cops. It was in the eyes, always in the eyes that said I don't give a shit, bring it on. He led the Saint Paddy's day parade, his chest covered with medals. Played the bagpipes too. Captain Hawks told Nick that it was as natural for Sonny McCabe to be a cop as it was for Sonny to breathe. Hawks loved the guy, would lick the soles of his feet. For years Sonny and his partner Eddie Moran were so close one couldn't floss his teeth without elbowing the other. McCabe and Moran, a latter-day version of Butch and Sundance.

Sergi Monserette said, "Nick, we need help getting the warrants, that's what we need. We need your help, buddy, that's what we're asking."

McCabe nodded and turned away, looking at the blackboard, an eraser sticking up out of his fist like a club.

"Why help?" Nick said.

"Robinson is a hardass," McCabe said, "as you well know. Tell you the truth, I don't think he likes white guys."

"Yeah?" Nick said. "What the hell am I?"

When Sonny did not answer, Captain Hawks said, "Anyway, we've had some problems with him before. He likes this case, don't get me wrong. He sees six o'clock news here."

McCabe shook his head. "He won't give me a warrant."

"C'mon," Nick said.

McCabe made a face and waved off any suggestion that he was exaggerating. "I don't want to get into the problems I've had with the man. I'm telling you Robinson won't give me a warrant."

"So how can I help you?" Nick said.

"Let me ask you," Captain Hawks said. "If you went to Robinson, applied for the warrants yourself. Said please and thank you, how would it go?"

"If I had what it takes, he'd give me the warrants. Look," Nick said,

"I don't get this, you have three other people here. If Andre don't want to deal with Sonny, for whatever reason, I don't really care why, but let's say that's true, that's a fact. You still have three other people here."

"We want you to apply," McCabe said. "Trust me on this, will ya? It'll be a whole lot easier, trust me here."

"Fine," Nick said. "It's fine with me. I'll get the warrants. What's the big deal?" He leaned back in his chair and folded his arms across his chest, nodding in agreement with himself.

Captain Hawks shrugged and threw Nick an apologetic smile. "You know, I knew you'd come through. I told them, I told them all. The other night, one night last week it was, anyway I'm down at Post Time, sucking down a few," Hawks said. "I'm sitting at the bar between these two guys from narcotics and your name came up. I didn't tell them we were working together; I wanted to hear what they thought."

"Did they say I was a screwup or what? I didn't get along too well there."

"Yeah!" Hawks said with a great laugh. "They said you didn't get along, but they liked you. Said you did your job. Look Nick, they said you were a tough piece of work and a stand-up guy. Just strange is all."

"Yeah?" Nick said. "What does that mean?"

"Strange? I don't know, how're you strange, Nick?"

"Not strange, forget strange. I'm not strange. Most of the people in this job are strange, not me."

"Hey," McCabe said, "you got to admit, Nick, you got some rep in this job. You know, anytime people talk to people about strange, your name comes up."

"Sonny, I don't give a shit about strange, never have. Stand-up guy— what does that mean? I'd like to know what you think that means."

"You're a weirdo, a bit of a whack job, but no rat," McCabe confided. "Like, you're almost one of the guys, you know. Almost. If you wanta know what almost means, don't ask me."

Everyone laughed, thought that was a hoot.

"Look," Nick said, "I'm going to tell you guys something. You ready? Okay, now listen to me, because I'm only going to say this once so pay attention."

Hawks shrugged and the others threw Nick sideways glances. The vibes in the room were more of interest than resentment.

Nick said, "I'm no sleeper here. I want you guys to understand just where I stand. If I hear something, I heard it. I see something, I saw it. You get my meaning?"

"Nick, Nick," Captain Hawks said. "I'm paying you a compliment, like those guys from narco were paying you a compliment. So you're a little strange, who isn't? But you're a stand-up guy. That's your rep, it's followed you everywhere in this job. Believe me when I tell you, you wouldn't be in this office if you hadn't been checked out. You're an oddball and you got some bizarre friends, but you'd go to the wall for another cop. That's good enough for me, and I'm the boss here."

Nick winced. "Look," he said. "I do my job. I've always done my job. I do a legit job and I won't be put in a jackpot for anybody. Now if you all can live with that, let's get on with this. Let's cut the crap and put some bad guys in jail."

There was a long silence. Finally McCabe said, "Listen, Nick, I'm saying and the captain's saying, we need you to apply for these warrants."

Nick was staring at his pen so hard that it blurred and became two. "I'm on this case three weeks," he said, speaking to everyone in the room. "I've made some observations, I've listened to the bug. I meet the snitch, hear him out, and I'll apply for the warrants. It's not like I haven't done it before."

"Um," Sonny said, his face twitching in an attempt to smile.

"I know how to get a warrant, for chrissake," Nick said. "Let's do it, set up a meet with the informant, I'll be there, get what I need and then we're off."

Captain Hawks sat up, took a pad and pen, did a little circle within a circle thing. "Explain it to him Sonny," he said. "Tell him about this snitch."

Sonny hesitated. "The thing is, Nick, the informant, he don't want to meet anyone. I mean he'll talk to me but—I mean this guy, I say, 'You have to talk to another detective,' and I think *he* thinks, like many of them do, that I'm bailing out on him, screwing him over or something, you know? I say, 'Meet this guy, he's a good guy, just like me.' He says, 'I ain't meeting with no one but you.' I say, 'C'mon don't be a jerk, just meet with the guy, talk to him and hear him out.' He says, 'I told you I'm meeting with no one but you, talking with no one but you, trusting no one but you, and that's that.' Then I explain, as best as I can explain to a numbnuts from another country, about the warrants and all, and I tell him it's complicated in America, but he has to understand the way we work here. And then he says, 'Fuck man, then we don't do it. I meet with you and only you.'"

Sonny McCabe spread his arms in defeat. "So that's our problem, you see what our problem is here. We got a headache with Robinson and the snitch too."

Carl Suarez, the second Spanish-speaking detective, trying to act cool and calm like an innocent bystander, said, "Maybe you can be there, you know, across the street in your car when Sonny meets the snitch. This way you know there is an informant and he's got this information, you know?"

Nick said, "Hold it a minute," and had Carl, who habitually wore a hooded sweatshirt and high-tops and granny sunglasses, even at night, and who thought it was not unusual for a detective to swear to a bunch of affidavits based on information from an informant he hadn't spoken to, explain it again.

"It's not like you'd be making up the informant out of thin air," Carl said. "C'mon man, he'll be there, you'll see him, Sonny will be talking to him. And, Nick, Sonny will be wearing a transmitter."

"I have to swear under oath that he told me, me directly," Nick said. "What're you nuts or what?"

Everyone in the room looked at him: Captain Hawks, Sonny Mc-Cabe, Moran his partner, the two Spanish-speaking detectives, like Nick didn't understand English.

"What I'm saying," Nick said, "how'm I supposed to swear to a goddamn search warrant affidavit if I don't speak to the informant? I won't do that, what do you think I am, a new kid in the neighborhood? I'm not going to swear to anything unless I speak to the man and hear it from his lips. You know, his lips to my ears."

McCabe said he'd make a call, see if he could change the snitch's mind. But he doubted it, thought it was a waste of time.

"Lemme get it straight," Nick said. "I sit in a car and listen when Sonny talks to the snitch. He gets the information, then I go to court and swear the guy told me directly? Captain, you go along with this?"

Basically, he could tell that Captain Hawks would go along with anything McCabe wanted. McCabe ran the show here, that was it, end of story.

"Look," Captain Hawks said, "this is no big deal."

Nick closed his eyes, resting his chin in his hand.

"Sure we'd be doing it a little on the sly here," Hawks said. "You'd have to take the stand and swear you heard this and that from the informant. And you would have, you'd have heard the whole story. You could answer any question, and it *won't be a lie. You would have heard it.* You can tell us no, no I won't do that, and jeopardize our whole case. It's up to you."

Nick sat up and laid his hands flat on the table. "Listen," he said. "Sonny, you set up the meet with the informant, convince him to talk to me. He talks to me I'll get the warrants. He nuts up, won't talk with me, case closed. I'm not going to commit perjury for this or any other case."

"For Christ's sake!" Sonny held his fists in the air, like a prize fighter. "Okay Nick, look. Let me call the snitch, okay? Okay!"

Nick said, "You got your fists clenched tough guy, what's with that?"

"We're brother cops here, and there are bad guys out there. You hear me? You listening?"

"I'm not deaf, maybe you think I'm dumb?"

"Look," Sonny said, "bad guys are trying to put their hands on a whole lot of guns. Big-ass guns, machine guns, all kinds of automatic weapons. Now, we see our job maybe a little different than you do. We see that we got to get those guns, get them off the streets and put a bunch of jerkoffs in the slammer."

McCabe stood there, fists still clenched. "We got to be together," he said. "We've got to be strong, stronger than the mutts. We play by the rules we lose, fuck the rules. Name of the game is squash the mutt."

"That's how you see it?" Nick said.

"That's the way it is," said Hawks.

Nick looked at Hawks. "I don't see it that way captain. Never have," he said.

"You are wrong," Sonny said.

There was silence around the table. Nick said, "Sonny, you make that call. Set the meet. This snitch will talk to me. I'll convince him to talk to me, that's what I do best, make people talk to me. Set it up and let's do it."

"I told you he won't."

"I hate to insist, Sonny."

McCabe said nothing.

Nick said, "I'm sorry but make the call, set up the meet."

"All right, all *right*, I'll try."

"You'll do it," Nick said. "And Sonny, open your hands. You stand like that, I got to think you're threatening me."

McCabe laughed, pink coming into his cheeks. "A tough guy, yeah I heard you're a tough guy."

"Call the snitch. You'd better tell me his name. You can tell me his name, right? I mean, I'll be swearing that this character is well known to me. At the very least I should know his name."

"Punto," McCabe said. "His name is Rodrigo Punto, one hell of a snitch, a hell of a stool and a dynamite guy." As if reading Nick's mind, McCabe said, "You know what they say, they say a detective is only as good as his snitch. That's what they say, and they're right."

There was silence again, a long moment of silence. Nick bent his head, drew a little box on his pad, looked up and said quietly, "I've known cops, all kinds of cops, and the cops I've known to get jammed

up, got jammed up and dragged off to jail because of their snitches. I
don't trust informants, none of them. And any cop that does needs to
get his head checked."

Sonny McCabe said, "Uh-huh. Okay, I'll make the call."

"Set it up, let's go and see just how good this Rodrigo Punto is.
Then I'll get you your warrants, how's that sound?" Nick said.

"Sounds good."

"This Rodrigo character is reliable, huh?"

"The best," Sonny said, and told Nick how he met Rodrigo, how the
guy was a cop in Havana, how he snagged him with a loaded .45, then
cut him loose when Rodrigo told him he'd rat out big-time bad guys.
How it was that Rodrigo hated these renegade creeps, bums who were
in the criminal life in Cuba and stayed in the life when they came to
the States. McCabe told him everything.

Nick shrugged, keeping whatever he felt about it to himself, thinking
it was a good story.

McCabe went to the conference room door, Nick's eyes on him,
telling Nick to sit tight a minute, saying to him, "Who knows, maybe
I'm wrong and Rodrigo will meet with you."

After about five minutes he came back, a big half-witted smile on
his face. "He'll meet us, eight o'clock, at Fisher's, it's a dairy joint on
the Lower East Side. He figures there won't be any Cubans, Italians,
or Colombians in some Jew dairy joint," McCabe said. "He made a
point of telling me, just me and you. Nobody else, just us two, that's
all he wants to see there."

See that, Nick thought, not at all surprised but not bothering to say
anything about it, seeing how happy McCabe and his crew were. What
he said was, "What are we doing for this guy, Rodrigo? What are we
paying him?"

"Nothing," McCabe said. "I told you the guy's a dynamite snitch
and I meant it."

"Sonny, you don't want to take me for a fool. Don't do that, it's
insulting." Meaning that there wasn't a snitch born that didn't hustle
something. Money, protection, credit for an outstanding case, vengeance. Something. Nick knew of no snitch, nowhere, no how, that did
his thing free of charge. It didn't get any kind of comment, just a silly-
ass grin from McCabe and a bunch of shrugs from the others.

Chapter 2

It wasn't that Diego Cienfuego was slim and taller than most of the Cubans, Dominicans, and Colombians in Jackson Heights. It wasn't that his hair was thick, the color of polished silver, and fell to his shoulder blades. It wasn't that he could play classical guitar, sing and dance flamenco as if he were a living, breathing spirit of Andalusia, a magnificent phantom that had stepped whole from ancient Alhambra. It wasn't that his teeth were pure white or that he had an elegance and a sort of grace rarely seen in New York City, forget Queens. It wasn't the way he talked to women, the way his striking sapphire eyes filled with emotion and genuine empathy and understanding when he spoke to them. More than anything it was the extraordinary, almost mystical connection he had with them. The way they made it perfectly clear that they wanted to ride him, each and every one he met. Irrational, illogical passion—that is what jammed him up, that is what destroyed Diego's life.

About eight weeks back, Diego and Natalia began to toss puckers at one another. For a talented guy, a bright guy it was a foolish move. Natalia was married to a jealous, dangerous man who had a reputation for violence, carried a gun, and hated Diego with a particular malevolence. Nevertheless, Diego had this problem with women that he had never been quite able to work out. It may have been that his damned feminine side was just a bit stronger than his masculine side for his own good. It may have been no more than that.

In any event, Diego Cienfuego had been diving in women's panties from the time he was twelve. And the women he'd known, all the women he'd known, treated him as though he were the man to end all men. They would touch him, poke him, follow him around. Skinny Carmen Melendez, the sister of Oscar, the bartender at Los Campos, she sent him the most lascivious note and a dozen roses. The woman was a grandmother, had eight grandchildren, for chrissake.

Diego Cienfuego came down the iron steps from the El at 108th Street and Roosevelt Avenue heading for the Hatuey, a tingling feeling between his legs. Thrill of thrills, maybe Natalia with her exquisite ass and marvelous breasts would be boiling milk behind the counter. And if God were kind maybe her husband, that big dumb mulatto bastard, Rodrigo, would be off somewhere folding his money.

The day after he arrived in New York from Miami, Diego walked into the restaurant and glanced at Natalia Punto, and she puckered those pouty scarlet lips of hers. A small quick pucker, no big thing, but a pucker nonetheless, a signal Diego took to mean I like you mister, I like you a lot.

That pucker pumped his Latin chest, and he jerked his chin at her and sent her a pucker of his own. They'd played their little game for two months now and it had not gone unnoticed by Rodrigo.

Lately when he saw her Diego hissed like he was calling a cat, and when he did Natalia would roll her shoulders, throw out that famous chest, and give him a pucker for the memory book.

Diego figured it would not be much of a problem to arrange something with Natalia. Rodrigo was hardly ever around, and clearly the lady had the itch. He could orchestrate an afternoon in one of the motels near the airport, the one with the mirrored ceiling and walls, the one with the double tub and phoney gold spigot. But Diego Cienfuego had never violated another man's wife and told himself he never would. He was the type of man that lived by rules he considered honorable. He simply loved to flirt, especially when the teasing entailed a little risk. And feigning love games with Rodrigo Punto's old lady put more than a little pepper in the play.

Diego's dead wife's first cousin, Benny Matos, told him, kept telling him, that Natalia's husband Rodrigo described Diego as a Stalinist fag. Said he was one of Fidel's butt boys, a *maricón* that should have stayed in Cuba. Benny admonished him to stay away from Natalia.

Afterward people would ask, pop-eyed with astonishment, why didn't Diego listen? Why did he not take Benny's warnings seriously?

Diego Cienfuego took very few things in this life seriously. People who knew him well described him as a space shot, a dreamer, a playful and fanciful man from another era, one that had never existed in Jackson Heights. The guy was a poet, as gentle as a lamb, a babe in the woods, meat on the streets of New York. True, all true, and another reason he would find himself in a shitstorm the likes of which you wouldn't believe.

So, on a cool, pleasant Friday afternoon in the spring of 1979 Diego strolled along Roosevelt Avenue, scanning the street and the El overhead. He walked along the avenue carrying his schoolbag like some student half his age, thinking about Natalia, about Rodrigo, the gentle breeze brushing his face. Two blocks off was the Hatuey, two blocks off was Natalia. He picked up his pace. He heard a train overhead boring out of the east, heading for the city like some gigantic enraged steel beast on a mission of vengeance.

Six months in America, three months in New York City, and the sounds of the place continued to unsettle him. There was much in this city that he liked, but plenty that he hated. The awful noise of steel on steel, for example. The howling police sirens, the whoopers and whistles of fire engines all hours of the day and night stunned him.

The train passed overhead and the store windows rattled, he could feel his legs tremble. Standing on the street, feeling the shaking of the passing train beneath his feet, he had a fleeting and sweet image of Palma Sorino, his home in Cuba. The serenity of the place, the pleasures he'd had there, the wife he buried in the rich soil. All that was part of his past, New York was now his world, he was in the city's grip, its immensity, its downright chaos of sound and smell and hordes of people, some of whom looked like they fell from another solar system. The strange young people that stank of violence and had the flat dead eyes of desperation. Among these people he would make his home.

Diego in the whirlwind, the thought made him smile.

He stood for a long time waiting for the sound of the train to fade, he stood looking to all the world like a man that had come to the end of something.

He walked past the Puerto Rican bodega and on to 111th Street. Afternoon shoppers in swarms crowded the narrow sidewalk; two young black policemen in their blue caps and tunics sat in a police car parked at the curb. One was talking to a red-faced young woman who was pointing to a group of teenagers who stood at the corner, their arms folded.

A big black Buick turned the corner, made a U-turn, and parked in front of the Hatuey. The car belonged to Diego's wife's fat cousin, Benny Matos. It was not a Cadillac or a Mercedes, but fancy enough, with its rolled leather seats and tinted windows. Diego figured that Benny could have owned any car he wanted, the man had no morals and boxes of money.

Benny Matos owned Los Campos, the finest Latin nightclub and restaurant in Queens. Diego was Benny's maître d'. Benny had offered him the job, for which he was well suited, when Diego arrived in New York. The club was in a long flat building on Corona Avenue. Diego worked there from six in the evening until closing, spending those hours seating patrons and entertaining stoned guests with his guitar.

The past Friday night, the club had remained open late for one of Benny's private dinner parties. Benny had been drinking and smoking a little reefer. Something had happened during Benny's meeting with two Colombian guys; Diego remembered the yelling and the pointing of fingers. One of the Colombians, a redhead in a straw fedora, started shouting at Benny, "You talk to much, you have a big mouth." Later that night Benny asked Diego if he knew what was going on with *ev-*

erything. Diego told him he did not know anything was going on. Benny smiled, saying that's good, that's fine, that's smart. Benny Matos whispered to him that it was not wise to have your friends and family fasten themselves to the idea that you're making too much money. Cubans, Benny said, were a jealous fucking people.

"Oh, yes," Diego had told him. "You're right."

Diego had no idea what in the hell Benny was talking about, the man sounding like he was warning him. What for? Diego was simply the maître d', he seated people and picked his guitar. He had no interest in the business of Benny's business. Diego did know that Benny was a bit of a buccaneer, buccaneer his word for gangster.

Benny intercepted Diego in front of the Italian bakery with the big red door on 110th Street.

"I'm glad I caught you," said Benny. "I've been driving around looking for you. Where the hell you been?"

"I got lost in Manhattan registering for school," Diego told him truthfully. "I told you last night that I was going to register at the college. I told you that."

Benny was one dapper guy, dressed head to toe in white. He was a Santero, had an altar in the basement of his house where he killed chickens and goats and left offerings for Ochun and Chango. Diego thought that Benny worshipped Satan.

"Aha, so you did? You registered?"

"Yes, for two courses. I'm going to learn English."

"Your English is fine. I understand you perfectly."

"I speak to you in Spanish."

Diego hardly ever spoke English in Jackson Heights; he knew very few people who did. He'd had several conversations with his German landlady, and those didn't go well at all. Ingrid did invite him to supper in her apartment. Ingrid was a woman with well-formed thighs and muscular legs. Thirtyish and plump. Not fat, nicely round. Sexy, with much hidden fire. Huge hazel eyes that were, Diego considered, receptive to hints.

"Whatever," Benny said. "Listen, I need you tonight. Oscar is sick or something, you'll have to tend the bar. Maybe you could bring your kid, have Justo give you a hand cleaning up. I'll pay him fifty dollars for the night. That's good huh? What the hell, if I can't pay my nephew fifty bucks to help me out, what kind of man am I anyway?"

"Sure," Diego said, "I'll ask him."

"Diego, he's your son. You don't ask him, you tell him. Be strong with your children, Diego. You are," Benny said, "the world's softest man. I don't know how you live with yourself."

Benny went to his Buick and opened the door, saying, "I knew that if I passed by the Hatuey, I would find you here. I told you to stay away from this place. From that woman."

"I'm going for a coffee."

Benny looked at him, amused. "You know," he said, "Rodrigo was a cop in Havana for Batista. He's a no-good bastard." There was something burbly and loose in his voice, a slightly hysterical sound, as if he were frightened. "We know that he has friends here with the police," Benny said. "The son of a bitch could kill you and get away with it."

"I like the coffee here," Diego told him.

"Friends," Benny said, "Rodrigo Punto has friends with the police."

Diego couldn't think of an argument for that. He waved a half-hearted good-bye.

"Rodrigo Punto," Benny said finally as he got into the car, "is a *bedejo*. The man is touched by evil spirits."

Diego knew that Benny said that about everyone he didn't like, and Benny Matos liked Rodrigo Punto about as much as Rodrigo cared for Diego. Nevertheless, Diego felt that tightening in his stomach and groin, not pleasurable, but a shadow of pleasure, a promise of pleasures to come. He raised a hand again and smiled at Benny, bending down to tell him he liked the coffee and the company in the Hatuey. He had no plans other than to have a coffee and share good company and nothing more than that; he sounded as though he meant it.

Diego walked into the Hatuey. Natalia was standing behind the counter, chatting with Dolores Delgado, a friend who worked as a school crossing guard on the corner near Diego's apartment. Dolores was a large lively middle-aged woman who wore her hair long. Diego smiled, said good afternoon, and went to the counter. Dolores was telling Natalia that she loved to drive into the mountains this time of year. "The air is so fresh and cool," she said. She was leaning on the counter, smoking a cigarette, puffing clouds of smoke in Natalia's face.

Sipping from a cup of coffee, Dolores glanced at Diego as though she knew some dark secret. A woman's secret. Diego stared at the women in the mirrored wall, grinned at Dolores and let his eyes lay for a long moment on Natalia.

The image of Natalia caught in the mirror turned and smiled back at him when he took his seat. And bingo, there it was, the pucker. He placed his schoolbag on the floor by his feet.

The rich scent of coffee and roasting pork filled the air; the breeze from a small portable fan cradled the fragrance and carried it to Diego. He opened his nostrils and inhaled, leaning against the counter.

"Can I get you a coffee, Professor?" Natalia said.

"Yes please, when you have a moment. I'll have the usual, and maybe a sandwich."

"Professor," Dolores said. "What can you teach me, Professor? What can you show me that I don't already know?"

"Ah, that depends on what a luscious, sensitive, tender woman like yourself would care to learn. I'm at your disposal. You ask and I'll deliver."

"*Dios mío*," Dolores said, "*que hombre bueno.*"

Out of the corner of his eye Diego could see Natalia giving him signals, talking to him with her hands, telling him to be still and not say too much. She examined her fingernails, then signed again with her hands. Diego caught the sense if not the meaning: *be quiet* was what she was saying. Behind Dolores's back, Natalia made faces, puckered her lips, and signed, *This woman has a big mouth.* Natalia then made a sign with her hands, that mouth of hers, her facial expression telling him she was in some unbelievable pain. All those looks, those expressions, led Diego to believe that on this day Natalia was up to something serious. She nodded at the kitchen, pointed to the room behind the curtained door. Dolores was talking a mile a minute about men, hard-hearted and spoiled by their mothers, men who act and make love like children. As she spoke she stretched out her hands like she was about to touch something precious.

Not until Natalia reminded her that the schoolchildren were about to be released from the late session did Dolores stop to catch her breath. Natalia leaned against the counter, her arms stiff, her hands whitening as she gripped the edge. Diego thinking, Benny was right, Cubans are a jealous people.

Dolores backed out the door, gesturing flamboyantly, saying loudly, "If I had a man like you, Professor, I would treat him like a prince, a prize, something rare and fine."

While Natalia prepared his sandwich Diego got up and wandered around the Hatuey. It was a small place, with a ten-foot counter and six stools, and two tables against a wall hung with photos and a map of Cuba in green and red. A jukebox stood in the corner, and Diego flipped through the selections. Natalia asked if he would care for a salad and Diego said yes, thank you, knowing it would please her. Natalia made wonderful salads.

He dropped a quarter into the jukebox and selected Tito Puente, then went to his schoolbag and took out a book.

Diego was sitting at the counter reading short stories by Mark Twain, "Man and Machine" his favorite, when he heard "*Hombre!*" He looked up and saw Natalia smiling at him.

Natalia had an outrageously beautiful face, with round black eyes and a straight nose that you didn't notice because of those lips. Hair the color of honey fell to her shoulders. But what hooked Diego was the smile. Natalia had the kind of smile that was overpowering, a smile that ruined all other smiles for you.

"You know, Diego, you're gorgeous. I could stand here all day and look at you, gorgeous as you are. That is, I could but I can't. I don't know for certain what time Rodrigo will get back from his trip to this place called Massapequa. We should not waste what little time we have."

"You're right," said Diego, flashing for a second on his oath not to violate another man's wife. Natalia's voice, he thought, was as inspiring as her smile.

Coming out from behind the counter, Natalia stood next to the kitchen doorway, which was hung with a curtain of light green material. She leaned against the doorframe, crossed her legs, folded her arms underneath her breasts, and stared at him.

She wore a loose-fitting peasant skirt, very long, it hid her legs, which to Diego's memory were perfect, and a flowered T-shirt. Her skirt fell to an inch above her leather sandals.

"I think you destroyed poor Dolores. I know her. She is daydreaming this very minute about what she would like to do to you—I mean, for you."

"She is married, isn't she?"

Natalia gave him a long slow smile, saying, "To a man who works for the post office and has smelly feet. I don't know that, I couldn't know that Dolores's husband has smelly feet. I only repeat what I've been told."

"Does her husband know the way she talks to men?" Diego asked gently. "The woman likes to play."

"Talk, Diego, talk is easy. Dolores is all talk. The difference between me and Dolores is that she loves her husband and I don't love Rodrigo."

Except for Tito Puente's soft mambo coming from the jukebox, the restaurant was quiet and still. For a moment they listened to the music.

"That's sad," Diego told her finally.

"Don't feel sorry for me, I'm no one to be sorry for."

Natalia took his sandwich, salad, and coffee from the counter and brought them to him, saying, "I once had friends, many friends. Rodrigo doesn't like me to have friends, he likes me to work for him and that's it."

"That's it?"

"Well . . ."

He stared at her.

"We could go into the kitchen," she said.

Natalia went and climbed up on a stool sitting with her back to the counter. She pulled her skirt to her knees, and Diego felt slammed again by that strange mixture of passion and conscience.

"I'm sorry you're unhappy, Natalia. I am." He couldn't keep his eyes off those legs of hers.

"Don't be. Rodrigo is a provider, and I know what it's like to be out on your own. I'm not unhappy. Just a little needy, if you know what I mean."

Diego looked up, about to answer. Then he caught himself and remained quiet, his heart going like a hummingbird in a small box.

"I'm not playing, Diego, I want you. I want you to think of how we can be together. It could be here, it could be now."

Diego made a face. "Someone could come in," he said, "anyone could come in here."

"Hardly anyone comes in this time of day, and there's the bell on the door."

Natalia seemed to rise within herself, passing Diego and logic, going off somewhere, to a place where some sweet adventure lay. There was a private, faraway look in her eyes.

He ran it through his mind. Told himself that he had taken an oath, his oath never to put his hands on another man's wife. A little play was fine, some teasing and flirting was healthy. Careful, he told himself, you are about to take that first step on the long downhill road.

Natalia made a sound in the back of her throat, as though she was experiencing a small pain. "Diego?" she said.

A smile touched the corners of her lips, and she turned her head.

"I'm going into the kitchen to prepare some soup," she told him, and got down off the stool. "If you like, you can come with me."

Diego followed her. He didn't say yes and didn't say no, he just followed her.

Chapter 3

In the kitchen there were pots and pans and metal trays suspended from a black iron rack that hung from the ceiling. The walls were painted yellow with red trim, it was clean, cleaner and neater than Diego expected. In the corner near the stove was a wooden table and a beach chair. He went to the chair and sat.

Natalia came and stood in front of him as if she were waiting for something, her hands on her hips, that smile on her face. She was quiet a long time. When she started to tell him how nervous she was, Diego reached out and touched the curve of her leg. Natalia bent her head. He put his hand on her face, ran his hand around her cheek and she stood very still, then she knelt in front of him. His hand went to the back of her head and she leaned toward him, kissed him quickly, deeply, pulled suddenly away and stood up. Natalia smiled with her eyes closed and her lips parted.

"*Por fin,*" she said.

Her left hand reached down and took his right hand and placed it between her legs. Sweat was gathering in the small of Diego's back. Through her skirt he could feel that she was wearing nothing underneath. And if it made any difference to Natalia that his hand was touching her it didn't show in her face.

The powerful aroma of Natalia seeped into Diego's blood, heated up, and started to sizzle. He wanted her so bad his bones hurt, but he couldn't enjoy himself, couldn't relax, he had never been so paranoid in his whole life.

For a couple of minutes he alternated staring at Natalia and staring at the green curtain. She made that pained sound again, ending with a nervous exhausted "Diego."

The door opened, the bell rang, and he got to his feet as if he had never heard of gravity.

Natalia spoke quickly, whispered, "Diego, even if it's just for minutes, I'd like to be set free. I tell myself it would feel so good to make love to a professor, a man of books, an aristocrat. I can't wait for your body to be on me."

She looked him over admiringly; he didn't know what she might be thinking. Diego felt a rush of panic. He thought he saw the curtain move. "Someone is in the restaurant," he said very softly.

He heard Natalia groan as though her heart had been pierced by a sword. She caught his eye for a second, then looked away. When she turned back to him, she lightly tapped him on the chest, saying, "Don't you move, don't you go anywhere. I'll be right back."

He watched her turn and go through the curtained doorway into the restaurant.

Diego pulled himself together, stretched and looked around. From the restaurant came the sounds of Natalia talking to a woman and pouring coffee. The thought struck him that hanging out here was silly—dangerous was what it was. Leave, he told himself, enough of this. He didn't want to make love in a kitchen. Not to a woman who had a husband, a husband that carried a gun. Except, why not admit it would be a sweet and special sort of revenge. Rodrigo was no friend, the man always making him feel surly and put-down.

In the kitchen was a closet; he opened the door. A white cotton drawstring bag hung from a hook on the inside of the closet door. He found himself taking the bag from off the hook, opening the bag.

A yellow cat appeared from beneath the stove, came over to him, and smelled his shoes.

What he found in the bag raised his spirits, made him smile. Black net stockings and a garter belt, gold panties and a halter top. Then the sound of a door opening, the bell, and then the door closing. Diego felt immense relief.

The curtain moved and Natalia stood there all smiles. Then the sweet sound of "Diego" on her lips. And Diego a little antsy now, glancing around the kitchen, wanting to leave.

They stood for a long moment in the center of the kitchen, arms around each other's waists, the yellow cat circling around their feet.

"You like those things, huh?" Natalia said, pointing to the cotton bag.

"I would love to see you dressed in these, but not here, not now."

Natalia paused for a second, then laughed. Leaning against Diego, she took the bag in her hand, examined it, smiled, and laughed again. "They're beautiful, aren't they, nice things, sexy, huh?"

Diego shrugged, saying, "They are very beautiful. Feminine."

She was much shorter than he, maybe a foot. He rubbed his cheek against her hair, inhaling the sweetness of her. She touched him and he was instantly hard.

"Rodrigo," she said, "he likes to wear them."

"You're lying. Natalia, you're kidding me; not macho Rodrigo?"

Diego threw back his head and laughed. Natalia joined him, both of them laughing until tears ran, laughing like kids without a care, like refugees from an insane asylum.

Diego thinking that in the Cuban world, the nation of machos, Rodrigo fancied himself emperor. The man always strutting around with the collar of his shirt turned up, around his neck a wide gold chain that got buried in the black coils of hair at the V of his open shirt. A bruiser of a guy always talking about his money.

Rodrigo Punto owned the Hatuey restaurant, a Laundromat, a bodega in the Bronx, and a medallion cab, which he drove nighttime all around the city because "That's where the money is."

Rodrigo feared no man. He carried on his hip an ancient pearl-handled Colt .45 military special, told everyone that he'd use it in a flash on any creep that gave him a dash of shit. On the pinkie of his left hand he wore a large golden ring with a black stone.

Diego gathered that Rodrigo had been a soldier in Cuba, then a cop. Benny had told him that Rodrigo killed people.

Diego avoided Rodrigo Punto the way you would a street where pit bulls run free. The thought of the brute parading in his garter belt and stockings drove him wild.

"No," Diego said, "no no oh God, I don't believe it. I don't."

"Believe it," Natalia said. "Believe it."

Diego was ecstatic, turning his head this way and that, his mouth gaping in delight. He pressed his palms together. "How long," he said. "When did he start wearing your underwear?"

"On our honeymoon."

Diego pounded on the side of the stove in a laughing frenzy. Natalia was walking in circles as if she were stunned. "On our honeymoon," she repeated.

Diego's wild laughter frightened the yellow cat, which jumped up onto the stove to see what the man was so broke up about.

"I like cats," Natalia said. "Better than people. With a cat at least you always know where you stand."

Diego went back to the beach chair and sat. He dropped his head into his hands, laughter bubbling out in hoots and howls. He listened to her laugh as well.

Natalia clucked her tongue and shook her head grimly. "You never know," she said.

"Crazy stuff," Diego said, "crazy stuff."

Then Natalia was in front of him; she pulled him to his feet. Now she was pushing against him, working her pelvis up and down against him. Unzipping his fly. She said, "Make love to me, Diego."

Diego felt embarrassed and stupid. Wake up, he told himself. This woman is Rodrigo Punto's, her choice. And in this life people generally get what they deserve.

He leaned against the stove, regarding Natalia and feeling a vague ripple of fear. It was time to go. Then her hand, those lovely long fingers reached inside his trousers.

"Diego?" she said, her mouth curving into a private, self-satisfied smile.

Natalia stood with her back to the stove now, her eyes half closed. A heated stillness came over her, and Diego watched her eyelids, slowly dropping shut like window shades.

"Natalia!" Rodrigo called out. "Natalia?" His voice sounded heavy and everywhere.

Natalia grabbed Diego's arm, her fingernails digging into it, saying, "Oh God, it's him, it's Rodrigo. I didn't hear the door. Did you hear the door?"

"Natalia?" Rodrigo called again.

Diego removed Natalia's hand and closed his fly.

"In here, I'm in the kitchen," Natalia answered, her eyes wide.

Outside of the tingle where Natalia's lovely hand had gripped his arm, Diego didn't feel anything. For a moment he stood quietly watching as Natalia reached up and pulled at her hair. She stood there hunched over, both knees together, elbows pressed against her sides, quick-frozen in fear. She looked to Diego like a stunned deer caught in a hunter's spotlight. His eyes went to the curtain, waiting.

Diego floated off outside himself briefly, just floated, and when he came back and landed he could hear Rodrigo saying something about a canceled trip, his voice almost a singsong.

Diego was slightly embarrassed by his own lack of concern, reminding himself that he was in fact with another man's wife and there was this thing in his pants making a tent. Spooking himself sober, Diego realized that Rodrigo was only a few feet away, standing just the other side of the curtain, his hand most probably resting on his pistol. The tent in Diego's pants took a hike.

All right, he thought, remain calm.

He was dressed, his fly was closed, and Natalia, although panicky, appeared fine.

God knows, Diego had always been a sucker for a dramatic moment. He rolled his eyes upward, thinking sweet Jesus, what I have here now is a dramatic moment.

Back in Palma Sorino everyone knew everyone else; no one would believe that Diego would violate another man's wife. The possibility would not even be discussed. Only this was Jackson Heights, this was Queens, this was New York City.

The curtain moved and Rodrigo stood in the doorway.

"What the fuck are you doing?" Rodrigo threw the curtain aside, almost reaching for his gun when he saw Diego.

"Easy, easy." Diego held his palms up.

Natalia described how Diego happened to be in the kitchen, speaking fast, hunched over, her hands in her armpits. And to Diego, Rodrigo seemed to listen. And the more she spoke the more Rodrigo listened, and the more he listened the better the story got. Natalia held Rodrigo's attention like a magician throwing tigers in the air, repeating the good lines, saying she was about to teach Diego to make soup, describing how she'd told him which spices to get down from the top shelf.

Rodrigo looked at him and then back at Natalia, his head turning like he was watching a tennis match.

Rodrigo Punto ran a hand across his mouth; he glanced at Natalia. He stood motionless, amazed, as if he were talking to a fare in his cab, complaining about traffic, and the fare, the traffic, all the people on the street had suddenly vanished, leaving him alone but intact behind his steering wheel in the middle of Fifth Avenue. The man looked astonished.

For a moment Diego found himself believing Natalia's outrageous story, and he thought Rodrigo did as well. He always had a hard time knowing what other people were thinking, so he assumed that they thought pretty much what he did. If he could believe Natalia's story, surely Rodrigo did too.

Natalia it seemed could sense Rodrigo's mood better than Diego. She ducked, but she was way too slow—taking one quick step toward Natalia, Rodrigo brought the palm of his hand hard across her face.

Natalia doubled up, then sank to the floor of the kitchen, sat still as a stone. She looked both scared and numb; her skin white as snow, her eyes focused on nothing as she just sat there in a kind of solemn haze.

Diego was stunned. He stared at her for a long moment, the anger in his chest building, building. She seemed to feel him looking at her and began to cry. It was the crying that blew Diego away.

"You bastard," Diego said, "why did you hit her?"

"I was talking to Diego," Natalia said. "Just talking." She looked at her fingernails as she spoke, avoiding their eyes.

"Are you going to tell me that too, Diego?" Rodrigo said. "Are you going to tell me you came here into this kitchen to have a little conversation with my wife? You pretty-boy fag bastard, that what you want to say to me?"

Not sure what point he wanted to make, Diego had to force himself to look at Rodrigo. The truth of it was, he had been so worried for Natalia he hadn't really thought of his own safety. "No, Rodrigo, no. I wanted to make love to her."

Rodrigo leaned toward him. "For those words," he said softly, "I should kill you. This city is a jungle, Diego, and you're a cripple. Me, I'm a tiger—you know what a tiger does to a cripple?"

Diego grunted and nodded in an understanding way. He was overwhelmed at how calm he felt. He was doing his best to stay alert, to do right by Natalia. Sooner or later she'd have to go home with the bastard.

"You have a good woman, Rodrigo," Diego said. "You don't deserve her."

The smile on Rodrigo's face faded until there was nothing there but hatred.

At such a time, Diego told himself, what's required is discipline, style. Protect Natalia. But from the look of him, Rodrigo was beginning to lose it.

Rodrigo Punto went about five ten, eleven, weighed around two-twenty. There was an abundance of fat, but plenty of muscle too, and he'd been banging on people most of his life.

"Sweet-mouthed pretty boy, you are going to pay. Big time."

Frenzy grew in Rodrigo's eyes, flaring up, up, incandescent heat, searing black heat, his eyes the eyes of Satan, all-seeing Satan, something comical about the sight of him, frightening and funny at once. Rodrigo turned his head from side to side, distracted for a moment, looking at Natalia, then back at Diego. He touched his side, grabbed at the place where he carried his pistol, as if to reassure himself, hesitating, then deciding that there was no way to go but at Diego, there was no turning back, he was all tension, out of control.

Rodrigo bent his head and charged at Diego, smashing his head into Diego's chest, his blind grasping fingers in Diego's hair, sending him crashing into the wall, knocking Diego down.

Diego managed to get to his feet. He felt tight and could not breathe, he felt as though he'd been hit in the chest by a sledgehammer. He began to move slowly around the edge of the kitchen, shoulders hunched and fists clenched. Rodrigo stalked him. Diego had no intention of going down again, knew he wouldn't. Natalia was watching.

"My wife wanted to open her legs for you," Rodrigo shouted. "She fucks you with her eyes, I see it, I see it all the time."

Diego was so sunk into himself he could hardly focus. The look of Rodrigo and the sound of him made his skin crawl. The man ranting incoherently, a thread of saliva across his chin, his eyes afire.

You didn't think of this beforehand, Diego told himself. Of course not, you don't think at all. Diego's face suddenly spread into a grin, as the vision of Rodrigo in garter belt and stockings flew to his mind, quick, instantaneous, he saw him in his golden outfit, Rodrigo the bull in that getup.

I know who you are, you crazy son of a bitch, he told himself, and he maneuvered his way around the kitchen calmly, coolly, a just perceptible smile on his face.

Diego was a gentle man, not a natural fighter. He was also the sort of man, as his wife's cousin Benny Matos would tell you, who, when he set his mind to a fight, the fight in him could surprise you.

"There are some people," Rodrigo snapped, making a gun with his thumb and forefinger, "that make you think, I mean the way they behave, they make you think that they want to die."

Diego set himself and waited to see what Rodrigo would do.

"I'm going to punish you, Diego. I'm going to punish you in front of this bitch who I have to call my wife."

Rodrigo threw a punch at Diego, powerful and awkward. Diego ducked under it and moved to the side, graceful as a dancer. Diego was six foot four, thin but strong. An easygoing man but nobody's pushover.

Rodrigo stumbled into the stove, he tripped over Natalia, who sat now with her arms covering her head. Catching himself, Rodrigo turned, wiping at his nose with his forearm. He nodded, smiled, bit his bottom lip. Then he lunged at Diego, arms outstretched, mouth agape, letting out a scream of both pleasure and pain.

Diego paused, gathering his strength, he dropped his left shoulder and came up with a ferocious right, catching Rodrigo square in the ribs. Rodrigo farted like a stallion and dropped to his knees. Diego bent his legs and struck downward, a piston stroke that landed on Rodrigo's forehead. Rodrigo fell forward onto the floor, gasping.

Rodrigo stayed down, twisted on his side, wrapping his arms around his stomach, making small crying noises.

"Natalia told me that she would not betray you, you fool," Diego said. He bent and poked Rodrigo's nose, saying, "You should kiss her feet."

Natalia looked up at him quickly, as if Diego might be asking her something.

Rodrigo looked up at Diego. "Commie bastard," he said. His mouth and chin glistened with spit.

Diego squatted next to Natalia and stroked the back of her head gently.

"You'd better leave," she told him.

Diego stood up breathing hard, his hand hurt and he was shaking.

"If he hits you again you come and get me." He looked at Rodrigo. "Rodrigo," he said. "You should learn to behave like a man, not like some gangster."

He went through the curtain, picked up his schoolbag, and walked out of the Hatuey, wondering if he should have stayed longer with Natalia. Deciding that in the end he would have to leave anyway. She was not his woman, she was Rodrigo Punto's.

Out on the street, he glanced at his watch. It was five thirty. He'd be late getting home.

Somebody screamed from the doorway of the Italian bakery. Diego turned.

Rodrigo stood on the sidewalk about thirty feet from him, that .45 in his fist.

"I'm going to kill you, you bastard," he bellowed.

Everybody on the street ran, but Diego took a step forward. Rodrigo yelled wordlessly, all his hate and anger going into it.

"What are you going to do?" Diego said. "Shoot me for talking to your wife? Go ahead, shoot me, you crazy son of a bitch."

Overhead he could hear a train coming, more steel on steel. Then there was a siren.

Rodrigo pointed at him with his gun. "You're a dead man!" he shrieked. "A dead man!"

Diego didn't answer. He was entranced by the gun in Rodrigo's hand. He stood still, one hand on his hip, the other holding his schoolbag. About six people were standing along the curb of the street and Diego watched them scramble when Rodrigo waved his gun in the air. Diego didn't move.

What was he supposed to do, turn and run, get shot in the back by a madman? He considered charging Rodrigo, pray the crazy man would miss when he took his shot. Thought better of it. The insanity of the situation made Diego feel as if he were in a movie theater watching some dull and pointless American cowboy film.

A small skinny woman with long braids and no teeth came out of the Italian bakery, walked out onto the sidewalk, took a look around, spotted Rodrigo, dropped her loaf of bread and ran off.

Rodrigo was still screaming, both arms in the air. Diego stepped back, sliding toward a large mailbox, hoping to get behind it.

Rodrigo leveled his gun.

The realness of that pistol made Diego want to yell for help, for the police. He had heard a siren—where were the police? He crouched, got down on one knee, tried to get his six-foot-four-inch frame behind the blue mailbox.

The police were nearby, had to be, Diego reasoned, this was a city where police were everywhere. Someone must be calling for help, there were about fifty people running all over the place. Diego peeked out from behind the mailbox, studying Rodrigo, now twenty feet off, entranced with the vitality of his every gesture, the absoluteness of his resolve. Diego tracked Rodrigo as he slowly approached. He could feel his heart pound, imagined he could hear it above the sounds of the street.

Benny Matos's big black Buick screeched to a stop at the curb. The door flew open and Benny, looking fat and wild in his white outfit, jumped out of the car, a baseball bat in his hand and Rodrigo's name in his mouth.

"You want to shoot somebody Rodrigo? Hey man, you hear me, I'm talking to you."

Benny was midway between Diego and Rodrigo, who stood in the center of the sidewalk, nodding violently, his eyes glittering with out-of-control rage.

"I don't want you," Rodrigo said, "I want that commie fag behind the mailbox."

"What you want don't matter no more, man. You got me is what you got. Me, Benny Matos, and I'm going to bust your fucking head."

Diego's eyes went from Rodrigo to Benny and back to Rodrigo. He saw Natalia come out of the Hatuey, her arms wrapped around her. Across the avenue people were lined up as if they were watching a parade. Everyone on the street looked extremely demented to Diego's eyes, laughing and pointing. Some were shouting, "Shoot him, shoot him!"

As Benny approached Rodrigo he slapped the bat against the palm of his hand, saying, "Man, I'm going to drive that coconut head of yours across the street."

Diego felt a fleeting pang of envy, seeing Benny's coolness, his downright courage. He wondered what it would be like to smash someone in the head with a baseball bat. Watch his head crush like a melon.

Rodrigo dropped into a shooter's stance, both his hands around his pistol. Benny kept moving forward.

A young black kid wearing an I-Love-New-York T-shirt loped over, almost running into Rodrigo, making a gun with his hand, the kid going, "Pow-pow-pow!"

The kid danced away, laughing and pointing, laughing and pointing.

Diego ran his hands through his hair, thinking half a brain, this city is full of people with half brains.

"I'm a man," Rodrigo shouted. "I'll show you what kind of man I am."

Diego stood up and rested his arms across the top of the mailbox. "Rodrigo," he shouted, "you are crazy. I did nothing. We did nothing."

"Get down!" Benny yelled. "Rodrigo," he said, "I'm coming to get you now."

Natalia dropped to her knees, crossed her arms over her stomach, and bellowed, "Rodrigo, we are innocent!"

Puzzled, Rodrigo turned.

Benny was on him. He smashed Rodrigo across the shoulder with his bat, sending him pirouetting into the window of the Italian bakery, his gun flying into the street.

The black kid in the T-shirt shouted, "Going, going, gone!"

Benny raised the bat again and began rhythmically banging on Rodrigo. Clutching his schoolbag, Diego ran toward Benny's car. He found himself unable to resist feeling sorry for Rodrigo. "*Hombre*," he said aloud, "you have had one bad day."

Benny steered Diego by the shoulder and planted him in the front seat of his car. As they drove off Benny threw his arm out the window, his fist in the air.

"I told you, I told you," he said.

Diego looked out the car window at the people waving, applauding, laughing, jumping up and down, howling like a bunch of zoo monkeys. Some stared at him for a second, then quickly turned away.

"Christ," he said. "They all act like we are heroes or something."

Benny laughed. "Yeah."

"A crazy place. This country, this city is crazy. Doesn't anyone care what you do here?"

"No." Benny laughed again.

Diego felt a strange dizziness come over him. He knew right then that no matter how he tried, the sight of those people standing on the curb shouting, "Shoot him, shoot him!" those people laughing and applauding, throwing their arms in the air, that sight would always be living behind his eyelids. This is the whirlwind, he thought, this is for real.

Chapter 4

Across the Williamsburg Bridge from Jackson Heights, in Fisher's Dairy Restaurant on Essex Street, in the heart of the Lower East Side, Rodrigo sat in a booth opposite the kitchen, his arm in a sling, and watched as Nick and Sonny McCabe came toward him.

The restaurant was deep and narrow, with six tables in front, twelve booths in the rear; there were no patrons, three waiters clustered around the cash register. Above their heads hung a blue cage in which a yellow and black canary chirped periodically like a telephone answering machine. The waiters were chitchatting in a language that Rodrigo had never heard, making him feel anxious and nervous, and he was already agitated and tense enough.

Nick watched Rodrigo try desperately to come off cool and loose. Sitting back, one arm draped along the back of the booth, Rodrigo affected a curious sneer, as if the fact of his being there was nothing but an inconvenience, a busy man with little time to waste.

"Rodrigo, my man. Hey, Rodrigo Punto, meet Detective Nick Manaris." McCabe slid into the booth, pulled a Marlboro from the pack Rodrigo had left on the table, and lit up. Nick remained standing for a moment, squinting at the menus on the wall. After a moment he sat down next to Sonny.

"I told you, Sonny, that I didn't want to talk to anyone but you. I told you that. I guess what I want don't mean nothing," Rodrigo said. The canary chirped and whacked its wings around like it had taken a hit of cocaine. Rodrigo flinched.

A tall skinny waiter with a chin beard walked over and asked if they were ready to order. He wore a white apron, blue jeans, a faded red Harvard T-shirt, and ankle-high sneakers.

"Oh, yes, man," Rodrigo said, "I'm hungry. How about a nice ham sandwich with some melted cheese?"

The waiter smiled. "I'll tell you what. You guys read the menu, I'll be back in a few minutes. You want coffee, something to drink?"

Nick said he'd have a celery soda and Sonny asked for root beer. Rodrigo said, "A celery soda?" Told the waiter he'd have a coffee, black, and forget the menu, he'd eat later.

"Hey, Rodrigo, what you want is important, very important to us," Sonny said. "But lemme tell ya, we got rules, things we gotta do. Hell, you were a cop, you understand."

"I was a captain. I made the rules. Nobody told me what to do until the fucking commies came. That's when I go man. I don't take rules."

Nick leaned across the table toward Rodrigo, talking gentle right at his eyes. "I have nothing but respect for you, Rodrigo. What you're doing takes heart, I respect a man with heart, with courage. You know, a man with balls."

"Uh-huh," Rodrigo said, and eyed Nick.

Nick thinking, cold, one cold bastard.

"You and Sonny, you guys good friends?" Rodrigo asked.

The waiter returned before Nick could answer.

"We're brothers," Sonny said. "All cops are brothers."

"I knew brothers who killed each other. Don't give me that brother shit."

"We're close," Nick said. "Me and Sonny go way back, been friends a long time." He threw Sonny an amused look.

"You dump that cannon you were carrying?" Sonny asked Rodrigo. "I don't want to see you get pinched for a gun." He exhaled smoke through his nose.

"Hey man, I carry the fucking gun. Not now, I don't mean I carry it all the time, just when I'm working. I tell you I rather get arrested than killed. You know killed is killed, killed is dead. And where I go the niggers are everywhere, they all got guns. I work nights, I have to protect myself."

Sonny said, "Sure," as if this made all the sense in the world. "You're right. You got to be careful, always on the lookout. Just don't get your ass busted, okay."

Nick picked up his soda and drank some, taking his time. "Why don't you get a permit?" he said. "We could help you out, give you a hand with the forms. We can take care of it for you."

"Nick," Rodrigo said. "You don't know your ass from a hole in the ground. They don't give people like me permits. If you're a gringo, you own a jewelry store and have a friend or family with connections, they give you a permit. A Latino like me, it don't happen man."

"Ey," Sonny said. "When this is over, we make this case, we'll owe you one. Whatever we can do we'll do. You got my word."

"I'm hungry," Rodrigo said. "What kind of restaurant is this anyway, a restaurant that got no food?"

"You picked it," said Sonny, staring flat-eyed at a menu on the wall that offered cottage cheese, sour cream, fruit cocktails, cheesecake, steamed vegetables, herring in wine and herring in cream.

"Yeah, well, I dropped a fare here last night, looked around and saw nobody that looked like me. I figured it was a good place to meet you, Sonny."

"The hell happened to your arm?" Nick said.

"Accident."

Nick found himself thinking again about McCabe and this case, this snitch, Hawks and the others, how badly he wanted off this team, but also how he had recently felt this need to team up, be one of the guys. He sat there with his soda, looking at Sonny and Rodrigo, the two of them laughing, fooling around, kidding with each other, and felt stabbed through the heart with a longing, a need to shake himself loose from this feeling that everyone around him was up to something. Wounded by the memory of ten years in the job and never being able to fit. Never a partner, never someone to laugh with.

Partners going back to back; the image had never found an easy home in Nick's mind. At his graduation from the academy, his class sergeant put his arm around the new rookie cop, pointed to his classmates walking off in twos and threes, as giddy as if they were on a honeymoon, saying, "Nick, make a friend, find a partner. Until you're teamed up, you're nothing but a loner. That ain't no way to go through this job." At the time it sounded reasonable, almost memorable, but thinking about it and trying to act on it later, Nick had realized that although he vaguely wanted to belong, to be included, he had a hard time seeing himself as one of the boys, he had never thought of himself as a joiner. His mother died when he was ten, he was raised by his father, passed around on weekends to various relatives so his father could have some time on his own. Always feeling like a trespasser, fighting with cousin after cousin. And now, ten years in the department, he still considered himself more an intruder than some uniformed soldier propping up the thin blue line.

Sitting back in the booth, he watched Sonny lean across the table and whisper in Rodrigo's ear, Rodrigo giving off a hell of a laugh. Something was funny, he was funny, he was the joke of the moment. Nick was desperate both to be there and be gone; he took out the case folder and positioned it in front of him on the table. Then he picked it up and tapped it against his chin. Rodrigo was sitting directly across from Nick but somehow the man managed to casually avoid Nick's eyes.

Nick felt tense, hurt, a bit pissed off. "You guys want to talk about this case now?" he asked.

"Sure," Rodrigo said. His voice low and confiding.

Sonny finger-combed his hair, saying, "That's what we're here for. It sure ain't the food." Nick took in Sonny's incredulous smile: everything was a joke to this guy.

"It's getting late," Nick said. "If I'm going to type these warrant applications, let's get moving."

Sonny shrugged. "Go to it."

"Okay, so what do we know? Who's expecting what and where is it going?" Nick began to regret starting this, but he hung in. "I understand you've seen some of these guns, samples, huh?"

For a second Rodrigo looked confused. Then he jerked his head back, spread wide his good arm and yawned. Sonny was smiling.

"Is there something funny here?" Nick said. "Did I say something funny?"

"Will you lighten up?" said McCabe.

Nick smiled tightly at him, then turned and looked at the empty restaurant, one waiter now sitting at a table near the door, drinking, it seemed to Nick, a glass of tea.

"How long do you know these people, this Benny Matos and those people?" he said finally.

"Too long," Rodrigo said.

"You've seen him with a gun, an automatic weapon?"

"Sure."

"And the others? The Italian, Tony Bellatesta, the Colombian? You've seen them all with guns?"

"Sure."

"All right, where did you see the guns?"

"Benny has them in the trunk of his car, boxes of them. I seen guns, I seen them in the club, in the basement of the club."

"What kind of guns? What've you seen?"

"I don't think you should get specific, let him tell it," McCabe whispered.

Rodrigo gave Nick a hesitant look. "Guns man, automatics. Machine guns."

Nick pulled a few mug shots from the case folder. Benny Matos first. "Have you seen guns in this guy's car?"

"I just told you man, that's Benny, I seen guns in his Buick. And in his house, I seen them there too."

"You've been to Matos's house?"

"Of course, how would I know the guns are there?"

Then the Colombian's picture. "This guy, you know his name?"

"Medina. They call him Cano because of his red hair. Sure I see him, and the Italian guy you got there too. I seen them all with guns. But there's one you don't show me. The important man, the big man. The man with the brains."

"Yeah? Who's that?" said McCabe.

"You forgot, hah? Maybe you were drunk? But I told you; Cienfuego,

Diego Cienfuego. They call him the Professor. You get him you got
the top guy. And the bum, I got to tell you, he's so cool, so slick. The
man lays back, he don't get involved in the bullshit. But he's the man
that gives the orders, he's the boss."

Nick looked away for a moment, thinking back on all that time spent
with snitches. If he believed this character, he would have to prepare
an additional warrant. Which meant he had a ton of work to do tonight.

Nick loosened his collar, ran his hand around his neck, through his
hair. It came back damp.

"Diego Cienfuego, huh?"

Rodrigo cocked his head at Nick. "Get the Professor, Nick. Get him
and you'll be doing some good. Make yourself famous like Sonny and
they'll write a book about you too."

"A book?"

"Sure, they're writing a book about Sonny. Right, Sonny? Tell him,
man. I thought you two were friends?"

"A book, Sonny?"

"You know how it is, people talk and nothing happens. Just talk."
Nick could see that McCabe wanted to slide away from the subject.
"Meanwhile we got this player, this Cienfuego, in the hopper. That's
another warrant, Nick."

Nick looked down at his case folder again, telling himself, the more
the merrier. Sonny tapped him on the shoulder, his voice low and
smartass.

"Robinson's your buddy, your pal, right? He'll sign whatever you put
in front of him."

Nick muttered, "Jesus Christ. So, Rodrigo," he said, "you don't like
these people, huh?"

Rodrigo leaned over and whispered, "I don't like them? I hate them."

Hate. Nick could hardly imagine a better reason to be a snitch, a
stool, an informant, a fink. Telling himself, in the street it's every man
for himself, like it always has been, always will be.

"Rodrigo," he said. "Tell me, as best as you can figure, how much
time we got?"

Rodrigo glanced at his watch: it was eight ten. "I can hang around
another hour, no more. I got work to do."

"I mean with the guns. When do you figure Matos will get them?
Tonight, tomorrow, when?"

"I don't know for sure. I'll call you."

"Take a guess," Sonny said.

"Tomorrow, tomorrow night, Sunday maybe? Monday? I bet Monday. The restaurant is closed for business on Mondays. On Mondays they go there to clean up. Nobody's around on Mondays. They deliver those guns Monday, I bet."

Rodrigo was getting a bit agitated now. There was a glossy film across his forehead.

Nick nodded and finished his soda.

Driving the cruiser away from Essex Street, Nick had the persistent notion that McCabe was studying him in a sly way, shooting him sideways glances. They were heading south on the FDR Drive. Sonny, his head back against the headrest, his eyes opening and closing, taking a small nap. Every so often Nick would glance at Sonny and catch him watching. Sonny would turn his chin into his shoulder and shut his eyes like a mischievous kid.

This guy McCabe gave him a laugh, what a piece of work. A real hummer, but with the undeniable charisma Nick always associated with the Irish.

Nick considered the way cops like McCabe constantly seemed to be in complicity with their informants, no matter how strange the snitch was. In a way, he thought, it was the cops that worked for the snitches. It made him wonder, the way so many things in this job made him wonder: just who in the hell are the bad guys around here?

He found a spot a block from the office on Old Slip and South Street and parked. Sonny looked at him sideways and in the space of that moment it was possible for Nick to see just how peculiar Sonny McCabe was.

"Where are we?"

"Where do you think?"

"At the office?"

"You weren't sleeping, who you kidding?"

Sonny sighed, rubbing his eyes. "You know," he said, "I can never figure guys like you. What's your problem?"

"I got no problem."

"Sure you got a problem. You look at me like you're better than me, like you think I ain't worth looking at. And here's the big one, you always think I'm running a game on you. I'm a liar is what you think. I was sleeping."

Sonny's jaw muscles were twitching. That good-looking face of his, so easy to read, self-incriminating, a face like a clear night sky over the ocean, there was the Southern Cross and the Little Dipper, the Milky Way.

Grinning like a little kid with a new toy on Christmas morning,

Sonny stretched and yawned, saying, "Ohhhh God, guys like you make me fucking nuts."

"Guys like me? What do you mean, guys like me?"

"You know exactly what I mean, guys like you. You know what I'm saying." He said it softly, as if someone passing in the street might hear. "So," McCabe said. "You up for a pop or two? Whataya say, let's go over to Post Time, some of the guys will be there. I know Moran will be there, the man lives in that joint. Hawks too, he'll be on his perch at the corner of the bar telling war stories."

"I need to get going," Nick said.

"See, you see? People want to be friendly and you just back off. Where you gotta go?"

"Excuse me, hotshot, but there's these warrants. You know what I mean? It's going to take me a couple of hours of typing at least. Then I have to call the DA. I don't have time for Post Time."

McCabe mumbled something like sure.

"You going to do the typing?" Nick glanced at Sonny, feeling a vague anxiety. He'd had enough of this guy, like a toothache.

"Me? Fuck no. It's up to me I throw the clerical man upstairs a double sawbuck, have him do it. The guy types like a broad. Write them out in longhand real quick and give it to Flynn. The guy's a typing machine."

"I type my own warrants."

"Hey, me and you, we're first-graders. We shouldn't be typing warrants."

Nick shrugged and said nothing.

"Okay, let's go."

"I'm not going to Post Time."

"I know, I know. C'mon, let's me and you go upstairs and type these warrants and get it done with."

McCabe opened the door of the cruiser and got out. Bending at the waist, hands on his hips, looking back in at Nick and saying, "Well, whataya say? Let's get it done."

Nick hesitated, thinking how to answer him.

"Nick?"

Nick said nothing.

"You need help doing these warrants, am I right?" Sonny said, as if the thought made him angry.

Nick nodded, hoping to come off thoughtful.

"What are you, a masochist or something? I ain't going to let you go upstairs by yourself and do all this work."

"I'm a good typist," Nick said, his voice small.

"Yeahhhhh, I bet you are."

"I am."

"You are, good. Then we'll get done in no time and go grab a cup."

Nick waited a respectful moment, then said, "Okay, let's go." Angry at having been overrun by this guy, this McCabe. Feeling unable to help himself.

Climbing the stairs to the OCCU office, McCabe said, "I want to say something. Can I say something?"

Silence from Nick.

"I don't know who you worked with before. I mean, I don't know how you and your partners worked. As for me, I go anywhere, anytime, do anything and do it right for my partners. In this job there's partners and then there's partners." Sonny tapped him on the shoulder. "You understand what I'm saying?"

"Sure," Nick said.

Nick looked around the office, found an empty desk with a typewriter on it, hunted through some drawers for search warrant applications. He noticed Sonny talking to the clerical man, saw Sonny go into his pocket, take out a roll of bills and peel one.

Sonny marched over to Nick.

"What kind of stunt did you just pull?" Nick asked him.

"Nothing. Less than nothing. Listen buddy, Flynn will type the warrants. Okay?" Sonny sounded almost amused. He picked up the case folder with Nick's notes and brought it to Officer Flynn.

Nick was about to call out Sonny's name but then let it go, thinking screw it. He sat up in his chair, began to straighten up the desk. Flynn started typing; the guy was fast, real fast. The hell with it.

Chapter 5

Diego told Justo warmly, as any man might tell his son, I don't like you wearing blue jeans and T-shirts, tennis shoes. I give you money for clothes, this is America, a dozen stores on every street, buy something decent. He glanced at Justo from the corner of his eye, seeing his dead wife in his son's face.

Silence from Justo. He gave Diego a look. When listening to things he didn't want to hear it was Justo's custom to stare like a hypnotist into the eyes of the speaker.

Diego said, "It would be nice to see you in a suit and tie, a good pair of shoes."

Justo was smiling at him; he put his hands on Diego's shoulders. "Papi," he said, "Benny wants me to come to the restaurant to help in the *kitchen*."

"I didn't mean for tonight. There are other times you need a suit and tie."

Justo told him he had no time to shop, what with school and looking out for Mariaclara and Miguel. Diego said make the time, a man is as good as he looks. You look like a bum, a street kid, a gringo with no class. And listen, don't argue with me.

They were standing at 108th Street and Roosevelt Avenue watching the streams of Friday night cars, waiting for the ride that would take them to Los Campos. It was Benny Matos's habit to send a car for him, the car always driven by this Puerto Rican guy named Hector Perez who was both a revolutionary and a junkie.

Hector generally picked Diego up around six and drove him home after closing Los Campos. Diego would get in the car and they would have this running conversation about the state of the world, American imperialism, Cuban communism, and the politics of cocaine. Diego half suspected that Benny and Hector were in the drug business together. He had never asked.

His first week in New York, his first night of work, Benny sent Hector and Hector told Diego, "It's hard here, New York is not an easy city, but it's way better, man, than Havana."

First of all, he had told Hector, he didn't come from Havana. And second of all how would Hector know how it was in Cuba?

"I know that no one in their right mind is swimming south, if you get my meaning," is what Hector had said.

Glancing at his watch, Diego folded his arms. Justo strolled over to the corner shoe store and stood at the window, jiggling the change in his pocket, his face up against the glass. His eldest son was a practical, handsome, kindhearted young man, to whom education and music were important things. The boy was sixteen, appeared older, and lived to take care of his younger brother and sister, helping to dress them, preparing their food when Diego was off seeing the sights of New York. Justo complained a lot but smiled a lot, too; his face lit by his mother's huge black eyes, he had her cleft chin and overbite, and Diego's light cinnamon skin. His black hair was wavy and he wore it to his shoulders, it broadened his face and made his high cheekbones stand out. A lady-killer, another Cienfuego lady-killer.

The sky above the city had grown dark, there were no stars or moon, just the corner streetlight. Justo, admiring leather boots and loafers, expensive things, smiling, his face caught in the circle of light, had the expression of a child in front of his birthday cake.

Standing there, watching his son, Diego thought of himself as a good and virtuous man, a man in a new country with a new life, a man, he told himself, that could care for his family. A man on the road to success.

He would have to swear off flirting, at least for a while. And even if he didn't swear off it all together, maybe a few here and there just to be polite, but Natalia Punto, no thanks. He gazed at his own reflection in the store's window. You're a Cuban, he told himself, you're as good as you look.

Diego turned on his heel, hearing a train overhead, experiencing a small rush of excitement, thinking of the afternoon, Benny standing there, the bat slapping the palm of his hand. Thinking of something that happened when he was living in Miami a few months back, something he was not very proud of. Jesus, when you've been frightened, every other fearful moment you've had in your life springs out. He replayed the scene in the kitchen in his mind, beautiful Natalia on her knees in front of him. Rodrigo, his gun, his golden getup, the entire episode so much craziness. Poor Rodrigo, poor bastard. To live knowing your wife has eyes for other men.

He came up behind his son and Justo met his eyes in the reflection of the store window.

"Papi, what a city, I love this place. There is nothing you can't get here. It's all here, everything. New York is paradise."

"They say that in paradise there was a snake, a serpent," Diego told him. "But you are right, this is a wonderful city. Only it will not be easy to find this city's secrets. It is not Palma Sorino, not our home. At least not yet."

"This city has no secrets, money is the answer here. The question, of course, is how to get some."

"Justo, you are resourceful and gifted, you understand things. Money is important but you can't allow it to turn your head."

"Don't you worry, that's not going to happen to me. I get some money, it'll be because I earn it."

"I hope so."

"I'm not Uncle Benny."

"Benny is not your uncle. He's your second cousin."

"Uncle, cousin, it's the same thing. Family. He calls me nephew, I call him uncle. Who cares?"

The car arrived and they got in, Diego in the back seat, Justo in the front next to Hector. Diego considered the night that lay ahead. It would be a late night, always Friday was a late night. Los Campos had a small dance floor, a long bar, and a dining room with fifty tables. With his guitar, Diego was the strolling house band.

Benny's friends, those gangsters that moved like panthers, were sure to show up. And that Colombian guy, that Cano, would ask Diego to play and sing a bolero, and when he did the women sitting at the bar were sure to squeal. Diego liked that, the squealing women, he liked being a star.

Relaxing in the car, his elbow resting on the leather seat rest, his head in his hand, Diego considered his two younger children, Miguel and Mariaclara. They were, for the time being, in his landlady Ingrid's good hands. The thought of his children contented and happy made him feel that life here would be fine.

As they approached Los Campos, a yellow cab sped passed them on the right, close enough for Diego to make out the driver and the passenger in the front seat. It was Rodrigo's cab, he was driving, and his passenger was Oscar Melendez, Benny's bartender. The man Benny had told him was too sick to come to work. What in the hell was Oscar doing snaking around with Rodrigo?

"Hector, hey Hector, isn't that Rodrigo and Oscar in that cab?" Diego said.

"You're right. What are those two doing together?"

"I thought he was sick," Justo said.

Hector said, "That Rodrigo is a Fascist pig. He was a cop. You know that Diego? The son of a bitch was a cop in Havana."

"I know. I heard. And let me tell you, he's no friend of mine. That crazy man hates me."

"Why?" Justo asked. "Why does Rodrigo hate you?"

Hector laughed, shook his head, turned around in his seat, flashing wide watery brown eyes at Diego, making Diego wonder how this Puerto Rican could drive without looking where he was going. Saying, "Rodrigo don't like you, don't take it personally, he doesn't like anyone. That fucker is somebody's pet alligator that grew too big. Somebody should straighten him out."

Diego held his hands up. "I did nothing to that man that he should hate me," he said. "Christ, I wonder if Benny knows that Oscar is spending time with Rodrigo."

Hector broke into a laugh, you could say it was not a happy laugh. "Rodrigo is the enemy," he said. "He is a brutal and insatiable enemy, like the imperialist United States itself. He must be pounced upon and defeated, and all the accomplices of that enemy, who betray their blood, must be defeated too."

He looked wasted and flushed; there was pain in his eyes, compounded by cocaine and booze.

"Jesus," Justo said, "that's some speech, Hector."

"From the top of my head, one of my short ones. Would you like to hear another?"

Diego smiled. "You have two ears and one mouth," he said. "Maybe what you should do is listen more than you talk."

"You are a smart man, Professor," Hector said. "Just not smart enough."

"No one is smarter than my father," said Justo. "No one."

Hector fidgeted in his seat. "Man," he said, "I feel fucked up."

They turned off Roosevelt Avenue onto Corona and pulled into the parking lot alongside Los Campos. The restaurant, which looked like a factory among the neighboring two-family homes, was a one-story cement block building painted green and black. In the front, on the street side, were two large picture windows, one to each side of oak and brass double doors trimmed in wrought iron. In one window was a red neon shape that bore a resemblance to the map of Cuba.

Parked at the curb in front of Los Campos on Corona Avenue was a black Mercedes. Seeing the tinted windows, Diego knew who the car belonged to: Cano, the Colombian bolero lover. He had arrived early.

Diego and Justo got out of the car and stood in the parking lot. Hector got out on the driver's side, saying, "You know, it becomes more clear to me every day. I mean, your uncle, your uncle Benny is a saint." Hector was stretching, yawning, his hair hanging in his face. Suddenly he pulled up his shirt and showed Diego and Justo where he was shot three times a few years back and left for dead.

"Two Puerto Rican brothers from East Harlem gave me this. Benny found me and took care of me. The man's a saint."

"What happened to the two guys?" Justo asked.

"Justo, c'mon," said Diego, "we don't have time. We are already late."

"They lost their will to live," said Hector. "Imagine that? A colorful but small funeral at Ortiz's on One-hundred-and-sixteenth Street. I was there, it was very nice, family and friends. A little music and some weeping, nice."

Hector kept talking, moving around, almost giddy with pleasure. The drugs at work.

Diego clapped his hands and said, "You eat talking candy tonight, Hector, is that it?"

Impatient and eager, Diego and Justo walked through the restaurant's back door. Hector was off again, on another mission for Benny. Diego scanned what he could see of the dining room, a few couples and a family of four. Friday evening people arrived late. Justo walked off toward the kitchen, raising his hand, saying, "Papi, I'll see you later."

There were Benny and Cano in the cocktail lounge, standing at the bar throwing down drinks, whispering, their heads together like a couple of lovebirds. Benny glanced at him, what's going on? And Diego shrugged, straightening up as Cano looked over at him.

Cano was a small, thin, birdlike man with intensely red hair. Wearing his usual sky blue guayabera with fancy lace trim, sipping his rum, smiling, waving at Diego, telling Diego to come join them. He was not a nice-looking man. However, Diego thought of him as intelligent. Cano's Spanish was faultless.

"¿Qué tal, Professor?" Cano said as Diego approached. And Benny smiled, looking slightly surprised; Diego thought Benny might be angry. Diego extended his hand to shake Cano's thin, bony, cold fish of a hand, seeing it was seven thirty, and he was a half hour late.

The cocktail lounge was done in Chinese art deco and separated from the main dining room by a shoulder-high peach-colored wood-paneled divider. There were large round tables in the dining room, where coral-colored walls rose to a deep blue ceiling. On the wall behind the bar was a huge hand-painted mural of Havana harbor.

"I'm sorry I'm late," Diego said. "I had to see to my children, and you know Hector." For a moment Diego was tongue-tied. "I brought Justo," he managed to say.

He went behind the bar. There was no one else in the cocktail lounge but Benny and Cano.

With a sudden paternal smile and then a laugh, Benny told Cano of the day's adventure on Roosevelt Avenue. Saying yes, the bitch was rolling around in the street, screaming we are innocent, we are innocent, don't shoot him. Diego squinted, trying to come on shocked and bewildered, talking to Cano, saying the son of a bitch wanted to shoot me.

It was Cano's turn to laugh. "Shoot you," he said, "what for?"

Benny saying, "This guy, this bastard Rodrigo, he thinks my cousin here is trying to fuck his wife."

A mistake, Diego knew it immediately; he saw Cano's expression tighten just a little.

Cano said, "It's true, you been fucking this man's woman, his wife?"

"Of course not," Diego said. "I go to his restaurant, the Hatuey—you know the Hatuey—because I love the coffee and sandwiches she makes there."

"Coffee and sandwiches?" Cano said.

"This woman has an ass and a pair of tits that are perfect, man," Benny said.

"You mean," Cano said, "this woman, this Natalia is beautiful?"

Diego felt a stirring in his stomach. "Beautiful, yes Natalia is very beautiful. She says she loves me, thinks about me all the time. Sometimes when she is lying in bed at night, she tells me she dreams of having me inside her."

"And you tell me you go to the Hatuey for the coffee and sandwiches," Cano said.

Benny said, "This woman is a *puta*, man, you'd better stop it, Diego. This woman is bad for you, like a bottle of poison."

Diego held up his hands, his face open, innocent. "To this moment I have done nothing wrong, nothing to be ashamed of. Sure, Natalia is a perfect woman for me, but she is married."

"The perfect woman," Cano said, "is a life-support system for a pussy. Nothing more than that."

Benny said, "What he means, Diego, if you got no plans to take this woman to bed and screw her until her eyes cross, then what the hell are you doing with her?"

Diego couldn't help himself, he smiled.

"It's not funny," Benny said. "The woman has a husband who wants to put a bullet in your Cuban ass. Wake up, will you, man? I'm going to have to kill this fuck, this Rodrigo, so you can have your coffee and sandwich in peace."

Cano grunted.

"Is that what you want? You want me to shoot him, boom-boom? Fuck him, man, I'll go kill the son of a bitch."

"Please," Diego said, "let's not go crazy here. Sometimes Benny you talk crazy."

Benny waved his drink in the air, saying, "Diego, if you don't want to take Natalia, then leave the bitch alone."

Cano was staring hard at Diego, like he couldn't believe it.

"That is exactly what I'm doing," Diego said. He turned and inspected the bottles on the bar, tried the Coke, beer, and soda taps. "You know," he said, "I just saw the man in his cab, and his passenger was Oscar, your bartender."

"Hold it," Benny said, and held up his hand. "What?"

"I saw Rodrigo in his cab on Roosevelt."

"And Oscar was with him?"

"That's what I said. Maybe you don't treat him right, maybe he's looking for a job."

Benny stared at him.

"Who is this Rodrigo?" Cano said. "Is he anybody?"

Benny shook his head.

Diego said, "Benny told me Oscar is too sick to come to work, that's why I am here behind the bar tonight." He looked past Benny, past Cano to the three Americanos coming through the door, the Italians from Brooklyn. They looked very much alike and none of them appeared to be over twenty-five. He looked at Benny, *Dios*, the man was still staring at him.

"I don't know what Oscar is doing with Rodrigo?" Diego said. "Maybe you know, huh?" What the hell was wrong with Benny, staring like that?

After a moment Benny said, "Oscar knows my business, much of my business."

Cano cocked his head at Benny. "What do you mean he knows your business? I am asking again, who is this Rodrigo?" He put his hands on the bar.

The three Italians walked into the dining room and took their usual table in the rear, across from the men's room. They all wore zippered leather jackets and had vacant, steady smiles on their faces. One of them Diego knew as Shorty; it was how he introduced himself.

"Oscar knows my business and he's halfway to a moron," Benny said.

Cano looked dreamily at Benny for a beat, as if wondering where to take it. "And this Rodrigo?" he said.

"He's a lying, thieving, big mulatto bastard. He drives a cab, runs the Hatuey. I'm told he has friends with the police."

Cano turned to Diego, who shrugged helplessly. "Sounds to me like you got problems here, my friend. Problems you had better take care of. Maybe somebody should go to the *botánica* and get some poison for these guys."

The words came out hard, outraged. Diego stepped back, shocked, caught by surprise. He stared at Benny.

Benny saying, "Shit, Cano, I don't want my enemies to die because when they do I'll be lonely and have nothing to live for."

And Cano, smiling now, saying, "Don't you worry, I have enough enemies to cheer the both of us."

Diego kept still, he knew that Benny and Cano meant exactly what they said. Benny now saying, "It's good you saw what you saw, Diego. It was good. Oscar and Rodrigo together is bad news. If I didn't know that then maybe I'm in the wrong fucking business."

"You asking for my opinion?" Cano said.

Benny looked at him. "No," he said.

Chapter 6

Nine thirty P.M., Nick was crossing the Queensboro Bridge; the harbor and Manhattan skyline were gloomy beneath an overcast sky. A thunderstorm had broken over the city and a hard rain battered Nick's car as he drove in the direction of Queens. After the day's events he was tired and anxious, but his spirits had lifted the minute he left McCabe and the others at Post Time. McCabe in his element, running around in his Italian loafers handing out drinks, pounding people on the back; the jester on stage, everyone's champion. Nick had watched him a long time.

Nick drove along thinking about the last moments, the way McCabe came after him when he was leaving Post Time, threw his arm around his shoulders, smiling at him, saying whataya think, pally, we had a good day, didn't we? The way McCabe pinched his cheek, telling Nick he should learn to relax, saying God love ya Nick, you'd be one hell of a guy if you could only learn to chill out. Sonny McCabe walking him to his car, Sonny's arm draped over Nick's shoulders, speaking in that confiding, side-mouthed way of his, explaining that OCCU was a great detail, a terrific place to work, and that Nick was going to love being a part of their team. Asking Nick if he would like Sonny to tag along, maybe give him a hand when he met with the DA. They were partners, Sonny said and he didn't like to send any of his partners off on their own. Halfway across the bridge, in the dark of his car, the rain coming straight down, the city beneath him, Nick felt himself smile.

Relaxed except for a distinct wariness in the back of his mind about the case, Nick considered that he was doing fairly well.

Starting out, Nick Manaris had been a patrol officer in East Harlem. After two years, a stint in Brooklyn Youth Patrol, promotion to detective, and a move to the Manhattan North homicide squad. Two more promotions, then assignment to the Narcotics Division. A year that was like a century in narcotics. The division had been a madhouse of corruption and wildass cops. Nick wanted no part of that. He made no friends there, had little to say to his fellow narcotics detectives. He asked out.

Transfers were not easy to come by for a first-grader. But Nick "had weight." He went to Andre Robinson, his rabbi. Andre made the call and bingo, Nick was out of narcotics and into the OCCU.

He felt exhilarated, looking down at the East River now, two tugs holding their bows into the current, the water moving fast, its surface pushing and swelling against the resistance of the cement and stone pilings of the bridge. Stopped dead in traffic, looking out at the river, he found himself thinking of Renata.

Nick had married a girl from Westport, Connecticut. She hated Nick's work, hated The Job. They were childless, and she was distressed. He was twenty-nine when she fled, left him for a professor of English from Jersey. In his fourth decade, bereft, brimming with grief and frustrated love, Nick Manaris was in a long, lonely angry dance with this life of his.

He had been unable to connect with women for years. Renata, his most recent shot at a relationship, had bolted and was heading south. He hoped she'd come back, yet at the same time he'd been thinking, what's worse, a bad relationship or none at all? Anyway, his instinct told him Renata was history, the end, another end.

Once he had convinced Renata to go on a fishing trip off Block Island. Funny that a woman who was a star athlete in high school and college, who loved the outdoors and ran five miles a day, did not like boats or fishing. She tried though, Renata tried. But she complained that the ocean frightened her, the rough seas, that she couldn't use the head and finally as Nick was casting with light tackle for some surface blues, that she wasn't having any fun.

Renata's idea of excitement was to spend a good chunk of her day searching out bargains. A night's fun was a video, and pizza delivered from Ray's. Eating out was important, a major deal. That is, if there wasn't anything good in the video store. Her professional life was so draining, she said, exhausting. A special-education teacher with the New York City Board of Ed, Renata spent her days in hand-to-hand combat with underprivileged and underdeveloped children, profoundly challenged midget gangsters, Renata's words. She was not a good teacher, she put herself through agony every day. A tall blonde, mercurial in an erotic, erratic way, she could pass sex by. I can take it or leave it, she had told him. Making love was not one of her passions. A real problem there. He flashed on Renata standing in the kitchen, her fingers pinching the bridge of her nose, saying that he simply was not around at the right time, he worked insane hours. Besides, the wicked baby criminals exhausted her. And the topper, he was gone too many weekends, fishing.

Nick did admit to being a compulsive fisherman, extreme. Up at two A.M. on his days off, driving about three hours north to a certain beach for surf casting. Sometimes he'd meet E. Z. Brochard and go "offshore" on his boat. Renata grew up in the city, her parents grew up in the city. The woman had no sense of adventure, and to Nick, a good boat, big fish, a day spent on the ocean with people who thought as he did was sublime. And when, halfway up a ten-foot swell, Renata, all blue around the gills, that morning in the boat, when she asked, Nick, what is it about this that you like? And he had told her I love it, Renata. I goddamn love it. His eyes searching the sea over her head while he sought the right words. This is real, this is peace, this is me. C'mon, she had said, c'mon. Renata, he had said, for me, this boat, this place, this ocean is flat-out celebration. I feel purely alive, I can feel every nerve and fiber of my body unwind. Maybe it was at that precise moment that Renata decided to flee.

It was when he made that easy left turn at the foot of the Queensboro Bridge that he caught sight of a black BMW with tinted windows. The same BMW he had noticed parked on the street not far from Post Time. For a moment he had the notion he was being followed. Nick kept watch, reflecting that there was no more menacing sight than a black BMW with treated windows. Satan on your tail. At Woodhaven Boulevard the Beemer hung a right and was gone. Coincidence, for sure, the driver most probably a Queens guy and there wasn't but one way to get to Queens from downtown, if you didn't want to spring two bucks for the Midtown Tunnel. He didn't get the registration, but to be frank, he had other things on his mind.

Nick continued on Queens Boulevard eastbound, fighting his way through the rain-slowed Friday night traffic. It had been several months since he had been to Andre's apartment and he felt lighthearted, on his way to see one of the two people he could truly call a friend.

The Queens Towers was on Austin Street in Forest Hills, thirty stories overlooking the city; it had an underground garage, valet parking, and an elevator that played show tunes. On a clear night there was a spectacular view of Manhattan from Andre's twenty-fourth-floor apartment. Nick pulled straight in and nosed the cruiser into a row of parked cars. He took his attaché case from off the front seat and handed the keys to a uniformed black teenage attendant.

Nick entered the elevator, punched twenty-four, stepped back, and waited, not sure what he was feeling, whether he wanted to impress McCabe, Captain Hawks, and the others, whether it mattered one way or the other. These thoughts of his going round in his head as he went down the hall to Andre's door. The door opened and there was Andre, suave and formal, impeccable in chinos, soft leather loafers, and a red cashmere sweater, just as impeccable as he was in pinstripes. The sounds of Big Bill Broonzy's guitar came from behind him. Andre asking how the hell have you been? you don't call, you don't write. Throwing his arm around Nick, giving him a hug, pulling Nick into the apartment with, as always, a good deal of confidence and charm.

Nick and Andre were twenty minutes into their conversation, drinking in the living room, when Nick said, "I've been here, what, ten, fifteen times? And you know, I never noticed that before."

"What?"

Nick eased himself off the sofa and took a turn around the room, looking at the bookshelves that lined the walls. "Your books are alphabetized."

"Yeah, so?"

"So? Are you serious? There are maybe a thousand books here, floor-to-ceiling books, and you alphabetized them?"

"So?"

Nick laughed and shook his head. Andre told him he'd been doing it since he was in grade school, he didn't think it was any big deal. No one else had ever mentioned it. Your LPs, and tapes, those too? Nick asked, and Andre told him sure, why? What's the problem? Goddamn, it's something, Nick said. I'm surprised is all, you know? I'm surprised. He looked at Andre for a response, but Andre had picked up the warrant applications, avoiding Nick's stare.

"So you met with the CI. What's your opinion, the guy reliable or what?"

"Reliable? What's reliable? He's a snitch."

"Don't be cute, he reliable or not?"

"Attached to the last application, the one for Cienfuego, there's a list there. Arrests and dispositions, information from this character Rodrigo Punto. It's all there. Five arrests, four convictions based on Punto's information."

Andre glanced up from the pages of notes in front of him. Without his glasses, he had to squint at Nick a little. "Do you believe all of this?"

"I prepared the applications, signed the affidavits."

After a very long moment Andre grunted. He dropped his eyes and continued reading the forms in his lap. "These are well written," he said. "I could get these signed by a judge, no problem."

"Good."

"Tomorrow is Saturday, Janeway is sitting in the arraignment part. If I approve them, he'd sign off."

Bruce Janeway was a criminal courts fixture, a heavy-duty drinker and a world-class womanizer. Nick had always known him to be a defense-oriented judge. A man chock full of concern for the bad guys, with his ponytail and red Jeep convertible, throwing spectators in his courtroom the peace sign, ripping cops at the drop of a hat. The guy always coming on like a one-man compassion clinic, a real pain in the ass.

"Janeway?" he said. "That guy's no bargain. When did Janeway become our ally?"

"The night he hit on a hooker at the Stadium Lounge, across from Shea. You wouldn't believe the curious tricks Janeway was into. Anyway, the hooker was an undercover, part of a sting we were running. We had a little private conversation, me and the good judge. Ten minutes and bingo, Janeway went from Cut-'em-Loose Bruce to Jam-'em Janeway."

"Serves him right."

"Politicking," Andre said.

"You're good at it. A natural."

"We'll soon see. I plan to make a run for DA next year."

"The last time we spoke you weren't so sure."

"I am now. I'll announce sometime in the spring. These Queens Democrats, they're a tough bunch to please, but in all modesty, I know how."

"Really?" Nick said. "How?"

"Politicking. Raise bullshitting to an art form. You do it with a smile. Tell them you're hungry and have a burning need to win. Tell them you're a Democrat but still believe in the death penalty, an important

Queens issue. Then you talk about Roosevelt and Kennedy, how those guys affected you on a deep personal level. How Reverend King, Bobby, and Jack changed your life. Say you're ready to support Democratic issues all over the city. Tell them you want to go all the way. Tell them whatever they want to hear—nothing beats good old-fashioned bullshit."

"So what's the bullshit? It sounds like you," Nick said.

"You'll recognize it when you see it. It wont take you long. Listen," Andre said, rearranging himself on the sofa. "This works for me, the election and all, I'll want you here. With me. I'll want you as my chief investigator."

"Well, beautiful," Nick said. "I hope you go all the way. District attorney, mayor, governor. New York's first black senator."

"The district attorney would be just fine for the time being."

"Hell man, this city can do a lot worse than you. Christ, they've *done* a lot worse than you."

"Now that's what I call a ringing endorsement."

"Hey, for what it's worth, you got my support."

Andre smiled suddenly, throwing Nick a quick and wistful look; you could see the kid in him, the kid he'd been. Drop-dead good-looking, smarter than hell, a scholar-athlete. "I appreciate that, I do," genuinely touched.

As if it were a confidential aside, never before uttered aloud, Andre saying when you were at Fordham Law you impressed the right people. Me for one, and that Jesuit, Father Raymond. We expected a lot from you. You would have made a hell of a lawyer. Nick saying shit man, there's more than enough lawyers in this country, more than enough good ones. I like being a cop and I love to fish. The loves of my life.

Andre studied him for a moment, saying finally, "Speaking of the loves of your life, how's Renata?"

"Gone. She went off to Miami, her college reunion." Feeling nervous now, Nick turned away and scanned the walls of books. "Things haven't been going great for us."

"Sorry to hear that. I like her. Smart lady, a pusher. Someone you need. I liked what she said about your going back to law school. It makes sense."

"There was a whole lot she wanted, a whole lot. Most of which I can't deliver." Nick finished his beer, threw it back like he was washing down about a pound of potato chips.

"You want another one of those?"

"No thanks. So I'll meet you in court tomorrow morning. There are four warrants there. It shouldn't take long."

"I want to throw something at you," Andre said. "Just sit a minute and listen, okay? If it's no, just forget I said anything."

Nick eased back onto the sofa and folded his hands in his lap. Andre's eyes were steady on him.

"I'll get these warrants for you. You want me to get them, I will. But first I'm going to tell you how I feel about your Captain Hawks and the others. That guy McCabe, Moran, that whole crew over at OCCU."

Nick sat very still.

"Look, I got you assigned there for a particular reason. You wanted out of narco, right? Me to you, off the record, I knew you'd never last there."

Nick puffed out some air and stretched. "No, well, you were right. I didn't like it there. At all."

"You see, I knew that, I know you. I'm just glad that I could help." Andre leaned forward, elbows on his knees, lacing his long fingers together.

"We've known each other ten years, right? I was with the attorney general's office five of those years, spent a couple years off on my own, and three years here in the DA's office. I've never reached out, never come to you and asked what you knew or didn't know about certain things in the PD. Never gone to you and said, 'Hey, what the hell is going on?' I kept feeling, wait for him to make the move, wait for Nick to come to me, he'll come to me in time. But I can't wait any longer."

"What are you talking about?" Nick said.

"See, lots of things have happened over these years. I'm sure you've noticed. Christ, you're the smartest cop I ever met."

Nick returned Andre's grin.

"How many beefs do you think came across my desk over these years? I get two or three a week, people accusing cops of doing this and that, taking their money, beating on them, helping the drug dealers. Nick, for as long as I've been in this city there has been the smell of sin around the police department."

Nick shifted on the sofa and raised his chin, saying, "I don't know where this conversation is going. It makes no sense to me."

"Hold it a minute. Hear me out. I think you owe me that much."

Nick was silent.

"Nick, what I'm saying is your department is in deep shit. Has been for years. What can I do about it? you ask. And why would I want to? Okay, well, you can make a difference, you can make a real impact."

"Oh, man, you got to be kidding. You're not serious, Andre."

"Hey look, don't make a judgment until you hear me out. What am I asking, a few minutes of your time. Christ, we're friends, aren't we?"

"G'head, g'head," Nick said brusquely, looking around the room, wondering just what kind of man alphabetized his books, for chrissake.

"Okay, just stay with me. Now, the department has had its share of investigations. Mostly small stuff, a precinct here, a precinct there. Uniformed cops, nothing major. Okay? Now, here's the thing." Andre paused, trying to catch Nick's eye. "You ready?"

"Just say it, Andre."

"Okay. This Captain Hawks, your CO. He's been bad for years, they got a sheet on him going back ten years. He gets promoted, then on top of that they give him a highly sensitive command like the OCCU. Like this guy is going to change his ways, you know?"

Nick's eyes were focused on the carpeting.

"Change his ways—he brings Sonny McCabe, Eddie Moran, and a bunch of other outlaws to the command with him."

Nick threw Andre a furtive glance, then looked away; he was desperate to be gone.

"Can I ask you Nick, how do you get along with those guys?" he said almost shyly.

"Fine, I get along with them just fine."

Andre laughed, baring his teeth. "I don't believe you. You're not being straight with me."

Nick ignored the comment. "I've been in the job for ten years. I mind my own business, do my work, and go home. This job is not my life. Sure I like the job, it's been good to me. Pays me well, I get plenty of time off, and every so often I can do something special."

"That's not what I'm saying. You know—I know you know—the OCCU is a flea market of misconduct."

"Andre, you're setting me up for something here and I don't like it."

Andre bent his head and rubbed his forehead with the back of his hand, saying, "This character, this Captain Hawks, and the others, they're a slick bunch. They make their own rules and do as they please. Take my word for it, they are one investigation away from a grand jury themselves."

"I don't think we are supposed to have this conversation, Andre. I'm not in Internal Affairs, and neither are you. If you have reason to suspect something, what you should do is notify the IAD, let them handle it."

"We've been friends for ten years, Nick, right? Have I ever come to you for a favor? The reason I am talking to you now, to be frank, is that I need a favor."

Nick had to force himself not to avoid Andre's eyes. He was getting tense, about an inch from angry. The truth of it was, he'd never have expected this, not in a million years.

Andre got up from the sofa, went into the kitchen, and returned carrying two more beers. He handed Nick one bottle and raised his own in salute.

"There's a lot of political twisting and turning going on in the district attorney's office. Santoro is one cool piece of work. He says he'll tap me to succeed him, but he hasn't. The party leaders here say they'll back me presently, but they haven't yet. Also the race issue is a hot one in Queens, no matter what they say in public. I know what they say to each other in private. It won't be easy for me, Nick."

"And what can I do, Andre? I'm just a cop."

"I want to make the choice for the party a simple one. I need a huge case, Nick, something with a lot of pizzazz. Front page of *The New York Times*, six and eleven o'clock news. I need your help."

He took a swallow of his beer, keeping his eyes on Nick.

"Listen, Nick, I want to know what Hawks and the others are up to. They're up to something. I know them, they're up to no good, and I want to nail them, nail them all to the wall."

Nick's spirits sagged. He moved his head around as if to relieve neck pain, saying, "We put this Los Campos thing together, you'll have a big case."

"Yeah, well, it's not the case I want, not what I need. You know what I need. Don't give me this razzmatazz."

"Wait a minute," Nick said, feeling charged now. "What in the hell are you talking about? What are you saying? No, wait, wait. You are asking me to be an informant, to spy on the people I work with. I would have to be crazy. I would have to be evil and a bit out of my mind to do something like that. What the hell are you trying to do, Andre, send the messenger of misery to my house?"

"You're part of their team, it would be the easiest thing in the world for you to keep an eye out. Watch what they're up to. Nick, c'mon, these are money guys. They don't work a case unless there is some payoff. The thing is," he went on before Nick could object, "it's me you'd be doing this for, me. You're going to be in a position to really help me out."

"Andre, the last thing I ever thought you'd do is ask me to do something like this. You're my friend."

"It's an imperfect world, Nick. People have to take sides. Look, these guys are a shiv in the side of the police department."

"What you're asking . . . If what you're saying is that you want me to be an informant, then I'm telling you, we are not friends, have never been friends. We are strangers."

Andre gazed at him sorrowfully. "Okay, Nick, look, maybe I should have put it another way." He pressed his palms together, prayerlike. "Okay. What I mean, if things are going to work in this city, cops like that bunch have got to be put down. It's important that it gets done, you know?"

Nick took a very long draw on his beer. He started to say something, hesitated. Wondered if he should excuse himself, get up and leave. He raised his eyebrows. "You arranged to have me transferred to OCCU thinking I'd spy for you?"

Andre nodded. Nick thinking strange, it is really strange, you thought you knew Andre Robinson and you didn't know Andre Robinson at all. He felt rattled, he had to wrap this bullshit up and be gone.

"This conversation," Nick said, "is depressing the shit out of me, because it reminds me that we are truly all users out here. All of us with our own agendas, everybody out to screw everyone else. Total vindication for the don't-ever-give-a-fuck crowd. Man, and people want to know why I love the honesty of the ocean."

"Look," Andre said. "If I insulted you I am sorry. I thought since we were friends and had the same moral view of the world, our friendship and shared convictions justified my asking a favor."

"I'm going to tell you something, Andre, your justifications are bullshit. You were prepared to turn my life upside down to help your political career. Sorry," Nick said. "No thank you." He stood up.

Andre rose, walking him to the door, draping his arm over Nick's shoulders, tugging at him like Sonny McCabe. They stood together at the apartment door. "My intentions were good and honorable," Andre said.

Andre liked to talk, he went on for about five minutes, describing the pressures he felt, the plight of the black man in America. When he got around to asking about Captain Hawks again, Nick decided he'd had enough.

"I don't want to hear any more of this," Nick told him. "You tell me you had good intentions. Everyone has good intentions, maybe even Hawks and Sonny McCabe. What I want to know now is, what are you going to do about these warrants?"

"Meet me at the courthouse in the morning. I'll get them signed for you."

"Good, that's good. Then I can go out and do my job and arrest some bad guys."

"Make sure no one gets killed, will you? McCabe and the others are a bunch of cowboys."

"No one is going to get killed, not if I can help it."

"Good, good. Hey, look, who can tell. After you work with these characters for a while you may feel different about what I asked you. So if things shape up the way I think they will with this team of yours maybe sometime I'll ask you again."

Nick only smiled. They shook hands.

"I'll see you in the morning," Nick said. It was not until he was about halfway home that he heard the suggestion of threat in Andre's final words. He thought again of the ocean, the sea, the blue, mako, and great white sharks. Nick had caught plenty of blue shark, which he tagged and set loose, and mako, which he ate. Once about two years back, over the Mud Hole, about twenty-five clicks west of Block Island, he had met a great white. The fish had been feeding on a dying, floating whale. He recalled watching the monster rock and roll, his great jaws tearing loose huge chunks of meat. It was a bright day, the sea was flat, tuna birds danced along the top of the whale, taking their own bits and pieces. He recalled how he had felt at that moment, his heart going out to the whale, the way he felt right now, almost without friends, alone.

About a half hour later Nick dropped his car in the police parking lot two blocks from his apartment, thinking again about Andre, how the man had shocked him. Not because of what he'd said, though that too had unnerved him, turned his stomach to ashes. Andre speaking so smoothly, trying to absorb him, trying to pull him in. Andre knowing goddamn well the consequences of what he was asking, that Nick would be harmed by what he was asking. The fact that he was willing to ask. Son of a bitch.

But the guy's all-out need to come out on top, that had also been a shock. He would be the DA, and yeah, maybe even the mayor. This, the same guy that used to speak of politicians with disdain, with distaste. Still, it was more than that—Andre had as much as said that he had planned for a long time to turn him into an informant. A snitch. Now Nick wasn't sure if he had handled it right. What he was feeling was that he should have thrown a fit. Got in Andre's face and let him have it. Christ, a stool pigeon, Andre Robinson wanted to turn him around.

Son of a bitch.

Funny thing was, Nick didn't feel as though he could complain. For years Andre had been his hook, his weight in the department. If not for Andre Robinson he would still be ducking bricks in the youth squad. He just wished Andre had never talked to him that way. It was weird, he felt embarrassed, ashamed that anyone could think of him that way, that he could be a fink. And he was equally ashamed that he was giving it some thought, since that was what Andre had thought he might do. That he would be just one more snitch. It drove him nuts. He would have liked to think that when Andre spoke to him about the OCCU the guy would have done it in a thoughtful way. Like a buddy, like a friend, maybe asked his advice about this and that. Not like a prosecutor, the guy's face all twisted. Jesus! How fast Andre could switch from one to the other, from friend to prosecutor, it blew his mind. Telling Nick he was the smartest cop he ever met. What a bunch of crap.

In his apartment, Nick examined himself in the bathroom mirror. His right eye hurt, it was killing him, bloodshot as hell. He needed some sleep, a good night's rest, seven, eight hours. Turn on the answering machine and turn off the ringer on the phone, get into bed, not a thought about Renata, no lying back watching late night news, which he was inclined to do. Nick Manaris had all the news he needed. Tomorrow he would get the warrants signed and that was that.

In bed, trying to find sleep, he tossed and twisted. Wondered whether Andre could read his face. Nick proud of the fact that no one could ever read his face if he didn't want them to read it. He curled himself up in the blankets, thinking of Renata in that black bikini of hers, the way she stuck her thumbs under her breasts, giving them a boost, laughing, giving Nick a jolt. His heart banging in his ears now, a roaring in his ears. Andre saying *Maybe sometime I'll ask you again.*

Son of a bitch.

Chapter 7

Diego spent the early part of the evening serving drinks, engaging in small talk with the Cubans, Puerto Ricans, and Colombians that were Los Campos's regulars. Slick, lean, young street men out on the town with their women. Spaced-out sharpies who stood with weird frozen smiles, as if all the mysteries of the night were known to them. Men who hissed and called out, "Party time, Professor, how about a Scotch and water, a sloe gin fizz for my lady here." A handful drank top-shelf Scotch, mostly they drank Cuba libres, rum and Coke with lime.

Men in dazzling shirts and slacks of silk and linen, good costly haircuts and jewelry, shoes from Italy and Spain, clapped hands and rolled their shoulders to the music of Prez Prado and Mongo Santamaría. They seemed the prosperous hombres but in fact were little more than boys. And although Diego cringed at the sound of their Spanish, he found them entertaining, even charming. There were no bearded men, and no one wore a suit.

At the far end of the bar a black Cuban with a harelip had his arm around a woman in a cheap green dress, his hand on her fleshy hip. The man's name was Montoya, he wore a sporty black sports jacket and seemed to Diego to be unhappy.

Montoya smiled at him. A little later he came over and softly asked Diego if he were going to sing. Diego had already told a number of the others that he would do a bolero soon, and he told Montoya that too.

Later, around three o'clock in morning, when the club's action was winding down, Diego carried a barstool and his guitar to the dance floor.

In a circle of light, Diego sang "Bésame Mucho" like a heavenly spirit, he sang his heart out. An old-fashioned crooner, he touched the hearts of every person in the room, brought back thoughts of bygone days and past loves. Couples out of the circle of light, in the darkness, moaned and kissed and ran searching hands between parted thighs.

When Diego had finished the last verse he returned to his post behind the bar. He was feeling transformed now, misty-eyed, loose, trying to look the star for the dozen or so single women who still remained and were moving around in their sexy outfits, throwing smiles at him, puckering their lips. Some leaned against the bar while others sat at tables, alone or in pairs. A few were high-roller prostitutes; rocking idly, they sized up the single drunk dudes. Some held glasses of ginger ale bought by men whose brains were so fried they thought they were buying champagne. For these women there would be some money later from Benny.

The late hour and neon bar lights shrouded in thick, wafting cigarette smoke, the outrageous smell of marijuana seemed to Diego to give the club a certain Bohemian atmosphere. It was a quality he found pleasing.

Diego heard Benny call to him from his spot at a table in the center of the room. "Diego," he said. "That was beautiful, man. You are a great talent."

In his white silk suit, Benny sat with Cano, their faces illuminated by the red glow of a candle. The Vasserman brothers from Manhattan and Tito Roman with his Bronx crew were seated at a table behind them. Stone gangsters. Diego had often overheard them talking of guns and cocaine. He thought of them as trash people. People it was wise to steer clear of.

Chino, the younger of the Vasserman brothers, had a wide open face with these Asian eyes that made him look innocent, soft. But the way he curled his lip and nodded when he smiled told you he was anything but. Mambo, the older brother, seemed to Diego to have adopted this New York street style of the averted eye and firmly closed mouth. Mambo had the face of an owl and the neck of a pig. Benny's friends, Diego considered, moved around like a school of predators on the bottom of the ocean.

"Hey, that was pretty good, my friend," Cano said. *"Ven acá conmigo."* Come over here with me.

"Thank you," Diego called out. He scanned the room, searching for someone cheerful and lighthearted, needing some excuse to go somewhere, anywhere other than Cano and Benny's table. He took a sip of his vodka and orange juice; it was too strong.

"Ven acá," Cano called out. He sat with his fingers laced behind his head. Next to Cano, Benny was hunched over in whispered conversation with pig-necked Mambo Vasserman.

Cano stared at Diego. Diego was reluctant to look at him, but when he did he was surprised to see the Colombian smiling, as if he'd just discovered an amazing secret.

Suddenly the jukebox began to pound out a salsa tune. In one corner of the club a group of four women twisted and squirmed like professional cabaret dancers.

Diego tried to appear casual, sucking down his drink. More and more he was feeling anxious, frightened.

"Ven, Professor," Cano shouted.

Diego crossed the room to Benny and Cano's table.

"Hey, Professor," Cano said. "I heard that you were a Fidelista."

Diego cleared his throat. "What's that?" he said.

"I said, I heard that you were a commie. That true? You were a friend of Castro, huh?"

"No, no. No friend. I believed in him once. He had dreams and gave himself to his country. That was before. A long time ago."

"A *Pionera*, huh? I bet you loved that commie fag bastard Che, huh?"

Diego looked at the suspicion building in Cano's eyes. He watched him pour himself some Scotch from the bottle in front of him.

"Love? Yes, I suppose you could say I loved him; he was a man of dignity. Then they killed him, and you know, times changed."

"So what are you doing here? Man, you should be in Havana. Not here with these traitors and imperialists."

The Vasserman brothers had left their table and moved toward the dance floor. They stood now practicing dance moves.

"You know, Cano," Diego said. "I'm not a political person. I came here looking for the good life for me and my kids. Just like you, huh?"

Standing, swaying a little, Cano put his hand on Diego's arm. "Like me? Man, you are not like me. I hate commies, I hate cops, I hate every motherfucker that ain't with me. You with me, Professor? Tell me, what side are you on?"

Benny held up his hand and smiled, saying, "Cano, Diego was my cousin's husband. He's family, man. Since when you talk politics, I never heard you talk politics. What is this, some kind of joke?"

Cano did not look amused. He turned from Benny and stared at Diego, got up real close to Diego. Diego could have bent and kissed his forehead. The Colombian's breath was stale from drink and smoke and the bitter foul juices that rose from his stomach and filled his throat. Diego turned aside, buried his chin in his shoulder. He felt queasy, and the fear that ate at him was growing and moving like a snake in his gut.

"This man," Cano said, "is a fool, Benny. Your cousin here, your family here, is a pussy without a backbone, without the stomach to be a man." He threw Diego a grin.

No one had ever called Diego a coward before. He was rattled by the Colombian's words, the manner in which he spoke to him. Diego had been a coward in Miami—Cano froze him, frightened him as he had been frightened then. He stared at Cano, then glanced around the room, stunned by the vividness of the memory. "You know, Cano . . ." Diego hesitated, sensing he was about to get himself into trouble, but forged ahead. "I think maybe you drank too much."

"Hey man, fuck you," Cano said. "Tomorrow, what are you doing tomorrow?"

"Cano," Benny said.

"Shut up, Benny. I want him here tomorrow. Three o'clock. You hear me, Professor? Tomorrow at three, here."

Both Diego and Cano stared, Cano turning to Benny and saying, "You are a stupid man. You talk too much and trust everybody, even a fucking bartender."

It confounded Diego—did Cano mean Oscar Melendez or him?

Benny shook his head, smiling. "No, I don't." He lifted his rum and coke; Diego saw his hand tremble.

"I'll be here," Diego said.

Cano patted Diego's arm in a friendly fashion. "Who knows?" he said. "Maybe you'll prove me wrong."

Diego began to laugh.

Cano grinned happily.

Diego and Justo stood in the parking lot waiting for Hector to pick them up. Cano appeared from the club's back door, he came up to Diego and walked him off a few feet.

"Listen Diego," he said. "I need to talk to you."

Diego shrugged in a way that could have meant why not? or about what?

"You're a man who people say is very smart. Maybe that's true, huh?"

Diego shrugged again.

"I am going to tell you about my experience in this life. Maybe you can learn something."

Diego folded his arms and tried to calm himself. How to play this guy? What to do? "I never pretend to be a smart man. I am what I am," he said, wondering what in the hell these people, this Colombian wanted from him.

"Have you ever been arrested? Ever been to prison?"

Diego felt a tremble of apprehension. "No."

"I have. And let me tell you, Professor, prison can be good. It can be very good. Like a university, time in prison can teach many things."

Diego didn't answer.

"When you become familiar with prison you gain a new love of the free life. The night sky is more beautiful, more brilliant." He suddenly thrust a finger into Diego's chest. "The color red becomes more red for you. Suddenly you fall in love with the morning air, the miracle of a woman's body and her passion." Cano's hand touched his cheek, lingered, then moved away. "You know, I'll never go back to prison. Never."

Diego looked at Cano, who spread his hands wide.

"Your wife's cousin Benny is a tough guy," Cano said, "real tough. But the words 'smart' and 'Benny' should never be used in the same sentence. Do you understand me?"

Diego hesitated, not at all sure what Cano was saying. "I understand," he lied. "A man like you must be careful." To Diego, Cano seemed very drunk, stoned, very dangerous. Exactly like the men who had humiliated him in Miami.

"You know, people say be careful, but I don't care what people think. I figure I get one shot in this life, and I'm ready to take my chances now."

Cano reached up and put his hand on Diego's shoulder. "You did a good thing tonight. You warned us about Oscar and Rodrigo. That was good, a very good thing."

Diego looked away. "It was no big deal," he said. "They were just riding together in a car. No big thing at all." He tried to put a casual spin on it, tried not to admit to himself that he had for sure put Oscar and Rodrigo in harm's way.

Cano grabbed him by the wrist. "You be here tomorrow at three o'clock. Okay my friend?" he said.

Diego did not answer.

"I want to see you here tomorrow, okay?" Cano repeated.

"What for?"

"Hey man, because I ask you. It's like a test, you know?"

"A test," Diego said. It was more an unhappy statement than a question.

"You are a frightened man, Diego. I want to see just how afraid you are."

Diego jerked his wrist free, frantic to be gone. "Listen, Cano," he said in a whisper, "you are reading me wrong. I'm not afraid."

"Fear," Cano said, "stinks like pussy. You got the smell of pussy all over you."

"What is there for me to be frightened of?"

"You tell me. Maybe death, everyone's afraid of death, huh?"

"You are wrong Cano. Death does not scare me. I have lived long enough to know that it may come tomorrow or it may come later, but it's bound to come to everyone in the end. Even tough men like you." Diego took a few steps backward.

"Are you going to show up tomorrow?"

"Sure." Diego vibrated at the thought. *Tomorrow at three*, the sound of those words rang in his soul like a mantra.

———

"He's crazy." Diego stared blindly out of the car window. "The man drinks, and smokes way too much reefer. And I think he does a whole lot of coke too."

Hector said, "Shit man, he's a wizard, Cano is the wonderman. He digs you, man. Cano told me himself that he thinks you're cool. You should be nice to him, Professor, he's an important man."

Diego didn't answer. His mind replaying the bizarre conversation. What to do? Cano was a madman, a for-real crazy. What does he want from me? he thought. Just what does this redheaded wild Colombian have planned? He wanted him at Los Campos—for what?

Diego sat still, talking to himself, as Hector drove too fast along Roosevelt Avenue. He sat wringing his hands, wondering, having a debate with himself, the dead quiet, early morning sidewalks rushing by. The smell of fear. He felt as if he was a clown, and he imagined Cano and the Vasserman brothers back there laughing. Diego tried to pump himself full of courage, but it was like wishing he was a ghost and could disappear. Cano had told him to be at Los Campos at three o'clock and he said he would be there; it was hopeless. He had to show up. He imagined explaining to Cano that he had made other plans. I would have shown up, but I had to take my kids to the zoo.

Diego turned and saw that Justo had spread himself out along the back seat. The boy was exhausted, his eyes were puffy and closed from nine hours of shoveling detergents into pots and pans in Los Campos's kitchen. Diego stared at his son, thinking the boy had seen so little of life, and yet so much.

Benny's Buick was parked at the curb in front of Diego's house. Diego felt instant relief, like a warm bath when you are bone tired.

Hector double-parked, and Diego woke Justo and led his testy, distressed, and overtired boy by the elbow up the front stoop and into the house.

Sunrise ran in a narrow pink and gray line along the edge of the early morning sky. It was five A.M. when Diego joined Benny in his car.

"Jesus Christ, I'm tired," Benny said.

"Me too. Are you going home now?"

"Sure."

"Listen," Diego said, "I am glad you stopped by. I need to talk to you."

"I figured you would. I figured after talking to Cano, you wouldn't be able to sleep. Cano can do that to you, he can do that to anyone. Make them not sleep. It's fucking five o'clock in the morning," Benny complained, glancing at his wristwatch.

"This is a bad man, Benny. This Cano is evil."

"Fucking bum. When you left he tells me he is going to straighten you out. You know, teach you something. He gave me this speech about prison, how he is never going back."

"First he called me a coward, then he made the same speech to me. I am no coward, Benny."

"Hell man, I know that. Didn't you stand up to Rodrigo, the guy pointing a gun in your face? You stood there, man. You stood your ground. Cano don't know you. Thinks everybody is a punk but him."

"Yeah, well, he's kind of right. I am not like him. Not a criminal, a gangster. The man is smart and crazy. A crazy smart man is very dangerous. You had better be careful."

"Fuck him, man," Benny said, anger coming into his face now. "That's the problem with these Colombians, give them a gun and they think they are Superman."

"I have met some very good Colombian people, my friend," Diego said.

"Is that right? I haven't."

"He wants me at the club at three tomorrow."

"I know, and you told him you'd be there. It's a problem."

"I wanted to spend some time with my kids. Mariaclara and Miguel are alone too often. It's not good, not healthy."

Benny gave Diego a weary ugly grin. "You already told Cano you would be there."

"Yeah, talk, talk," Diego said, thinking Cano was so loaded the man most likely would not remember their conversation. Thinking of Cano's eyes, those crazy Colombian blue eyes, turning that image off real fast, thinking of Cano, Cano staring at him, hissing at him like a redheaded viper. Saying *he's a pussy, he has no stomach to be a man.* Like the people in Miami, the black American kids who showed him their guns and took the money from his pocket, his watch, his daughter's necklace. The way they made that clicking noise when he begged them not to hurt his child. Mariaclara standing there on that Miami street, stone-faced, not a trace of emotion, without fear. Even when they tore the necklace from her throat, never a sound. Seeing himself now as those ferocious teenagers saw him, on his knees, begging, pleading, in sheer terror. Remembering his daughter's impassive black eyes watching her father, seeing himself through his daughter's eyes.

"Look man," Benny said, "it's up to you. You want, you can spend the day with your kids. I'll handle Cano."

Diego leaned back against the car seat and saw Miami again. "Why does he want me there? What's going on at three o'clock?"

"Business," Benny said. "Just some business we need to do."

"But I am not involved in your business."

"My friend, you are around it. You may not know that you are around it; however, you are."

Diego frowned. In Benny's smiling face he read the word *trouble*, and the word sounded in his tired head with a merciless resonance.

"You know, you could make some money," Benny said. "People trust men like you, so cool and educated. You're not a street bum like me, and not a miserable bastard like Cano. You could make real money, the kind of money you could use for your family."

Diego imagined having the kind of money Benny and Cano seemed to have. Being able to do things for his children, to pay for their education, buy himself a car. It was foolishness. He was an honest man and if the honest man believed in something, really believed in it, then he must act on it. Still, Diego understood enough of this life to know that in the end there is little hope for the honest man. If I walk away from Benny, he thought, I'll be lost here in this city. He was confused, and no answers crawled up out of the gutter into his lap.

"What do you think, Benny?"

"It's up to you. But you can't work at the club any longer unless you join us. You have to be with us, or you have to be gone. Cano won't have it any other way. Listen Diego, Cano don't care if a man is smart or dumb, as long as he knows whose side he's on."

"And he's the boss?"

"Yes, yes he is. You know, if you don't work at Los Campos there is not much you can do in this city. Sure you could wash dishes, bag groceries. Maybe if you're lucky you could find a job singing somewhere. But I doubt it. You have a good thing here, Diego. Think about it."

Diego shrugged, thinking that that was probably true.

Benny took Diego's hand and put folded money into it. Diego looked down and saw the zeros.

"You're a smart man, you understand what I'm saying. What you got there is for you and for Justo."

Diego counted out three hundred-dollar bills.

"You always pay me by check, and it's always on Tuesday."

"That is for Justo, and a little something extra for you."

Diego felt the money in his hand, felt a few hundred dollars of extra spending money.

"Why don't you just try it for a while? Hey man, you might love the business."

"Yes? And what business is that, Benny?"

"Come by today at three o'clock and find out."

Half an hour later, knowing he would not sleep this night, Diego got quietly out of bed and went to Mariaclara's room. Her magic candle flickered on the night table. He stood for a moment or two, watching his daughter sleep, and then went to his son's room and glanced in. Then he went into the kitchen and made himself a cup of coffee, took a book and began to read. In short order he felt a flash of enthusiasm, and he took his pad and pen and began to write. He wrote for quite some time, a *décima guajira*, a folk poem; Cubans have always expressed their most passionate feelings of love and hate and fear in the ancient form. Diego wrote hastily, eagerly. When recited, the *decima* is read in a pleading, crying voice.

From far across Roosevelt Avenue, from some incalculable distance, came the wail and howl of a dog, first one, then others, wild and desperate and forsaken.

Chapter 8

Seven forty-five in the morning. Four stories below Nick's window three police officers stood waiting for their midnight-to-eight-A.M. tour to come to an end. Nick guessed that they were from the nearby station house. They were standing on the corner beneath a grocery store awning. From a distance the cops appeared young and in good shape, their bodies well cared for. Their uniform brass, silver, and leather was new and polished; it gleamed in the somber morning light.

It had rained all night and it was still raining, a depressing rain now, not hard but steady, as if it was settling in for a week. The cops were chatting, nudging and playing with each other, dodging in and out of the rain, and even from four stories up it was apparent that they were pals. The walking traffic was heavy for a Saturday morning, a few ragtag homeless passed before the cops, but mostly it was a crowd of New York quick-walkers starting their day. A yellow cab rolled into a bus stop and parked in front of the cops. A black man wearing an army fatigue jacket and green beret got out on the driver's side. Glancing at the cops, the cabbie ran to the grocery with his hand on his beret as if it were a prize that might be stolen. The policemen turned and smiled at him. One of the cops took a slow turn around the taxi as if inspecting it. Then pausing a moment, glancing up and down the street, he dropped down into a squat, took a knife from his pocket, and with a quick, violent stab popped the front tire of the cab. Nick watched as the cop stood, looking around as if he'd done it all before. Then he waltzed over to join the other three. They looked at each other and laughed. Together they strolled up the street, heading for the station house. Nick thinking that it was a day's work figuring cops, but he sure as hell knew that as long as cops are human beings and remain both human and beings, there will always be some that are loony. And what the hell, you have the balls to park in a bus stop right in front of three cops who just worked eight cold, rainy hours, you asked for it.

Nick was standing at the window drinking coffee, watching the cab-driver change his tire when it occurred to him that, against all reason, safety, and common sense, he felt a mounting urge to work this case with Sonny McCabe and the others after all. Maybe Andre was right about them, and maybe Andre had it all wrong. He would find out for himself. An adventure was what it would be, an antidote to the current emptiness of his life. It would be interesting to see such cops in action, he thought. It would be interesting to see cops who believed in things he had never been able to understand. It would be different. He owed nothing to Andre, he would not be his spy. Whatever he might do and whatever he might see with McCabe and the others would be no one's business but his own. A cold and nameless excitement possessed him. He finished his coffee and watched the street below him surrender to a heavy rain.

He had waited at home in the expectation that Andre would call him, but it was eight fifteen and no call had come. He suspected that it must be because Andre was expecting him at the courthouse. Screw him, he thought, getting dressed. Nick had made his feelings known— what more had to be said? Only Andre wouldn't quit, the guy was a politician and being a politician makes good people turn peculiar. Politicians manipulate people as they wish and don't care about the price, the bastards.

How angry he had become. His own bitterness surprised him.

Shaking himself out of his ruminations, Nick wandered back into his kitchen and began to clean it up. There was a note to himself on the refrigerator door. Damn— It was Saturday morning, he had made plans the past week for a fishing trip with E. Z. Brochard.

E.Z. had been a narcotics detective out of Providence. Nick had gotten to know him eight years earlier, when they both attended an organized-crime seminar at the FBI Academy. Retired now, E.Z. ran a charter fishing business out of a village called Wickham. He was bearded, a bit heavy-handed, solitary, and unsociable, but Nick had taken an immediate liking to him. They had been fishing buddies for years.

Nick didn't know how long it would take, how many more years he'd be playing cops and robbers, but there was no doubt in his mind that someday enough would be enough, and when that happened he'd pack it in and head north and E.Z. would be there.

Nick took the phone into the kitchen and dialed, figuring he would be stuck with this case for another few days at least. E.Z. picked up on the third ring, Nick telling him that a job had come up very suddenly, this new office he was working, he'd be up in a week or so.

"I us'ta worry about you years ago. I stopped worrying. You'll get here when y'get here. It's a miserable day anyhow." E.Z. seemed to frame his response to himself.

"I hope I didn't hang you up," Nick told him.

"Naw, I'm gonna have some breakfast, maybe go and check the boat, then kick back and chill out. Listen," he told Nick, "do yourself a favor, finish up with those N'yawk criminals and get your ass up here."

"I'll do my best."

"By the way, buddy, the old Allen place at the end of the road, the green and white cottage near the salt pond—you know the place?"

"Sure."

"It's going on the market next month."

"They'll want a ton of money for that house. And they deserve it, it's in a beautiful spot."

"You can get it for a hundred and a half."

"E.Z., that cottage is worth a quarter million. More."

"The Allens don't need the money, Nick. Hell, man, all Peggy Allen wants to do is unload the place and head south so she can be with their grandkids."

"How much land?"

"Five acres, maybe a bit more you count an acre or two of salt marsh on the north end."

"A hundred and fifty thousand," Nick said. Trying to picture the cottage in his mind. He gave an embarrassed laugh.

"Like ya said, worth every penny and then some. And listen buddy, those people like you. They told me they like you. Folks up here try and sell to people they know, and if they like you they'll make accommodations."

"E.Z., I don't have that kind of money."

"Well keep it in mind anyway," he told Nick.

Nick assured him that he would indeed.

At nine he left his apartment, and as he went along the hallway toward the elevator, he realized that he felt more refreshed and stimulated than he had in a very long time. The question was why? McCabe and the others were nutsy, that was a given, that was for sure; Andre with his be-my-spy bit was from outer space. And he was in the middle, Nick Manaris, a man without a country. What was he trying to prove? Nick was beginning to feel sorry for himself, but then he figured go with it man, go with the flow, put a little adventure in your life. Take a walk through a minefield, what the hell. It occurred to Nick that being a New York City cop can bring you the kind of exhilaration that the visitor with a return ticket gets when he travels to a war zone. A hell of a rush, was what it was, the kind of rush he hadn't experienced in years.

Chapter 9

Where the fuck is Nick?"

Ten o'clock in the morning on a windy, miserable, rain-swept Saturday, the kind of day you're goddamn happy to be a detective and out of uniform, and what am I doing? Waiting for a guy who couldn't get laid in a whorehouse with a fist full of fifties. Some kind of reborn dipshit.

Sonny McCabe sat on a bench in the first row of the Queens County Criminal Court's arraignment part, the row reserved for cops and lawyers. A familiar spot in a familiar courtroom, wall-to-wall lawyers and bondsmen, the usual snakes, slipping and sliding, looking to turn a dollar. Sonny was more curious than angry, turning his head like an owl, trying to spot this goddamn partner of his. He appeared for all the world to be precisely what he was, a hotshot first-grader. His gold detective badge was draped over the breast pocket of his five-hundred-dollar sharkskin suit. A woman detective sat beside him, Sonny telling himself, man what a pair of lung warts on this broad. Christ, I ain't seen tits like that since Mrs. Radu and the eighth-grade picnic. He'd been sitting there for an hour, waiting for Nick, watching the preceding night's collars cruise in singles and pairs from the bullpen to the well in front of the judge's bench.

A few minutes earlier, restless and annoyed, he had gone through the door into the bullpen looking for the assistant DA, thinking that maybe the guy had seen Nick Manaris.

The bullpen was a ten-by-twenty holding cell where about fifty men prisoners were packed together, row upon row, in sweaty closeness. A steady, riotous noise billowed from them, combining with the stench of urine and a tide of flatulence to produce a single seamless, encompassing and overpowering aura, which Sonny McCabe hardly noticed. Sitting in the courtroom, he flashed on the days when he was in uniform; what had horrified, impressed, and bewildered him then was no longer amazing, impressive, or mystifying. His rookie naiveté and wonder were almost annoying in retrospect.

For Sonny McCabe the world was divided between genetic foul balls and real human beings. Skels and cops, to be specific. He did not find the assistant DA, and he hadn't seen Nick. So now he sat edgily, eager to hook up with Nick. Hoping his partner had the search warrants and they were ready to be signed by this half-a-fag judge. The guy sitting there with his ponytail, tall and thin with these brown moles that dotted his face. One the size of a dime on his forehead, between his eyebrows. To Sonny, it appeared that the good judge had been popped between the eyes with a forty-five.

The weekend arraignment calendar, Sonny concluded, was a procession of beasts, mostly dis-cons and DWIs. There were the usual number of drug and gun possessions, a precinct anticrime unit had nailed a couple of street gorillas for robbery and the Public Morals Unit had snapped up a hooker in a cowgirl outfit. A cop from the Far Rockaway precinct had a house burglar, and there were two mopes up for assault on a cop, wearing their bandage turbans. Some dunce shuffled in front of the judge in his pajamas; they had him for assault on his wife with a hot curling iron. Caught her sucking tongue with the pizza delivery boy, everyone cheering at that. Then came a huge colored guy with a shaved head and motorcycle boots, busted for raping this high yellow bimbo, the bimbo crying these big tears, saying she was a schoolteacher and so on, Sonny thinking, a colored guy for rape of a colored broad doesn't seem so much of a crime somehow. About a dozen senior citizen courthouse groupies stood under the windows along the wall, killing time while time killed them.

The Saturday morning menagerie, all cuffed behind their backs, paraded before Cut-'em-Loose-Bruce Janeway. Pete Hawkins, a sergeant from the safe-and-loft squad, had once told Sonny that Janeway sexually preferred men to women and money to either. Sonny remembered thinking so what's wrong with that?

Judge Janeway hardly ever looked up. He talked in a monotone, banged his gavel, then came down like the hammers of hell with either sky-high or no bail at all. The Legal Aid was a man with a boy's face who, Sonny figured, spent his off time raising poodles and singing Peter Allen tunes. A real sweetie. You couldn't fool Sonny McCabe, not after four good years in the Public Morals Unit. Sonny, proud that he had faggot radar, pleased that he could nail a queen in a heartbeat, watched the Legal Aid huffing and puffing, looking at the prisoners with an expression of mild disgust. The guy playing to the judge with small smiles and little cutesy winks, doing his song-and-dance bail-and-probation routine. The assistant DA, a sallow kid, maybe twenty-five, with a blond military haircut and one of those cheap, off-the-rack suits, did slow turns with his hands on his head. It all gave Sonny a laugh, everything was a circus act.

The woman detective hadn't shut up since she sat down, but Sonny could hardly hear what she was saying, what with all the arraignment commotion, the spectators, defendants, and victims' families, the cops in uniform gabbing like hell. She lowered her head to rest her chin in her hand, saying Jesus, I go round the clock tracking this creep, snatch him at two in the morning, now I got to sit here all day. Hey, but you know, what else I got to do?

Sonny told her that maybe what she should have done was take the test for the fire department. Though it'd be a hell of a trick getting that chest of hers up a ladder. Sonny, you're a riot, she said. You're a regular comedian. What you got going? He told her he was waiting for his partner.

"Lookit," he said, "there he is now, see him standing over there with that big dumb shit-eating grin on his face? That's him, that's my prize partner."

"Nick Manaris?" she said. "You work with Nick? Lucky you."

"You know him, you worked with him?" Sonny glanced at her, saw her eyes narrow.

"I worked the youth squad with him," she said. "That guy will take the smile off your face. Talk about hardassed."

Sonny waved at Nick, watching him shift from one foot to the other, looking around. "Yeah," he said, "you're right. Ol' Nick got no sense of humor. Now you on the other hand, you sweetie, you're just chock full of comedy. What you need is a vacation, a trip to Puerto Rico or something."

"A vacation?"

"Or some coke. Maybe what you need is a good sporting fuck."

"You know," she said, "it's depressing to spend fifteen years as an asshole spending time with other assholes."

He laughed and nothing more had to be said.

Desperate now to get to Nick, Sonny worked his way through the crowded aisle. He believed the woman cop, whose name he didn't know, that not being at all unusual. Sonny McCabe knew the names of about half the people that knew him, famous as he was. Still, he figured the big-breasted broad judged Nick Manaris correctly as hard-assed, but fuck it, he'd work the guy, straighten him out. Nick Manaris, by Sonny's lights, had potential.

Sonny's way was blocked by the crowds of cops and lawyers shuffling their way down the aisle to the bridgeman. He threw Nick another wave, Nick smiling, standing there with that busted nose of his, and shit, there was ADA Robinson behind Nick, in earnest conversation with a pair of lawyers. The guy working the room like a seasoned campaigner. Sonny was sure he had heard that Robinson was about to be tapped by the Democrats as the next DA of Queens County, but maybe the reports were exaggerated. He hoped so, he hated the smart-talking black son of a bitch. Sonny feeling a little tense now, a tightness in his chest. Seeing Robinson grab Nick's shoulder, whisper something, then turn and walk out of the room. The guy wearing a three-piece suit, a dark blue pinstripe, the expensive kind. Sonny had a suit just like it, knew the price. Talk about your uppity nigger. Fucker with his small grin, big-ass college ring on his right hand, meaning he's educated, which Sonny knew meant diddly-shit in the street, in the real world.

Nick stared distantly at Sonny, expressionless, save for a beating tension in his jaw.

"I've been waiting here an hour," Sonny said.

"Sorry, I went straight to Andre's office, he called the judge's clerk. As soon as Janeway takes a break, we'll go into chambers."

Sonny grabbed Nick by the elbow, a grin exploding across his face.

"So we're all set," Sonny said, the words whispered and quick. He pulled Nick from the courtroom into the corridor.

Andre Robinson followed, stood off about twenty feet or so, his back to the wall, reading the search warrant applications.

"So what do you think?" Sonny asked Nick.

"About what?"

"The warrants. You figure Janeway will sign them or what?"

"Why not? Of course he'll sign them. They're good warrants. We're all set, just have to wait for the morning break."

"Good, that's good," Sonny said. "Eddie Moran and Captain Hawks are over at the wiretap plant with Suarez. Monserette and a team from the office are set up on the club. We'll stay close now until we hear from Rodrigo and this thing goes down." Sonny stopped, looked up and down the corridor. "I can smoke in here, can't I?" He hunched over and lit a cigarette. Nick noticed that his hands were shaking.

"Christ, did we have a night last night. Didn't get in till six this morning. You should have come back."

"I was beat. By the time I finished with Andre, I'd had it."

"We went over to Dan's. You know the joint across from the phone company on Church Street?" Sonny glanced slyly at Nick. "Ever been there?"

"Once." Nick passed his hand over his mouth, turned to glance at Andre. "A couple of years ago with two guys from narcotics."

"Man we had us a time. Must have been a slow night. There were whores everywhere."

"You did good?"

"If you can't score at Dan's then you're in a gang of trouble."

The habitués at Dan's were high-priced call girls who used Dan's Bar and Grill as a place to wait for clients. Nick understood that the spot had been in action since prohibition. Danny Tomazzo, the most recent proprietor, a disappointed Mafia wanna-be, was on the pad from head-quarters to the courthouse. Detectives who knew of the place dropped by after hours and drank at the bar on tab. No cops paid. Many of the women who worked the joint lived in the suburbs. Worn out at the end of the night, they'd hitch a ride home with a cop. The grateful whores tipped with a quick blowjob.

Nick and Sonny strolled along the corridor, killing time, Sonny telling and retelling the story of the previous night, his arm around Nick's shoulder, giving Nick a squeeze, a hip bump, muttering in his ear. Andre against the wall, his eyes casually avoiding Nick's.

Nick floated off in an agitated bubble, certain that Andre had Sonny right in his sights, telling him again this morning, you be sure and keep an eye out. What the hell did *that* mean? Telling Nick that McCabe was bad news, a train wreck waiting to happen.

Nick had been surprised to find himself defending Sonny. "Christ, cops are cops," he'd told Andre. "McCabe's no different than hundreds of others. A little mouthy is all."

Sonny's distorted expressions of concern and warmness were comical. Still, he kind of liked the guy. Kind of. What he liked best, thinking about it, was not so much that Sonny was so easy to nail but the look Sonny gave him when he did. The eye contact, the smile. You dealt with Sonny McCabe you felt like somebody gave you a ticket to a comedy club. The guy found humor in everything, and he made you feel as though you wanted to laugh right along with him.

The truth was, Nick's reaction to Sonny surprised and alarmed him. Nevertheless, the down and deadly feeling he had experienced the day before had gone topsy-turvy. His luck was shifting, he could feel it shift, the way it did sometimes in a fight, the momentum leaves the other guy, goes over to you. The brain turns off and the body takes over. For reasons he couldn't explain, Nick felt as though his life was changing and this guy McCabe was at the center of it all.

So earlier, when Andre had battered Sonny, Nick had taken it personally. "Put yourself in a McCabe's or any cop's shoes," he had told Andre. "Deal with the day-to-day shitstorms for a while and let's see how you behave. Sure McCabe is a clown, a floor show, a regular circus. Listen, maybe that's the way Sonny McCabe has learned to deal with it."

"What? What is he dealing with by being a thief?"

"Goddamn it, the insanity of the street, and the sanctimonious hypocrisy of the fucking politicians. That's what," Nick had told Andre, thinking, people like you.

Nick guessed that Andre probably was not going to let up on this pressure he was laying on him. Andre wasn't especially good as an administrator, but he was superb in a courtroom; it really impressed Nick. Andre never threw in the towel, the man didn't know how to quit.

When Nick had walked through the courthouse doors, Andre had been standing there waiting. They had gone directly to Andre's office, and once there, Nick had told him, you know, I didn't sleep last night. I sat up thinking about you and that game you ran on me. You know what I think, Andre? he'd said. I think you believe you own the truth. You're an arrogant son of a bitch is what I think. You keep leaning on me and I'll treat you the way I treat all the other DAs. Like mushrooms—keep them in the dark and feed them bullshit. Andre saying I find it interesting that you have never spoken to me this way before. Restraining an impulse to say that there is always a first time, Nick pointed out that Andre had not asked him to be a fink before.

"Nick," Andre said. "Do you know what you sound like? I mean, you know, like some rockhead cop."

"Maybe what I should do is go with the flow for a while. Maybe that's exactly what I should have done all these years."

"And you'll start hanging with those characters just to see how deep you can get in. Is that what you want? C'mon, c'mon wake up. What's wrong with you?"

"Look, nothing is wrong with me Andre. I think it's time for a change is all."

"Hook up with McCabe and that crew, you'll be doing your changes in the joint, smart guy."

Nick started to answer but let it go. "Are you going to have Janeway sign these warrants or not?"

"I said I would. Now why don't you go down to the courtroom. I'll meet you there in about ten minutes." For a moment it seemed that Andre was fussing over an invisible problem. "Listen," Andre said finally. "If I'm off about Captain Hawks and Sonny McCabe, heaven and hell have changed places and everything I know about human nature is wrong."

"Everyone is wrong about something sometime," Nick told him. "Can I get going now? We don't have all day, Counsellor."

"Do me a favor," Andre had said, all smiling and friendly. "Remember that we all sow the seeds of our own destruction."

"Christ, you're giving me a headache. What in the hell does that mean?"

"You're a smart guy, a first-grade detective. Figure it out, Officer."

Waiting in the corridor in front of Janeway's chambers, Nick stood shoulder to shoulder with McCabe. Across the corridor, Andre tilted slightly forward, his hands behind his back. He kept squinting at Nick, then looking around the corridor. Nick turned from him, refused to make eye contact.

Sonny was totally relaxed, humming a little jig, singing to himself, holding a cigarette, sizing up the passing parade of lawyers and cops, complainants and defendants. Despite the hubbub, Nick could hear Andre breathing through his mouth. He looked irritable and strained. The judge's door opened and Janeway came out, accompanied by a clerk, and ushered them into a carpeted, comfortable office with two windows, the walls covered with about twenty standard pictures of the judge with his arm around local political stars. Sitting alongside Janeway's desk was this woman stenographer drinking from a container of coffee, chomping on a bagel.

As they walked into the room Janeway took Andre's arm, saying, "I read all the applications, they're fine. No problem. We need Detective Manaris here to go on the record and you can have your warrants."

Nick looked around the room, then over at Sonny. Sonny grinned and winked. Then he glanced at Andre, locking eyes with him across the room.

Back out in the corridor ten minutes later, Sonny McCabe studied Nick as Nick chatted with DA Robinson, wondering why he was drawn to the guy. Sonny thinking, the guy's not so slick, and it's not because he's a mover, a money guy. Nick unquestionably was not. It would make things easier if Nick were a mover, but Sonny didn't care about that either. He lit another cigarette. Maybe he could put a change in the guy, show him the light. He figured it was possible, he'd seen it happen plenty of times. Uptight straight guy, like a worm turning in an apple. Put the big bucks in front of them, show 'em how.

He was convinced it was possible, there was something for sure in the air between them. He was curious about this Nick, this first-grader who wanted you to think he was as pure as the driven snow. Sonny's experience telling him that there was no such thing, a completely honest person, especially a cop, specifically a cop been around as long as Nick. Nick every so often throwing him that look, coy and hard at the same time. That look that goes through you like a knife. Anyone could see that the man had a way with people, he had something and knew how to use the something he had. Not sharp but smooth, about a million times smoother than Sonny's steady partner, Eddie Moran. Eddie getting slow and lazy, dipping into the booze more and more, for chrissake. Cops love ex-jocks, fighters and so on; Sonny had heard that Nick had once been a pro, a club fighter. Most cops love ex-jocks because they remind them of what they would have loved to have been but could not.

Most cops don't make any sense. Most cops are profoundly stupid and sheeplike in the face of authority and superior rank, and ex–professional jocks. He was no different himself. Mickey Mantle, Sonny couldn't utter a word the night he met him. Acted like he was a stone retard, mumbling and shit. No different than anyone else—except when it came to his cop bosses. He didn't give a shit about bosses, half-a-humps always with their hands out.

Sonny stood in the corridor talking with this homicide, a guy who he had worked with in the Public Morals Division. But he wasn't paying attention to the guy. He dragged deeply on his cigarette, glancing at Nick and the DA. Nick grinned at him. Sonny smiled at the homicide's story, but the last thing he wanted to hear was a cop's war story, or stories about other cops, other than his partners. This Nick Manaris, he thought, had a special kind of confidence, and the balls of a grizzly bear. That's what Sonny saw, and that is what he wanted to be around. Sonny decided he'd romance this new partner of his, see where it went.

Chapter 10

When they came out of the courthouse the rain had stopped. It had turned from a gray into a golden sort of day, bright and windy, white tatters of clouds running across the Queens sky. Nick got in the passenger seat of the cruiser, Sonny drove.

Sonny was going on about Robinson and Janeway, saying that every time Andre saw a group of two or three he did twenty minutes. The guy's a liberal leech politician, pure and simple.

Nick kept quiet. The way he'd been feeling about Andre lately, he didn't mind Sonny saying it.

Nick figured they'd head straight over to the wiretap and surveillance plant, but it looked like Sonny had other plans.

They drove to an Italian salumeria and sandwich shop on Metropolitan Avenue in Glendale. Sonny parked behind a precinct radio car. There was a COPS FOR CHRIST decal on the back window, and on the bumper a: We-Love-New-York sticker.

"Hey Nick," Sonny said, "c'mon."

"Where are we going?"

"To get lunch, the fellas must be starving." With that wholesome honest face, putting him on.

Nick glanced at the shop. "There has to be eight, ten people waiting for us."

"So?"

"Counting me and you that's ten, twelve people. We're going to pick up a dozen sandwiches?"

Sonny smiled at Nick, showing his teeth, putting him on again. Nick thought this guy, this Sonny likes to play Santa, everybody's big brother.

"What I'm wondering," Nick said to him, "is how do you know what they want to eat?"

"Trust me. You're gonna come with me or what?" His voice soft and quiet, out of character for Sonny McCabe. Nick crossed his arms and studied him.

"C'mon," Sonny said, "I know these people here, we're talking world-class, great, guinea hero sandwiches."

At one in the afternoon the place was crowded, people at the counter and little round tables, most of them city employees. About a dozen sanitation men and six uniform cops from the local precinct, everybody busy rolling their eyes, munching on these huge sandwiches.

Sonny walked through the door ahead of Nick and made a broad sweeping motion with his arms as if he were getting ready to direct a band. He shouted, "Hey, cuz, I'm here. What the hell can I eat that won't poison me?"

The man behind the counter wore a baseball cap and had a Roman nose. He yelled into the kitchen, "Sonny's here. Hey Anne, it's Sonny McCabe."

A woman came bursting out of the kitchen, squealing, "Sonny! Sonny!" And suddenly everybody in the place hustled over to shake Sonny's hand, saying hey, hey guy, how you been, big time? The scene a wild surprise party. They kept Sonny busy there in the middle of the floor for five minutes. Shaking his hand, patting his shoulder, pinching his cheek. Anne threw her arms around Sonny's neck and planted a kiss on his lips.

"No tongue, no tongue," Sonny yelled. "Your husband will cut my heart out." That brought down the house.

A fat forty-year-old uniformed cop strolled over and slapped him on the back. "Fuckin' Sonny." Behind him came another cop, and they bear-hugged. "We missed ya, tiger, where the hell you been?"

"Fuckin' up the bad guys, where else."

Sonny gave Nick a brief, blank, wide-eyed stare.

Nick laughed for the first time in days, suddenly feeling like he was onstage, a member of a rock and roll band, backing the lead singer, Sonny McCabe.

Anne took Nick's elbow, turned him this way and that, grinning, giving him the up-and-down, checking him out.

"Who are you?" she said.

"My new partner," Sonny told her. Explaining that he and Anne had gone through elementary and high school together. Her husband, Carmine, the muscle man with the baseball cap, owned the place.

"Hey, hey," Anne said, "you were supposed to call my brother."

"No," Sonny said, "Richie was supposed to call me."

"You're lookin' great," she told him. Sonny nodded but didn't return the compliment.

Nick sat down among three of New York's finest, thinking that this Anne has a warm smile and sad eyes and look at those curves. In jeans, boots, and a turtleneck, Anne looked like somebody'd drawn her. Tremendous brown eyes, with a curious child's stare, and that hair, long and black, pulled back tightly from her high forehead. And that trick she did with her lips, pursing them before she spoke. Anne, Nick figured, was not someone Renata would have liked.

Three years living with an uptight special-ed teacher, three years of listening to moans and complaints about her female high school students. The silent neighborhood gal-friends of the midget gangsters, she called them. Needy bitches in heat. Their boyfriends, hot-blooded goof-balls whose brains were in their pricks. Hell, he could still hear her. Renata hated the girls only a bit less than she hated their boyfriends. Creeps that jumped the girls in school hallways when they were twelve. At fourteen the girls were getting shit-faced and diving into the back seats of cars. The little twits. Funny, a woman that hated to make love always talked about the lovemaking of other people. Three years of watching Renata pace around the apartment, those long fingers of hers up alongside her nose. Every day whining about how her midget gang-sters lived for sex. Putting up with and listening to that shit every day had worn him out. Sent him fishing. Being alone was better, better than having to listen to some neurotic broad. Forget Renata, Nick thought, no more Renatas.

Sonny called out, asked Nick to go and get a couple of six-packs of Bud from the refrigerator. Sonny telling him that Monserette and Suarez liked hot sandwiches. He'd get them meatballs and sausage, throw a ton of hot pepper over it. Spics loved that hot shit. Okay, now the spics are taken care of. Eddie Moran and Captain Hawks ate roast pork covered in mayo with tomatoes and lettuce. Four ham and cheese for the other team. As for himself, Sonny told Nick, he was a roast beef kind of guy, asked Nick what he'd like. Nick told him anything, maybe the Genoa salami, with provolone and a bit of mustard and some let-tuce. That honey mustard? Sonny said.

Now they both were smiling. Nick saying, whatever.

Sonny placed the order, Nick asking about the others, the other de-tectives from the office. Sonny saying excuse me, what do I look like a fucking lunch wagon? They'll eat ham and cheese. He paid the tab with a hundred-dollar bill, asking Carmine to put the names of each of the detectives on the sandwich wrappers. Carmine nodded in an under-standing way. Nick went to the cooler and got the beer, two sixers of Bud and a St. Paulie Girl dark for himself.

The fat uniformed cop walked over to Nick, saying, "You don't know how lucky you are to team up with Sonny McCabe."

"Yeah?" Nick said. "Why's that?"

"I know ten, twenty people the man's helped out. Sonny McCabe's a saint. You need him, you call him, the man's there."

"Really?" Nick said. "A good guy, huh?"

"The fucking best."

Sonny, with his bag full of sandwiches, was waving and shouting good-byes, heading for the door. As they went out, Anne fish-eyed Nick.

Nick held the door for Sonny, saying hey, I want to pay for my own sandwich, handing Sonny a five-dollar bill. Sonny saying ey, don't insult me. It's no big deal, you wanta pay for something, tonight you can buy me dinner. How's that?

"Dinner?"

"Okay, lunch tomorrow, whatever you like."

"You know, Sonny, you play the big spender. It don't look good, it's asinine is what it is."

"It don't look good to who?"

"People, that's who. You're a cop, you carry a wad of cash in your pocket, you look like I don't know what. A wise guy, a high roller. You paid for these sandwiches with a hundred-dollar bill. People notice that shit."

"Listen," Sonny said, "you ever see a moving van behind a hearse? You can't take it with you, Nick. You know what I mean?"

"That's not the point. You go around towing a spotlight. You're like a goddamn billboard. Pockets full of cash like that. You have to be loose in the head."

"The hell you talking about? How the hell do you know where I get my money?"

"Sonny—"

"Sonny, my ass. What if I told you I do construction work on the side? What if I told you that I work every weekend from five in the morning till five at night? What if I told you I own a construction business? What if I told you that, hah?"

"You do? You have your own construction company?"

"What're you, nuts? When could I find the time? Besides, do these hands look like the hands of a construction worker? Christ, you are nuts."

As Sonny bent to open the door of the police cruiser, Nick saw that grin on his face. Jesus, the guy truly was a floor show.

Sonny came around the car and handed Nick the keys. "You drive," he said. "I'm tired."

As Nick pulled out into traffic, Sonny said, "Christ I love guys on the job, I do. They are the only people with any brains. Cops know who all the liars are. In my life I've been drawn to cops the way I've been drawn to no one else. My wife and kids included."

A part of Nick felt that way. He used to call it the wisdom of the badge. An emotional bond with all cops everywhere. A bond that had really never existed for him but should have. And if the truth be known, it was a major disappointment in his life.

"I got you thinking now, don't I? Got you wondering, huh?" Sonny said.

"Maybe."

"Sure I do. A guy like you couldn't figure a guy like me in a thousand years."

"You're right about that."

"You don't have to, let's leave it like that. Now step on it, those guys are starving and I don't want their sandwiches to get cold."

"You want I should hit the siren and lights?"

"That's the smartest thing you said all day partner."

"That right?"

"That's what I said."

"Sonny McCabe," Nick said, "you are something else."

"That I am, Nick. You know, buddy," he said smiling, "you shouldn't believe everything you hear about me."

"I'll keep that in mind," Nick told him.

"Well, you hear stuff. People say things, some good, some bad, and you wonder who dreams that shit up. I can't figure it."

"All I know is what I see. And what I saw back there was a dead ringer for Santa Claus."

"Well," Sonny said, "it's all natural, it's no act."

"What I think, it's a routine," Nick said. "I have to figure you have a lot of routines and that was just one of them."

"Of course you'd figure that. But it isn't really that way."

Feeling strangely relaxed, Nick drove the cruiser through the Queens streets toward Los Campos. You're looking to understand this guy, he told himself, you're a fool. You're trying to get a make on this six-foot stick of dynamite, this Sonny McCabe, and you can't even figure yourself. Talk about a dumb move.

But you got to hang in there, he thought. You got to hang in because you want to feel what it's like to be sucked under a surge of time and things. It's not too smart good buddy, he told himself. It's not smart at all.

Chapter 11

Late in the morning, around eleven, Justo got up and got the Queens Boulevard bus with Mariaclara and Miguel, to go shopping at Alexander's. Diego lay in bed drifting in and out of dreams. Rain pounded his bedroom window; he would awaken for a moment, twist and turn, thinking of Cano, Benny, and Rodrigo, and within seconds fall back into an uneasy sleep. He had decided in the early morning hours that he had little alternative but to warn Rodrigo. It would not be an easy business, his trying to explain Benny's and Cano's uneasiness to the wild mulatto. Their concern about whatever it was Rodrigo knew of their business, the rumors of his association with the police. But he had no other option that he could see. In the moments that he was awake the events of the previous night came back to him in sharp jabs of memory. He had to face what he had done, and what he had done was to put Rodrigo and Oscar on the tip of Cano's nose.

He drifted just below the surface of sleep, conscious of a dream, and as that dream went on he saw himself standing between Benny and Cano in a large loftlike room. All three wore elegant white suits. The room was windowless, and it too was completely white; it had a cathedral ceiling beneath which a huge wooden crucifix stood in an diffusion of blood. Terrified, Diego stretched his hand before him. Skewered on the cross was Rodrigo, dressed in his golden outfit. His head was outrageously swollen and deformed, like the head of some papier-mâché caricature at carnival, his eyes bulging out in a horror of agony. The image rolled and whirled behind Diego's eyelids. When it formed again he could see that someone had smeared lipstick across Rodrigo's upper lip and nose; there was silky green eyeshadow on the anguished man's eyelids. He wore his garter belt, and his black net stockings had been split at the knees. Blood was spouting from a wound in Rodrigo's chest. Diego cried out to God in his sleep.

Cano glanced at Rodrigo, then turned to glare at Diego with a sort of insane patience, and Diego looked at the floor.

After a moment, Diego was conscious of music, not in the loft but from behind a closed door to the rear of a golden tabernacle. The music was just beyond hearing, and he kept turning his head, trying to make out the melody being played. Diego stepped forward; he felt frightened, angry, on the very edge of panic. He strained his neck and ears and heard the faint sound of a guitar. "Bésame Mucho," he thought, it was "Bésame Mucho." That is my song, he told Cano. Is that you playing?

Cano asked him. His dead wife's fat cousin, Benny, was doing tiny dance steps in time to the song. From somewhere nearby he heard a siren, then the pounding of charging boots, an assault. The Communists, he told Cano, want you to surrender your intellect. I'd rather die than surrender my brains.

Of course you say you would. But you would not, said Cano. You are a coward, I know you are a coward because your niggers from Miami told me so.

He looked back toward the place where Benny had been dancing. Benny was gone now, and in his place stood the four young gangsters from Miami, smiling.

You are a bastard, Diego told Cano.

Ah yes, and more evil than you can know.

Then the rain, actual wind and rain, he could hear windows rattle. He was awake, curled up in his bed, the melodious chords of a guitar in his head.

He got out of bed and went into the kitchen and found water at a low simmer and an espresso pot prepared for him. There was a note from Justo, *I took the money, Papi. I am going shopping with Mariaclara and Miguel.* On the note Mariaclara had drawn a heart with a smiling face.

Diego made himself a pot of coffee. When he looked out the window the rain he expected was not there; the street below was wet but the sun was high at midday. He stood looking out at the street, hearing the click-clack of the El two blocks off at Roosevelt Avenue. His heart was beating outrageously fast.

He went back to the bedroom, sat on the edge of his bed, and finished his coffee. With a sudden chill he remembered the dream, the crucifix, Rodrigo. He glanced at his watch. It was twelve noon.

Christ, he thought, I'm running out of time; there was hardly any time at all. He finished his coffee, had another, showered and dressed. For a while he stood before the bathroom mirror, combing his hair, then tying it back. Maybe he should get it cut? But it takes so long for it to grow, he thought. He nodded at his reflection in the mirror as if both he and the likeness knew it would never happen.

Diego went out into the street and breathed the unfamiliar and fresh taste of autumn-scented air. Walking along Roosevelt Avenue he thought of a poem he had once read about a deer that was so frightened that it went to a lion for protection. But he was neither an animal nor a coward; he would handle this Cano, this Colombian. The man was deranged, he most probably heard voices. The way he glanced at Diego, always those quick looks.

In spite of it all, Diego had no fear of the Colombian. Anyway, he no longer trusted Benny enough to protect him. Benny, it seemed to him, was playing both sides. When push came to shove, Benny would stand with the man who had the power. Benny was beyond help, he cared only for money. He'd brought his troubles upon himself.

Diego was headed for the Hatuey, wanting Rodrigo to be there. As he walked his determination increased, then suddenly vanished. Why not just call Rodrigo at the Hatuey and leave a message, a warning? Too late for that now. At one-thirty he reached the restaurant. It was closed. He stood grimly searching through the window, his hand shading his eyes. The restaurant was dark, but there was some light escaping underneath the curtain at the kitchen doorway.

Diego looked up and down the street, getting anxious now. He clenched his fist and knocked halfheartedly on the window. Maybe Rodrigo or Natalia was inside, he thought. Or maybe Rodrigo was already dead, Cano's doing. Or maybe Natalia and Rodrigo had fled, now that word was out about his meeting with Oscar.

"Rodrigo," Diego shouted at the dark window.

He went to the front door with its Closed sign hanging on it and thumped, harder this time. After a moment or two he knocked again, then paced to the corner and back in helpless agitation. The door opened and Natalia appeared, looking flushed and slightly out of breath, wearing the same peasant dress she had worn the day before. Diego's stomach heaved and his mouth got dry. Natalia smiled and shook her head. Diego put his hands into his pockets and looked away. He felt both embarrassed and happy.

"I hope I didn't disturb you. I'm looking for Rodrigo."

"Rodrigo never came home last night," she told him. Diego went past her into the restaurant, absently going through the curtain and into the kitchen. He looked around.

"Have you heard from him? Did he call you?"

Natalia closed and locked the door, pausing to pat her hair in the mirror. "No," she said. "It is unusual, but it's happened before. But not for a very, very long time." She went into the bathroom, leaving the door open. "I have water on. Would you like a coffee?"

"No. Yes—maybe. Listen, when did you last hear from him?"

"I drove with Rodrigo to the hospital—you know that Benny broke his arm? I waited with him in the emergency room, then he told me to go, to take a cab and go home. That's the last time I spoke to him."

"Strange," Diego said after a moment. "Isn't that strange?"

Natalia shrugged. She pulled down her panties, raised her skirt, and sat down on the toilet.

"You should close the door," Diego said. "It's not polite."

Natalia laughed. "I'm an independent woman, Professor. Maybe you feel threatened by a woman like me."

Diego turned his back. The sound of the toilet flushing distracted and aroused him. He didn't answer her. He held himself still, leaning against the wall, trying to recover the energy and determination to warn Rodrigo that he had felt earlier. But it was gone.

Natalia came out of the bathroom. She came over and stood alongside him.

"I'm trying to find your husband," he told her.

"That's nice. What for?"

"I want to speak to him."

"He does not want to speak to you, Diego, he wants to shoot you."

"I'll talk to him, explain things."

"It won't do any good. Rodrigo won't listen. Diego, the man hates you. His love for me is so wild, he is jealous beyond belief."

"I don't call that love, Natalia, I call that crazy."

"Wild love and craziness, you tell me the difference. Anyway, maybe if I had given him a child—"

"Natalia, I need to speak to him. There are things I must tell him."

Natalia smiled, she just smiled.

Standing there Diego began to weave schemes, ways to approach Rodrigo. He would behave honorably and warn the man. Late the night before, sitting in Benny's car, he had known he must, and he had known it again this morning.

Diego and Natalia stood side by side, both leaning against the wall. He checked himself, considering how honorable it was really to want to raise yourself above another man's wife. Natalia glanced up at him; she looked a little frightened. Diego considered that it was best not to think at all. Warning Rodrigo about the danger he faced was one thing, but wanting his wife was another. His *pinga*, erect and quivering, chased all thoughts of honor, brought visions of Natalia's breasts, her thighs and buttocks. And he understood then how the honorable man comes apart, divides into two. Diego felt more delighted than dismayed.

"I put the Closed sign on the door," she whispered.

Natalia rested her head against his shoulder, the feel of her straightened his spine. He glanced at her, and she ran the tip of her tongue across her lip. She reached down and caressed him through his pants. Suddenly she thrust her hips forward and her shoulders rocked back and forth, round and round, her breasts shaking. "C'mon," she said, "enough of this, let's go into the kitchen." He followed her, looking at his watch. It was two o'clock. Walking behind Natalia, behind the brazen wiggle of her ass as she led him by his *pinga* past the curtain, effortlessly, as if he were a young boy. Studying that exquisite ass that had stirred him from the moment he first saw it. At that moment Diego Cienfuego believed it was possible he had fallen in love. Certainly a part of him had. She turned and put her arms around his neck. The look in her eyes, Diego considered, was more one of submission than concern.

"Aren't you afraid that Rodrigo will corner us again?" he whispered.

She put his hand on her breast and drew him to her. "No," she said, "I cannot tell you why but I am no longer afraid of Rodrigo." Taking his face in her hands, kissing him full on the lips.

For a moment they stood completely still.

There was no sound except the purring of the yellow cat at it encircled their feet, the cat and their own strained breathing. The kitchen was warm, they were alone, isolated and safe, lost in time.

"I want you to touch me right, Professor," Natalia told him. "I want you to touch me. I want you to lose control, you would lose control if you touched me."

Suddenly Diego put his hand on the nape of her neck, under her hair. He lifted her and carried her to the table as if she were a child. Whatever fear was left in Diego subsided as his desire for Natalia rose. He set her down on the table, but his hands did not release her. She whispered his name over and over again, making a bright song that filled his heart with joy. "Talk to me, Professor," she said. "Tell me of the red mountains of the moon and white powder sand, palm trees, and warm, soft blue water. I want to remember all of this, I never will let it go."

But Diego felt that he had no time for talking or poetry. He slipped both hands up her skirt, cradling her, he ran his palms over her thighs, then grabbed her underpants, and pulled them off. She drew him down, pushing and heaving against him, her arms wrapped around his neck. Diego felt her body under his hands, a simple, smooth, wonderful body. Both of them now uttering small sounds. He undid his trousers and grabbed her buttocks, strangely cool and extraordinarly firm, in his hands. He shut his eyes in joy, raised her, to be inside her, the pure sensation of it, the jolt of it, always new, and thoroughly familiar. Diego pressed Natalia hard against the table, she opened her legs, then her lips, her mouth forming a perfect circle. He pushed himself into her and her thighs gripped him with surprising strength; she lunged at him as if to push him off, at the same time striving to travel with him. Finding harmony, they worked in exquisite unity, a perfect bolero, as though they had danced together for years. Pure pleasure for Diego now and no thoughts, nothing of Rodrigo Punto, no thoughts of anyone now, and even Natalia had become unrelated to the pure delight of it, the viscous beat of skin on skin. He came first, ferociously, with shudders that ripped through his whole body, and he stayed with her, inside her, until she sighed and called on God, dear God, and on Diego, her hips moving in a fury, her mounting tension turning in an instant to tremors, her back arching, grabbing at his hair, pumping until they dissolved together in the blaze they generated.

Their table ballet did not last long, just long enough. And when they were through, Natalia looked at Diego quizzically, tilting her head, her arms still circling his neck.

"You know," she said. "It was just as I expected. Perfect, hombre, perfect. I think I will love you forever."

Diego thinking of a line Benny had told him back in Cuba, in Palma Sorino. Diego, he had said, you know a man should consider himself very lucky if his love lasts as long as a good fuck.

Good old Benny.

They lay still for a long time, Diego circling Natalia's cheeks, eyebrows, the bridge of her nose with his fingertips. He carefully raised himself off her and took her panties from the floor. He lifted the skirt of her dress and gently slid her panties up her legs and thighs. Natalia sat up on the table and Diego put on her shoes, first one and then the other.

The revolutionary junkie driver, Hector, was waiting, parked at the curb when Diego walked out the door of the Hatuey. He had left Natalia sitting at the counter drinking a coffee, telling him that he was nothing like Rodrigo. Diego did not want to think of himself and Rodrigo. Dealing with one painful, drawn-out, oppressive spasm of conscience now. He had watched as Natalia twirled strands of her hair between her fingers. He saw that she was crying.

Leaving Natalia he felt a horrible falling sensation, reminding himself of the dilemma of the honorable man, telling himself, now hombre, finally, Rodrigo can have his wife back.

Chapter 12

It took Nick a couple of minutes to figure what the hell Sonny was talking about. He wanted Nick to think that having a writer, a civilian come along on a raid like this one was not at all extraordinary, but he was too self-conscious to pull it off. Sonny talking nonstop. Nick barely listening.

They were stopped at a red light on Corona Avenue. One thirty on a Saturday afternoon, light traffic, a bus, two trucks, and a yellow cab on the road in front of them. Nick noticed the people waiting at the bus stop, out of five none were white, all South American. One, a short fat man, what you would call Indian-looking. A Mayan, Nick thought, a Mayan in a baseball cap and zippered green windbreaker. A Mayan waiting for the Q41 bus. The neighborhood was changing fast. Not that Nick thought that change was bad or anything, just recognizing the changes.

Five minutes later, the two of them sitting in the cruiser, parked now two blocks from the surveillance plant. Sonny asked him if he knew Frank Kurtz. Nick, reaching over the seat for the bag full of sandwiches, said yeah, I heard of him. Sonny told him he'd probably get to meet him today. Did he ever read one of his books? Nick said no, he didn't read police novels. Sonny said, oh right.

"Yeah, you'll meet him today, this Kurtz," Sonny said. "This guy who is writing this book about me."

Nick recalled that Frank Kurtz had written several police novels, and one, he remembered, had met with some success. He had read a couple of paragraphs somewhere, maybe in a *New York Times* review. He remembered thinking that it was not very good, the writing was not very good at all. "Really?" he said.

Sonny looked at him. "Yeah. He got approval from downtown to ride along with us."

"On a no-knock crash warrant? Are you kidding? There could be trouble here. These people got guns, does he know that?" Nick straightened up in his seat, holding the sandwich bag in his lap now, experiencing a small rush of apprehension.

"Listen, first of all the guy's an ex-cop, a clerical lieutenant from Brooklyn. So he's not a street guy; he knows the score. And let me tell you, when I run a take down, I do it cool and easy. I'm not into shoot-'em-ups. We'll take these guys out nice-nice. No gunplay. No need for it."

"That's the smartest thing I heard you say in a while," Nick told him.

"I say a whole lot of smart things. Maybe if you weren't so high on that white horse of yours, you could hear me."

"I hear you, Sonny. Believe me, I hear you."

"Yeah, right. Kurtz, he writes these books about cops—you heard of the guy, right?"

"I told you I did."

"But you never read one of his books. *Shadow Precinct? China Blue?*"

"Sonny, I don't read police procedurals, I live 'em, for chrissake. But now that you mention it, I think I did read an excerpt of something he wrote. He's no Jimmy Breslin or Saul Bellow, I'll tell you that."

Sonny studied him thoughtfully, as though confused. "Who's Saul Bellow?" he said.

"A damn good writer."

Sonny ran his fingers through his hair. When this guy's nervous, Nick realized, it came out as anger.

Sonny saying now as if talking to himself, "Yeah, well, Kurtz's books are good, real good. They plan to make a movie out of his last one, *Shadow Precinct*. Got Paul Newman to play the lead role. Anyway, this is going to be the guy's first work of nonfiction. This book he wants to write about me, it will be the real stuff."

"The real stuff, huh? He writes the truth about you, you'll end up making little rocks out of big ones. Who you kidding, the real stuff."

"Will you get off that? Whataya think, I'm a damn criminal or something?"

"Sonny, what I think don't matter. But listen, you can't be serious. You can't bring some civilian on a hit like this."

"Nick, the man's retired from the job what, two, three years? He's no civilian. Besides, he got an okay from downtown." Sonny, it seemed to Nick, was real tense; still his voice was friendly and light.

"Captain Hawks know about this? What's he say?"

"Hawks? Hawks? The captain had his teeth capped, cost him three grand. The man's taking acting lessons. I sort of promised they'd find him a small role."

Nick nodded, telling himself you thought you could make it with this crew of whack jobs? "Terrific," he said. Nick sat frozen, bewildered. Hearing Andre's voice now, the warning.

He looked at Sonny, who stared back at him, his eyebrows doing that dance on his forehead again. That smile of his spreading, Sonny saying now, "Books, movies, TV. I'm going to be fucking famous."

Sonny's eyes shining, fixed on Nick. Big blue eyes, expressive, the man still liking the sound of his own voice, or seemed to, the pride in his face, saying all the wrong shithead things you could count on him to say.

"Sonny, you *are* famous, and from what I can tell, that's your problem."

"You know," Sonny said happily, "I'm sorry we didn't team up years ago. We make a good team."

"Yeah?"

"Fuckin' right. I'll tell ya, you wouldn't be wearing those shit-ass clothes you're into." He looked at Nick and shrugged, saying, "You may not believe me, but I was like you once. A long time ago I was just like you. Until I saw where the truth lay."

"Hey, Sonny," Nick said, "you're doing it again."

"What, what am I doing again?"

"Tugging that signpost, dragging that spotlight." Might it be, Nick wondered, that this Sonny McCabe had no sense whatsoever of the heat he drew on himself? The thought made him shake his head. He laughed a little but he was getting pissed off.

"What are you thinking, what's wrong?" Sonny said.

It stopped him. Nick said, "Nothing's wrong. C'mon, these sandwiches are getting cold."

As he turned in his seat to open the car door it occurred to him that it might be possible to talk some sense to this guy, to this Sonny, wake him up, tell him that there were people, important people, who saw him as a target. But there was no time, too much to explain, too many forces at work now. He puffed out some air; it was a worried sound. Shit, this guy McCabe was a mystery to him.

Nick got out of the cruiser, putting all questions on hold for the time being. He figured there was no way to tell if Sonny was putting him on about Kurtz getting the okay to ride along. Nick thought he'd ask the writer when he met him but had the feeling that it was probably true. Like with everything else in this command, Sonny asked and Hawks delivered. It was as if Captain Hawks was a phantom in his own office, bowing to the needs of a detective, who was what, three, four ranks beneath him? Bizarre stuff.

He saw Suarez waiting alone on the sidewalk in front of a jewelry store. The apartment above the store was vacant and had been converted into the surveillance plant. Suarez stood, head down, arms folded, his eyes fixed on Los Campos across the street. He stood as if waiting for a bus, glancing every so often at the club's parking lot. Nick and Sonny walked up to the detective but Suarez didn't acknowledge them, apparently afraid of drawing attention to himself. Not wanting to disturb him, Nick passed Suarez by.

Sonny smiled a big hello, then sidemouthed, "We got sandwiches, buddy."

" 'Bout time bro," Suarez said, and turned and followed them into the building.

The stairway to the second floor was dark. Sonny loped up the stairs ahead of Nick and disappeared into the apartment. Suarez took hold of Nick's jacket from behind, gave him a light tug. "I hope you got a good night's sleep. It's going to be a busy day. Let me tell ya, things are moving across the street." His voice coming out in a smothered monotone, as if he were out of breath and trying to whisper.

They reached the second floor and went into the apartment. It had been close to a week since Nick had last been at the plant. He walked into the apartment slowly, taking in all the activity like a visitor, waving to Eddie Moran, who stood at the window peering though venetian blinds. On a straight-backed wooden chair in a dark corner of the room sat a tall thin man with a full beard and granny glasses. He stood and waved at Nick, saying, "Hey, how ya doing buddy?" Nick could see how tense he was.

"This is Frank Kurtz, Nick," Suarez said. "He's gonna ride along."

"Listen," Kurtz said, "I'll stay out of your way, I'm just here to watch."

Nick smiled, saying, "We have some sandwiches. They're huge. I'm sure we can find something for you if you like."

"Great," Kurtz said, "I'm starved. So what do you think, you guys going to do some business today?"

"We've been waiting for the informant to call," Eddie Moran said to Nick. "It appears he's among the missing."

"Did you try his house?" Sonny asked.

"The house, the Hatuey, I spoke to his wife. Man, her English is awful. She tells me she hasn't heard from Rodrigo since yesterday afternoon."

Sonny stood near Captain Hawks, who was studying a diagram layout of Los Campos. Sonny fingered a portable radio, called out to the men on foot and those in the surveillance van in the street. "Come on in, soup's on," he said into the radio. Sonny sighed deeply. "Hey, maybe Rodrigo got busted. He's always carrying that cannon of his. Anybody check?"

"I checked," Moran said. "He didn't get pinched. Christ, this is one bitch of a case. I hate working people I can't speak to or understand."

"You're right," Sonny said. "This case is your basic hummer. Do something for me, will ya, Eddie? Spread these sandwiches out on the table there. They're marked by name and there's some brews here, for whoever wants one."

Eddie Moran took the sandwiches from the bag and spread them out on the table. The one marked *Hawks* he carried to the captain. Hawks winked at Nick and motioned with his head toward the window.

Nick peered through the blinds at the street below. There was a white van and about a half dozen cars in Los Campos's parking lot. Benny Matos, the club's owner, had left his Buick at the curb. Nick spotted the black Mercedes behind the Buick; he knew it was the ride for the Colombian guy, Medina.

Sonny and Kurtz joined Nick at the window. They took note of a pair of well-dressed men who stood guard at the club's front door. Sonny turned away, barely interested.

Plenty of action, Nick was thinking, way too much for a Saturday afternoon. Something was going down. The front door opened, he saw Benny Matos walk out onto the sidewalk, a kind of sentry or something, hands on his hips, his head on a swivel.

"Check this guy out, Sonny," Nick said.

"Will ya look at that hippo son of a bitch all in white," Sonny said. "Now, you gotta know that sometime this morning ol' Benny there got dressed, stood in front of a mirror. He checked himself out and said I look good, I'm ready. Man, was that sucker wrong or what?"

Everybody bent over with laughter.

"You know, fellas," Sonny said. "Those mambo-dancing fools down there are waiting, they're waiting for someone."

"A bunch of them began arriving about eight this morning," Hawks said. "The van in the parking lot, that showed about eight thirty. They pulled right up to the club's back door. Our line of sight was blocked, Suarez didn't see a whole lot. Right Carl?"

Detective Suarez was assaulting his sandwich with concentration. "They took something, or someone, out of the van. There were four of them. Medina, the redheaded Colombian, was there. But I couldn't make out what they were up to."

"Anything on the wires?" Nick asked.

"Nothing of interest on the phone," said Eddie Moran. "And it looks like they're staying out of the office. The bug has been quiet."

The apartment was empty of furniture save for two tables that stood along an interior wall. On one was the reel-to-reel tape recorders, one for the telephone at Los Campos and one for the bug in the club's office. Nick was a firm believer in room bugs. Others might swear by telephone taps, line bugs, pen registers, various phone eavesdropping devices, but he had never used a room bug that didn't produce. Besides, there were few things in his life that he enjoyed more than sitting down and listening to the enemy when they were relaxed and chitchatting. It was like fishing for shark, they were right there at arm's length, never guessing they were about to be speared and tagged.

Working with wiretaps and bugs over the years, Nick had been privy to the wildest and most riveting details of the criminal life, but after a few years you could drown in it, and what had once made you step back in wonder could begin to slip past your ears, as unheard as air.

"The way I see it," Nick said, "we have to talk to Rodrigo. No doubt something is happening down there. Could be a major deal, could be nothing at all." He looked through the blinds again. Too much action in the street; in the club's parking lot there were men standing around, waiting. "Sonny, we need to know what's happening down there. And we need to know soon."

"We'll find out what those banditos are up to. It's only a matter of time," Sonny answered patiently.

"I figure they got some kind of sit-down going on," Suarez said.

"What else you figure?" Sonny asked him.

"Well you can't tell anything from the wires. I don't know what to figure." He looked around the room. "I've been listening to these people for six months. They talk, talk, talk, and all they're talking about is guns. A little dope rap, but mostly guns. Those fucking people down there could be armed to the teeth, you know?"

"Carl," Sonny said, "you're the best interpreter around. Only putting together what you hear and what's going on has never been your strong point. We got pages of conversation here, and still we don't know what's happening." He turned to Nick, "What do you make of this?"

"First of all, I think the guns are here now, or they are arriving today. We've never seen this much activity around that club during the day. Still, I'd like to know where the hell is Rodrigo. I don't know about you, but I don't like the looks of that, the fact that he's not around."

Nick went to the table and took a half of his sandwich. "C'mon Frank," he said to the writer, "there's plenty here, help yourself. What I want to know," Nick said, "is how long do you figure to sit tight? Hell, they could get those guns and move them out while we're sitting here having a picnic."

"He's right," Captain Hawks said.

"We can't hit them blind," Sonny said. "If we go in blind, we're liable to blow the whole thing."

"We won't go in blind," Suarez said. "When Monserette gets here, let him grab something to eat, then me and him will take a little stroll across the street. We can get close. Maybe we can overhear something, check the joint out."

"Well," Sonny said, "that's a good idea. As good as any. What do you think, Captain?"

Captain Hawks nodded, munching on his sandwich, saying, "I wish that goddamn snitch would call."

"The pigskin-eating pain in the ass calls me every day around noon," Sonny said. "I called the office, he hasn't checked in."

"Maybe he's tied up," Frank Kurtz said shyly.

"I guess so," said Sonny.

"I don't like the feel of this, Sonny," Nick said.

"Me neither, but let's not panic. Maybe I'd better take your panic pulse, are you panicking?"

Nick was charged up, his instincts telling him it was time to plow through that door across the street, time to cinch the vest and do it. It had been a while since he'd done anything that could even remotely be considered dangerous police work. He was eager and couldn't figure out if that was a good or a bad sign. "I'm not panicked," he said. "I'm pumped and ready to go. How about you, Sonny, you up for this?"

"Hey buddy, when this war party lands, just don't get in my way."

Everyone in the room laughed; Nick found it embarrassing.

"Jesus," Frank Kurtz said, "you can't make this shit up." Taking some notes now.

Nick heard the street door open, the sound of feet coming up the stairs.

The other team—Monserette and four more detectives—arrived and went straight for the food. Sonny and Captain Hawks took the diagram of Los Campos and moved off to another room, closing the door behind them.

Standing by the table with the tape recorders and receivers on it, Nick found himself drinking a beer with Frank Kurtz. One receiver was tuned to the office in Los Campos. They could hear music and some laughter, a faint shout. Apparently no one was in the office, but the bug planted in the suspended ceiling was powerful enough to pick up conversation and sound from the hallway nearby. Kurtz, it seemed, liked his beer; he drank two bottles of it.

"You know," Kurtz told him, "in my twenty years I never worked a wiretap or a bug. I mean when you think about it, getting that close to people, it's something mystical almost."

Nick smiled, thinking mystical, yeah it's mystical all right.

"So Nick, how long have you been on the job?"

"Going on eleven years," Nick told him. He had decided to allow himself this one beer. No way to tell how this hit would unfold, and he wanted to keep his wits about him. Still, he felt a little bad for Kurtz; the writer looked a bit lost, so a little conversation with the guy seemed the decent thing to do.

"Man, let me tell you, the second ten go like a shot," Kurtz said. "The first ten years in the job drag, but the second go with the speed of light. You married?"

"Nope. Been there, tried that, it didn't work."

"Divorced?"

"Right."

"Too bad. The cop's dilemma"—he held up his bottle of beer—"booze and broads."

Nick smiled, thinking maybe he should go find Sonny and Hawks.

Kurtz finished his beer and gazed around at the gathering of detectives with affection. "You know," he said, "after you throw in your papers, you'll miss this. The fraternity of cops."

"So they say."

Kurtz stared at Nick and tapped him on the forearm with the flat of his hand. "Take it from me, this is what matters, this is all that matters, walking into harm's way with people you care about, people that care about you. The brotherhood."

Nick stared back at him, thinking, how the hell would you know, a clerical lieutenant? For years he'd been hearing this back-to-back stuff from people who never got out from behind a desk.

"I'd give my right arm to be back here with you guys."

"You mean to be here all the time or long enough to write a book?"

Kurtz shook his head in confusion. "You're right," he said. "Most times the job can bore you to death. And taking shit from bosses—Christ, I don't miss taking shit from the brass."

"I've never been bored," Nick told him.

Suddenly there was a voice on the open receiver, the voice sounded close and clear. Both Nick and Kurtz turned; it was as though someone was with them.

"Hey, ¿dónde ésta Manny? ¿Dónde Manny, man?"

"That bug is something," Kurtz said.

"If it's set right, I mean in the right place, and there's no major interference, it's like they're whispering in your ear. A lover saying, do me, do me."

"Whooooo, that's good." He took a ballpoint pen out of his shirt pocket and opened his notebook.

Nick laughed.

"C'mon Nick, how do you see it? You think you'll hit today?"

"Yeah, I think so. Still, I'd love to hear from the informant. Without the snitch you're tossing the dice. It becomes a crapshoot, and in this business you don't want to shoot crap unless you have to." He watched Kurtz stare at him. "So you're writing a book, huh?"

Kurtz nodded. "I've always wanted to do a real police book, a true story."

"The world of Sonny McCabe. A cop's cop," Nick said.

Kurtz laughed, but Nick thought he had embarrassed him. "What is it for you?" Kurtz asked. "I mean, they told me you're a first-grader, top of the line. You must love this too."

"There is no answer to that. For everyone it's different."

"Right, but what is it for you?"

Nick smiled at him. "Frank," he said, "you were a cop. You don't have to ask those questions. If you want to know why a cop loves being a cop and whatnot, ask yourself. You were a twenty-year man. I'm not going to give you the words, you're the writer."

"Ever read one of my books?"

"I read part of your last one. It was good, a good read."

"Don't misunderstand, I appreciate your being kind, but I hate when people say that."

"What?"

"A good read. It makes me feel as though I've written a *Kojak* episode."

"Sorry. Anyway, I like Kojak. You know, the man with the lollipop, he can break any case and delivers justice with a smile."

The writer raised his beer in acknowledgment, saying that Kojak was good, but fiction. Sonny McCabe, now Sonny was the genuine article, talking about the first time he ran into Sonny McCabe, leaning forward, bringing his face close to Nick's, whispering, telling Nick that Sonny had come into his Brooklyn precinct late one night, all beat to shit. The man had three gang-bangers in tow. Young guys, street-running guys, no-shit bad guys. Sonny took the three of them down and never pulled his gun. Reciting it in a way that Nick found riveting.

When Kurtz straightened up and finished his beer, Nick said, "You tell one hell of a story."

Nick stretched and yawned, seeing the tale of Sonny McCabe in the hands of this guy, seeing Sonny's life vindicated and raised to legend in a book. Kurtz glanced at Nick and the look he threw at him led Nick to believe that he knew what Nick was thinking.

"You know," he said, "Sonny led the Public Morals Division in arrests three years running."

"One hell of a cop," Nick said.

"The best," said Kurtz. "By the way," he said. "We do the movie, we're going to need technical advisors. Could be a spot for you there."

"Really? I can't imagine anything I'd rather do," Nick told him.

Kurtz winked and slapped his shoulder.

Chapter 13

Benny told me where to find you," Hector said during the short ride to Los Campos. He did not say much else. It was three thirty in the afternoon.

The car rolled into Los Campos's parking lot. As Diego got out he saw pig-necked Mambo Vasserman standing at the club's back door; his brother Chino stood just behind him, whispering to him. Diego followed Hector to the door. The Vasserman brothers backed away, Mambo telling Hector, "They are waiting for you in the basement, chico."

Diego could make out about a half-dozen men, more standing in the hallway and in the kitchen. He glanced over the crowd and recognized among them Tito Roman from the Bronx. Tito was staring at Diego, and his stare was vicious. As far as Diego knew, Tito knew nothing about him other than that he was the club's maître d', but the look he gave Diego told him something else. It was an evil stare, and evil, he thought, was what these people were all about.

There were more men at the bar, and two stood guard at the front door. Paco Morales, a man who worked every so often in the kitchen, waved as Diego came in. As he shouldered past them, Diego considered that in fact he knew many of the people with whom Benny did business. Too many not to be involved on some level.

The door to the basement was opened by Chino Vasserman; he held the door open until Hector and Diego entered, then bolted it. Diego had never been in Los Campos's basement before.

Reluctantly, he followed Hector down the stairs to a large windowless room. There were whitewashed cement block walls, and an overbright light hung from the center of the ceiling, making the room feel like a vast jail cell. The walls glistened with dampness and the poured-concrete floor was slimy. Along one wall was a row of what appeared to be large gray footlockers. Six, maybe seven. In one corner two ma-

chetes, a lance, a bow, and a quiver and several arrows were tipped
against the wall. Diego glanced quickly toward the opposite corner,
where Rodrigo and Oscar were standing, secured by a wire cable to a
threaded metal rod in the cement block. A second, thin wire held
them together by the upper arms, the wire had cut the muscles below
their shoulders and looking more closely Diego could see that the wire
was turning their arms blue. He'd half-expected to find the two men
here, it wasn't that. But to see them in this condition stunned and ap-
palled him. Both men, it seemed to Diego, appeared to have been
hypnotized by the pain they had endured. They stood together on tip-
toe, totally naked, Rodrigo's busted arm hanging in a cast at his side.
The room smelled strongly of cigarette smoke and mildew, disinfec-
tant and urine. There was a table in the center of the room, and
Benny and Cano sat there eating sandwiches, drinking beer from bottles.

Cano thrust a hand toward Diego, saying, "You, Professor, are a half
hour late."

"He was busy," Benny said kindly, "busy fucking the rat mulatto's
wife."

Rodrigo let loose a small growl that was more of a moan.

"This," Diego said, waving his hand in the air, "is barbaric, immoral.
This is stone-age shit. What are you people doing here?" And for the
first time it occurred to Diego to wonder about his own chances of
leaving that basement alive.

"Morality," Cano said, "is an invention of the weak to keep the
strong in line. You know that, Professor. In this room, it is useless to
plead. So keep your mouth shut and sit down."

Diego looked around for a chair and found none.

"On the floor," Cano said, "sit on the fucking floor, Professor."

"Benny," Diego said.

"I can't help you now, don't ask me."

"The floor is wet," Diego said. "I will stand if you don't mind. I can
stand, it's okay."

"You will fucking sit, hombre, because I told you to sit." Cano removed from his belt a silver pistol and struck the butt on the table.

Diego stood still, thinking I've come to the end, this place is where
it will end.

"I told you, Cano," Benny said, "Diego is smart. Still, he has as much
balls as brains. An unusual man."

Cano looked at Diego and then at Benny. Benny had a calm half
smile on his face. "We will see, huh? We will soon find out if what
you say is true," Cano told him.

"Why am I here?" Diego said. He was disoriented and growing more and more fearful.

"We have confused you," Cano said. "You want to know what is going on. We understand."

"He is a good man," Benny said.

"Says you, man," Cano said. "Says you. There is something in men like us that makes men like you wonder if God is dead, eh Professor?"

"Cano," Benny said, "why don't you just ask him what it is you want without the bullshit?"

Cano finished his beer in one long swallow.

"Ask him?" he said. "I should be polite and ask the Professor?" Cano's eyes drifted to Rodrigo and Oscar. "I don't have to ask him anything. I tell him," Cano said. "He is a coward, fearful of his own shadow, a punk. Diego," he said, "we need the use of your apartment." Cano pursed his lips as though he wanted to throw him a kiss. "You, I love people like you. You will help us. Now you give me good simple answers, okay?"

"Go on," Diego told him.

"You have had no trouble with the police, the police don't know you. Am I correct?"

"Yes," Diego said.

"Not in Miami, not here?"

"That's right."

"Did you like it there? Was Miami a good town?"

Diego didn't answer him.

"I need your fucking apartment because it is safe," Cano suddenly shouted at him. "A safe place to put our lockers. These two rat bastards have made our little spot here hot. Do you understand me?"

"Look," Diego said, "my children are at my apartment. Do you think I will allow you to put them in danger? You would have to kill me first."

"Oh my friend," Cano said. "Don't go asking for something you don't want. I may give it to you."

"You don't frighten me, Cano, you never did."

Cano seemed almost embarrassed. "Listen," he said, "your children are fine. The young ones are with your landlady, and Justo is at this very moment upstairs in the kitchen."

An image of Justo in the midst of this madness spun in Diego's head and sent a wave of revulsion through him. "My only concern is for the safety of my children," he said.

Cano nodded.

"Diego, help me out, will you?" Oscar the bartender gasped behind him. "I've been falsely accused, please help me man."

Diego turned and looked at Oscar and then at Rodrigo. Rodrigo's head was down; he seemed to know there was no help.

"Oscar," Benny said, "tell Diego what you told me."

There was a cold edge in Benny's voice, a sound Diego had not heard before. Oscar lifted his head and then shook it. "I have never been in Rodrigo's cab. Never," Oscar said. "Diego must have made a mistake. It was someone else he saw, not me."

Benny nodded. "The man is calling you a liar, Diego."

Diego didn't answer.

"Benny . . ." Rodrigo said.

Benny turned his head slowly.

"Say we went for a ride. Okay, what does it matter?"

"I was never with you!" Oscar howled.

Benny, it seemed to Diego, thought that over. He thought it over and then nodded. "I was not talking to you, Rodrigo. Was I?" he said.

Rodrigo dropped his head.

Cano rose from the table and went to the corner of the room where the machete, bow and arrows, and lance stood. He took the bow and tried it out. Then he strung an arrow. The other men in the room stood around, waiting to see what Cano would do. Hector finger-combed his hair, a wild-eyed crazy smile on his face.

"You see," Cano said, "we know that Oscar was with Rodrigo. We know that Rodrigo is an informant for the police. We know that Oscar knows of our business here. We want to know what Oscar has told Rodrigo, what the rat bastard, Rodrigo, told the cops. We want to know what the fuck is going on."

"Listen, listen to me," Oscar begged. "I did nothing. I swear. Nothing!"

"Cano," Diego said. "Isn't it possible that they simply went for a ride together?"

"No," Cano said.

Diego looked away. He found the look of horror on Oscar's face truly unbearable.

Cano fired the arrow, catching Oscar in the top of the thigh. Oscar's scream went on and on, and behind it Hector laughed insanely.

Cano turned the bow in his hands, checking it, then he looked at Diego. He looked over at Oscar. "I missed your balls," he said.

Benny grunted unhappily.

Oscar's howling stopped only when Manny Vasserman sealed his mouth with a piece of duct tape.

Diego looked at Oscar's bulging eyes—these people were insane.

"Jesus Christ, Benny," Diego said. "Why would you bring Justo here? We are family, for God's sake." He looked into Benny's moon face. "Come on, Benny! You and this Cano live in a world of craziness, but I don't. What the hell can I do for—"

"Calm down," Cano said, loading another arrow. "I told you we need your place, your apartment."

Diego became panicky, really alarmed for the first time. It seemed to him that he had counted on the ultimate victory of the honorable man. He had been a true believer and vainly imagined that honor and right were on his side. Now, to his terror, looking around him, he could see finally that honor invariably will give way to circumstance.

"You are a phony bastard, Professor," Cano said.

Diego put a hand to his forehead, thinking this is agony, this is horror, this is hopelessness, the whirlwind. He had to get out of there, out of that stinking basement, out of this insane city. Take his children and run from New York as he had run from Miami.

The Colombian came forward and stood in front of Diego; there was a look of what seemed to be pure pleasure on his face. He tried to force the bow on him.

"Shoot that rat bastard, Diego. Go on, shoot Rodrigo. Hey man, you already nailed his wife, now you can nail him." His breath was hot and horrible, the breath of a lion fresh from a kill.

"I am no killer, Cano. I'll have nothing to do with your insanity. I am an honorable man, God damn it."

Cano laughed. "You are a fraud, Professor. You think you are a hero but you are not. You are the worst kind of hypocrite. You screw another man's wife, he threatens you as any man would. And then you come running to us, to Benny and me. You inform. Then you scream that you are an honorable man. I hate your guts, you hypocrite. You fake."

"Cano," Diego said, "you are crazy. Do you know that, hombre, do you know that you are a fucking lunatic?"

Cano drew back the bowstring, taking aim at Rodrigo, a small grin on his face. Diego glanced at Cano, saw all that fury, Cano saying now, "Crazy? I'm not crazy. I am smart, smarter than you, Professor. Rodrigo," Cano said softly. "You informed to the police. I know you informed. I want to know what you told them. Huh? Huh! Huh!"

Rodrigo started talking slowly about the police, that he didn't know any policemen, but Cano's expression quickly affected him and he changed the subject matter and Rodrigo started telling Cano what a good connection he would be to sell guns and just how much money he could make for him.

Cano told him he wanted to know about the fucking cops.

Rodrigo screamed, "I can help you! I know people, plenty of people who would buy your guns! You have guns to sell and I have the people who can buy them. Important people, people with money."

Cano's grin spread. He turned to Benny. Benny sniffed and drummed his fingers on the tabletop. "Tell me, Benny," Cano said. "How do you think this piece of shit here knows that we have guns?"

"Oscar told him," Benny said. "Oscar told him everything."

Rodrigo twisted his body just as Cano fired the arrow; it hit the cement block wall with a horrible twang. The sound of that arrow striking cement hung in the air, numbing the room.

"Shit, missed again. How could I miss that fat bastard?"

Hector approached Rodrigo, he twisted and turned, aping the man's moves, whooping. The Vasserman brothers stood off to the side entertaining themselves constantly with knives. There came from Rodrigo a long low moan that seemed wrung from his soul.

"For God's sake," Diego said, "tell them, Rodrigo, tell them what they want to know."

"Oh man, fuck you, you faggot bastard. Why should I give them the answers they want? No matter what I say, your friends won't let me live."

Diego laughed weakly. Jesus, he thought, this man is strong. Rodrigo truly had courage. Diego believed in courage.

Cano dropped the bow and arrow and strolled back to the corner of the room where the lance and machetes stood. He took the spear and brought it to Benny, handing it to him, and then he took his pistol from his belt. He went and placed the silver gun gently alongside Oscar's head. "You are right, Rodrigo," he said. "It is over for you, my friend. Your only concern now is how you die." Cano cocked the gun, and Oscar's eyes got wide. The Colombian fired point blank into the side of Oscar's head, blowing Oscar's entire forehead away, leaving his brain exposed. Oscar's feet made a quick convulsive shuffle. Blood stained the sleeves of Cano's guayabera, streaks of it ran down his wrist and over his fingers

Benny said, "I have to say, Cano . . . I have to say."

"Glad you approve, Benny," Cano said.

Diego looked around saying, "Oh my God, you crazy bastard. Lord, this is a terrible place to die!" he shouted.

Cano laughed, saying, "Do you know a good one?" He wiped his eyes with the back of his wrist, then took the spear that Benny held. Rodrigo rolled his head back; he looked at Diego and Diego had no choice but to meet his eyes.

"I fixed you, you bastards. I told the cops that you have guns here," Rodrigo said. "I said they got guns in their cars and in their houses."

Cano made a face, sighing deeply as if he knew all along where this was going.

"You are shit people!" Rodrigo screamed. "The cops will come, yes, they will come for you all!" He then turned his head toward the wall. Cano retreated, then walked in a slow circle around Diego, Diego turning, watching him, waiting. Cano stuck Rodrigo with the spear, he stuck him hard, drove the spear right into his side.

Rodrigo's eyes opened in amazement. He kicked out with his feet and fell sideways against the wall; the spear went with him. Rodrigo shouted once, shouted for his wife in a choked ghostly voice.

"Christ!" Diego shouted.

"Yes, Christ," Cano said. "You can call on Christ, the Virgin Mother, anyone you fuckin' want to." Cano grabbed his crotch. "I fuck the saints, I fuck you."

Diego locked eyes with Cano and a strange kind of calm settled on him. He stared at Cano and found that all at once the whole terrifying experience had composed itself into the Colombian's face. I'm there, he thought, I'm there. They got me. His mouth was dry and his chest felt tight from the beating of his heart and his body tensed with a strange, terrible excitement. Cano was smiling and in his mind's eye Diego could see him standing with the street gangsters from Miami.

Chapter 14

Apart from Sonny and Hawks, all the detectives on the raid team were sitting in the surveillance room, finishing their sandwiches and beer, laughter following a constant low rumble of conversation, everyone waiting for the captain and McCabe to make an appearance. Everybody lounging, listening to cop war stories, epic combats, an extraordinary love-filled ten minutes with a cop groupie in the backseat of a patrol car.

Nick sat with Kurtz at the far end of the room near the window so he'd have an angle on both the street and Kurtz.

"I feel a need to go and join those guys," Kurtz said.

"Go on," Nick told him. "Cops tell the best stories. Go ahead and take notes."

"They seem real young to be detectives," Kurtz told him. "Or maybe I'm just getting old."

"They are young."

Kurtz looked at them sideways over his glasses with a wide-eyed delighted grin. Most of his police career he had been an inside guy, a student. He brushed some bread crumbs from his sweater, then glanced at Nick. Telling Nick, I gotta hear this, he went to join the laughing group.

A young black detective, whose name was Lloyd something, was into his story, talking matter-of-factly. "So I'm out bouncing last Friday, I grab this chick and we do the dirty in the backseat of my car. I ain't going for no motel, hotel shit. Anyway, the bitch smells, man. I mean she stinks. It's not a real bad smell, she's wearing perfume, a great bod, but she's drenched in about a gallon of perfume."

Kurtz rocked in his chair, arms folded, his eyes locked on Lloyd.

Nick smiled. He would not get up and join in, but he had to smile. The cop going on with the story, a good-looking guy, reminded Nick a little of the young Harry Belafonte. Dressed for the street in jeans and sneakers and a red hooded sweatshirt.

Lloyd said to the group, "So I get home. Sneak in like the old burglar, my dog doesn't even open his eyes. I'm good, man, I'm home free. My old lady sleeps like death itself. I get undressed, drop my clothes on the chair, and slide into bed. Okay? Only when I wake up I find the wife sniffing my shorts like a goddamn anteater. She's sniffing and sniffing and wagging her head. I tell myself, I promise myself, I swear to myself that next time I'm going to toss those suckers out on the parkway. I'm going to bring a pair of fresh shorts and stash them in the glove box."

Laughter all around.

Kurtz asked is that it? and Lloyd said it? No that ain't it. Last night I'm out making the rounds, I bump into ol' smelly again. And don't you know it's back in the car, feet in the air. Going home, I can feel this stink all over me, and Kurtz said Jesus Christ. Why didn't you go and take a shower?

"Yeah, where? I'm in the South Bronx, man, it's four o'clock in the morning."

Frank said, "Go on, go on."

"Anyway, I'm breaking a hundred heading out to the Island. Toss the drawers out at exit forty, nice move if I say so myself, quick backhand flip. I get in about five, five thirty this morning. Pass the mutt, okay, but I'm exhausted, I'm wiped. I don't wash up. I jump into bed and pass out. Now, it's about six, seven in the morning, I wake up to the sound of sniffing. Now I'm frozen, I don't move, I just open my eyes and there's my wife, and her nose about an inch above my stomach. I mean you could really feel it. She's running that nose of hers the length of my body, right down between my legs. She got one hand holding the sheet of the bed, the other one's got my gun."

Frank Kurtz slapped his forehead. "Holy shit," he said. "Which gun?

"The gun, man, my service revolver. *That* gun. Busted! Busted!"

The group of cops exploded, Lloyd doing a quick moonwalk across the room, arms outstretched, shouting, "But Honey! But Babe!"

Kurtz's laughter was louder than anyone else's.

From his perch near the window, Nick glanced down at Los Campos's parking lot. A car pulled into the lot and two men got out. "Carl," he said, "come here. I want you to check these two guys out."

Detective Suarez came and looked out the window. "That one guy," he said, "the tall one. I think his name is Diego Cienfuego, they call him the Professor. The other little shit is Matos's gofer, Hector. A small-time dealer out of East Harlem. A junkie too, he's got a long sheet."

"Ah," Nick said. "The Professor." Three more men exited the club's back door. The gathering stood still a moment, hump-shouldered and serious like a circle of vultures, waiting. Nick saying now, "That guy, the tall guy, the Professor, the snitch said he's the top guy."

"What?" Detective Suarez seemed to pale a bit under his dark skin. "He told you what?"

"He said that this guy, this Diego Cienfuego is the head guy. He said you wouldn't know it, the man's low key, but he runs the show here."

"You telling me that Rodrigo told you Cienfuego is the boss?"

Nick nodded, wondering when the hell Sonny and Hawks would come back.

"If he said that, he's lying."

Nick winced. He looked at Suarez. "I don't get it. Why would he lie?"

"Well, you're the first-grader, I don't think this is a semi-almost-major revelation. Snitches lie all the time."

Nick turned and looked down at the parking lot, squinting, wondering. He watched the five men go in Los Campos's back door. "So you figure this character Rodrigo is bullshitting?"

"Look, I've been listening to these heroes for close to four months now. I think I know who's who, I've been in the club a dozen times.

Cienfuego seats people and sings songs. I got no doubt that the man knows what's happening, but he's no boss, no big-time guy."

"Why would Rodrigo run a game on us? The guy told me the Professor lays back, he's low key, but he's the main man. That's what Rodrigo said."

Nick watched Suarez look off, nodding, thinking about it. Carl said, "The guy in white, Benny, the guy with the belly so big you could name it, he's the boss, him and that redheaded Colombian, Medina. They run the show here."

"But Rodrigo—"

"Rodrigo was pulling your pud, don't ask me why. These Cubans are fucking nuts. I couldn't tell you what runs their engines. They're a different sort, these Cubans are."

"I guess," Nick said.

"And let me tell you something else. They don't forget or forgive. Rodrigo had better leave the planet if these fuckers ever find out he turned them."

Chapter 15

At three forty-five Sonny and Captain Hawks strolled back into the surveillance room past the group of lounging detectives and went to the window. They took a moment to glance through the blinds, then went back across the room. Captain Hawks saying, "Okay, we've been reaching out for the snitch, he's not around."

"We going to hit them anyway?" Detective Suarez asked.

"No way, not without word from our guy. But we came up with this idea that we'd send you and Sergi down into the street to sniff around."

Detective Sergi Monserette, the other Spanish-speaking detective, thought that wasn't a bad idea. Only how would they stay in touch? Hawks saying we'll put a transmitter on you, you talk we'll hear. You figure we should move in, let us know. I don't know what else to do. I figure we sit tight until we hear from Rodrigo. Detective Monserette saying he had enough of this sitting still and watching. Shit, maybe Rodrigo took a hike out of town.

Eddie Moran distributed the raid jackets and vests and bought out two shotguns. Suarez stood in the middle of the room pulling off his sweater and T-shirt. He stood still while Monserette taped on the body wire. Suarez grinned and held up his arms as Monserette ran duct tape over his chest and across the antenna and microphone. Nick knew that tape would rip and tear and hurt like hell when it came off. The guy had a chest like a bear.

"Okay now," Captain Hawks said. "I want you all to listen up."

Sonny turned to Lloyd and his crew of detectives and said to them good-naturedly through cupped hands, "C'mon, listen up here. The captain is going to lay this out."

"I want to make sure you all understand," Hawks said. "Carl and Sergi are going into the street for a look-see. Carl is wired; if they hear something and think that we should hit, we go."

To Nick it seemed that everyone was getting nervous, drawing together in the center of the room, the adrenaline starting to pump.

"If we hit, I want this to go down easy. We're not a SWAT team," Hawks said. "We announce our purpose and authority, nice-nice. I don't want this to turn into some kind of frontal assault."

Everyone was starting to pace like cats, taking out handguns, checking them. Eddie Moran jacked a round into his shotgun, the metal-on-metal sound getting everyone's attention. Kurtz was taking notes like crazy.

"There are two entrances, front and rear," Sonny said. "Eddie and I will take Lloyd and his team and go to the front door. Nick, you and the captain will hook up with Carl and Sergi and take the back door."

Nick exchanged a quick smile and wink with detectives Monserette and Suarez, Saurez mouthing *boom-boom*.

One of Lloyd's team, a short and stocky man with shoulder-length blond hair, said, "If Carl and Sergi are in the street and something hot comes over the wire, who's going to translate?"

Hawks walked in a small circle, his arms spread, frowning with frustration and bewilderment. "Okay, does anyone else here speak Spanish?"

"I do," said Kurtz. "I'm not Carl or Sergi, but I can get along."

"Thank you, Lord," Sonny said. "Turn up the receiver over there and listen up. See, ya see, Nick, ol' Frank here is going to come in handy."

Frank Kurtz stared at Nick for a moment as if asking a question.

"Radios?" Nick said.

"I'll have one," Sonny said, "and you'll have one. We'll leave another on the table so Frank can reach us, or raise CB if he needs to."

The plan was to ease up to Los Campos's doors, enter front and rear, round everyone up, and rendezvous in the dining room. Rodrigo had told them that the guns were in crates stashed in the basement.

The preparations for the raid complete, detectives Suarez and Monserette left the apartment.

Nick sat in a wooden folding chair at the window. Eddie Moran came to him and handed him a shotgun.

"I hate to bring this up," Nick said, "but did anybody think to call the local precinct and tell them what's going down?"

Hawks and Sonny exchanged glances, quickly shook their heads. "I don't want anybody to know what we're doing until we're into it," Hawks said.

"Why's that?"

"Nick," Hawks said, "we don't know who knows who here. Get my meaning?"

"It's not for me to say," Nick said, "but I think we call the precinct, tell them we're executing a warrant, and maybe ask for a car or two. It can't hurt to have a little backup."

"We have ten people." Sonny lit a cigarette. "We don't want this to turn into a cluster fuck. We won't need any help."

Nick turned to the window, feeling a little anxious in his gut now, feeling like he had to pee, not liking the feel of this at all. "It's up to you," he said, "but I'd like to see a uniformed presence on a raid like this. We don't want these people to think that this is a stickup. They could lose it and start shooting."

"Ey," Eddie Moran said, "we're all wearing raid jackets. It says NYPD here, don't it?"

"It's not the same, Eddie. Those two guys are wearing sweatshirts." Nick pointed out the window at Sergi and Carl, walking across the avenue. "They're going to be right in the middle of this."

"They're pros, they know what they're doing," Sonny said.

Nick twisted in his seat, the Remington pump shotgun cradled in his lap. He was surprised at how heavy it felt. Either he had grown a whole lot weaker since the last time he carried one, or he had forgotten the heft of the weapon.

Nick got up and went to the table; he took twelve rounds of double-0 buck, put six in each of his jacket pockets. Then he took his shield from his badge case, put it on a chain, and put the chain around his neck.

The raid, it seemed to Nick, had started out with the usual eager and cheerful confusion. It was fun, it got to your head. Like walking into a ring, the announcer going it's time to rock and roll. The anticipation pump was putting one hell of a charge in his blood. The action pump was why he loved being a cop. The truth was, he cherished the contact, his mind asking him, how healthy is that?

The thing about this sort of raid was that you were dealing with evidence that could not be destroyed. Guns were not drugs and could not be flushed away. There was no urgency for a quick crash entry. Once they were sure the guns were in Los Campos, they simply had to announce their purpose and authority, show the warrants, and enter. It should all go easy.

It was also true that a raid like this one could go bad. That was one of the things Nick didn't like to think about, didn't like those thoughts at all.

"Christ, we could sit here all fucking night," Eddie Moran told Sonny.

"Just do your job," Sonny said.

"Testing, one, two, three. I hope you guys can hear this," Carl Suarez's voice said through the receiver.

Eddie Moran stood at the window, squinting hard at the club's front door. He played with the venetian blinds, staring at the street and the parking lot beyond. Nerves, butterflies. He glanced over at Nick and cocked his head toward the window but saw that Nick was lost in thought, so he called Sonny.

"They're right in front of the club," Moran said, "Sergi is knocking on the door."

Like Detective Suarez, Sergi Monserette was a translator-investigator. A soft-spoken guy whose parents had been born in Barcelona. Thin and muscular, Nick figured him late twenties, early thirties at the most. He had a mane of flowing light brown hair that he brushed straight back. His movements were leisurely and controlled, and it seemed to Nick that the guy's mind was always off somewhere, not moving with his body. He had pegged Monserette as a deep thinker, a man with a past. And although they had both been assigned to the Narcotics Division, Nick had not gotten to know him; as a matter of fact, they had never met before Nick's assignment to the OCCU. In general, Nick thought, Monserette ignored him.

Captain Hawks had told him that Monserette had been in some heavy shit with a DEA task force, a joint investigation that brought him to Arizona and then Mexico. A crazy, wild fed case that left a DEA agent killed and Monserette himself badly wounded. The guy got himself the department's Medal of Honor, pinned on him by the mayor while he was in the hospital, recovering from his wounds.

"Sergi's knocking," Moran said. "Nobody's answering."

"Hey! *Oye!* Anybody home?" Carl Suarez's voice said through the listening device.

Pow!

"That was a gunshot!" Frank Kurtz screamed, wild-eyed. "A shot, a shot, I heard a gunshot!"

"Play it back, play it back!" Sonny yelled.

Pow!

"Christ," Hawks said, "that is a gunshot."

Spanish voices now, words coming through the receiver in a rush. Kurtz saying wait, wait a minute. Sonny yelling c'mon, c'mon, what the fuck is going on? Kurtz saying, they said that's one down, two to go. That's what I heard, one down . . .

Carl Suarez's voice came over the receiver. "We heard a shot from inside the club!" he shouted. "*A gunshot from inside the club! We're going in!*"

"Okay," Nick said, "let's go."

"Wait," Captain Hawks said, "wait a minute."

Carl called again. "Sonny, we're going in."

Hawks stared at Sonny in panic. Sonny ran to the window and pulled up the blinds. "They're banging on the front door," he said. "They're really trying to get in. Who told them to do that? What the hell are they doing?"

Nick joined Sonny at the window. Sergi and Carl were at the club's front door, and Carl was banging on the door with the flat of his hand; Nick could see his pistol in his other hand. "Police! Police! Open this fucking door!" one of them cried. To Nick the voice sounded half hysterical.

Nick took his shotgun and went to the door, opened it and stood by it. "Captain," he said, "we are not going to get a written invitation."

"Okay, let's go, let's go!" Captain Hawks shouted, his voice booming in the room. "You know where you have to go, do it."

"Should I call CB," Frank Kurtz said, "get some cars here?"

Hawks looked at him sullenly. "Yeah, yeah, maybe you'd better."

"C'mon," Nick said, "what the hell are you doing standing there, Sonny? All of you, for chrissake they could be shooting people across the street."

"Aw shit," Sonny said with a bland smile, "we messed this up."

Nick ran down the stairs carrying the shotgun in one hand, using the other against the wall for balance. He was slightly out of breath when he got out on the sidewalk, and he could feel himself break a sweat. Nonetheless, he felt no fear. To his astonishment all his fear had disappeared, like windblown clouds in a clearing sky. He stood on the sidewalk a moment, and then he ran, ran across the avenue toward Los Campos.

The front door was wide open. Carl and Sergi were nowhere to be seen. Nick started for the door but Sonny was behind him now, saying, "Take the back door, we'll go in the front."

In the club's parking lot a tall lanky black kid charged around on a skateboard. He glanced at Nick, Nick yelling now, "Police, get out of here!" The kid scooted off without anything coming into his face.

Nick was ten yards from the back door when it flew open and a man in a pearl gray suit and a cowboy hat charged out. "Police!" Nick shouted, more in surprise than anything else. He motioned with the barrel of his shotgun to the ground. "Get down, get down!" he said.

Nick heard Captain Hawks behind him. "I'll take him, keep going."

Hawks dragged the man to a parked car and handcuffed him to the door handle.

The club's back door was open, and Nick could see light in the hall-way. From somewhere in the club came pistol shots, the *pop-pop-pop* of automatic weapons fire, the explosion of a shotgun blast. Nick charged through the open door and Hawks came after him, pulling the door closed behind him.

Chapter 16

Suddenly, Diego felt as though he were in control of his fear. The agony vanished, and he was amazed to feel as strong as he did. He knew that everything in that basement was real. Yet at the same time it seemed to him that he was standing on a corner in Miami. The teenage gang-sters appeared before him. He could see them, he could see and hear them all. They were there and real; he could see their vicious faces, their drugged-out yellow eyes. For a moment he thought he would scream. He sprang toward Cano, slipped once on the wet concrete of the basement floor, but in two quick steps he had him.

Diego grabbed Cano by his blue guayabera and threw him across the room, going after the Colombian like the avenging angel of the Lord himself. He was close to a foot taller than Cano and stronger, much stronger. And Diego was fast—but not fast enough. Cano scrambled to the corner and grabbed one of the machetes. Still Diego didn't feel fear, he wasn't afraid at all. Crouched in a fighter's stance, Cano laughed a little. Waving to the others to stand back, saying, "Leave us be. Let me see what this big tall skinny bottle of piss has in his guts."

His nostrils flared, his eyes were wide and grotesque and savage. Cano paused a moment, gathering strength, then he went for Diego.

"Wait!" Benny yelled.

Foolishly, Diego turned to Benny. Chino Vasserman came up behind him and threw his arm around Diego's neck, a strong heavy arm.

"Wait!" Benny yelled again.

Noises came from above—loud crashing, scuffling and running feet, shouts, sharp thumps, what sounded like glass breaking, then a gunshot.

Chino took his arm from around Diego's neck and went carefully to the foot of the stairs, leaving Diego standing in the center of the room. Chino looked confused and frightened, he took a pistol from his belt, holding the gun awkwardly. "*¿Oye dime, qué pasa?*" Chino shouted. He was answered with the sound of more running, a bang on the basement door. There was another gunshot, then another, then a burst of automatic weapons fire.

"What the fuck!" Benny yelled, his voice coming from down deep, out of control.

Cano walked in small circles, holding his machete in the air, shaking his head to express his utter confusion, his incomprehension, his inability to understand what was going on. He made no sound, but his look conveyed pure terror.

The basement door crashed opened.

Tito Roman, the Bronx drug dealer, stood at the top of the steps. He looked down at them, gasping in a total panic. "The fucking cops!" he screamed. "The police are here!"

Hector sprinted up the stairs, followed closely by the Vasserman brothers. Cano and Benny were running in three directions at once, looking hopelessly for a way out, both of them shouting, "Cops! Cops! Cops!" Benny doing his fat man's shuffle. The panic on Cano's face, and the terror in the Colombian's eyes gave Diego a pulse of pleasure. Above him there came more automatic gunfire, the blast of a shotgun. Diego's head was going bad. The whitewashed walls, the mutilated, hanging bodies overwhelmed him. He pictured his child, his son Justo, in the very center of the battle and horror consumed him. Diego was so frightened for Justo he thought he might vomit.

Desperate, he made for the stairway, taking the steps two at a time. The door to the basement was open, and he saw a police detective standing on the landing holding what appeared to be a shotgun. He was well built, with a face that was full of malice and viciousness. Someone sometime had smashed his nose. Around his neck was a silver chain on which hung a gold badge. He wore a blue zippered jacket with NYPD emblazoned across the front. He brought the gun up even with

Diego's head and smiled—or seemed to smile. "Move, motherfuckah, and I'll blow your head off." The two men stared at each other. Loud noises and screaming swept through the club, and the stairwell filled with the smell of gun smoke as the echoes of the firing died away.

Chapter 17

Nick found Carl Suarez sitting on the hallway floor, his hands curled around his pistol, the pistol resting in his lap. He looked as though he had been crying. Nick squatted down next to Carl and touched his face. Detective Suarez's body stiffened in a sudden spasm. Hawks stood behind Nick, his breath coming in fits and starts. There were yelling and crashing sounds coming from the dining room at the end of the hall. Nick saying are you okay?

Hawks yelling now, "What the fuck happened?"

Carl buried his face in his hands and began sobbing, "Jesus Christ, Jesus Christ. They killed Sergi, they just shot him in the face. Christ!"

"I have to get in there," Hawks said.

"No, no," Carl told him earnestly, "they all have guns, they're fucking crazy. Nick, they thought we were stickup men. They didn't ask any questions, they just started shooting."

"All right, all right," Nick said, "you're going to be all right. Captain, you stay here with Carl. I'll go."

Nick started to get up but Captain Hawks flew right past him, accidently kneeing Nick and kicking Carl in the head, slamming Nick down on top of Detective Suarez.

Hawks charged down the hallway, screaming, "What the fuck is going on here? What the fuck is going on?"

Carl groaned a little.

Nick thinking that Suarez had become completely unglued and now Hawks had panicked. And a panicked man in a combat situation, as anyone would tell you, was capable of astonishing acts of courage and stupidity.

"For chrissake, Captain," Nick shouted, "get *down*, will ya!"

Hawks turned to him, screaming, "Why you stupid bastard! I have to lead my men! You stay here with that fucking coward!"

A figure in a straw fedora leapt into the hallway, fired a shot *whap!*

and Hawks folded in two like a puppet, his arm, his gun hand going straight up. He fell back against the hallway wall and then slid to the floor. *Kaboom!* Went Nick's shotgun and the shooter flew straight back into the dining room.

Putting his free hand on Carl's shoulder, Nick stood up and started down the hallway. He got to Hawks and turned him over, not knowing what to expect. The captain's chest was covered with blood. He had never seen such a thing, not in all his years on the job, a shot cop. Captain Hawks whimpered, "Alice," and then the light in his eyes went out.

Nick crouched down, crooning to himself what a fuckup, what a mess. And now the fear of death, which had not been there before, came for him.

There was another pistol shot, then Nick's ears were hammered closed by the blast of a shotgun. Somebody shouted "Don't shoot!" In the distance, Nick thought he heard sirens and wasn't sure if the sound was real or imaginary. Nearby the sound of men shouting, swearing, someone called on God. Eddie Moran's voice, Lloyd's voice, Sonny McCabe.

Nick stood and quickly made his way along the hallway, staying close to the wall, holding the shotgun firmly to his chest. He went to the end of the hallway, which opened into the dining room, and looked in. His eyes found the man who shot Captain Hawks, the man he himself had shot. He was dead. Part of his face and shoulder were gone, but he still wore his fedora. An amazing trick, Nick thought, amazing.

A teenage boy lay nearby. He was draped across a table, not quite dead, shot in the legs and stomach. Four men lay on the dance floor, head to toe. Two were dead, two badly wounded, almost dead. The dead lay very still. One of them was Detective Sergi Monserette. Tracked, Nick thought, Sergi Monserette had been tracked from Mexico by the spirits of the dead and nailed in Queens. A cold breeze swept over him from an overhead air-conditioning unit, and Nick hugged himself.

Sonny McCabe stood in the middle of the room. He shook his head as if embarrassed. "Check the basement," Sonny said. "Careful, Nick, there're people down there."

He would both remember and not remember going to the basement landing, seeing a man coming up the stairs, bringing his weapon up.

"Move, motherfuckah, and I'll blow your head off."

That he would not remember.

But he would remember forever going down into that basement, seeing the dead, tortured men hanging. The erect posture, the bare bodies stretched on wire. That would become the most intense and deepest and most profound memory of his life. And in the hours, days, months, and years through which the life of Nick Manaris was evolving, never would there be more terror mixed with pain than in the hours of that Saturday afternoon in Queens.

Later Nick found himself again in Los Campos's dining room. There were seven bodies; two were policemen. The sight made his mind shudder to a complete halt. He watched the man they called the Professor wring his hands, the man couldn't keep his hands still. He kept running his eyes across the faces of the people standing around; the man covered himself with anguish, letting out ghoulish moans and a long wailing cry. Nick held his breath against the man's pain. He felt the need to touch him, but there was no point in it. Yet he could not take his eyes from the man, or shut his ears to his lamentation.

"*Mi Justo. ¿Qué le has hecho ha mi muchacho, mi hijo, mi niño?*"

Sonny McCabe, breathing heavily through his open mouth, staring at the man, then suddenly yelling at him, "Whose fault, whose fault?" Sonny grabbing the man's wrists, twisting them behind his back, snapping on the handcuffs.

Chapter 18

It had been two hours since the team had hit Los Campos. Nick was sitting alone at a table in the club's dining room, attempting invisibility. He wasn't sure what to do with himself. The fact that he had seen so many dead and dying in one afternoon would not settle inside him. Captain Hawks, Detective Monserette, and the civilian bodies had lain around for what seemed to him an eternity. Two hours now and he was still sitting and thinking, and wondering what the hell happened here?

Earlier, as he came up the stairs from the basement, Nick had spotted the police commissioner and Andre just as they came through the club's front door. Certain that Andre would corner him and ask questions, questions he was not at all sure he was ready to answer, Nick made himself scarce. He went to look for Sonny McCabe. When he caught Sonny's eye he beckoned him into the bathroom.

Nick held Sonny by his arm, saying, "How the hell are we going to explain this?" His nerves were coming undone, and the anger had hardened in his stomach.

Sonny smiled gamely. "What the hell are you taking about?"

"Two dead cops and five dead civilians, that's what I'm talking about."

"What I see is three dead gun-dealing bastards, two tortured informants, and two murdered hero cops. That's what I see." Sonny sighed and glanced down at his wristwatch.

Nick studied Sonny's face, trying to figure out what he saw there. Was the guy angry or frightened? He suspected it was a little of both. "Look," he said, "there's going to be some tough questions, and we'd better have answers."

Grinning, wagging his head, Sonny gave a little shrug. "Hey pally, we did our job. Think about it, we did nothing wrong, nothing." Sonny spoke more softly now. "C'mon man, you're a cop for chrissake, you were there, we did what we had to do. Those scumbags started shooting, what the hell were we supposed to do, run?"

"Seven dead people. I've never seen anything like it."

Sonny shrugged, looking bewildered. "I can't figure why in the hell Suarez and Monserette started banging on that door. They did that on their own, no one told them to do that, bang on the door like that. It was fucking stupid."

"We should have had a uniformed presence," Nick said, trying to come off positive and strong. "We should have called the precinct for help."

"That was Hawks's decision. What're you doing, trying to lay this off on him?"

Nick stared at him, mute and grim.

Sonny's eyes shifted toward the bathroom door. "The man went down a hero. I won't have anyone throw dirt on him now."

"I knew this was going to go bad," Nick said. "I could almost smell it."

Sonny looked at him thoughtfully. "Hooray for you. Funny, don't you think, that you kept those thoughts to yourself. These feelings you had, you didn't say anything."

"Yes I did, I told Hawks that I thought he should notify the precinct. Get some help here."

"Bullshit."

Nick saw the anger building in Sonny's face and let it slide.

Sonny turned his head away in annoyance. "Goddamn, who the hell's side are you on? The man's dead for chrissake."

"Bad," Nick said, "this is wrong."

"Bad, huh? I'll tell you what's bad. Check out those two guys hanging in the basement like a couple of sides of beef. The people that did that are the people we're dealing with here. Now that's what I call bad. C'mere," Sonny said. He put his hands on Nick's shoulders, pulled him in close. "We lost two partners today, and we're going to see to it that they didn't die for nothing. Those gun-dealing, torturing fuckers are going to pay. We're going to make them pay. You hear me, you with me? And that's no bullshit, that's a guarantee."

Silence from Nick.

"Goddamn, can't you feel the evil here? C'mon man, this place is a horror chamber. And those bums Cienfuego, Medina, and Matos ran it. The question is, where the hell are you coming from?"

"I don't know," Nick said. "I have questions."

"Yeah, well I have explanations, and no answers," Sonny said calmly.

When they came out of the bathroom, Nick went and stood for a long time at the edge of the dining room, near the door to the street. What he needed was to get out of there, out of the club and go somewhere to think. Hawks, Monserette, Rodrigo, and the other poor bastard hanging in the basement kept revolving in his head, a scene from some horror movie. And the other guy, that Cienfuego, the way he screamed over his kid. Nick didn't understand Spanish, but he understood lots of pain. A nightmare like that, all you want is to forget. He couldn't shake it, the look Cienfuego gave him. Like he wanted his pity, like he needed his help.

It took some real concentration for Nick to take notes, get his thoughts together. Sonny was talking to Carl Suarez at the bar. Andre stood with his arms folded talking with the police commissioner and the chief of detectives.

A dozen detectives and half that many police brass moved around the club, contemplating the scene of battle with narrow eyes and wagging heads. A police photographer set up his tripod. The chief of detectives called out, "However many pictures you plan on taking, take twice that number, okay?"

Nick leaned against the doorframe and looked out the window, watching the gathering of TV and print reporters clamoring for news outside. There were floodlights, cameras, and microphones from every television station in the New York area. Steve Stern, a tall trim guy with red hair, emerged from a car. He approached the two uniformed cops who were standing guard at the club's front door. Nick knew Stern pretty well; he had covered the police department for years for a local ABC affiliate and once had interviewed Nick about youth gangs.

"Crime scene," the uniforms chimed in chorus.

The three of them stood together on the sidewalk and watched an ambulance arrive. Two well-muscled black men rolled a pair of stretchers past the cops and reporter into the club. A uniformed captain approached them. "Take the two officers first."

The two men straightened up and gave the captain a look of patient annoyance.

"I said, make sure you take the two officers before you take any of the others."

The attendants said nothing, waiting to be told exactly who was who.

"Nick," Andre called out.

Nick put his notebook away. He didn't want to talk to Andre, wasn't sure what he would say.

"Detective Manaris," the chief of detectives said, "c'mere for a minute, will you?"

Sonny looked up from his conversation with Suarez. He gave Nick a cautionary glance. Nick turned to Andre, locking eyes with him for an instant, an acknowledgment, *I told you so.* Nick started across the room, thinking *I hope to Christ he's not going to ask me anything I can't handle.* His mind flew off somewhere for a moment, just flew, and when it returned, the chief of detectives was saying something about the need to be careful with those notes.

Nick nodded. "I just took a few, not many, just a few."

He understood exactly what the chief was saying, his personal notes would one day be evidence, evidence that would be made available to a defense attorney. His words could be used against him.

"Make sure you talk to your partners, make sure you're on the same page," the chief said. His eyes were deep brown, black almost, and they seemed to Nick to be sympathetic.

The chief had been a detective for close to thirty years, nothing that had happened that afternoon could surprise or shock him. His name was Jack Ludwig. He was the son of German immigrants from Bavaria who owned a bakery in Ridgewood. A big burly man who coached high school football and favored imported beer and expensive cigars. He was wise in the ways of crime, wise in the ways detectives could screw up. He had an aversion to media people and politicians and thought little of priests. Jack Ludwig judged a man by the look in his eyes and the sound of his voice, and whether or not he had anything intelligent to say. Even though the chief had been raised to his lofty rank by the current police commissioner, rumor had it that he didn't have much use for him.

"The thing is," Andre said to Nick, all formal and professional, "I don't want you giving any statements to anyone until I Q-and-A you. That goes for your partners, that goes for everyone here. I don't want this story told a dozen times a dozen different ways. You understand?"

"Sure," Nick said.

"I'll be late meeting the mayor," the PC said. "I'd better get going. We need to get to Captain Hawks's and Detective Monserette's families. You know," he said, "it's ironic, but I put the Medal of Honor on Monserette about a year ago. Jack," he said to Ludwig, "DA Robinson will pull this together. Take direction from him; the DA's office should run the show here."

Jack Ludwig smiled tightly at the police commissioner and nodded. Nick thinking, this man has a real problem hiding his anger.

The commissioner winked and shook Andre's hand. He was a short thin man in his late forties dressed in a blue blazer and gray slacks, with neatly trimmed blond hair. More like a TV anchor than a police commissioner, Nick thought. No bulge anywhere, no gun.

The commissioner aimed a finger at Nick's chest. "Detective," he said, "I bet that when you woke this morning you'd never have guessed that death would come so near you today."

He looked expectantly at Nick.

"That's true."

The PC studied him for a second, then turned to the chief of detectives.

"You see, Jack," the PC said, "a police officer never knows when God is going to tap him on the shoulder."

They all nodded in faint agreement.

"We never know when the golden book opens and our name is at the top of the page." Hands clasped as if in prayer, the PC regarded them each in turn. "That is why I'd love to see all my officers in a state of grace." The commissioner took a long breath. "Tell me, Detective Manaris, how many of your brother officers standing around here right now, how many of these men do you think are in a state of grace?"

The question was so blunt and so dumb that for a moment Nick didn't know how to respond. "I don't know," he finally said. "I would guess a few."

"And you, detective, how are you?"

"I'm fine," Nick told him.

"You killed a man." The PC stared at him solemnly.

Nick hesitated, daring himself to speak his mind, but said only, "He didn't give me much choice."

The PC waved a hand as if to declare the subject dead, and Nick felt relieved.

Andre shrugged. "You killed a man who had just murdered a police captain. The way I see it, you're a hero."

"That you are," the chief of detectives said, smiling a little.

Nick said nothing.

The bodies of Sergi Monserette and Captain Hawks were lifted and placed on the stretchers, and the straps were drawn tight. As the attendants rolled them through Los Campos's front door, the press closed in around them.

The PC mumbled something that Nick didn't catch and then turned to Andre. "We'll hold off on the press conference until later this evening."

Andre glanced at the PC. "At my office?"

"I think police headquarters would be better."

"This is our case. District Attorney Santoro should hold the conference."

"I think not. Two police officers were killed, one a police captain. I don't think a police captain has been killed in the line of duty in fifty years. The conference should be at police headquarters."

"I'll talk to Mr. Santoro. Maybe we should both hold one," Andre told him.

"Well, what can I say?" The PC turned his head. "It's a free country."

"That it is," Andre said.

The PC gave Andre a long stare. "Jack," he said to the chief of detectives, "walk me to my car."

Not caring about any of this, worried about questions and answers, and about the state of Detective Suarez's mind, Nick casually looked around the club, which was becoming more and more crowded as more and more detectives and police brass arrived. There was something so warped, so self-serving and political about the way Andre and the PC were going about this, in reducing all this suffering to who would hold the news conference, who would benefit. Nick experienced a moment of pure clarity: he would never make it in their world, never rise above street detective, because he simply didn't have the blind ambition and the heedless, overpowering animal need to come out on top that Andre had, that the PC probably had. Andre would be a winner; the PC, Sonny McCabe, the chief of detectives, the reporter Steve Stern, maybe even the writer, Frank Kurtz, they would end up winners too. Not because of brains or guts, but because they understood that in order to prevail you had to believe that no one else's life mattered but your own, that what really counted was coming in first at all costs, always, in all things.

Andre looked around the club. "Gather up your team and report to my office as soon as possible," he said to Nick.

"Detective Suarez is really shook. He could use some time off," Nick said.

"*He's* upset?" Andre said. "For chrissake, he should be. Look, look," he said, "nobody is getting any time off. You can forget that. You're all working till I take all your statements and we set a grand jury date."

Nick simply nodded.

Andre sighed, gazed dreamily down at his feet, shook his head with melodramatic regret. "I knew that this team would find trouble. It was only a matter of time."

Nick told him they were still counting guns downstairs in the basement. Largest haul he'd ever heard of. Five, maybe six hundred automatic handguns. Andre reminded him of the seven dead people. Nick said right, right, tell me something I don't know. Andre said this was not the place to get into it, but he had some questions. Like who the hell made the call to charge through a door into a place where all the bad guys are armed to the teeth? Things like that. Nick just listened.

"I simply cannot understand how experienced detectives made the judgments that were made here today. Can you? Seven dead people, Nick. Seven."

Nick didn't know how to answer, he'd said all he could say.

"Make sure you have your stories straight. When I ask questions, I don't want to hear any mumbling. I expect clear, concise statements concerning all your actions."

"We did our jobs, that's all I know."

"Well, friend of mine, you and your team best be prepared to do better than that." Andre grinned, giving a backhand wave toward the club's dining room. "Try and be at my office in an hour or so. I can't wait to hear what you all have to say."

"We'll be there," Nick said quietly.

Andre mentioned again the fact that seven people had been killed, though of course, most tragic were the deaths of the two police officers. And when he held his news conference later on in the day, he'd make that point. The point that two cops died heroes. Nick muttered that yes, that was good, that Andre should tell everyone they were heroic. Finally saying he'd hang loose here for a while, then he'd round everyone up and—

"Make sure *you* have your story straight," Andre said, and then reconsidering, he said, "Everyone's battered here, stunned. Too astonished to think straight. They're going through the motions right now. I'm counting on you to pull them together."

Nick coughed, cupping his hand over his mouth, looking around. "I'll talk to them. I'm worried about Suarez, the guy's a mess," he said, but so quietly, so softly that Andre could hardly hear him. Andre continued talking, his voice remote, then angry, chiding the Police Commissioner for wanting his own press conference, when the conference should rightly be held by the DA's office, and wasn't this their case, the DA's case? He could, Andre pointed out shrewdly, just have called a press conference without informing the PC, but that wouldn't be right. There were after all two dead cops here.

"What were their names? Hawks, right? Captain Hawks, and Detective Monserette."

"That supposed to be funny? You knew Captain Hawks."

"Right, I sure did."

"And Monserette? You knew him too? Those two men died heroes. I was there, Andre, I saw it happen."

"Uh-huh. I knew Detective Monserette." Andre shook his head, smiling, as if Nick just didn't get it.

Nick raised his chin, getting angry now. "What the hell's so funny?"

Andre said something under his breath that Nick didn't catch.

"What?"

"I said, I warned you."

Andre stared at him. Nick wanted to take it further, but Andre went by him, saying over his shoulder, "C'mon. Walk me to the door."

At the club's front door Andre said, "All I want, Nick, all I want you to do for the time being is prepare yourself and your partners for my Q-and-A." Andre paused, head cocked, he seemed to be deep in thought. "Does this raid, the action you guys took here, does any of it make sense to you?"

Nick was about to answer but Andre cut him off, saying never mind, just think about it.

"We did our job," Nick said, sounding a little trapped.

"And now it's time I do mine," Andre's voice going flat and sullen, a slight shakiness there too. He glanced quickly at Nick, opened the door, went out, making his way to his car through a gauntlet of reporters, waving them off, announcing his plans for a press conference later that day.

Nick watched Andre, trying not to be too obvious about keeping an eye on him but needing to watch the guy leave.

He saw two stocky well-built men in suits get out of a black BMW with tinted windows that was parked just behind Andre's car. Andre went to talk to the pair. Nick remembered the BMW, he'd seen it parked on the street across from Post Time, and then again on the

Queensboro Bridge. He leaned against the doorframe, noticing how friendly Andre and the two suits appeared, and felt a vague ripple of apprehension. Now Andre went and got into his own car, started it up, made a U-turn, and headed down Corona Avenue toward Roosevelt, with the BMW following. Who the hell were these guys? Nick was getting a feeling now that told him there was a whole lot more here than he knew. Yeah, that was the car he saw on the bridge, damn right it was.

Nick figured that the cop stationed in front of the club was young, a rookie. He was a big guy, six two or three, alert, bright-eyed. But he found out after talking to him a minute that Pete Schmidt had ten years in the job. "Been in this precinct the whole time. Happy here, steady days now. A conditions man, plenty of work. You want collars, a little OT, we got all you can handle." Standing in front of the club, Officer Schmidt told Nick his father had a plumbing business, but he himself was no plumber, too much work, and it was dirty, and hard, and in the winter, man forget the winter. He'd taken the cops because half his buddies had gone to the fire department, but forget that crap. He wasn't about to run into any burning building.

It was a shame, two cops—one a captain. "I do steady eight-to-fours on Roosevelt Avenue. Both sides, One-hundred-eighth Street to One-hundred-twelfth. One of the stiffs they carried out, that guy Rodrigo Punto, I heard he was on the job in Cuba. Anyway, Punto owns a coffee shop on my post, the Hatuey. A fucking madman. I'd been looking to run into him, people told me that the nut job had pulled a piece on some guy, right there on the avenue. Billy Zito, a good kid, a hell of a football player in his day—went to Hofstra, made Little All-American— anyway, he owns the bakery next door to the coffee shop. Billy told me this guy Rodrigo was ready to pop some guy, thought the guy was banging his old lady, fucking nut. Well, somebody got to him," Pete said. "Can I help you with anything? I know everything that goes on down here. It's my post, man."

"You know who the guy was, the guy he wanted to pop?"

"I can find out for you. Give me a day or two, I'll ask around."

Nick handed Pete his card, told him to give him a call. They stood in front of the Los Campos, drinking coffee out of the club's cups. "I was wondering," Nick said, "the black BMW, the one that parked right out here, the one with the tinted windows; you ID the driver?"

"Hell yeah. They pull up, park right in front of a crime scene. I'm thinking, what balls. I was about to chase 'em off when they showed me their tins. Feds. Imagine driving around in a car like that. And I made 'em for a couple of bad guys, drug dealers or something. Shows you what I know."

"Feds? What kind of feds?"

"Hey, I see big gold badges, special agent, U.S. government, that's good enough for me."

Nick paused, "Pete, can I ask you something?"

"Ask."

"The black guy, guy came out of the club a few minutes ago."

"Sharp guy, got into the department car?"

"Right," Nick said.

"I've seen him around. I don't know who he is, but I know I've seen him."

"He's an Assistant DA."

"Seen him in court, right. What about him?"

"You hear what he said to those two guys, to the feds?" With real interest. "You hear what he said to them?"

Pete Schmidt thought, tugged at his gun belt, shifted his weight from one foot to the other. " 'They're being held at the precinct. We'll stop there, then go to the office.' That's what he said."

Chapter 19

Sonny McCabe spread his arms out in welcome. He said hey, where the hell you been? I'm standing here holding Carl's hand, trying to keep the guy from going round the bend. Moran, Lloyd, and Lloyd's crew are helping to transport the prisoners and I'm wondering where the hell's my partner? What've you been up to? We need to go over this, make sure we know who's going to say what.

"Where's your writer friend? Where's Kurtz?"

"I haven't seen him."

"He's probably still at the plant."

"I'll call. Look, we going to go over this or what?"

Nick glanced at Sonny, and the guy gave him a shrug, that silly-ass grin, then straightened as Eddie Moran and Lloyd came through the door. Nick told Sonny to track Kurtz down, tell him we're going to the DA's office. Sonny lit a cigarette, glanced around, saying maybe we should go over this first. Nick saying what for? We tell it like it happened, just the way it happened. No need to come up with any story here. Eddie Moran standing at the bar, a beer in his hand. Sonny turned from Nick, walked over to Eddie and whispered something. They were a pair, those two. Nick found Detective Suarez, put his arm around his shoulders.

"How you doing, brother?"

"I'll be all right."

"We've got to go over to the DA's office. Make a statement, do a Q-and-A. You squared away, anything you want to tell me?"

"Hey, I go knock on a door. I hear a shot, I bang on the door. Next thing I know the door's open and some big fucker is pulling me through it. The bastard grabs me by the collar, pulls me inside, tosses me around like I'm a fucking doll. Sergi's yelling cops, cops, we're cops. I hear somebody scream fuck you are. And the son of a bitch shoots Sergi right in the face. I run into the hallway, and that's where you found me. What else do you want me to say?"

A couple of things came to mind immediately, but Nick let it go, saying, "Okay, all right. That's the way it happened, that's the way it happened."

"The way it happened? Fuckin' right that's the way it happened." Detective Suarez squinted. "He called me a coward, Nick. Captain Hawks, God rest his soul, the man called me a coward. But I swear, I'm no coward. I'm out here every day, all I do is go into those streets and lay it out, lay my life on the line every fucking day. And he calls me a coward. It's like he killed me. Goddamn killed my heart. I heard him, I heard him tell you stay with the fucking coward. Well goddamn, I'm no coward, you know?" He looked at Nick.

Nick saying, "I've seen you in action, I saw you in front of Los Campos banging on the door, trying to get in that club. That wasn't the move of a coward, that was a heroic move, that was a guy with balls."

"Yeah." Detective Suarez put his hands to his face, rubbed his face in circles. "I never figured anybody would ever think of me that way, not a chickenshit, not me, man."

Lloyd, the story-telling detective, took a seat in the back of the cruiser, and Suarez joined him. Nick got behind the wheel and Sonny sat in the passenger seat. Eddie Moran, half in the bag now, brought up the rear with two members of Lloyd's team.

Moran being half gone was very much on Nick's mind at the moment. The guy was icy, an irritable and mean Irish drunk. But just like

Sonny McCabe, for all his problems, Eddie Moran was one hell of a cop. If shooting people and kicking ass was your idea of what made a good cop. Between the two of them they had taken out four people at Los Campos. And neither of them probably gave a damn, either.

"So, Lloyd, you got a funny story for us?" Nick sought out his eyes in the rearview.

"I wish I did, man, I wish I had something funny to say." Lloyd slouched down, peering out the window, watching the Queens streets go by.

"Christ," Sonny said, "you ever see anything like what happened to Rodrigo?"

"I can't believe Sergi and Hawks," Carl said, "I can't believe it. Can you believe it, Sonny?"

"No. No, Carl, I can't."

They drove to the Queens County Court House. Nick pulled into the garage and parked, and everyone sat up straight, apprehensive and sullen.

Nick had the feeling that Detective Suarez was about to lose it. The guy looked tortured, his mouth moving, his eyes opening and closing like one of those amusement park puppets. Suarez kept turning to Lloyd as if he wanted to say something. The poor bastard had seen Detective Monserette shot in the face, and Nick suspected that unspeakable nightmares lay ahead for the guy.

The garage was a squat building attached to the courthouse, DA's offices, and Queens County Jail. Four stories of cement block with rooftop parking. Weekdays you'd play hell finding a spot to park, weekends it operated at about twenty-five percent capacity. There was reserved and numbered DA's parking on the first floor.

Nick took note of the four cars parked nose in; three were official county cars, the fourth a black BMW with tinted windows. He parked alongside the Beemer. Eddie Moran pulled in alongside him.

Nick took a moment. Lloyd and Suarez worked their way out of the cruiser's rear doors. Sonny sat still, staring at Nick. "What are you looking at?" he said.

"That BMW."

"What about it?"

"I'll tell you later."

"Hell you will, tell me about it now." Sonny seemed about to say something else but opened the door and got out. He stood alongside the BMW, hunched over, looking in the window, his hands in his pockets. Nick stood next to him.

"I've seen this car before," Nick said. "I've seen it more than once."

"Yeah, where?"

"It was parked on South Street, across from Post Time. Then on the Fifty-ninth Street Bridge. It was following me."

"C'mon? What the hell would it be following you for?"

"A good question."

Sonny put his hand on the roof of the car and walked around it. Nick followed him.

There was a red magnetic roof light flasher inside the car, and the customary federal radio, a good one. Nick checked the license plate: Ohio. He took down the number, not that it would do any good. The records on this car had been pulled, that was a given. He could feel Sonny watching him. "It's the feds' car," Nick said.

"Really?" Sonny said, tapping the roof with the flat of his hand. He said to Detective Suarez, "Carl, you got your blade? Let me have it for a minute."

Suarez went into his pocket and came out with a switchblade.

"Gimme it, I'll give it right back to you."

Suarez handed Sonny the knife, he didn't seem to care. Sonny tried the passenger door, it was locked. Then he walked slowly around, went to each tire and jabbed, using the knife like he knew what he was doing.

"Sonny," Nick said.

"Got some balls tailing a partner of mine," Sonny said.

Nick heard the voice before he saw the guy, and what he heard was, "Hey, the fuck you doing? Get away from that car." It was one of the two men he had seen earlier with Andre. He was walking toward them now, a wary look on his face like what the hell?

"You know what," Sonny said, "I think somebody slashed your tires."

"Yeah, well it better not have been you, buddy, that's a government car."

"What government?"

Up close the guy seemed bigger than Nick remembered. Not bad-looking, very presentable in his blue pinstripe. A little suntanned, and clean-shaven. He turned to Nick and said, "You see who did this?"

"Did what?"

The agent narrowed his eyes, glanced down at his tires. "I'm a federal agent."

"Good for you. What the hell were you doing following me the other night?"

"What other night?"

"On the bridge. First I saw you parked on South Street, then on the bridge. Don't lie to me, you were following me. I know you were, so cut the crap."

The agent shook his head, taking his time. "You're crazy, or drunk. Why would I be following you?"

Sonny said, "My partner's not drunk and he's not crazy, but tell you what, I am. I'm more than a little crazy, and if I catch you in my rearview, I'll blow your ass up."

Nick was impressed with the way Sonny stood in there, got nose to nose with the agent, no bullshit. More than a hint of looniness in those eyes of his, backing the guy up. Sonny saying now, "Think about it, pally, we're New York City detectives, got plenty of enemies out there. Now, you're driving this slick, flash car with dark windows. How the hell are we supposed to know you're not the enemy?"

"Hey man, calm down, will ya? Look, I haven't been in town but a few days. I haven't been following anybody."

"I saw you at Los Campos," Nick said. "I saw you there."

The agent stood backed up against the BMW, his shoulders hunched, watching them. "You all had better back the fuck off," he said. "That's not me talking, that's Uncle Sam."

Sonny McCabe said, "You can tell your uncle, your aunt, your grand-mother, you can tell them all for me, Sonny McCabe. You can tell your whole goddamn family, I catch any of you in my rearview, I'll run your ass over."

The agent was smiling at them now. "You guys scare me to death, you know that?" he said.

Nick hesitated, thought for a minute. "Well then," he said, "you should know what it feels like."

"I hear that," the agent said.

"Good," Nick told him, "that's a good sign."

They walked through the garage, no one said a word till they reached the elevator that would bring them into the court building on Queens Boulevard. Sonny said to Nick, "You saw that half-a-hump at Los Cam-pos?"

"Uh-huh."

Eddie Moran, swaying a little, rocked back on the heels of his snake-skin boots, eyeing the elevator button. When he rolled forward, he shut his left eye and aimed his thumb at UP. Carl Suarez made faces at his reflection in the elevator's door. Lloyd and his two partners stood around, heads bowed, hands in their pockets.

When they walked out of the elevator on the fourth floor, the DA's floor, the security guard said, "Well what the hell we got here, an invasion?"

"Hey pally, buddy of mine," Sonny said. "You wouldn't believe the day we've had."

"I probably wouldn't," the security guard said. "It's all over the radio and TV," he told them. "You guys are famous."

Sonny became so excited he began to turn in circles, smiling, clapping his hands. Nick watched him dancing in the hallway, thinking once again, what is it with this guy?

Sonny winked at Nick, smiled, wagged his head. Nick saying, "I don't see anything that happened today worth smiling about. Then again, I could be wrong."

Sonny said, "You know what I think when I hear you talk like that? You know what I feel?"

"Tell me."

"I think you worry too much about things you can't change. You're a worrier, Nick, and you're depressed. That's your problem."

"Sergi and Hawks are lying on a refrigerated slab, facts like that depress me."

Nick was about to hold forth about the human condition, the world of assholes, but decided to let it go; either you understand or you don't. "This is the worst day of my life," he said, "and the kicker is, it's not over yet."

Sonny did not appear to have heard him. After a moment he said, "I knew Hawks ten years. More. Sergi half that many, don't preach to me, Nick. You think you know me, but you don't know me at all."

"And maybe I never will, huh?"

"Oh you will. In time you will. What I'd like to know, what's got me thinking, is that fed. What in the hell do you think they're doing hanging around? I don't like that picture."

"I understand."

"Do you?"

"Yeah, I know how you feel."

Chapter 20

Diego stood on the sidewalk in front of Los Campos, a detective on either side of him, waiting for a cruiser to take him to the precinct. The cop on his right, the black one, held him gently by the nape of the neck, and every so often he'd squeeze. It was almost friendly. Almost.

Cops in uniform moved about, erecting barricades to keep the inquisitive back. Detectives went back and forth, going into Los Campos and then returning to stare at him, having conversations among themselves, conversations Diego did not understand. A pink-faced police sergeant with rust-colored blotches on his cheeks directed traffic. From time to time this crazed Spanish-speaking detective approached Diego and shouted curses in his face and spat at his feet. There were newspaper reporters as well; Diego could not see them but he could hear their shouted questions and the click-click-click of cameras somewhere behind him. A number of high-ranking police with much gold braid were appearing now, exchanging salutes with the patrolmen. The senior officers seemed despondent and enraged. Unlike the detectives, none of the higher-ups paid any attention to him.

For Diego, the remorse and mourning he felt was like madness—it was madness. It was difficult to breathe, his chest hurt and he was panting. Diego felt cold. He shivered, feeling as though his life was disappearing before his eyes. He was very tired and couldn't think clearly, couldn't concentrate. His neck was sore and his back too. His arms had been twisted behind him, his wrists held tight by handcuffs, causing his shoulders to ache. Motivated by some urgency that was like hope, he constantly looked around the street for a familiar face but found none. His mind filled with visions of his two remaining children, Mariaclara and Miguel. Who would explain Justo's death to them? Who would tell them why the police killed their brother? Who would care for them? Diego was confused and wanted nothing more than to be with his children now. He could not make real the notion that his Justo was gone. He himself was convinced that given the opportunity, he could explain to the authorities the circumstances that brought him and Justo to Los Campos. If they would allow him to explain, he was certain the police would realize he was an innocent. Anyone would. But no one seemed interested, they only sneered and ridiculed him, shouted and cursed at him.

More police gathered around him now, and Diego felt battered by the waves of their strident sarcasm. He was angry that he understood so little. He heard someone say, "Are all the bodies gone?" Diego repeated the words to himself. He didn't understand the words, and it made him dizzy. He had lost all sense of time and place, his mind wandering back and forth, full of visions of Justo. The boy that loved life so much and had lived so little.

Presently a police cruiser pulled up. An officer slid out of the passenger seat. He came and got Diego and brought him to the car; placing a hand on his head, he opened the rear door and pushed him down onto the back seat. Diego sat on his hands, his knees drawn up almost to his chin, sobbing. After a while the cop, who was almost as tall as Diego, got into the car and told him to shut the fuck up.

Other police officers came to the car to look at him and make comments. The police talked among themselves for a few minutes, and then Diego was driven to the precinct house.

He was led through the stationhouse and brought to the second floor and placed in a holding cage. Some uniformed cops came up to the cage and spoke to him. Diego stood in the corner, there was no place to sit. He didn't understand what they were asking or saying, so he said nothing, just looked at their faces and wagged his head. The crowd of police officers swelled, and now detectives came over to the cage to shout at him.

A uniformed sergeant whose name tag said RAMOS dragged him from the cage, telling him in Spanish that Detective Monserette had friends in this precinct. Ramos held a wooden club, a nightstick, and urged Diego to look at it, told Diego he was going to shove it so far up his ass that it would come out his mouth. Diego looked into Ramos's eyes, just looked at him.

Ramos removed his handcuffs and led him to a fingerprint board, telling him to stand still while he printed him. Later Diego would not remember much. Certain things, certain images, clerks and civilian assistants, mostly overweight black women, who moved around him. Some worked at typewriters, others stood near file cabinets or carried folders. A pretty one with skin the color of Coca-Cola smiled at him and wagged her head as if she were sorry for him. Or maybe she was trying to tell him she thought he was lost, done for.

When he finished with the fingerprints, Ramos handcuffed him again and sat Diego in a straight-backed wooden chair alongside a desk. Ramos put a form in an electric typewriter and asked him questions; his name, his address, his age, where and when he was born, his height and weight, the color of his eyes and hair, whether he had ever been arrested before. Diego answered all the questions and when Ramos was done, he stood Diego up and led him back around the precinct, down a flight of stairs, past the front desk, and through a door into a cellblock. Ramos put him into a pen with a man from Tito Roman's Bronx crew whose name was Felix Caban.

Felix's hometown was Havana, but he had been in the States awhile. Diego knew him to be a bit crazy, a cokehead like Benny, worse than Benny. One Friday night in Los Campos's bathroom, Diego had found Felix sitting on a toilet snorting cocaine from the lid of a juice jar. His head was back against the wall, the lid in his upturned hand, as if he were waiting for an offering. One of Benny's hookers was sucking him, going at him with a distinctive professional style, and Diego remembered standing and watching, thinking this woman knows what she is doing. At the time he'd thought that Felix had overdosed, his lip and nose were covered with a thick layer of powder and his eyes were wide open in a death stare. Benny told him later that Felix could do up the product of half a Bolivian mountainside and still ask for more. In the bathroom, Felix had urged Diego to try some. Try some of the woman and the cocaine. Diego worked up the courage to tell him he did not like cocaine, did not like drugs at all. A day without coca is a day without sunshine, Felix had said to him. And the woman? Diego had told him, maybe later, man she was good.

"I am so sorry to hear about your son," Felix told him. He held out his hand and Diego took it. "Professor, everything went crazy. I don't know what happened. I don't know how it started, but when it did, I was afraid I would die, and now I am sorry I didn't."

Felix told him that the idea of spending the next fifty years in prison because of that crazy Colombian bastard, that Cano, made him sick to death. And Tito Roman is dead, the cops killed him. I guess you know that. Diego said that along with his son, many people had died. Six, maybe seven people.

Felix saying the cops were running around like a bunch of madmen, screaming at everyone. "This Puerto Rican detective, he comes up to me spitting and cursing, telling me that his friend got killed. Like I give a shit. I told him, man, I told him I didn't give a shit about his friend. I told him we all have families. I told him I was worried about myself, I said I didn't do anything. I think what I said upset him, the Puerto Rican. Because when I told him how I felt about his friend, I saw the man go all white, which is not easy to do if you're a Puerto Rican nigger."

Diego, on the side of the bench nearest the toilet bowl, glanced away from Felix. Officer Ramos was standing at the cell door.

Felix said, "I told that Puerto Rican fuck that, dead cops' families don't cry any more than anyone else's. I'm telling him that I am an innocent man, these Puerto Ricans think they're big men, you give them a badge and a gun. Listen to this, the bum tells me he gets a chance, he's going to shoot me, he's going to fuck me up. I tell him fuck you! Fuck you! Fuck you! I could tell you a lot about Puerto Rican cops. You want to hear it, man?"

Diego jerked his head toward the cell door.

Ramos said, "I have to tell you, Cienfuego, that you have a right to make a phone call. So I told you, okay?"

Felix looked at Diego. "You got someone to call, man? A lawyer or somebody?" He said to Ramos, "I didn't get to make a call."

"This is America, you got a right to make a call. But I didn't say you were going to make one. You shit cop-killing Cuban asshole."

Ramos left and Felix said, "What did I tell you? You give them a uniform and they think they are Superman."

Diego tried to get comfortable, pushed himself back against the wall, stretched out his legs, saying, "Man, if they are going to condemn me for my stupidity about what was happening at the club, then I'm finished."

Felix stared at him.

"I will not deny that I was stupid for not seeing what Benny was up to. If it is a crime to be careless, then I should accept my punishment without a word."

"Are you asking me or telling me?" Felix told him. "Because if you're asking me, I will tell you that we are all in some deep shit here. All of us, Professor."

Diego shook his head as if to clear his vision. "God," he said, "I don't think that to be ignorant is a crime in this country, because if it were, everyone would be in prison, even the cops. Especially the cops. Still, it looks to me that being stupid and trusting is going to make— cost me a whole lot. It's already cost me a son." Diego jumped up from the bench, crossed over and took hold of the bars, bellowing, "You bastards! You took my son!"

"Calm down," Felix told him, "calm down, let's wait and see what happens. These people should give you a pill or something to calm you down."

"You have been in prison before, right?"

"Sure, many times."

"So, what's the secret? How do you survive in a terrible place like this?"

"Professor, nobody knows what is going to happen to you, to me, to anybody."

"It doesn't look too good for me."

"Well, if you do go to prison, remember that Felix Caban told you the way you survive jail is to forget the outside world. Because, my friend, the outside world is going to forget you."

"Wonderful."

"Look, chances are you'll be okay. Benny will get you a lawyer. You'll get a chance to tell your story. Who knows, maybe they will believe you."

"Benny," Diego said. "Fucking Benny."

Chapter 21

Andre Robinson worked out of an office high above Queens Boulevard, a street of office buildings and shops, of bars and cafés where cops, defense lawyers, and ADAs made themselves comfortable with bail bondsmen and private detectives, journalists and politicians. Dark gathering places for Queens bourgeois sharpies, all of them convinced they were beyond cool.

As Nick, Sonny, and the team walked down the hall toward Andre's office, an assemblage of assistant district attorneys and DA investigators lined the hall, wanting to grab a peek at the cops who had survived the shootout.

A smiling young secretary met them at the door. He shook their hands, introduced himself as Mark Malone, and led them into the conference room.

The room was new and elegant, with mahogany paneling in a severe lawyerly style. There was a long table of the same wood, with a dozen chairs arranged comfortably around it. It was a large room, by no means simple, with a powerful political smell. The price of this impressive room, which had been paid by the taxpayers, was outrageous.

Andre, seated at the head of the table, directed his secretary to arrange coffee and sandwiches.

"Tell Mark what it is you would like and he will get it for you."

"Speaking just for myself," Nick said, "I'm not too hungry. But coffee would be good."

"I'm starving, you think maybe we could get some Chinese?" Sonny said.

"Tell Mark, he'll arrange it."

They took seats around the table. Mark put yellow legal pads and pencils in front of each of them. They gave him their lunch orders, and after the secretary went out Andre said, "I understand that none of the prisoners have been booked. They've all been printed and so on, but not booked. Have you decided who will be the arresting officers?"

"I'm taking Matos and Medina," Sonny said. "Nick will take Cienfuego, and Eddie Moran will take the Vasserman brothers. That leaves six others. Detective Lloyd Joseph and his team will take two apiece."

Nick looked across the table at Carl Suarez, who was shaking his head sadly. "Detective Suarez should have a collar," Nick said.

"I don't think so," said Sonny. "No disrespect, you did a hell of a job, Carl. But my feeling is you should hang loose on this."

"Fuck me, that's crap. I want one of these guys."

"I don't think so," Sonny said.

Carl didn't answer, but his lips twisted into a sneer.

"Look," Andre said, "I had hoped that you would get these things straightened out before you came here. You didn't, so I'll straighten it out for you." Andre touched his chest. "I'll tell you who the arresting officers will be."

Nick shifted in his chair. "I don't think I'm out of bounds asking why the chief of detectives is not here. It seems to me the department should have some input."

Andre shook his head. "Well, the ironic thing is, I invited him to be here and he declined. This is our case, so we'll proceed with that understanding."

"Fine," Sonny said. "It's your call."

Nick caught an appraising look from Andre and nodded, hoping his discomfort was not too obvious.

Mark, Andre's secretary, ducked in with a bag of sandwiches and coffees and passed them around. He made a face at Sonny as if he were annoyed. "Are you serious about the Chinese food?"

Sonny shrugged. "I'll take a sandwich."

"I have to consider what lies ahead," said Andre, taking the lid off his container of coffee, waiting for Mark to close the door. "There very well may be a trial and I need to lighten the load. I won't have five arresting officers. There will be three, Nick and Sonny and Eddie Moran. The rest of you will be carried as assisting in the arrests."

There was silence, everyone thinking.

"Nick," Andre said, "stop me if I'm off here, but the way I understand it, you arrested Cienfuego on the basement stairway."

"That's right."

"Then you brought him down into the basement, where you found Medina and Matos seated at a table."

"That's right, and I also found Punto and Melendez hanging dead on the wall like a couple of bats."

"All right, all right," Andre said, "we'll get into the specifics later. As for now, you found Cienfuego on the stairs and Medina and Matos in the basement. You held a weapon on them?"

"A shotgun."

"Well for all intents and purposes you placed them under arrest the moment you pointed the gun."

"I guess that's true."

"You know it's true. Would you have let them leave if they asked to go?"

"Of course not."

"Then they were under arrest. They make any statements?"

"Not that I could understand. I don't speak Spanish."

"No, I mean beyond that. Did you say anything and did they answer in any way you could understand?"

"No."

"You didn't Mirandize anyone, read anyone their rights?"

"You're kidding me, right?"

"Hardly. Okay, no questions and no answers."

"That's right. I did tell Cienfuego I'd blow his fucking head off if he moved."

"Did he understand you?"

"Hell do I know? He did what I told him to do. He put his hands on his head, turned around, and went back down the stairs."

"That's where you found the other two?"

"Right."

"Any conversation with them?"

"No. I motioned with my gun for them to get up. Told them to put their hands on their heads, then I led them up the stairs."

"You check the men hanging on the wall? Did you check and see if there was any sign of life?"

"Yes. Yes."

"When, Nick? When did you check the men hanging like bats on the wall? That's what you said, they were hanging like bats."

"When I got into the basement, Matos and Medina were sitting at a table. I motioned for Diego to go and stand near them. Then I backed up to the wall and glanced at the two men who were hanging. They were gone, dead. The front of Melendez's head was blown off. Rodrigo Punto had several wounds. Christ . . . Someone speared the poor bastard, there was a spear in his side. His eyes and mouth were open. . . . There was no pulse, no sign of breathing."

A moment passed.

"And?"

"I gathered up the three perps, walked them up the stairs, and turned them over to two uniforms from the precinct."

Andre nodded, his eyes focused on the table. "Okay, good. Nick," he said, "the man you shot in the hallway, the man that shot and killed Captain Hawks. His name is Tito Roman. We are ninety-nine-percent sure he is also the man that shot Detective Monserette. We have to wait for ballistics to be positive, but I'm sure Roman did both shootings."

Detective Suarez was shaking his head, smiling sternly, his eyes down. "The guy with the fedora," Carl said, "I saw him shoot both of them, I saw him, it was him, the fuck."

"Now, the four other dead perps," Andre said, "we are waiting for positive IDs from BCI on three of them. That's assuming they have criminal records and have been printed before. The fourth, the kid— well he wasn't such a kid. Anyway, he is Diego Cienfuego's son, Justo Cienfuego. The father ID'd him at the scene."

Sonny McCabe hunched forward, elbows on the table. "Look," he said, "I took out Justo Cienfuego, he's no kid. That bastard came out of the kitchen with a gun, he pointed that gun at Eddie, and man you know—"

"Sonny," Andre warned him. "When I want your statement I'll ask for it."

Nick glanced at Sonny, and McCabe nodded, looking sullen, and shut down. Those blue eyes narrowed, exposing him, all the anger right there.

Eddie Moran broke the silence, whispering, "The fucking kid had a gun."

Sonny nodded.

Andre threw Eddie a look, saying, "You'll each get your turn."

"The kid had a fucking gun," Sonny said. "For chrissake, Nick saw it." Sonny gave Nick a look, silently requesting that Nick come forward for him.

There were two quick knocks on the door. Andre held up a hand, saying come on in. Mark Malone entered, flipping through the pages of a pad, shaking his head. He seemed happy.

"Every TV station in town is here, and some national TV as well," he said, leaning on the long table. It was easy to picture him as Andre's right-hand man, a secretary and PR guy in one, tough and smart, someone who believed his future to be connected to Andre's. "I've been handling calls from all over the country. No question about it, we have the story of the day. Christ," he said, "I have calls here from *Nightline* and CNN."

"I told them I'd hold a press conference later," Andre said. "Did you tell them that?"

"Yes, but they didn't listen."

"Tell them again. Look, we will want to bring everyone into the tent on this one. But they'll have to be patient."

Nick sat, curious and amazed, what the hell was Sonny thinking? A gun in the kid's hand? What kind of bullshit was that? "You know," he said, "we haven't taken a statement from anybody yet. I mean, we can't keep them waiting forever before we book them." He was staring at Sonny, thinking what is it with this guy, pain in the ass. Eddie Moran and Carl watched him. Nick said, "Who knows, maybe I get one of them to flip, somebody might want to come over. This is a good time to cut a deal, work something out. They got to know they've been had. One of them might come forward to save his ass. I'd like a shot at them."

"You don't speak the language," Sonny said. A big smile on the guy's face.

"I'll bring Carl with me."

"Christ," Andre said, "what am I going to do about all this media?" He seemed relaxed now, merry at the idea of going onstage. "I'd like to call a press conference right now, shove it to the PC."

Nick remained silent, staring at Sonny, as everyone laughed. The kid had a gun—the bastard.

"Go," Andre said, touching Nick's arm to reassure him. "Take a translator and go and see Cienfuego. Do a good job, you're good at getting statements. Just don't offer him a deal, it's too late for him. Medina and Matos are at West Street, they're being debriefed as we speak."

"What the hell are they doing in the federal can?" Nick said warily.

"Well," Andre said, "you probably know better than I that these guys are major players. They made one call and that was to the DEA. I'm not at liberty to disclose just what it is they are offering; suffice to say it is major. That's what we've got working here."

"They tortured and murdered two people," Nick said.

"Cienfuego, they said. They say it was Cienfuego."

Sonny saying now, "Nick, Rodrigo told us Cienfuego is the main guy. The Professor, you remember. Rodrigo said he was the boss."

"No-good bastard," Andre said, pouring his coffee from a container into a large white mug inscribed with a blue DA decal. "I'll tell you something, fellas, it's a shame we don't have the death penalty in this state because I'd throw the switch on this Cienfuego character myself."

"Right on," Sonny said.

"Okay, get going," Andre said suddenly to Nick. "See if you can get this Professor to give it up. I doubt it, they're a tough sort, these big-time players are real tough."

Nick said, "This guy, this Diego, if he was such a major player, why would he have his sixteen-year-old son hanging around? The kid was working in the kitchen from what I understand."

"Who can figure these fucking Cubans," Sonny said. "The bastard tortured and killed my informant, one of his people killed two of my partners. Now, speaking for myself," Sonny said, tapping himself on the chest, "I get revenge for that sort of thing. I set their fucking hair on fire."

"Tell 'em, brother," Detective Lloyd said.

"I don't claim to be the best cop in the world, Nick, but I claim to seek justice. My kind of justice."

"Well said, Sonny," Andre said.

"It's true," said Eddie Moran.

"I took an oath," Sonny said. "And I am faithful to that oath by being loyal to my partners, by being loyal to the people who are loyal to me, without compromise."

Nick thinking Sonny was the coolest pro in the practice of charm he'd ever met. "I'm impressed," Nick said, "but personally I'd rather be fishing."

"Well one day," Sonny said, "we will all get together, and together we will have you take us on a fishing trip."

"Include me in," Andre told them.

Nick picked up his coffee and drank it, wanting to grab Sonny McCabe by the ear. Man the guy pushed his luck. He wanted to say *Christ!* loud as he could. But he clenched his jaw, remained quiet, listening, watching Sonny and Andre do their cute little dance of love, deciding they were both a pair of clowns in the circus act called New York justice. "All right," he said, "why don't Carl and I go and speak to Cienfuego."

Andre's face seemed drained of good feeling. He folded his arms across his chest and narrowed his eyes.

"You get an admission from Cienfuego, Nick, and we're home free."

Sonny laughed, it was more like a grunt. "Give me twenty minutes with him," he said. "I lay the McCabe on the bastard, he'll cop out to the Kennedy assassination."

Laughter all around. Nick kept quiet. He kept his seat until Andre rose from the table. Andre shook hands with Sonny McCabe and Eddie Moran and Detectives Suarez and Lloyd and each of the two members of Lloyd's team.

"I'll be in touch tomorrow," Andre said as they all headed for the door. "The way justice moves in this city, I had better get a grand jury started as soon as possible."

Nick told Sonny he would speak to him later.

"Now wait a minute," Sonny said, "I got this right? You're going to book Cienfuego, Matos, and Medina?"

"Cienfuego tonight, Matos and Medina when the feds get through with them," Nick said.

Andre said, "Nick will take care of Cienfuego. It looks as though the feds will adopt that part of the case that concerns the other two."

"Take them to federal court," Sonny said, "not here. I'm only a cop, tell me, can they do that?"

"If I agree, they can do whatever they want. They are, after all, the government."

"Well, then we can be sure that they own more than one car," Nick said.

"What's that?"

Nick said, "Never mind." He'd been going to mention the two feds and their BMW, but then he figured maybe he better wait. "I'll talk to you later," he said, standing.

He and Carl Suarez walked out, leaving the office door open, and went to wait for the elevator. "One hell of a collar," Nick could hear Andre telling Sonny. "You did some job."

"It's what I do," Sonny said.

"Don't let him kid you," Eddie Moran was saying, "Sonny had help on this one."

"I should let Sonny speak to the press people. Give them a little teaser," Andre said. "Maybe I should let him do that."

"Yes, yes," Sonny said as if it were a great idea. "The PC would go nuts."

"I'm sure he would. You know," Andre said, "every time the PC looks in the mirror he takes a bow. I can't stand people like that, media sluts. However, Sonny, I can't allow you to do that. It would cause me a ton of grief."

"I have my own connections, friends at Channel Four. Hell, I'll make the call."

Andre was laughing as the elevator arrived. He said, "Sonny Mc-Cabe's press conference, I should let him do it. Now that would be something.

"You think anyone at Police Plaza would mind if Sonny McCabe held his own press conference?"

Nick heard them laughing together as he got onto the elevator. The sound of their shared laughter did not make him feel happy, not in the least.

Chapter 22

Nick drove down Queens Boulevard back into Astoria, Carl sitting still as a stone in the passenger seat. If Carl had been disturbed by the meeting, the debriefing at Andre's office, he'd said nothing about it. But it seemed to Nick that the young detective was brooding and angry. He trusted this guy Suarez; looking at his dark, slicked-back hair now, he had a face you'd see on some rum commercial from the islands. And he had a feeling Carl trusted him. But he also had a feeling—one of those nagging ones that kept you thinking—the guy was wired tight, about ready to blow. And that Carl knew something more than he was saying. For most of the ride from the DA's office to the stationhouse, Carl was very quiet.

Nick parked in a reserved detective's spot and looked up at the building where Diego was being held.

It was early evening, the night would be clear. The elevated train tracks rising over the street hid the moon from view but its light lit the stationhouse's front door, the metal bars over the windows, the sidewalk and the alleyway that ran alongside the building. Radios in the police patrol cars parked in front of the precinct cracked out Saturday night calls.

The interior of the stationhouse was brightly lit. Uniformed cops, two women reporters, and a crew of about five detectives milled about. The desk officer was a large black man wearing lieutenant's bars; he stood behind the desk and acknowledged Nick and Carl with a faint smile. Alongside him a sergeant was bent over writing in the log.

Nick asked the lieutenant if he could have Diego Cienfuego brought up to the detectives' squad room. He'd need him for about a half hour, no more. Then he'd run him back to the desk to be booked. The sergeant looked up from his writing and regarded Nick in an unfriendly fashion. His name tag said RAMOS.

"You wanta tell me how in the hell you walk a bum in here that took part in a cop killing? You wanta explain that so I understand?" he said. Telling Nick that in his day, the bum would have been booked from the hospital, or better yet, the morgue. The lieutenant said those days are history. Pull that shit nowadays and you end up in the can yourself, watching the skel collect a million bucks from the city. Listen to this, there's a cop in this precinct getting sued by a stickup man. The cop and the stickup man get into this shootout. The cop nails him. The stickup man sues because he was shot with hollow points, says they're illegal. Crazy, right? Still, the bum's suing. See, today, these shitheads know their rights. Even know what kind of bullets they're supposed to be shot with. Fuckin' nutty city.

Nick said, "Excuse me, but can we have the prisoner, it's been a long day."

Sergeant Ramos left the desk in no particular hurry. Nick and Carl headed for the stairs to the second floor. They found the squad room empty, walked through it, and went to the detective's squad commander's office and knocked. No one answered.

"We'll talk to him in here," Carl said.

Nick looked at him and nodded.

They arranged three chairs around the squad commander's desk and took seats, Nick sitting behind the desk and Carl alongside him. The third chair they had placed directly in front of them.

Sergeant Ramos entered the room with Diego in tow, his hands cuffed in front of him. He looked around the place.

Carl half-rose from his chair in a cautious crouch, saying, "Nice to see you again, Professor, take a seat."

"This asshole's a teacher?" Ramos said. An edge of anger underneath the mockery.

"Thanks, Sergeant," Nick told him, "we'll take it from here."

Ramos side-mouthed something in Spanish to Carl and Carl nodded. Then Ramos turned and left the room.

Diego took his seat slowly and resentfully, like someone who is totally exhausted and wants you to know it.

Nick turned to Carl, who sat slouched in his chair, his face twisted in unconcealed anger. "Translate for me, Carl, word for word. Don't leave anything out and don't add anything. Okay?"

Carl nodded.

Ramos had left the case folder with the arrest cards, prints, DD10, and 61 on the desk. The 61 was a general crime report, an outline of the arrest, and the DD10 was a MO, or method-of-operations sheet. Nick went through the papers, glancing at Diego, about ready to get things rolling, forty-four-year-old guy, lost his kid, poor bastard seemed self-conscious, vulnerable. Diego sat with his legs crossed, his cuffed hands folded at his waist. He wore a blue shirt and gray slacks, he had no belt or shoelaces.

"Tell him who I am, and that I'm going to be his arresting officer. Tell him he doesn't have to speak to me. Tell him he doesn't have to say anything without a lawyer present. Tell him if he can't afford a lawyer, we will get him one. Tell him I'm sorry his son was killed."

"You want me to mention the kid, right?" Carl said.

"Word for word, Carl."

"Okay." Carl nodded, staring across at Diego. He opened his mouth to speak but then stopped and turned to Nick. "You know," he said, "I think this guy understands English."

"No, no," Diego said. "I understand a little. Just a little. Please speak to me in Spanish."

Carl took a breath. "See," he said, "these fucking guys understand what they want. Smart bastard."

"Please," Diego said, "I understand only a very little."

"Go on Carl, go on in Spanish."

Carl's voice dropped into a husky monotone and as he spoke Nick watched Diego's face. The guy nodded, closed his eyes and nodded some more. He slid down in his chair, raised his cuffed hands over his head and began to sob.

Nick didn't move, sitting forward in the hard chair, hands laced together on the desk, staring at the guy.

Carl muttered something, got up from his chair, and took a stroll around the room.

"Tell him to calm down and relax. Ask him if we can get him something."

Carl spoke, no expression on his face, like he was reciting something.

Now Diego said to him, "My eldest son is dead. There is nothing you can give me."

"Ask him if he has any other children."

Carl spoke again. Diego answered, Carl saying, "He has two, a boy and a girl. The girl is fourteen and the boy is twelve."

"Does he have any other family here?"

Diego's answer went on for quite some time. Certainly more time than the question required.

"He said the only family he has here is his dead wife's cousin, Benny Matos. He said that he has no money for a lawyer and doesn't understand why he needs one. He keeps saying he did nothing wrong. He wants to know who will look out for his kids while he is being held here. He repeated that he is innocent of any wrongdoing."

Nick felt his face getting hot. "Tell him he was found—tell him *I* found him in a fucking place where seven hundred guns were being held. Tell him people were tortured and murdered in that place. Tell him two police officers were killed there. Tell him to stop this I'm-innocent bullshit or I'm going to lose my sense of humor."

"Nothing!" Diego shouted, "I did nothing wrong."

"Well, my friend," Nick said, "somebody did. Somebody did a whole lot wrong," sounding more concerned than hostile.

Diego turned to Carl, Carl repeated Nick's words. Diego stared at Nick a moment. He sighed heavily and nodded, speaking a long time, to Nick. Then silence.

"Well?" Nick said.

Carl let the silence hang for a few seconds, gathering his strength. Saying finally, "He said the police did wrong by killing his son. He said that he was a good kid and that the police should not have hurt him. He said he doesn't know anything about guns, has never held a gun. He said he thinks he should speak to a lawyer."

"You believe him?"

"I don't know." Carl sounded anguished. He extended his hand, wanting Nick to rise, eager to speak to him alone. Nick went with him to a corner of the room, Carl whispering, "I don't know, I don't know."

"You don't know what?"

"None of this makes any fucking sense, none of it. I'm telling you I was in Los Campos a dozen times, more. This guy was hanging around sure, but . . . Look," Carl said, "I never heard him on any of the wires. I never overheard him talking trash with Benny or Cano or any of the others. I know what Rodrigo told you, and you have to respect what the snitch said, but it just don't make sense."

"Diego," Nick said, raising his voice, "how well did you know Rodrigo Punto?"

Diego's mouth contorted into a private smile. He answered in Spanish, speaking directly to Carl, talking for some time.

Carl told Nick, "He says he knew Rodrigo from the Hatuey. Says that Rodrigo's wife often made him lunch there. He said that Rodrigo was a jealous and crazy man."

"Right." Nick said to Carl, "Ask him if he was banging Rodrigo's old lady. Ask him that. Then ask him if Rodrigo threatened to shoot him a couple of days ago."

Carl spoke to Diego.

Diego answered.

Carl said, "He said yes and no. Yes Rodrigo threatened him, and no, he wasn't fooling with his wife."

Diego glanced up at Nick. Nick held his eyes for a moment, then Diego turned away, his head slowly swaying from side to side. He seemed to Nick to be deep in thought.

"Remind him that I found him on the stairway, coming up from Los Campos's basement, a place where two men had just been tortured and killed. Ask him if he wants me to believe that he knows nothing about it. Go on, Carl, ask him, he's starting to piss me off. Tell him that too, tell him I don't buy his bullshit I'm-innocent story, and I'm about to get real pissed." Nick held up his hand, asking Carl to wait a minute. "Tell this jerk that his two other children are going to become wards of the state—wait a minute, don't tell him that."

"Well, what do you want me to tell him?"

"Tell him I think he's a fucking liar. I know he knows exactly what happened in that basement, and I want him to tell me. I want a blow-by-blow, no bullshit, no stories."

Carl spoke, and after a moment Diego looked up at Nick to answer, then caught himself and said nothing.

"Well?" Nick said.

Carl shrugged.

"Okay." Nick nodded amiably. "I want him to give me a statement as to what he was doing in the basement, what he saw there, and how he happened to be there in the first place."

Carl asked and Diego answered. This time his answer was short, and Nick saw him withdraw, retreating into himself, clamming up.

Carl saying, "He said he is an honorable man. He said he committed no crime and he doesn't think he wants to speak to you any longer. He said he wants a lawyer."

"What?"

"That's what he said, he said he's an honorable man."

"Tell him I said he should go and fuck himself."

Carl smiled as if they had shared a joke.

Diego said something. Carl told Nick, "He said you don't know anything about him or his family. You don't know anything about the life he's had. He's a respected man, he said, people respect him, he's no criminal."

"That's what he said?"

"Uh-huh."

"Yeah, well you tell him I may know nothing about his past, but I sure as hell know plenty about his future."

Nick continued to speak to Diego for another half hour, but Diego was through talking. He nodded, shrugged his shoulders, shook his head, said yes, no, I don't know, becoming more and more withdrawn. Distracted by thoughts of Sonny McCabe and Andre's curious new-found mutual regard, Nick grew tired of Diego's silence, tired period. Finally he told Diego he was calling it a night, explained to him that he had better get himself a lawyer, a good one.

Nick and Carl walked Diego through the detectives' office and down the stairs to the front desk. The lieutenant was the only one around now, talking on the radio, giving a job to a sector car.

"We're ready to book him now, Lieutenant."

The lieutenant held up his hand, telling Nick he needed a minute. Standing, waiting, looking around, Nick felt a sudden, sharp hit of sadness: Christ, six men and a boy, seven people who yesterday were eating, breathing, watching TV, planning how and when they were going to get laid. Seven of them were at that very moment stretched out on a slab somewhere, getting cut into sections by some ME who was probably eating a pizza and listening to Willie Nelson tunes. Jesus Christ, Nick thought. He wondered how all this started and where it was going. He glanced over at Diego and was mildly taken aback. The guy throwing him a small tight grin, standing there in some kind of shock. He felt a mixture of sympathy and bitterness toward Diego, with his sad, pain-filled face, a dead son, two other children unprotected in a strange city, an ocean of grief being neatly arranged for him by Andre. Still, there was no doubt, the guy had been in that killing hole, that basement.

The lieutenant signed off the radio, cleared his throat and looked directly at Nick as if waiting for instruction.

Nick put the arrest cards up on the desk and gestured with his thumb. "All set, Lieutenant. For purposes of the booking, I'm giving him murder one, twice."

Chapter 23

At first I thought I could talk to them," Diego said. "You know what I mean? That they would understand and maybe help me out."

Felix said, "Cops help you out? No chance. The one that spoke Spanish, he sounds like the detective that spit at me."

"I don't know. For a little while they seemed to understand. I thought the American guy would listen to me. I don't know why, I just did."

He lay on the metal bunk, a thin blanket pulled up to his neck, his hands laced behind his head. Felix was half asleep on the bunk across from him.

"But after a while I could see they were not there to help, they were there to make trouble for me, more trouble than I already have."

"You're smart, Professor. Don't talk to them, don't say nothing."

"I need a lawyer, a very good one," Diego said. "They are charging *me* with the murders of Rodrigo and Oscar."

There was a slight pause. "You got some money, something stashed someplace?"

"No. No, I don't." Diego told him how much Benny paid him. And even with tips, which could be very good, sometimes a hundred, a hundred fifty on a busy Friday or Saturday night, he still couldn't save anything. Children are expensive, he had to raise three, it costs. "God," he said, *"Dios mío."*

"Benny got plenty of cash, man," Felix told him, "he'll help you out."

"What do you think about Benny and Cano?"

"What about them, Professor?"

"Where are they? I haven't seen them."

"Probably they keep them someplace else. Tomorrow we'll all be together. Tomorrow, when we go to court."

"These detectives, this Nick and Suarez, first they made me feel they would help me out. You know, if I told the truth, what I saw, what I know. But hell, I don't know anything. That other Puerto Rican, the cop Ramos, you know what he said?"

"Tell them what you know, tell them everything you saw," Felix muttered, sounding like he was angry and had heard it all before. "Think of yourself, think of your family. Same shit all cops say when they try and make you rat."

"He said, 'You're going to go to jail for a hundred years. You are going to die in prison, and get buried in a hole in upstate New York. A place where it is freezing cold all winter and stinking hot all summer.' I told him, 'I don't plan to die in this country.' He said, 'You are already dead, you just don't know it.' "

"Fuck Ramos, fuck that coconut head," Felix said.

"Tomorrow I will talk to Benny. He must get me a lawyer," Diego said. "I need a good lawyer. Somebody who is interested in my troubles, cares about me. He doesn't get a lawyer for me then I'm going to tell the cops everything I know. I don't know much, but what I know I'm going to tell them."

Felix said, "I don't think that's a good idea. You know what I mean? I mean, people would get very angry at you, Professor."

"Angry at me? The whole world is angry at me now. I saw Cano kill Oscar, he shot him in the head. I was standing right there, me and Manny, we were right there. Then he killed Rodrigo with a spear—a spear, can you believe it? The man is a beast. I owe that man nothing."

"Yes, I would have to agree with you," Felix said. "On the one hand Cano is an animal. On the other, he takes care of the people that take care of him. Business, man, it's all business."

"He is evil."

"Fuck with him, Professor, and you'll find more trouble than you have now, times five. Look, Professor, you can't take none of this personally, it's business."

"Business. My son, Justo, my boy, what kind of business was that?"

"Cano didn't shoot your boy. Listen, Cano is a man of the street," he said. "In spite of what you think, his judgments are fair."

Of course, Diego thought. Absolutely, we are all fighting for our lives and we all know it, don't we.

In any case he wondered just how smart it was telling Felix his thoughts. Probably not too smart at all. Felix was one of Cano and Manny's people. Then again, he thought, I'm in jail, I'm here. As Ramos had said, he could be in jail for a hundred years. He glanced around the cell and wondered if Ramos was right. He wondered if jail was any more secure than the streets were in this crazy country.

That night the rain came again. Unable to sleep, Diego lay on his bunk and listened to its lonely music. In his mind's eye he saw a beach, and on that beach he could see healthy, happy children running along the sand.

Chapter 24

Nick was more than a little wobbly after a night of popping aspirins, trying to kill a headache that kept him awake till three in the morning. A bitch of a headache initiated by Diego Cienfuego, and then topped off when Renata called at midnight, to describe the tranquillity of St. Petersburg, Florida. As it turned out, Renata didn't have plans to return home any too soon. The peacefulness here cannot be fully described, she told him. It was useless, Nick decided, to speculate about what Renata might be thinking. Who knew what was going round in her wacky head. She seemed friendly enough, concerned about him, but there was no way to tell. In any event, he was becoming used to being alone. The feeling was not altogether bad. So Nick Manaris made a promise to lay off women for a while, not forever, nothing like that, but for a while.

He was walking toward Andre, and halfway across the floor of the Queens County Criminal Court complaint room he stopped short. Steve Stern, the TV reporter from Channel Seven, had come through the courtroom door and was approaching Andre, moving quickly, a microphone in one hand, a tape recorder in the other. Andre looked at Stern with only mild interest and went back to his reading. Nick saw that Andre wasn't paying attention, saw him sitting there going through a stack of yellow prior-arrest-record sheets, as Stern came right up to him, stuck the microphone in his face, saying, "District Attorney Robinson, do you have a comment as to why Medina and Matos were arraigned separately last night. Arraigned in the Eastern District of federal court, no less?"

The half dozen clerks, complainants, and cops standing around watched the scene with amazed interest.

Surprised, Andre stood up, shouting, "Hey, hey, what are you doing? Get that out of my face!"

"Secret private arraignments don't happen in cases when police officers are killed. And they certainly don't happen in federal court. Why the mystery?"

Nick took a seat at a desk near the door, deciding to let this play out, watching Andre trying to deal with the spunky guy, to find some way to answer the reporter, to find a way to counteract all the curious looks and open mouths.

"Don't you dare put a microphone in my face like that again. You were at the press conference last night. I said then and I'm telling you now, the federal government has a vested interest in this case. This is an ongoing investigation, a joint investigation by the Queens County district attorney's office along with the FBI and the DEA."

"You're saying Matos and Medina, two major Latin American crime figures, are now cooperating with the government?"

"No, you're saying that."

"Are you saying that their cooperation—"

"Listen to me. I didn't say anything about cooperation, *you* said cooperation. Don't put words in my mouth, Steve, don't do that."

"The people of the city of New York would not be happy if a deal is cut with cop killers. And who can blame them?"

"There have been no deals cut in this case."

"I have a source that tells me there have been. My source, a high-ranking police official, reported to me that the Queens County DA's office has cut a deal with these major gun and drug dealers. Men who it would seem are responsible for the death of two cops. Can you comment on that?"

"I just did."

As Nick watched, Andre took a pen from his pocket and scratched something out on a piece of paper. He handed it to Stern. Stern glanced at it, nodded his head, and said, "Would it be fair to say that you have no comment?"

"No, Steve, it would not. I have a comment, my comment is that your information is incorrect. There is an ongoing investigation, and that is all I am willing to say at this point."

Stern nodded and shut off his mike and recorder, saying, "You wouldn't bullshit me, Andre, would you? Because—"

"Call me later," Andre told him, standing.

Stern nodded and headed back through the door into the courtroom, everyone standing around watched him go.

Nick stayed seated for a few minutes, watching Andre pacing across the room from him. Andre looked furious, but a bit self-conscious too. He picked up a telephone and tapped out a number, waited a moment, then slammed the phone down.

Nick leaned back in his chair, watching and waiting. When Andre at last sat back down and looked around the room, Nick smiled at him, arms folded across his chest, trying to come off like what's going on, hotshot?

Andre waved him over, then began tossing papers around the desk, drinking his coffee, glancing about the room, wagging his head.

Nick sauntered over to him. "Stern was a bit hard on you."

Andre didn't answer.

"So what's the story, you cut a deal with the feds?"

"You know, your chief of detectives is feeling feisty, smart bastard. I'll show him—what are you talking about, cut a deal with the feds?"

"What am I talking about? A day before we make the arrest I catch a pair of feds tailing me. The same feds show up at the arrest scene. Makes me feel like a criminal, some fucking fed following me. Why the hell didn't you tell me about them?"

Andre's eyebrows rose. "Did you slash their tires? Was that you? Upset that guy, really frightened him, somebody threatened him, personally threatened a federal agent with bodily harm."

Nick had trouble keeping a straight face. "You're kidding."

"A DEA agent, I'm not kidding," Andre declared, nodding.

"A federal agent?"

"I'm telling you, the man made a full report. A team of New York City detectives threatened him."

"Is that right?"

"It's not funny."

"You see me laughing?" Nick shrugged as if it didn't mean anything. "You want to tell me what's going on here?"

"First of all," Andre said, "I want to tell you that I'm sorry about that conversation we had the other night."

"Which one are you sorry about?"

"You know, the one about . . . forget it."

"No, which one are you sorry about? The one where you suggested that I spy on my partners?"

"Right, that one. Forget it."

"I did. So what's up? You and Sonny now the best of friends?"

Andre seemed ready to get into it, going through the papers lying in front of him, glancing around, looking right and left. Nick curious, not wanting to let this go.

"Why didn't you tell me the feds were working these guys?" he asked.

"I can't tell you everything."

"I don't expect you to. But there are some things. You know, we are friends. At least I used to think we were friends."

"Look, it's just that, you know, I'm fighting for my political life here."

"I don't get it. Explain to me how by not telling me what the hell is going on, it helps you. I mean, I don't get it."

Andre turned to look around the room. Everyone had left except the complaint clerks.

"C'mon Andre, talk to me."

"The U.S. attorney in the Eastern District, Paul DaSilva, he is going to make a run for governor, and he's a lock." Andre leaned back and extended his entwined hands. "The man's a lock, Nick, and he'll come out and support me for district attorney. The man's a national figure, a close friend of the president, got the entire Democratic Party behind him." Andre brought his face close to Nick's. "With support like that, I can't lose. He tells District Attorney Santoro to tap me, I'm golden."

"Andre, listen to me—"

Andre waved him quiet. "You helped make a great case, Nick. I mean in some ways it was tragic, police officers were killed. I understand your feelings. Believe me, I understand. However, let me tell you, these guys Medina and Matos, they have been doing business with major international players. We're talking important government officials in the Bahamas, in Colombia and Mexico. They cooperate, well, there's no telling where it will go. You can see why this case of yours should go federal, can't you?"

"Sure. But, hey Andre—"

"Look, we're going to prosecute Cienfuego and the Vasserman brothers. Focus on them as the major players. The guy who shot and killed Captain Hawks and Detective Monserette is dead. You killed him. Everyone's saying you're a hero, as they should. Let the feds worry about Medina and Matos, use them up and throw them in Witness Protection. Who cares?"

Nick flinched. "Fine," he said, "that's fine. But what if Cienfuego is a witness and not a conspirator? What if the guy was simply at the wrong place at the wrong time? It happens."

Andre gave Nick a breathy "C'mon," then shook his head. "The snitch named him, described him as the main man, and who's going to argue with him. The snitch is dead, Cienfuego probably killed him."

"It's not strange to you that the feds don't want to talk to Cienfuego, that nobody's interested in the guy?"

"We can't have everybody flipping, Nick. Somebody's got to take the weight."

"So tell me, why were the feds following me?"

"They were running a parallel on your investigation. I guess they wanted to be near the action."

Nick smelled a lie but let it slide. "So," he said, "you got McCabe off the tip of your nose, right?"

"What do you mean?"

"You were so hot on the guy."

Andre gave Nick a little smile. "That was then, this is now. This case you and McCabe brought me is a whole lot bigger than another bad-cop case. And to tell you the truth, jamming up cops don't make me a hero in Queens. Besides, somebody will nail Sonny sooner or later."

Nick laughed. "Maybe not."

"Look, I know the guy's a rascal, but he has something of the hand-some wild teenager in him, he has his silky side."

"Silky, yes. Silky is good," Nick said.

"I figure that maybe his past is past and who am I not to give some-one a second chance?"

"Talk about the worm turning."

"Okay, you have me there. But I have to tell you there is something disarming in the way McCabe lets you know exactly where it is he's coming from."

"Tell me about it. I know that I've never been able to get the hang of it, the way he charms people. It's something. I've seen him in action, the man's got something going, that's for sure."

"Look," Andre said, "can I be candid with you? I mean, forget pros-ecutor and cop. Christ, you're one of the two or three people I know whose opinion I trust."

"Sure."

Andre lowered his chin, making himself smaller, his eyes going from left to right. "I'm serious."

"I know you are. Go on."

"DaSilva loves this case, wants it like crazy. It will make him a hero in Washington. He'll owe me, big time."

"Okay, I understand that. What does that have to do with the price of beans?"

"You mean McCabe?"

"Yeah, right, Sonny McCabe. The guy who you described as walking evil. Not that I agree, not that I ever agreed with you about Sonny."

"Look, as far as McCabe is concerned, for the time being I prefer to live between the hemispheres of light and darkness. It's a dimly lit place between knowing and not knowing, a place where you find your own truth. Right now, I need Sonny McCabe. Can you understand that?"

"Sure I do. I understand, believe me I do."

Andre's tone softened, but his dark handsome face showed worry. "We've known each other for years. You know me, I can't lie to you. The truth is I've never been part of that moralizing elite who aspire to perfection."

Nick looked straight at him. "Andre," he said, "I have to wonder if I know you at all."

"C'mon."

"C'mon? You'll admit that you've been popping out of one trick bag after another lately. You're beginning to confuse me."

Andre leaned forward, saying, "What do you mean, confuse you?"

"You've been coming at me from three different directions at once. A real politico, if you get my meaning."

Nick caught an appraising look from Andre and smiled.

"Compromise, Nick, it's what I'm learning. It's what this political life is all about. But you need real friends, Nick, one or two people who will maintain moral restraint and watch your back for you. The fact is that you have always been that for me."

Nick felt himself blush.

"Can I count on you?"

"Count on me?"

"That's what I said."

"I guess," Nick said. He tried to picture the old Andre, the guy who thought that politicians were only a little less sleazy than pimps, but decided he was being uncharitable and petty. "Okay." He nodded, ready to get going. "Okay, I'm off to arraign Diego Cienfuego."

"See you at the circus. By the way, we'll give him a plea if he wants to cop out. He takes us on, we'll put him away till he's old and gray. You think he'll do that?"

"What?"

"Cop out, take a plea to a lesser charge, and maybe do seven and a half to fifteen."

"I don't think so."

"No?"

"No. I think he thinks he's innocent."

"You're kidding."

"Why would I kid you?"

To say that there were no words to describe the hallway and courtroom 1A would be inaccurate. There were words, Nick thought, words like *a judicial circus gone batshit,* and *minicam madhouse.* In the hallway outside the arraignment part, as Nick entered it, there was a churning mass of clawing humanity—cops, complainants, lawyers, media people—gathered in conspiratorial groups, all eyeing Nick as he passed through.

Normally, Sunday morning was busy, with the just-arrested making their first formal appearance before a judge to have bail set. But this Sunday was supercharged. Along with the usual rank-and-file perps held for rape, murder, madness, drugs, and guns, there would be a group of notable gun dealers and cop killers. The air filled with the voices of camera- and sound men, producers with their assistants, reporters with their hair. Families of the arrested—mothers, brothers, wives, girl-friends, friends—shouted and rubbed shoulders with off-duty cops.

Even the cops from the twelve-to-eight tour, who stood around craning their necks, rolling on the balls of their feet, had no trouble keeping themselves awake.

Inside the courtroom people lined the oak walls, the straight-backed benches were filled. A persistent din continued to pump up the air. Even with beefed-up security, the place was wall-to-wall bedlam.

Nick had made his way along the wall to the front of the room; he stood now beside the judge's bench with Sonny and Eddie Moran, Lloyd Joseph and the detectives assigned to Lloyd's team. Everyone tight as a bowstring, waiting to see the defendants, the cop killers.

Nick spotted Andre working his way down the center aisle. As Andre approached, Nick noticed the reporter, Steve Stern, immediately behind him. He was smiling, and it occurred to Nick that it was the kind of reassuring smile you save for the terminally ill.

"Good morning fellas," Andre said. "Okay, we're first up. It should only be a minute or two. In the meantime, there are a couple of things I want you all to remember. First of all, keep your mouths shut. No talking to the media."

Nods all around.

"No matter what you think, these people are not our friends."

More quick nods.

"Next, you all were given yellow pads. During the next day or two I want each of you to write out your own accounts of everything you did, leading up to and including the raid. Will you do that?"

Sideways glances and more nods.

"I want as much detail as possible. Do it soon. Today, tonight. Do it before you forget. All right?"

The door to the judge's chamber opened. A court officer exited and held the door open for Judge Janeway.

To Nick, the court officer seemed very young. He was a short thin black man with a huge Afro, and he wore a uniform that looked as if he had just taken it out of the box. He had a baritone voice that belied his size. "Take seats," he shouted, "everyone take seats."

Nick heard Andre mutter, "Okay, okay."

The judge rapped his gavel, saying, "I am Bruce Janeway, this court is now in session. We have a full calendar, so let's move this first arraignment as quickly as possible. I have allowed one pool camera in the courtroom; other media and TV people will have to work off that. I can see that the camera is ready, so let's begin. Clerk, call the calendar."

A reverberation, a grumble, an immense enraged mutter rose from the row of sitting and standing off-duty police officers, and a single high female voice shouted, "Bring him out. I want to see the man that killed my husband."

"Oh f'chrissake," Sonny said. "Oh beautiful. Hey Nick, take a look at that, will ya?"

"Who is it?"

"I think it's Rodrigo's wife. Hey Eddie, her English is not so´ bad."

Nick looked up. About eight rows back stood a spirited and chic Latin woman. She seemed dazed and was flushed from arguing with a uniformed policewoman, who was tugging and pulling at her coat. The woman stood staring at the judge over the heads of the people sitting in front of her. And the thing that Nick noticed about her, the thing that really got his attention, was the way she held the hands of two children, one standing on either side of her.

"I didn't know Rodrigo had children," Nick said.

"He didn't," said Sonny.

Nick said, "His wife is standing there with her arms around two kids. Wait," he said, "I bet they're Cienfuego's."

"Got me," Sonny said.

Janeway pounced on her at once; he rapped his gavel and pointed, saying, "You, you sit down or I'll have you removed and arrested. And any more of this and I'll clear the room."

The woman sat.

The judge banged his gavel again, saying, "Let's get on with it. Call the calendar."

A series of names followed a series of numbers and Nick watched the parade of defendants come out of the pen area into the courtroom. They stood in front of the judge smiling, smiling, nudging each other, looking around at all the gathered media and friends, and newfound enemies. Smiling . . . Nick thought, what the hell could be going through these guys' minds? Maybe they just were holding back their fear. Somebody yelled, *Mira! Mira!*

The judge saying, "There is assigned counsel solely for purposes of the arraignment. I'm going to hold all the defendants without bail pending action by the grand jury." And then Andre's announcement that the grand jury presentation would be within forty-eight hours. When the group moved past him, shuffled in a slow stroll before the judge, Nick could see that Diego was the only one not smiling, and he seemed to be in some pain, his belt and shoelaces were gone, he was holding up his pants and one foot kept popping out of his shoe.

Nick heard the judge say, "I'll take them one at a time, starting with Julio Vasserman." He heard the interpreter repeat the judge's words. Heard the judge say how do you plead? Heard one of the assigned lawyers say, say not guilty. Heard Chino Vasserman announce, "Not goddamn guilty."

A resounding, "Awwwwww bullshit," from a string of off-duty cops standing along the wall. The judge's gavel went bang! bang! Nick was clenching his hands so tight his forearms hurt. Looking at Diego, seeing the frightened, glazed look on his face, the man was lost. Nick sweating a little inside his clothes now, staring at Diego Cienfuego, Diego having a hell of a time with his shoe as he stood there, head bowed. Hearing now a young girl's voice, a sharp anguished voice, call out Papi! Everyone turning toward her as if she'd just produced a gun, Nick seeing Diego come upright, shoulders back, head turning quickly. Nick's eyes were fixed on him. Hearing the girl's voice again, louder this time, the judge's gavel going bang! Diego's bright, blue eyes searching the room, peering into the crowd, opened wide as though he had been shot. Diego glanced at Nick; he seemed about to say something but turned from him back to the crowd.

"Qué pasa, Papi? Papi, qué pasa?"

The words pierced Nick's heart, the young girl crying out again and again. And Diego seemed pale now, white as a ghost, sweating, his chest heaving as if he couldn't find air. Nick thought the guy would go into shock. Janeway's gavel banging away. Nick turned to look at the child and saw all that anger and hatred coming right at him. The girl just staring at him. Then she screamed again, Papi! like a cat poked with a stick, Jesus, Nick thought, Jesus. The other defendants seemed to take a certain pride in their calamity. They turned to the audience, big grins on their faces. It was a terrific show, many people seemed to be enjoying it immensely.

Diego stepped up onto the bus that would bring him to the prison at Rikers Island. He was handcuffed to Felix Caban. The Vasserman brothers, already on the bus, paid him no mind, and there were others, others from Los Campos, four or five others, they too behaved as though he wasn't there. Diego sat in the first seat, nearest the driver, his eyes fixed straight ahead, working himself into a tight-lipped, stomach churning rage.

"Why am I here?" he demanded of Felix after some time.

"Calm, remain calm," Felix told him. "Things are being taken care of. You'll see, you will be fine."

"Yes, really? Taken care of? And my children, who will take care of them?"

Felix put his finger to his lips. "Quiet," he said, "remain calm."

It was a little before midnight when the bus rolled out of the bay of the Queens County Jail. Diego had been awake for more than twenty-four hours. In that time he had eaten only a sandwich of cheese on white bread, and he'd drunk at least a dozen cups of watered-down coffee.

"Why were Benny and Cano not there today? Where are they? What's going on here?"

"Quiet," Felix said again. "Remain calm. We are going to Rikers Island prison now. You will need to be smart, Professor. But we will be together, we've already seen to that. I will watch out for you."

Diego laughed. "It's kind of you, Felix. I appreciate your interest in me. That is very nice, but we are going to prison."

"Things can be done here. Everything can be done in this city for money. Do you understand me? It will not be so bad. Are you listening?"

"The thing is, what about Benny? He must get me a lawyer."

"Relax, we will take care of you."

Take care of you. The words made him tremble, and he repeated them to himself with fascination, his blood growing cold. Diego Cienfuego was going to be taken care of by a bunch of gangsters and killers and gun dealers. He could see it in their eyes, Mambo and Chino and the others too. See what Felix meant when he said they would take care of him.

Feeling a sudden crunch of depression, Diego decided he would call the detective the first chance he had.

By the time the bus arrived at Rikers Island, Diego was so exhausted he could barely move. When the driver parked the bus and the correction officer up front shouted "Up, up, everybody up!" he had trouble standing. Felix helped him to his feet, yanking at his handcuffs.

They were first off the bus. It was cold in the courtyard, and there was a misty rain falling. They walked into a gloomy antique of a building, into a large, well-lit room with peeling gray walls, one battered desk, and a filing cabinet.

Diego was shivering so badly that the officer had trouble taking the handcuffs off. It was the first time in hours that they'd been off, his wrist hurt like hell and he had a small cut on the back of his hand. Everyone from the bus was in the room. A few were black, there were two Puerto Ricans, cousins, they said, from the Bronx; they had been arrested for possessing a large amount of drugs. In this room the blacks were outnumbered, they stayed off by themselves and said nothing.

Diego stood in line with Felix, Mambo, and Manny Vasserman and the others from the club. Two corrections officers stood in front of them. Suddenly Diego was overwhelmed by a sudden stench—someone in the room could wait no longer for a toilet.

"Vasserman, Manuel and Eduardo. Cienfuego and Caban. You four come with me."

The corrections officer was a man named Tommy Carbone, whose mother had been born in Ponce. His father was a Howard Beach Italian-American. Tommy was so happy when he heard that the Vasserman brothers were going to arrive at Rikers he broke into a two-step. Tommy spoke some Bronx Spanish. He called their names from the cards he held and directed them through a gate into a small bare room with an anemic light that hung from a wire in the ceiling.

"All right, fellas, strip down," he said, "and put your clothes along the wall. That's all your clothes, your shorts too, everything."

"C'mon man," Mambo said, "what's this?"

"Do it," the officer said. He threw them an amused look.

Mambo walked toward the officer, his arms outstretched like a priest's. "Hey, Tommy, c'mon."

"Just do it, Manny, do what I tell you and then we can get outta here."

Felix sought out Diego's eyes and winked.

Diego removed his clothes, feeling humiliated, feeling as though he were living some sort of ghostly dream with evil spirits circling his head.

A second corrections officer entered the room, followed by a huge man with eggplant-colored skin and a lab coat. Tommy saying now, "Raise your arms."

Tommy checked Diego's armpits and mouth, fiddled with his long hair, which it seemed he found pleasing, giving everyone a laugh. He snapped on a pair of rubber gloves, pinched Diego's scrotum, and lifted his feet, checking the soles.

The man in the lab coat held up a hand as large across as two of Diego's, and Diego had big hands. He too was wearing a rubber glove.

"Okay," he said, "turn toward that wall, bend over, and spread 'em." In his other hand he held a flashlight.

"Fuck, man! Fuck!" Manny shouted. Then he laughed, the guard laughed back, unthreatening, a friend. Manny, along with everyone else, turned, Manny Vasserman heaving his massive pig-necked body around and facing the wall.

"Bend, c'mon, bend over. Real slow, real slow, real slow, that's it . . . stop."

Diego closed his eyes and dropped his head, trying to think of some pretty music, as a finger the size of a policeman's nightstick entered his rectum and probed, and probed some more. Diego felt as though he would cry, he was no hero.

Chapter 25

A few hours before Diego Cienfuego stepped up into the bus that would take him to Rikers, Nick Manaris walked through the door into the dimness inside Post Time. A Frank Sinatra tune was playing on the jukebox as Nick awkwardly shouldered his way through the crowd of off-duty cops standing around smiling, talking, shooting the breeze about sports and women. There were policewomen in pink lipstick talking men and partners, trying to look like they weren't really annoyed, though they obviously were. Gabbing about last night's tour, taking apart the details of their adventure, voices rising and spirits rising, laughing. Partners who together had faced the worst nightmares New York could deliver and had triumphed. There were buffs and cop groupies who talked more like cops then the cops themselves. Nick checked out a couple of guys standing at the bar and recognized them as civilian informants. He knew them to be a pair of kooks who carried fake IDs and store-bought handcuffs. There were a few anticrime guys in field jackets and work boots, a pair of homicide detectives in good suits, shirts, and ties drinking Manhattans. A crew of narcotics detectives stood near the rest room, jerking restlessly about in animated conversation about "a fucking buy that went bad."

Many times, coming into Post Time, Nick had tried to think of some way to get into it, be part of it, belong, and he'd come up with nothing. All at once anger swept over him. For Christ's sake, he should have headed home, he was exhausted. He stood there in the middle of the jammed joint, his chin up, looking for Sonny.

Through the smoke and noise he spotted McCabe dancing, his hands flat atop the jukebox, doing a solo, a little two-step to "Mack the Knife."

Eddie Moran was sitting in a black leather booth in the corner with Frank Kurtz. He bellowed, "Nicky, Nicky boy, here baby, c'mere, grab a seat and a libation, buddy boy."

Nick could see Moran clearly, his face illuminated in a small circle of white light from the candlelit bowl in front of him. Kurtz sat next to him, the writer's head resting against the wall, his eyes closed. They both seemed fairly tuned up, their table busy with empty beer bottles and glasses.

Sonny waved, telling Nick he would be right there, Nick should go and make himself comfortable.

Sinatra went on and Sonny continued dancing as if he were in no great rush to leave his spot. The song ended and Sonny spun on his heel, the guy knew how to move.

Nick slid into the booth across from Moran and Kurtz. The writer lifted his head and winked. "This story is so big," he said. "Forget TV, we're talking a major feature here."

"Hey, how's Carl?" Eddie Moran said. "How's the little guy doing?"

"He's doing fine. Well, not fine, he's doing okay."

Eddie made a face. "May the Lord help the poor fuck."

"He's really shook up," Nick said, "he'll need some help."

"Naw," Eddie Moran said, "fucking guy's gonna be okay. He's one of the boys. Your basic Puerto Rican, full of emotion and bullshit, but he's still one of the boys."

A couple of hours ago Nick and Carl had grabbed something to eat in a Puerto Rican restaurant on 116th Street. They ate rice and beans and some fried chicken in a place that was half grocery, half restaurant. You could buy coffee from Jamaica there, and some kind of exotic rice. Nick tried to come up with some words of wisdom, something to ease the guy's pain, telling Carl it was all some plan or other, fate was what it was, fate and luck. It was Sergi's fate to die that day, nothing anybody can do about bad luck and fate. Carl telling him fuck me, fuck knows, maybe I could have done something, who knows? Fuck me. But I'll have to live with it, won't I? Just dead Sergi and me, wondering what the fuck? His face was on fire and there were tears in his eyes.

Nick looked up and there was Sonny McCabe, carrying a tray with four bottles of beer. Sonny smiled and sang out, "Hey Nick, good, you made it. We were waiting, figured you'd say fuhgedaboudit and head home."

"The guy's a sweetheart," Eddie Moran said. "A stand-up guy this Nick is."

"I believe that the world must be written about as it is, or not written about at all," Kurtz said.

"Don't pay any attention to him," Sonny said, putting the tray he carried onto the table, moving aside bottles, glasses, and an overflowing ashtray adorned with two crumpled empty packages of Winstons. "Kurtz here has been in his cups all day, the guy's gone, man, blasted."

Frank Kurtz beamed. He took this as a great compliment.

"How's Carl?" Sonny said.

"I was just telling them, he's a bit screwed up. But he'll be okay. At least I think he'll be okay."

Sonny passed the beers around, saying, "I've seen that before. A guy freezes in the street, same guy day before could handle a million screaming wackos. Who can explain it, it happens."

Eddie Moran nodded.

Nick said, "Yeah, well, Carl's good people, I trust the guy. Who knows what happened."

"So," Sonny said, sitting down next to Nick, "how you doing?"

"Me? I'm fine."

"Don't be so sure. You popped a guy today, your first one. Don't be so sure you're fine."

Nick allowed himself a smile. It gave him a chance to shake loose a little of the uneasiness he felt.

"I need to say something," Frank Kurtz said. "I need to tell you men that I'm proud to know you." He raised his glass to the smiling group, and it was clear to Nick that this guy, this Kurtz, more than anything else in the world, he wanted that moment to go on forever.

"Oh for Christ's sake, Frank. Come on," Sonny said.

"I mean what I say, just what I say. You men are heroes in my book, real American heroes."

Kurtz looked straight at Sonny as he made his toast with what Nick called a brother-cop grin, wide, warm, and ingratiating, showing you, the way cops do, that he is one of the strong, the undeluded, the aware. Kurtz went on for about ten minutes about the glory of the Los Campos raid, Sonny and Moran joining in with a laugh and a few quick words now and again, giving Nick a pain, a gnawing feeling that was on the edge of agony. He wanted out of Post Time, he wanted away from Kurtz and Eddie Moran, away from their silly-ass homage to Sonny McCabe. When Kurtz said, "Man I'm beat, I need to get home," Nick closed his eyes in relief.

"C'mon, another half hour," Sonny said, glancing at his wristwatch.

"Nick's here now, you guys got stuff you want to talk about. I'll call you tomorrow." Frank Kurtz stood, saying, "Ouuuuu." He had been drinking all day, growing more shaky with each swallow. "Jeeze," he said.

Sonny got to his feet and pinched Frank's cheek. "You okay, guy? You don't look too good."

"I'm fine."

"Fine my ass, you wait here I'll get someone to drive you home."

"No, no, no. I'll call a cab."

"Yeah," Sonny said, "I don't trust you, give me your car keys."

"C'mon."

"Hand 'em over."

Kurtz handed Sonny his keys. Sonny took the keys and as Kurtz began to walk off Sonny said, "Frank, can I ask you something?"

"Anything," Kurtz said. "Ask."

"Why do you write? I mean why do you write books about cops? I mean you're retired, you got away from it all. Don't you know it ain't wise to go back?"

Nick watched Kurtz look away, fold his arms, the guy trying to think of something smart to say. He took a moment and then said, "Writing is the best way I can think of to turn your deepest pain into money."

Sonny said, "The job gave you pain, huh?"

"It broke my heart."

"But you're making money?"

"Writing is a tricky, complicated business," Kurtz said. "Making money is not easy."

"Yeah? Well I bet I could make money. I bet I could be one hell of a writer. Shit, I got a black belt in bullshit. Tell all the shit I've seen, everything I know. Gives me goose bumps just thinking about it."

Kurtz shrugged, his head bowed. "Why not?" he said.

The writer walked off, weaving his way through the crowd of flushed-faced cops. Sonny watched him go, looking both amused and annoyed. "And what about you, Eddie, you gonna take a hike or you gonna sit here and write a book?"

"Where am I gonna go?" Eddie looked around the bar as if Sonny's words had another meaning.

Nick felt obliged to maybe ask Eddie Moran why it was that he had nowhere to go. Only he had never figured out how to start a conversation with a drunk that didn't sound half-witted. Moran solved that problem for him by simply standing and saying, "I guess I could drop in on Connie, maybe she'll put me up."

Nick thinking this guy's a mess, one sad and lost man, a self-destructor, a classic. He glanced at Eddie; his eyes were puffy, watery, his skin looked worn out. Eddie reached down, picked up a bottle of beer, poured himself a glass and drank it down. He continued looking around the bar, the crowd was thinning out, people going home, going somewhere else. Eddie had been banging down the brew since early that morning. "Sure," he said, "Connie will be glad to see me."

"Stay awhile," Sonny said.

"Naw, I'd better get going too."

"Up to you," Sonny said. "You okay to drive?"

"Fuck yeah." Eddie leaned on the table, trying to get his bearings. "I could drive to the moon." He sounded unwell, his voice flat.

"Whyn't you just hang loose?" Nick told him. "Me and Sonny got a few things to go over, be a few minutes is all. I'll drop you."

"Where the hell are you going to drop me? You live uptown, I need to get to Queens. Besides, I need my car."

Sonny sipped his beer. Eddie began to pack for his trip. He put his cigarettes in his shirt pocket, took some cash from his wallet and went to drop a twenty on the table, Sonny saying, "Keep it, I got it. Go out and wait by my car, I'll drop you. Leave your car here, don't worry about it, we'll pick it up tomorrow."

Eddie nodded. Somebody down the bar called out, "Hey Eddie, Eddie Moran, you got two more today, didn't ya? You're a regular Wyatt Earp you are." Eddie Moran smiled, he held up his hand in greeting, and made his way through the crowd to the man at the bar, who stood with his arms spread as if giving a blessing, showing his teeth in a great smile.

Sonny put a cigarette in his mouth and lit it.

"I want to talk to you about Justo Cienfuego," Nick said.

"Yeah, I figured you would," Sonny said, but his face showed that he wanted no such conversation.

"Look, Sonny, I don't want to keep you guessing, I want you to know my boundaries straight off."

"The hell you talking about?" Sonny said. "Hey, you wanta get something to eat? The food here's pretty good, want a sandwich or something, a roast beef, something like that?"

"No thanks. Listen—"

"C'mon, I'm buying, grab yourself a sandwich, you gotta eat, man."

"I ate, it's fucking midnight, I'm not hungry. The hell you saying I saw the kid with a gun? The hell you say that for?"

"See those guys standing by the bathroom, those three guys over there?"

"What about them?"

"They're from narcotics, I know them. You know them?"

Nick glanced at three young men in leather jackets, all of them in their mid twenties, long hair, jeans and tennis shoes. One, a short guy with an earring and stringy blond hair, looked like one of those wacko kids liked to hang out in the East Village. He seemed angry, jumping around like he had to go to the toilet.

"Can't say I do," Nick told him.

"I know 'em. They come in here, hug each other, they whisper and then they go into the bathroom and come out smiling." Sonny grinned. "Young jerkoffs," he said.

"People do what they do, it's their business," Nick said. "We're not talking about wild-ass kids from narco, we're talking about what you told Andre, what you told the DA. I want to know why you said what you did. Then I'll tell you why I'm pissed. In case you didn't know it, I am, I'm pissed at you."

"You know," Sonny said, "when I came into this job twelve years ago, it felt like I was playing football again. I played sandlot, played in high school, had a full ride to South Carolina. Blew out my knee the first summer practice. Did one year in college and came home. Didn't stop me from getting on the job, but it killed me as a running back. Tell ya what, I bet I could still outrun anyone in this joint, even those kids from narco. Can't cut is all, can't make that cut, and if you can't cut, you ain't gonna run with the ball." Sonny leaned back in the booth. "How about you, Nick, you play ball, football, anything like that?"

"No, not me. My father hated team sports. I liked to fight though. Golden Gloves, some college. Sonny, I never saw the kid Cienfuego with a gun. He may have had one, but I didn't see it."

"All right, all right. We'll get to that, trust me."

Both Sonny and Nick turned as the bar exploded with laughter. Eddie Moran in a shooter's stance going, "Pow-pow-pow! Gotcha! When I kill people I use a shotgun, go for the legs, then finish them when they are down and rolling around." Moran had his rap going full throttle.

Sonny said, "Shitfa brains. Anyway, every September in high school I went out for football. In my high school, football was where it was at. The fame, the glory, the girls. And if you were any good, you got a free ride to college. Me, I was all-city, all-state, second-team high school all-American. Not bad for a white running back."

Sonny stared at Nick as if lost in thought, then let out a heavy sigh. "Your father wouldn't let you play, huh? Wouldn't let you be one of the guys."

With a quick nod, Nick poured himself some more beer.

"See," Sonny said, "I didn't have a father. My father was killed in Korea when I was a kid. When I was a kid the word 'father' meant nothing to me, I associated it only with God."

"It's getting late, Sonny," Nick said, staring straight at him, wanting to get into it, into why he had come to Post Time to talk to Sonny McCabe in the first place.

"Why, you got some place to go? You want to go home? You got no place to go, relax, okay?"

Nick nodded.

"So, here I am again in a stadium. The football field of the police department. I wasn't in homicide, Bureau of Special Services, or a DA's squad. I was in Public Morals, and now OCCU, some prestige, but not the big time, I'm still limping. But you see, something else happened along the way. I'm still all-city and all-state. I make more collars than anybody else and get my office in the newspaper all the time. They're still cheering, still yelling Sonny, Sonny, Sonny. I'm still the star, I still carry the team."

A faint, uneasy grin curled around the corners of his thin mouth. "Do you understand what I'm saying?" Sonny said.

"Yo! Hey! Yo!" Eddie Moran called out. "Whataya say, Sonny? It's getting late."

Sonny held up his hand, spread his fingers, five minutes.

Nick looked into those cold blue eyes. First with Sonny it's the eyes, the way he looks at you to make sure you got the message. Something in Nick, something stubborn made him lie, made him say, "You lost me, I don't get it, whatever the it is, I don't get it."

"Football."

"You want me to be a team player, is that it?"

"Hey buddy, it's a tough game, only the strong survive. Believe me I know. Sometimes, bullshit reigns and you got to ante up the family jewels, brother."

"What did I tell you the other day in the office, huh? Didn't I say don't fuck with me? I said I'll work with your team, I'll do whatever I can, but I see it, I saw it, I hear it, I heard it. You remember, you were there. I'm no sleeper here, I told you. I told you exactly how I feel, and I haven't changed the way I see things in the last two days."

"You know," Sonny said, "I finally figured out why I like you so much. Opposites attract. It's classic, predictable."

"Sonny," Nick said, "if I let you, you'd fly me right into a mountain. I ain't gonna let it happen, buddy. There's a lot about you that I like, but I gotta tell ya—"

"C'mon."

"No."

"Nick, cut this prissy paralysis bullshit that sends you moping, conscience-stricken, walking around like some asshole. You're not a priest, Nick, you're a cop. You're a good cop and I want you to stay my partner. We could do some great things together."

"You don't need a partner, you need a probation officer."

Sonny laughed, thought that was a hoot.

"Hey Nick," Sonny said, "you've been on this job for what, ten years? Man, I figure that by now you gotta see that this is all bullshit. There's us and there's them. Look under your shoe, that's where they are, that's where they all are, they're dirt. And, I mean everybody, your friend Robinson, Cienfuego, the feds, those creep sonsabitches Medina and Matos. Alla them shitballs."

"Yeah," Nick said, looking around, "that must be it, everybody's shitballs but you."

"No, Nick, no. Not me—us."

Nick looked up as four detectives he knew from the local precinct came in and stood at the bar. They waved at Sonny. Nick turned to see if Sonny had noticed, he should have known better.

"I know everybody on this job," he said, leaning toward Nick, "and everybody knows me. And what they know about me is that I'd do whatever I could for them, for any cop."

"Just cops?"

"Who else? You figure there's somebody else I should give a shit about?"

"What about DAs? You and Andre, yesterday you two seemed to be the best of friends." Nick could feel his face flush, anger flooding into it. But anger at who? At Andre, at Sonny McCabe, at himself. Anger disguised as interest, always a cool move.

"You think maybe I don't know your friend Andre Robinson's story? You think maybe I'm stupid? I know what he thinks of me. His off-the-cuff friendly riffs are bullshit, don't you think I know that? Maybe he thinks I checked my balls at his office door. I know he's your friend, so excuse me when I say he's a phony, like the rest of them."

Nick looked at Sonny for a second. "You ever think that maybe you're the biggest phony of all?" he asked, just like that.

To Nick's surprise, Sonny smiled, all the intensity fading from his big handsome Irish face. Nick was beginning to think that this guy, this Sonny, wasn't so nuts after all. He looked a little embarrassed.

"Sure, sure I am. But your friend's worse than me, far, far worse. He sees himself down the road as the mayor of this loony-bin city. Sure he wants to be DA, but that is only his first step. And he'll do anything to get there, sleep with anybody, including me. He's a phony bastard and you know it."

Nick looked away, thinking that to a greater or lesser extent, Sonny was right. He sat there pondering the vagaries of friendship.

"C'mon," Sonny said, "I better get going. I have to drop Eddie off."

"And that's it?" Nick said. "That's all there is? We didn't talk about the kid, the gun, my seeing or not seeing it. We didn't talk about anything."

"Sure we did."

"I didn't see a gun in Justo Cienfuego's hand."

"Well either you did or you didn't. Maybe you just forgot, maybe what you got to do is think about it. Think about it and by the time you testify to the grand jury, your memory will clear a bit."

"Don't bet on it."

"Oh, shit man. I'd bet on you in a heartbeat. Let me tell you a little story."

Nick didn't say anything.

"When I was working patrol—I was in the Seventy-five, in Brooklyn, a real shithouse. Anyway there was a fire on my post, a bad one. There was this kid, this black kid, I loved this kid. I have to tell you, this Bobby had it all. Good-looking, growing like a tree. Man I had two kids of my own, I'd go home at night and creep into my kids' bedroom and smell them, see if they were breathing. I worried all the time about my kids. This other kid, this Bobby in the Seventy-fifth he had nobody, nobody smelling him. He was twelve years old and he'd be out in the street shooting baskets at one, two o'clock in the morning. Shooting baskets into some old wastebasket I nailed to a telephone pole in front of this firetrap he lived in. This kid was fucking twelve years old and he could dunk. You know what that is, a twelve-year-old that can dunk a basketball? My kids could barely tie their own shoes when they were twelve. Anyway, there's this fire, some asshole with a space heater. This kid, this Bobby gets burnt real bad. I mean real bad. His face, his hands, broke your heart. One day I got him sitting in the car. On the late tour, I'd have him sit with me awhile. So we're sitting there drinking Cokes. His left hand was gone, and his face, man his face was so disfigured you wouldn't believe it. I say to him, 'Bobby, if you could have one wish what would it be?' You know what he said? He said, 'I'd wish that everyone I knew had a face and a hand like me.' Well, I sat there, I didn't know what to say, what to think."

"You ever hear from him?" Nick realized that he was whispering.

"No, his mother took him down south. Mississippi, I think, or Louisiana, down there somewhere."

"Uh-huh," Nick said, feeling suddenly worn out, physically exhausted, as if he'd spent six hours pulling lobster traps, which he hadn't done in a while, which he missed doing.

"Whataya mean, uh-huh?"

"What do you want me to say? You want to hear some of my stories? I've been on this job ten years, I got a million stories too."

"Do you understand what Bobby was saying to me, telling me?" Sonny sounded disappointed. He waved his hand vaguely. "I tried to tell you something."

"Look Sonny, I know it's miserable out there in the streets, rough and miserable. People feel as though they're disconnected, alone. We all want to belong, to be part of something. I know that, I understand that. But you got this cockamamie idea that either I'm with you or you're my enemy. That's not right, it's wrong, is what it is."

"I'm going home," Sonny said.

"Yeah," Nick said, "me too."

They sat in silence awhile, both of them thinking.

"I'm gonna tell you something," Nick said. "Today in court, those kids, you remember the kids with Punto's old lady? The kids standing with her?"

"Yeah, what about them?"

"They were Cienfuego's kids. I don't know that for sure, but I bet they were."

"So?"

"The girl, she looked at me, and when she looked at me, stared really, what I saw reflected in her eyes was nothing short of God's judgment."

"Oh for chrissake."

"Her brother was shot to death, and her father is going to be put in the slammer, for who the hell knows how long."

"Yeah?"

"And I was a part of that. We, all of us, are part of that."

"The kid had a gun, Nick. He was pointing that gun at my partner— your partner too. Now what would you have me do, call time out? I couldn't call time out, Nick, nobody would have listened."

"But I didn't see it. The gun. I never saw it, Sonny."

"You told me that. But maybe you were too excited to remember exactly what you saw or didn't see."

"I know you, Sonny, how you think. You think you say the kid had a gun and Eddie will swear to it."

"He had a thirty-two revolver, Nick. Cut it out, you're starting to piss me off."

"Now normally that's good enough. Only with this case we got Andre Robinson, and although Andre would love to believe you, he's not so sure. Now if I say I saw a gun, then that's all she wrote, it would be case closed."

"Right."

There was silence.

Sonny said, "But there was a gun."

"I saw no gun. By the time I got there the kid was already dead, or dying, I don't know. Anyway, he was laid out across a table."

"So we'll leave it at that."

"Just so you understand."

"You mean you're not going to think about it?"

"What the hell is there to think about?"

"All right, all right, Christ you make me fucking nuts," Sonny said. "So what else? You got something else you wanta say?" Sounding bored now.

"This case we got, this case, it's got holes in it. I wanted to talk about that, about the fact that this case is full of holes."

Sonny picked up the check and read it; he stood, leaving a hundred-dollar bill on the table. "Holes," he said, "every case got holes. We'll close the holes in this case easier than most."

"Really? How you plan on doing that?"

He smiled. "We're smart and we're creative." He waved at Eddie Moran, who was standing alone at the bar now. "And we're New York City detectives, we can do whatever we want."

"That right? Sorry, I forgot."

"Listen," Sonny said with a weary sigh. "You'll testify to the grand jury the way you want. Let your conscience be your guide. I swear to Christ, I can't figure you."

"We got a problem here," Nick said.

"What the fuck do you want from me?"

A good question, Nick thought, the best of the night. "I figured you knew," Nick said. ·

"I thought I did too. Look," he said, "stay in touch. I'll talk to you tomorrow, the next day. Okay?"

Nick got up and started for the door.

Sonny McCabe stood with a beer in one hand, his car keys in the other; he rubbed his chin against his left shoulder, watching Nick go. "Hey, there was something I've been meaning to ask you," he said after him.

Nick turned. "What's that?"

"Your buddy, your friend Andre Robinson, he's a fag, right?"

"Excuse me?"

"You heard me. I asked around, nobody I know has ever seen him with any gash."

"With any what?"

"Gash, a broad. And those five-hundred-dollar suits he wears, neat

as a pin with that little red hankie sticking out of his pocket. That's a
code, man. I was in Public Morals five years, I know a queen when I
see one."

"Christ." Nick felt his legs go a little weak, and for a second it was
hard to breathe. Bright lights were going off in his head. "Sonny,
man . . ."

"Don't Sonny-man me. The guy's got a picture of James Dean in his
office."

"And Jack and Bobby Kennedy, and Martin Luther King."

"Yeah, and who said they were straight? Look, I'll call you in the
next day or two, we'll get together."

"Sure," Nick said, "I can't wait." Trying to sound funny, but the line
came out phony and forced. As he went through the door Eddie Moran
called out, "See ya buddy." Nick thought he heard Sonny say, "Shitfa
brains," but he felt too worn out to be sure, too fed up and heartsick.

Nick got uptown quickly, dropped his car, then went across the street
to Tio's, took a look inside and went to the bar. The place was empty
except for the bartender. Nick ordered a beer, then changed his mind
and said make it a Glenlivet, straight up with some water on the side.

Gay, he said to himself. So what, it's his business.

He sat at the bar and swallowed his drink and ordered another. So
why hadn't Andre told him? Christ, they knew each other ten goddamn
years, the guy never said a word. Maybe it was because there was nothing to say. But we're friends. So what is a friend? Poets and philosophers
have discussed that question for years. Nick pushed money at the bartender and asked for another, saying, "If it's a friend I need, I should
go and get a dog."

The bartender was drinking coffee from a glass, nervously smoking a
cigarette. "What's that?" he said.

Nick looked up and stared past him, through him, thinking McCabe,
what the hell does he know? What the hell does Sonny McCabe know
about anything? The guy's a flashy piece of white trash, a jerk with the
IQ of seaweed.

"So why the fuck didn't Andre tell me?"

"You talking to me?" the bartender said.

Chapter 26

Sometime around three o'clock in the morning, he couldn't remember when, Nick let himself into his apartment. He checked his answering machine and found three messages on it, one from Renata; one from the cop, Schmidt, the uniform from Los Campos; and one from Andre.

"It was ninety degrees today, but I ran anyway. I saw a pelican," Renata said. "They are wild, amazing creatures."

Nick went into the bathroom and washed his face. Smelled traces of her, her shampoo and perfume. He was pleased to be alone and figured that was a sign of something serious, that he'd be annoyed if Renata had told him she had plans to come home soon. He could just see her coming through the door, carrying a pizza or a bag of Chinese and a couple of videos. It would be a pain in the ass if that happened. It was stupid, really, when you thought about it, it was dumb to live with someone you didn't love. Loneliness was what did it. But he wasn't lonely, he was his own best company, always had been. Maybe Renata would find a job in Florida, at a private school, work with little blond kids, kids she could deal with. Nick went back into the bedroom, sat on the edge of the bed and took off his shoes. He leaned over and played back Schmidt's message.

"The DOA Punto, the screwball, he figured that this guy Cienfuego was humping his old lady. Cienfuego's the one Punto threatened. Listen, I don't know if this means anything, but the people out here, the people on my post, they say your guy Cienfuego is a real numbnuts. A country guy, you know what I mean? No criminal, nothing like that. But what the hell do they know? See you around."

Nick wondered what the people in Diego's neighborhood meant when they said numbnuts. But for some reason he wasn't surprised.

He hit the machine again. "Nick, listen," Andre's voice said, "call me when you get a chance." A long pause. "Lay your head down in peace, friend. You killed someone who needed killing, it was out of your control. You did what you had to do. I know you, know how you think. You had absolutely no choice. And listen, the feds got statements from both Matos and Medina. They laid the killings on Cienfuego, said they'd testify if need be. Goddamn cold son of a bitch, this Cienfuego. If you need me, need to talk, call me."

Fucked, Diego, Nick thought. You're history.

Nick didn't think about the shooting until later, in bed. Thinking, you get hit with double-0 buck and your fedora doesn't come off. Picture that. The bum killed two cops, he wasn't about to have nightmares over a hump like that.

Right before he fell through the surface of sleep, Nick tried to imagine what it would be like to live like Sonny and Eddie Moran, and couldn't. He began to think about Renata, found it disturbing, stopped. Lying there, his thoughts were of a small dark-haired girl, standing panic-stricken in a packed courtroom, staring at him, her terrible black eyes pushing a knife into him. He did not like to think about a child's anger. That in a matter of seconds, someone out there in the world, albeit a child, had decided to despise him. Nick did not like to think about that. Or his own guilt. He did not like to think of a child as an adversary. It was unnatural. It was the way Sonny McCabe saw the world. He imagined the feds taking statements from Medina and Matos, romancing them, turning them. He pictured Andre standing there, enjoying it, enjoying having his case so tidy, so neatly drawn together. Then the crew of them, laughing together afterward, the way snitches do, joking about it, walking around Andre's office, looking at the pictures on the wall, all of them together, good buddies now, like a family. It was ridiculous, it was a joke, was what it was.

Asleep—at least he thought he was asleep—Nick thought of Andre, of alphabetized books, tapes, and records and said to himself you know the man ten years and it never occurred to you. Some detective you are, a regular Sherlock.

Three days into his stay on Rikers Island, Diego lay in his underwear in the stillness of his cell. Three nights running he had been unable to find sleep. From the bunk across from him came the sound of Felix snoring peacefully. The cellblock was unusually quiet. Diego stared at the bars and thought of the two Puerto Rican cousins he had spoken to during the day. Diego decided that Puerto Ricans made the best Americans, though they didn't make very good Puerto Ricans. It seemed to him that most of the Puerto Ricans he spoke to thought of Puerto Rico as the end of something, and New York, America, as the beginning. As for himself, Diego thought of New York City as a cage with wild animals in it; the cage door was locked and he was inside. He considered that this was the way Jews must view the entire world.

Twisting beneath his sheet, Diego thought about what Felix described as the ladder of American prisoners. The bottom rung, Felix explained, is reserved for the child molester. A baby-fucker, Felix called him. It seemed to Diego that such a person would hold the lowest rung anywhere in the world. A step up is the rapist, then the petty thief and junkie, who is just below the drug dealer. Above the drug dealer is the murderer, above him the armed robber, near the top is the cop killer, and at the very top, the uppermost and final rung, king of all American inmates, the Mafia chief. He had heard Felix say that there was an important Mafia man in their block. In fact, their cellblock contained only those people who occupied the top rungs of the ladder. Diego was surrounded by men whose business was crime. And Felix was excited by all of it.

Because of the seriousness of their crimes, the seventy-five or eighty prisoners in B block were separated from the general population of the jail. B block was maximum security. All were awaiting the final outcome of their court cases, everyone held on bail in excess of one hundred thousand dollars, or like Diego, no bail at all. No one was allowed to leave the block, so there was no work, nothing to do but eat, sleep, masturbate, and watch TV.

The first day other prisoners didn't exist. Faces were like dark shadows floating before Diego's eyes; voices came out of nowhere. By the second and now the third night, he had reached a certain equilibrium. But not a minute had passed during the past days and nights that he did not think of poor Justo. And now all Diego knew was that he was alone, and his life was being taken from him; there was no happiness in sight, he was caught in a storm, a whirlwind of pain. This was the end. When he thought of the future all he could see was grief.

His first day at Rikers, he had gathered himself together enough to telephone his children. He found no one at home, and panicked, he telephoned his landlady. Diego, she told him, you had better get yourself a reliable lawyer quick. The police were here searching for Maria-clara and Miguel. Ingrid had told him that she refused to believe he was as bad as they had said on the television. Then she gave him a message, a phone number, he must telephone Natalia Punto.

Mío, the children are with me, Natalia had said. They are sleeping, they lay together on the bed holding each other tight. I will take care of them, don't worry about your children, think of yourself.

Diego sat up. He slid his legs over the side of the bunk and dropped his head into his hands. I will care for your Justo, Natalia had told him. Your son and my Rodrigo, they will be well taken care of. Rodrigo had money, plenty of money, Natalia explained, and she had taken some of that money, five thousand dollars, and had brought it in a paper bag to a lawyer by the name of Weisner.

Weisner will come to see you, she told him. Weisner promised he would come as soon as possible, so expect him. And then she asked him if he knew how her husband had died. Diego remembered that Felix had warned him the prison guards played many tricks, and one of the tricks they played was to listen in on telephone calls. He told Natalia that her husband was a brave man, more brave than he could ever be. You may not believe this, she told him, but I liked him. In the end I liked him too, Diego told her. We have the children to worry about, Diego. She said I pledge to you that I will care for them as if they were my own.

Diego had thanked her. He remembered that he had stopped breathing for a moment, and then he had whispered, "Natalia, please promise you will not let them forget me."

"Forget you, Diego? Your children and I will never forget you, be sure of that."

"I love you, Natalia," he had said, and at that moment he did, he loved Natalia more than he had loved any woman, ever.

"Diego," Natalia had said finally, "when you look at the black and gray walls around you, think of the flower-covered walls in our Cuba. Think of your children, think of me. Be strong, Diego. Be strong."

Felix walked into the cell carrying a sandwich. It was around ten o'clock in the morning. Chino Vasserman and another of the Bronx crew, a black man nicknamed Cubano, were watching in the corridor. Felix offered Diego some of the sandwich.

"I'm not hungry," Diego said. "I'm not feeling too well."

Felix said, "You have to eat. You didn't come to breakfast, we were waiting for you."

Diego bent his head and looked Felix in the eye. "What's going on?" he said.

Felix glanced down at the coins in Diego's hand. "You going to make a call?" he said.

"Yes."

"That's okay. But you need to talk to Manny and Chino. You're not being stupid, I told them. Just trying to find out how you can get out of here. It's natural. You just don't want to do something without talking to them first. Right?"

Diego's anger made him speak without thinking. "If it wasn't for these people, I wouldn't be here," Diego said. He glanced at Chino, who looked as though he were about to smile. "I'll talk to them later," Diego said, "right now I'm not feeling well."

"No," Chino said. "Now, bring him now."

"Just come on," Felix said. "They need to talk to you a minute, just a minute."

Diego shrugged his shoulders with an exasperated smile. "Well, okay, yes, I will talk to them."

"Manny is in the TV room, come with me, I'll bring you there."

"All right, all right."

"Look, we don't all stick together, we could have problems in here. Manny takes care of you, right?"

"I guess you are right." Calm now, resigned. Having said that much Diego glanced uneasily at Chino. There was a wide smile on the man's face.

The corridor to the TV room was dark and narrow and lined with men standing outside their cells. They watched Diego and Felix as they went by, their voices dropping. Diego heard sniffing sounds. The corridor walls were decorated with graffiti. Through a door on his right as he passed, Diego saw the corrections officer, Tommy Carbone, sitting in a chair behind a desk. His hair was neatly trimmed, expensively cared for; he looked as if he had just stepped off a Hollywood set. Tommy sat talking to a black inmate with a shaved head and a large gold earring, a tattoo of a small red bird on the back of his neck. Tommy, Felix had told him, ran coke and heroin into the jail. No marijuana, the smell of marijuana was too strong to hide. Tommy was organized crime, you want to see organized crime, forget those wops out in the street and take a good look at Tommy. The black man was listening intently as Tommy talked, Tommy saying something like, "You'll be here till the trial. Don't feel so bad, anybody can get themselves into trouble."

Diego walked down the corridor and through a passageway to a door with TV on it.

"Oye, Professor," Mambo Vasserman said, standing in front of the TV, arms folded, watching a cowboy movie, wearing new denim jeans and a red T-shirt, and a very nice pair of sneakers, high-tops. Manny had huge, thick powerful arms, Diego had not forgotten how powerful they were. With a flick of his hand, Manny waved Diego over.

Manny had been drinking alcohol, rum, by the odor. The smell put Diego in mind of Los Campos's basement, and his heart froze. Diego felt his knees tremble, he felt as though he were underwater and couldn't breathe. Someone turned the sound of the TV up, and Diego turned to look at it.

Manny watched him in silence for a moment.

"Professor," Manny said, "we are your friends here, and you want to betray us."

"I don't understand," Diego said. "What are you talking about?"

"You. You don't recognize your friends. Christ, man, you are going to call the cops. Fuck, man, what's that, calling cops on your friends?"

"No, no. I'm getting a lawyer. A lawyer is coming to see me."

"You told Felix you were going to call the cops. Felix don't lie."

"I don't lie," Felix said.

Diego was only half-listening, he looked around the room and saw several people he had not seen before.

When it happened, it happened fast.

Manny smiled, then hit him with a straight-armed right. In a second, Felix and Chino Vasserman had pinned him facedown on the floor. Manny put his knee into Diego's back and held him down, yanked his arms behind him. There were men around him, some already heading for the door, some standing there, staying to watch, they offered mainly advice. Cubano walked over to him, dropped into a squat. He grabbed Diego's hair with strong hands, and despite Diego's resistance, Cubano slowly pulled his head back, exposing his throat.

Twisting his head, Diego tried to struggle and was beaten and kicked. He heard his ribs crack. He tried to turn his head, tried to look around, as if being able to see would make some sort of difference.

Manny was humming now. A pleasant sound. Diego attempted to kick, to bite. His arms were pulled back with even greater force, and he heard another crack, felt something split. He was feeling sick from not being able to breathe. He grunted and a little stream of spittle ran down his chin; he took deep, snoring breaths.

From the corner of his eye he caught the gleam of a razor.

"Diego is an honorable man," Diego got out in a strangled voice. He couldn't think of anything else to say.

It did not stop Manny Vasserman. He cut Diego swiftly, his face, his throat. This done, Manny rose and demonstrated for the watching crowd a kind of macho dance step, the group laughing, Manny moving around the room with slow steps, hunched over, groaning all the while with the pleasure of it.

"Oh God," Diego cried. A bubble of blood broke over his lips. He could taste and smell it. You don't have to take it anymore, he thought. Let it be.

Exasperated, Chino Vasserman, Manny's brother, stepped back to escape the spreading pool of blood.

Nick sat in a windowless room at the Queens County courthouse, staring at the picture of Diego Cienfuego on the front page of the New York *Post*.

"Do we have any idea at all who killed him?" he said to Sonny McCabe.

Sonny shrugged. "Bronx homicide caught this, right? That means they'll stamp it in a week or so. Christ, with all the cases they carry, they'll never get to this. Lay it off on corrections probably. Unbeliev-able.

"Bingo, Cienfuego catches a dirt nap, and we close most of the holes in our case. Perfect." Sonny was reading Kurtz's final draft of his book proposal.

"Two for two. You and the feds, both happy that Cienfuego caught it," Nick said. "The feds won't have to bring Medina and Matos in to testify, and we can run a plea bargain past the rest of them." Nick dropped the newspaper onto the desk. "I wonder who killed the poor guy."

Sonny rubbed his palms together and turned a page. "Poor guy? Poor guy my ass. Give me a break. Anyway, the plea bargain is up to your buddy, Robinson. Probably give them a plea to the gun possession. I don't know. It's not our problem."

"So that's it then." The phone rang and Nick took it. "Hello, DA's office."

"Nick, I have Kenney and Cosgrove from Washington in my office," Andre said. "They would like to speak to you and Sonny."

"We're here."

"And, ah, the informant's wife, Natalia Punto, she's in the reception room. Wants to speak to me."

"No kidding."

"She has two children with her."

"Jesus." Nick snapped his fingers, trying to get Sonny's attention.

"They're on their way, Kenney and Cosgrove. Be nice, Nick, these are good guys."

"Of course."

"What?" Sonny said. "What?"

There was silence on the line for a moment, then Andre said, "Do you have any idea why Natalia Punto is here?"

"No, I don't. Maybe Sonny does. Hold on a minute. Rodrigo's wife is in the reception room. She wants to see Andre."

"About what?"

"I'm asking you."

"The hell do I know?"

"Sonny has no idea why she would be here," Nick said into the phone.

"Well, I don't want to see her," Andre said. "What can I say to the woman?"

"Hey Andre, I think those kids, there's two of them, right, a boy and a girl?"

"That's right."

"I think they're Cienfuego's. Cienfuego's children."

"That being the case, I certainly don't think I should see her."

"What'll you do?"

"I've already sent word that I'm busy. She didn't make an appointment. I'll have my secretary tell her to come back with a lawyer. I won't speak to her without a lawyer present."

"The agents are here," Nick said.

"All right. Give me a call when you free up."

The two federal agents entered the room. Sonny did not even look up from his reading and Nick could not resist a smile. "Nick Manaris," he said, "and this is Sonny McCabe. How's the government today?"

The agent they had run into in the courthouse garage appeared to recoil when Nick offered him his hand.

Nick had a full-blown flashback of the conversation he'd had with the agent, what was it, a week ago? Feeling a momentary buzz, half anger, half shame.

"Bill Kenney," the agent said.

"Jim Cosgrove," said the other.

Nick turned to Sonny. "We should thank these two men," he said, trying to ease the tension. "They've taken all the weight in this case."

"You thank them," Sonny said.

The two agents were both what you'd expect, well dressed and in good shape. Standard-issue feds.

"Thanks to you two," Nick said, "it doesn't look as though we'll go to trial. Give everybody a plea, let's make a deal, pick the right door and you're a winner."

Nick fully intended it to be all in good humor, but not only did it fall flat, it inspired a look of total disgust from Sonny McCabe.

They shook hands. Agent Cosgrove was an older guy, mid-forties, not DEA but FBI, working a joint task force with the drug people out of Washington. Nick thinking, a natural, looks like an accountant, a banker. No dummy. Good suit, always right, been around a while. Could be one of those Mormons the Bureau recruited from Brigham Young in the sixties. A hardened, experienced man with nothing unresolved. His partner, ten, fifteen years younger, hair a little longish, cowboy boots, looked like he just stepped out of the University of Texas, he stood ramrod straight throughout the introductions, thin guy with his college ring, very white. Agent Kenney, DEA.

Sonny standing now, facing the agents across the desk, with the book proposal in his hand. "So tell me, Kenney, ever figure out who slashed your tires?" A courteous tone.

"McCabe, maybe you guys thought that was a funny move. I didn't see the humor in it. Then again, I'm not from New York, when it comes to humor I'm a little slow on the uptake."

Agent Cosgrove moved in front of Kenney, as if to shield him from assault. "Bill," he said, "our tires were slashed by some New York City street slug. It wasn't police officers, it couldn't be."

Kenney shrugged. "I have no sense of humor, always been my problem."

Sonny saying now, "Hell, you got a sense of humor, you made those lying, killing little weasels, Cano Medina and Benny Matos, your guys. I think that's fucking hysterical."

Nick said, "I have an idea. Listen to this. Why don't we start over and try to be friendly? How's that sound?"

"We got no beef with you," Cosgrove said. "Look, we came here to explain what it is that we're doing. At least tell you as much as we can. You understand. There are things, you know, confidential. Whatever the hell that means. Anyway, we're not obligated to do that. We don't have to tell you guys anything. But I think it's the right thing to do."

Sonny muttered something. He sat down and went back to his reading.

Nick nodded sympathetically and kept his mouth shut.

The agents got comfortable, pulled up a couple of chairs and sat. Cosgrove said this was the kind of case, another example, it wasn't Mafia, La Cosa Nostra moving hundreds of guns, it was South Americans, specifically Colombians. "And it turns out Medina and Matos have been doing business with them for years."

"Excuse me?" Sonny said deliberately, still not looking up. "Are you guys going to tell us something we don't know?"

"What do you know about a city called Medellin?" Cosgrove said.

"I have to think it's in South America," Sonny said. "A little out of my jurisdiction."

Cosgrove exhaled heavily, then spoke in a precise manner. "You're right, Sonny, these people from Medellin are way out of your jurisdiction. At least for the time being they are. Okay, look, I know you're annoyed, and I know you're thinking, I collar a bunch of real shits with guns, the feds step in and scoop a couple of them up. Bad guys cut a deal, they give up a little, this and that, then walk away. Only that's just not the way it works, so now listen to me. You people, you and Nick and the others, you people did one hell of a job. For my money, it's you local guys who really put it out there every day."

Sonny was sitting hunched over, reading his book proposal, but Nick could tell he was listening.

"Nevertheless, let me tell you, it's 1979; we don't come down on these characters, in ten years, maybe less, they will become a scourge in our country, far more powerful and far more deadly then all your Mafia families put together, times ten."

Sonny said, "A bunch of Indians from the Amazon?"

"Excuse me," Agent Kenney said, "these people are not Indians."

Cosgrove saying now, "Matos and Medina were dealing with people who control a massive, highly disciplined organization. They are an intelligent, ruthless, cold-blooded crew that can deliver tons—and I mean tons—of cocaine, and enough weaponry to outfit an army."

Nick asked, "What about the Cubans?"

"They're in and out, active in South Florida. Pikers compared to the Colombians," Kenney said.

"Diego Cienfuego? What did you have on him?"

Sonny said, "The fucker just came up from Miami, you can bet he was busy there." He glanced quickly at Nick and then went back to his reading. "Cubans, Colombians, the same fucking tribe."

Cosgrove laughed and shook his head. "No, Sonny, they're not. I saw in the paper, somebody whacked the guy, huh?"

"Uh-huh," Nick said. "Cut his throat, the poor bastard."

"We don't have anything on him," Cosgrove said. "Medina tells us Cienfuego killed two guys at Los Campos, and I believe him. As far as Cienfuego being connected, I never heard of the man. What about you, Bill, ever hear of the guy? Bill's been working Miami for the past five years."

"I never came across him. That don't mean anything, the smart ones pop up out of nowhere."

"Bet your ass that don't mean anything," Sonny said. "This bum was an important man, heavily involved up here."

Nick listened to the feds, fascinated. He thought of clarifying one point; Medina lays the killings on Cienfuego, says he was the boss, the main guy, that he killed the snitch. Matos and Medina admit to being in business for years. But Cienfuego had been in the country less than six months, and in the city for only three. How could he have been the main player here? But Cosgrove kept talking, and when Nick thought about it again, he decided why bother?

"Well anyway," Cosgrove said, "I want to say that you people did one hell of a job. Congratulations. I think that Medina and Matos are going to turn some major things for us, and if not for you guys, it never would have happened."

"You know, you're right," Sonny said. "What our job needs is more genius detectives with a little humility, there are so few of us left."

Agent Kenney said, "There you go." He laughed, reached out and patted Sonny's shoulder.

"Let me ask you something," Nick said. "Say you finish up with Matos and Medina, they give you this and that, testify, whatever. What then? Witness Protection, is that what you do?"

Kenney said, "Oh yeah, this is 1979, a new era. We treat them like they're heroes, change their names and send them to Alaska. Maybe buy them a big house."

"No shit. New name, clean their records, new social security cards?" Nick said.

"Uh-huh," Sonny said, smiling, his eyes almost shut, "probably give them a private White House tour."

"These two, this Benny and Cano, they can deliver, big time," Cosgrove said. "They'll earn their protection."

Nick was feeling pretty miserable, his mind telling him, what a bunch of shit. He said, "Seven people died the other day, another yesterday. That's eight."

No one said anything.

"Two police officers killed, and are we going to nail anyone real bad here? I don't think so," he told them. "Nah, only the few street humps we got at Rikers. Certainly none of the major players."

Kenney said, "We're only starting. There is more to do."

Nick reminded himself that it was great to be so young and full of illusions. He said, "I can't believe it, all those guns, eight people dead, and nobody is going to do any real time."

They were silent, looking at each other, maybe all of them with the same thoughts, Nick wasn't sure. Sonny said, "What did I tell you the other night, huh? It's all bullshit, it's all a fucking game."

"We don't see it that way," Cosgrove said.

There was a long silence before Nick said to him, "He has a point."

"Yeah, well if he does, I don't see it," Cosgrove said.

"Put yourselves in our position. We're cops. We deal with this shit every day. You guys been playing this game for years, and when we look up at the scoreboard, we see the bad guys a hundred, the government zero."

Cosgrove looked distressed, and Nick felt a twinge of compassion. The agent said, "C'mon, we do what we can."

"Hey look, first it was the Italians, the Mafia, drowning us in junk," Nick said. "Then the blacks pouring that shit into their own neighborhoods. Then the Cubans. Now you tell me the Colombians are coming, look out you say, the fuckers are climbing over the wall. Well maybe you should make the wall higher, go over to Colombia or wherever and drop a net on these bastards before they get here. Because in the end, we're the ones, us, the cops, that are going to have to deal with them hand to hand. See, then I have to ask myself why, why can't my government, who can put people on the moon, why can't they come down on these foreign governments that are killing our kids? And I have to think they got another agenda, the government don't care. Well, they care, but not really. I have to think—"

"Hey Sonny," Kenney said, "your partner here can get real heavy, can't he?"

"Tell me about it," Sonny said.

"Maybe he should write a book, huh?" Kenney said.

"Nah, who would buy it? You want to read a book, read mine," Sonny said.

"What?" said Kenney.

"The book, when I write it, you go out and buy it, tell your friends to buy one."

"Hell yeah."

"I'll remember you said that."

Nick smiled and shook his head. "Sonny . . ."

About a half hour later, soon after the two feds left the office, Andre came by.

"Listen, that woman with the kids, she is still in the reception room. What the hell does she want?"

Sonny went to the office door, took a look down the corridor. He said, "Does she make you nervous?"

Andre said, "Her screaming does. Jesus, can't you hear her?"

"I don't hear anything," Sonny said, "wait, what the hell?" and stepped into the hallway. "Hey Nick, Nick, c'mere, will ya."

The security guard was in a red-faced shouting match with Punto's wife, both of them waving their arms and bellowing as assistant DAs closed their office doors, afraid to get drawn in.

The guard was scared because he had worked here ten years after retiring from the air force and he'd seen this before, a Puerto Rican fit, they called it, something like an epileptic attack. Foam coming from the mouth, eyes spinning, snorting like a bull. Self-induced, a cop had told him, these people can bring these attacks on themselves. Only this was no attack, no spinning eyes, no foamy mouth, and this woman wasn't Puerto Rican, she was Cuban, and she was pissed.

Nick, Andre, and Sonny stood in the hallway, off to the side, watching the show through the reception window. The assistant DAs' offices were cut off from the reception room by a locked, buzzer-controlled, frosted glass door, and Natalia Punto was dancing back and forth in front of it, shouting at the security guard and the receptionist. "I'm not mad at you!" she screamed. "I don't care about you, those son-of-bitch people inside have me waiting here for two hours!"

The security guard didn't know whether to be insulted or grateful. The guard, who was built like an overstuffed chair, would take these sneaky, hesitant steps toward her. He'd get too close and whoosh! the woman's handbag would pass about a foot from his head.

The leather couch in the reception room was occupied by the two children Nick had seen in court. Above them was a mural of the Brooklyn Bridge that ran the length of the wall. Both children were neatly dressed in matching navy blue outfits, clean. Nick thought they looked like an advertisement for a trip to Spain, quietly sitting there, staring at the carpet, holding hands. Real good-looking kids. Especially the girl, embarrassingly pretty with reddish-brown skin and large, soft, light jade eyes.

"Stay away from me," Natalia shouted. "I want to talk to Mr. District Attorney Robinson, and I no leave until I do."

"Lady," the security guard said, "talk to me calmly."

"I will talk to you, I will tell you the name of the man that your wife makes a bed for, you fat bastard."

"Sonny," Nick said, "didn't Eddie say that Punto's wife had trouble with English?"

"Uh-huh, yeah, that's what he said. I gotta tell him this woman speaks better than he does. Which, by the way, is not saying a whole lot."

"I don't plan on standing here, a prisoner in my own hallway, while this woman carries on," Andre said. "Let's go and talk to her. Get it over with."

The little girl's eyes widened as she saw the three men come through the door. She pointed with one hand and then the other. "He had my papi," she said, "that one."

"I'm Assistant District Attorney Robinson. Can I help you?" Andre said, which of course, did it.

Natalia screamed, "Help me? Help me?" She was heaving with outrage.

"Calm down, lady, calm down," Sonny said.

But Natalia was in no mood to listen. She looked at Nick and Sonny, turned to Andre, her face contorted with pain, shouting, "You know where I am taking these two children?"

Nick turned his head slowly, tentatively, to take a look at the children. He tried to force himself not to grin. For as long as he could remember, whenever he had been anxious, really anxious, which was not too often, Nick Manaris grinned. He tried to control it, he tried real hard but couldn't help himself. He glanced at the children, then gave a short tug on Sonny's jacket.

"Jeeze," Sonny said. "How old you figure she is?"

"Ten, twelve, about that." It was the eyes, Nick thought, a bruised look to the eyes, liked she'd been crying for days. The girl sitting there sizing him up, sizing them all up like she's, what . . . appraising them? And the brother, they looked like twins, same hair, same eyes and skin, long narrow noses, but Nick did not think they were twins, the girl seemed older by maybe a couple years.

Sonny said, "Jeeze, the last time a woman looked at me that way, it was my ex-wife. She was thirty, and she was Italian. I thought only nutty wop broads stared at you like that."

Natalia said, "I am taking these two children to a funeral parlor. To a house of the dead, so they can see for the last time their father and their brother."

"Please, Mrs. Punto," Andre said. "Calm down."

"I am calm. Do you want to see what it's like when I get mad?"

"No thank you."

"I have a question for you, Mr. District Attorney Robinson."

Andre closed his eyes and nodded. "Okay."

Natalia Punto exhaled, and when she spoke she spoke very softly. "Why," she said, "deader than dead . . . ?"

"Please, Mrs. Punto, please," Andre said.

Natalia began to breathe quickly and audibly, as if she was about to hyperventilate, saying, "Yes Mr. DA, yes." Her eyes opened quite wide. "My God tells me that the people you love do not die as long as they are remembered. I have a long memory, Mr. DA, a very long memory. I want you to know that. I want you all to know that."

"Guard," Andre said, "I think Mrs. Punto is finished here now. Show her and these two children to the elevator."

Mariaclara and Miguel got up off the sofa and stood behind Natalia. Natalia backed up as if the guard was planning to grab her, maybe grab the kids, which he wasn't. He approached her, hands extended, meaning only to guide her to the door. But Natalia was not one to trust a man in uniform.

The girl looked uncomprehendingly at Nick from behind Natalia, as if searching his face for some clue to something, anything at all. Suddenly Nick felt cut off from all the rest, as they were cut off from each other. He watched as Natalia Punto continued backing up, her arms stretched out to shield the children behind her. So long as she kept moving she would be all right, he thought.

Natalia stopped.

The guard said, "C'mon, lady, enough of this bullshit, take your children and leave."

"You are the one that is bullshit," Natalia told him.

Glancing at Nick, she nodded politely, then looked carefully again at the security guard. "You should be ashamed," she said.

The guard kept moving toward her.

Natalia said, "How would you like me to kick you in the balls?"

The guard stood still.

She grinned fiercely, her eyes moving from one face to the next. "We are leaving," she said, "we are going."

The guard started to say something; he faltered and stopped short.

A hell of a woman, Nick thought. For a fleeting second he was overwhelmed with sorrow for Diego, and Rodrigo too. They both loved this woman; he could see why.

Nick cleared his throat. "Natalia," he said. "Your name is Natalia, right?"

She gazed directly into his face. "*Sí, claro*," she said.

"You think we are your enemies here, but we are not," Nick said.

"Why do you care what I think?"

"I do, I do care what you think."

Sonny said, "Take his word for it, he cares."

"You, Detective McCabe," she said, "I don't talk to you, I don't look at you. I am talking to detective ugly nose."

"Forget it," Sonny said. He laughed softly, steadily. "Fuckin' beautiful," he said.

"You can hope that I forget. You believe in God, you can pray that I forget. But I never forget, we never forget that you murdered our Justo."

"Whoooooooo," Sonny said, "you scare me."

Natalia began to speak, then stopped and shook her head.

Andre said, "You should leave, Mrs. Punto. Consider the children."

"Yes, Mr. District Attorney, I will leave. But before I do, I want to give you something." When Andre only shrugged, Natalia said, "I have something for you."

Natalia opened her shoulder bag and took out a red-jacketed book. She handed it to Andre.

"What is this?" Andre said.

"Rodrigo's book."

Sonny said, "This is beautiful. Rodrigo was writing a book."

"All right," Andre told her. "If it makes you happy, if you'll leave I'll take it," he said, "I guess I can take your book."

Nick was watching Diego's daughter. Her hair was pulled tight behind her ears, she wore tiny golden earrings; when Natalia turned to walk out the door, the girl looked at Sonny. But Sonny paid no attention to her. Sonny was smiling triumphantly at Natalia Punto's back. When the girl caught Nick looking at her, she glared and stuck her tongue out very slowly.

In the months that followed, Nick found that thoughts of Diego, of Diego's children, and Natalia Punto kept coming back to him. He had to be careful, he was thinking of them too often, blurred pictures that jerked in and out of his head. He worked at it, worked at forgetting, and in time they became just one more cop story, one more thing that had happened to him on the job.

Chapter 27

After the election, when Andre Robinson took office as the chief prosecutor of Queens County, he went through some old cases and some new ones. He'd read the investigators' reports, drift off in confusion, and say shit. A number of big cases that should have been made were blown, early or late or halfway through. He found himself thinking that with the right telephone call two of New York's best detectives could be transferred from the Organized Crime Control Unit and assigned to his office. Of course it would entail some future debt, favors would eventually have to be repaid. He could live with that; Andre was skillful at that brand of politics.

Andre arranged lunch at Forlini's with the deputy mayor for criminal justice, a man named Schwartz. A tireless cigarette smoker and coffee drinker, he'd had a long and close relationship with the current mayor. Before picking up the tab, Andre gave Schwartz a piece of paper with two names on it. The following day the deputy mayor spoke to the mayor, the mayor telephoned the police commissioner, the police commissioner called the chief of personnel, and bingo, Nick and Sonny were transferred to the Queens County district attorney's office.

The transfer orders came through department Teletype on a Tuesday morning. Inspector Riordan, the CO of the OCCU, telephoned Nick with the news.

Excited and nervous like a pair of rookies, they arrived at the courthouse on Wednesday. Andre introduced them around and had his secretary help them fill out the necessary forms. Andre then directed Leo Turner, his squad commander, to show them the Kennedy Airport hijacking case.

Close the case out, Leo Turner told them, it's a dead issue, finis, done. Andre wasn't so sure; he asked Nick to read the case folder. Nick took the folder and sat himself at a desk and read it. Three wiretaps, one on a bodybuilder, an enforcer, a guy named Mario Mauro from Astoria; the second on Vincent "Kid Vinny" Calisi, a stickup man out of Howard Beach. And the third, the most important, on Little Anthony Rufino. Rufino had been an East Harlem street guy, a loan shark's collector. He was a mad hatter who prowled the streets with a baseball bat, rounding up late payments. Here was a hump who'd spent most of his life in a cold-water flat, an enraged man who found relief in violence. Little Anthony Rufino, information had it, had been inducted into the Bucci crime family, and after that he killed people on order. At the moment he was a man of some means, living in the trendy town of Roslyn, out on Long Island. He had his own loan-shark book and ran hookers out of a couple of West Side joints, and Little Anthony was the prime suspect in a half dozen murders.

After about five minutes of going through transcripts and detectives' observations, it looked to Nick like an eighteen-month hijacking investigation had started out hot and came up short.

The DA's investigators had given the case a good shot, twelve detectives going round the clock. But halfway through, they blew it by jumping too early and collaring Kid Vinny's brother with a Luger in his pocket and his ass in a stolen car. The remaining subjects panicked, and the following day the wires went dead. Two of the three targets fled the jurisdiction for parts unknown. There was nothing left to do but to have Rufino, the subject of the last wiretap, sign off on the notification, it being a state law that the subscriber of a telephone must be notified within ninety days of the tap being pulled.

Holding the case folder that first day, Andre had grinned, saying, "Maybe if we had you two stars working these hijackers, we'd have made this case. Anyway, the investigators earned a vacation, there's no one around to deliver the notification. Why don't you two do it?"

It's all in a day's work, Nick thought, saying, "Partner, we got our first job." Sonny had gazed briefly at Andre, a gaze that made Nick smile, a gaze that said Sonny was personally affronted. Sonny saying, "Excuse me, but I'm a detective first grade. I don't deliver messages."

Andre pointed to a chair in front of the desk Nick was sitting at, as if standing, Sonny made him uneasy.

Sonny remained on his feet, hands in his pockets.

Andre said, "Listen, I am very serious, maybe you can do something with this."

"One hell of a case," Nick observed, looking through the notes, reading some of the telephone transcripts, truly impressed; he slid forward in his chair to read on.

"Whoa! Whoa! Will you look at this," Nick said. There was conversation in the transcripts between Rufino's wife, Ann Marie, and a guy named Paulie. Andre saying the wife? Nick said the woman had a death wish, making it with one of Rufino's own people.

Andre nodded his head. "People could say that. And this Rufino is a shrewd piece of work, read it, you can see he suspects her. Look at her picture. Ann Marie was a *Penthouse* star, she stops traffic. Look at the one in shorts, she's standing in front of the house. The investigator told me that passing cars would actually stop. And the boyfriend, Paulie, he's Little Anthony's driver."

"Let me see," Sonny said, "let me see that."

Nick handed Sonny the file. Sonny read for a while, then smiled broadly. "Fuck me," he said, "you're right, these two are walking on the cheating side of town, man are they looking for trouble. Christ!" Sonny said, judicious. "Little Anthony is a moron, but he ain't stupid. These two people are insane."

Nick said, "We'll take a ride over to his house, ask him to sign the release."

Andre nodded. "Do it, give you something to do today."

"Man!" Sonny said. "Did you read this? I mean these two get to it, don't they? I'm getting a hard-on just reading this stuff."

Nick took note of the playful look in Sonny's eyes and smiled.

Andre said, "If the rest of that crew had gabbed like the two lovers, we would have had something. But they were cool, talked in codes, talked fast, dialect Italian. Then they stopped talking all together."

Nick was curious and asked if they had put Rufino into anything else, something other than hijacking. Andre told him that Little Anthony was using Kennedy Airport like it was his private shopping center. The guy was a wiseguy, a made man in the Bucci family, he'd do anything to turn a dollar.

"I tell you what I think," Nick said. "I think it's worth taking the shot. We go and talk to this guy, lay the feds on him, see what he says."

"Precisely," said Andre.

"Man!" Sonny said, still reading.

"Do you have any idea how much these characters were lifting from the airport?" Andre said.

Nick grinned. "As a matter of fact I do. I worked a case there about a year ago."

"Nuts, these people are absolutely nuts," Sonny said. "Anthony Rufino would cut this guy Paulie's balls off and stick 'em in his ear. And that would be for starters. C'mon, let's go and see Little Anthony. I'm dying to get a look at this woman in person," he said to Nick. When Nick was silent, he continued, "Me and Eddie worked Rufino when we were in Public Morals, he owned some massage parlors, screw shops over on the West Side." He waved his arm. "C'mon partner, this could be interesting."

"I'm ready," Nick said.

"Be very careful," Andre said. "Don't give up anything. Tell him simply that his phone was tapped for sixty days. Tell him that, and point out that the feds are interested in him. Keep in mind that what other people said on his phone, he is not privileged to."

Sonny was listening to Andre, his face expressionless. Then he said, "From her picture, Ann Marie Rufino is one of the best-looking women I have ever seen. From reading the transcripts, I know for sure she is one of the dumbest."

Andre nodded, looking carefully at Sonny. "Rufino is no fool, watch what you say."

"I was just thinking," Sonny said, "Rufino knows what he said, what was said to him. He took more than a few shots at some pretty bad and important people here. Said some shit he wouldn't want anyone to hear."

Andre kept on nodding. "Right," he said. "That's true."

In the cruiser they discussed it further. They were both irritable, Sonny because Eddie Moran was not interested in joining them on the DA's squad, and wouldn't Eddie be a big help on a job like this one. Moran knew Rufino, knew the guy well, had busted him when they were in Public Morals. And Eddie knew how to talk to these wop bad guys. Knew just what to say to get their engines going. And Nick was irritable because he did not want to talk or think at all.

"Nick," Sonny said, "I can't believe how stupid this guy Paulie is. You know, put your life on the line for a piece of ass." He sat back in the passenger seat and stretched. "And the wife, what can she be thinking? Can you imagine someone so hot to trot? They both have to be loony, right?"

Nick was silent.

"Goddamn Little Anthony Rufino," Sonny said. "Like shame on him, can't keep his shit together." After a while he said, "Listen, Nick, if you don't mind, when we get there, let me do the talking."

"Um."

"I know the guy, let me speak to him."

"Sure."

"Between me and you, this guy, this Little Anthony was on with PMAD, Nick, he was paying everybody. Not that he ever put money directly in my hands. I'd never let him do that, not a scumbag like him. But I worked there, and people came to me. I did what I had to do, I did what everyone did that worked there. Rufino was just another lowlife running a whorehouse and an after-hours joint. That was the old days, remember. You couldn't run a whorehouse without being on. It's not like it was unusual or anything. There were pads, PMAD had a huge one, just the way it was, ey Nick?"

Sonny opened a pack of cigarettes, took one out and lit up. "I said, it was the way it was, that was then, this is now, huh, Nick? You're not going to go off on me, get nuts about my telling you things, I hope?"

Nick was staring at the highway, moving right along in light traffic, thinking Sonny McCabe's corruption—in particular Sonny's kind of corruption, which might be described as so much a part of him that he himself recognized none of it—was about to make him nuts.

"Sonny," he said, "what you did back then is your business. I don't want to hear about it. What I care about is what you do now. Do not, I repeat, do not screw with me. Remember what I told you, I see it, I saw it, I—"

"Okay! Okay! Chill out, I hear you, I understand."

"I'll lock your ass up myself."

"You would not."

"Don't bet on it, Sonny. Don't test me."

"Ey, what did I tell you? I gave you my word, right? Didn't I say we partner up, work together, I'll do things your way? Shit, it's easier, believe me, takes the pressure off."

Nick smiled at him. "Look," he said, "it's been good these past few months. I like working with you, I like having a partner. I never met anyone who knows this job better than you. Just behave yourself."

Sonny's face flushed. "We'll do fine," he said. "Hey, did I tell ya? Kurtz got the book deal, and guess what, we had more than one offer."

"I'm happy for you, I am. I like having rich friends."

"Naw, there's no money in books. Movies, that's where the bucks are."

"So you'll make a movie."

"Bet your ass. I was born to be famous. Listen, I'm going to take a nap. Wake me when we get there."

Nick wanted to say something, but he had learned that the first rule in dealing with Sonny McCabe was not to say too much. Let him do the talking.

A couple of months back, the transmission on Nick's car went. The same day he had two court appearances, old cases from when he was in narcotics, one in Brooklyn and one in the Bronx. It was Sonny's day off, even so, Sonny picked him up at eight in the morning, telling Nick forget the subway, are you kidding? It's dangerous down there. He drove Nick to Brooklyn and stayed until Nick finished in court and then drove him to the Bronx and did not leave until Nick was through. The following day Sonny handed him his car keys, told him to use the car until Nick's was fixed, he had another car. For the first time that Nick could remember he felt as though he might have a partner. He had never met anyone in this job that did the kinds of things for him that Sonny did, and it changed Nick. Made him a bit more tolerant of Sonny. Nick had decided that he'd search for a way to bring Sonny around, make him see the right side of things. He realized that Sonny's behavior for years had been fed less by a kind of criminality than by his wacky belief that you had to go along to get along in this job. He'd show him that there were other ways. Eventually the guy would come around and see that Nick had been right all along. As for McCabe, he showed Nick what it was like to have a partner, someone in your life you can count on, and Nick liked the emotion, the feel of it. It was as though he was starting fresh, a whole new view of the job.

And what Sonny did for Nick, he did for others, many different people. He lived the words *brother cop*, when so many on the force just paid them lip service. Sonny had an eye for people that he could trust and be close to. Nick's mind strayed back over the past couple of months; he wanted to think about what McCabe had done to bring about this change, how his view of the man had been so reversed. Sonny chose his friends carefully, and once you were one, you were one forever. Sonny cared about you, he was proud of you, he was eager to tell you he would be there if you needed him. And, he had the greatest laugh, full-bodied, real, rich with the joy of being alive, of being a cop.

The way he ran the fund-raisers for Captain Hawks's and Sergi Monserette's families was the best example of Sonny's generosity. Nick had never met anyone who gave of himself the way Sonny did. On the phone four, five hours a day, getting people to show and to make a pledge. But what really altered Nick's view of the guy was his appearance before the grand jury in the Los Campos case. Everyone testified by the book, just the way it went down. Not another word to Nick from Sonny about the Cienfuego kid. As it turned out, the remaining defendants worked a plea bargain. Perfect. And now, teamed up, Nick and Sonny had been steady partners for what, four months? I can work with this guy, Nick concluded, just got to keep the reins tight.

Still, Sonny had a past, a long history, and although Nick felt that their new relationship was good, he knew that it could come apart at any time. Many years ago he had made a decision about how he would live his life, and that decision had, at times, brought him some pain. Nevertheless, he had gone too far along this road of his to change now. He drove the cruiser, glancing at Sonny, Sonny's head back against the headrest, Sonny asleep. Nick contemplated the round open face, that good-looking Irish face, so easy to read, and hoped that what he read there was true.

Nick drove the cruiser onto the Long Island Expressway and out east to Shelter Rock Road. Jumped off the highway and headed north into big money, past big homes, big, fashionable Jewish community centers. It was elegant living: large, neatly tended lawns and artistically trimmed shrubbery, Mercedeses and BMWs in the long driveways of huge, wood-frame, brick, and stucco houses with wide porches that went round and round. So close to the city, an hour at most, and no people, the neighborhood strangely quiet in the middle of the day. None of this was for Nick, he preferred the New England coast, small weathered cottages that faced the sea.

Nick parked the cruiser in front of Rufino's house, Sonny saying, "The little prick has done all right for himself."

The street was quiet, empty of people. A dog, a black Labrador, lay in the afternoon sun, tied by a rope to a tree. Music. Somewhere someone was listening to Motown.

"Boy," Sonny said, shaking his head, "look at that house and tell me crime don't pay. I bet that guinea bastard is in there, sitting at his kitchen table, counting my money." Sonny laughed. "Kidding, only kidding."

Nick smiled and shook his head; he liked to believe that he now understood what he thought of as Sonny's twisted sense of humor. They nodded at each other and headed for the front door.

There was no question in Nick's mind about what he was going to do. He would show Rufino the eavesdropping warrant, tell him his phone had been up for thirty days, the transcripts and surveillance information were about to be turned over to the feds. Explain to Little Anthony that he had two choices: talk to the DA, or deal with the feds. No big thing, his decision.

They went along a brick walk and up the steps to the front door. Opened the storm door, quickly and quietly, knocked. After a moment, Ann Marie Rufino appeared.

She was a tall woman with straight blond hair to her shoulders. Fair skin that had been sunburned, standing there in red stiletto heels and a short black jumpsuit. She smiled, said a pleasant, "Yeah, what is it?" A light voice like a kid's.

Sonny, his badge case already in his hand, said, "I'm Detective Malloy and this is Detective Manaris. We're from the Queens County district attorney's office. Is Anthony in?"

Nick had noticed her breasts while looking at her face; he wondered if they were real, thinking how could they be? Nick was looking into her eyes now, even in the shadow of the doorway he could see they were blue and clear, like the sky over Block Island on a summer morning. He felt a familiar glow and tingle, something he hadn't felt in a while, something he hadn't felt at all since he couldn't remember when. And for a moment he was overwhelmed by a burning feeling of something that had been lost. Self-consciously, he cleared his throat.

"We need to speak to your husband a moment. There's no problem, we just need to speak to him."

Ann Marie said, "I don't think he's home." She spoke softly. She turned her head to look into the house, then turned back again. "No," she whispered, "no, no, no. He went shopping."

"Then we'll wait," Sonny said.

She stepped inside, closed the door, then quickly opened it again. "Yeah, how do I know you're cops?"

Nick said, "You can check our IDs, call our office, or telephone the local police. Ask them if they want to come out here and we can all have a little chat."

"Can I help you?" Ann Marie said. "Is there something I could help you with?"

"No," Nick said.

"Well, I don't know what time he will be back, you can't wait out here all day."

"You want to invite us in?" Sonny said, a big grin spreading.

"I can't do that, I don't know who you are."

"Well, why don't we just shake hands and be friends," Nick said.

"Look," Sonny said, "look Nick, she's smiling. Ann Marie, you seem like a very nice person."

"I am."

"You're what?"

"I am a nice person."

Nick and Sonny stood still and did not answer.

She said, "Do you really plan on waiting here all day?"

"Listen lady," Sonny said, "tonight, you know, when the moon comes up, we'll still be here waiting and watching. Tomorrow morning, you know, when the sun comes up—"

"Oh please," she said, and shut the door.

For a moment it was in Nick's mind to get back in the cruiser and drive around this neighborhood with streets named after spices, Thyme and Cinnamon, and find a place to grab some lunch. He had been out this way before and knew there was a diner, a famous one out on Northern Boulevard, the Neptune, something like that. Hang out for an hour or so and come back and wait, maybe bring a couple of containers of coffee, a paper, and sit in Little Anthony's driveway until the little bastard came home. Except that the surveillance report said that Rufino drove a Lincoln Town Car, and there it was at the end of the driveway, black, shiny, and new. He's in there all right, probably standing behind that first-floor window, looking through the venetian blinds, watching a couple of guys who could be anybody. Maybe even a couple of shooters come to call, to blow his little ass up, hero that he is, sending his wife out to check. Probably has her start his car in the morning, punk. Nick could feel him standing there, the little shit behind the blinds watching them.

Sonny was right, they'd wait all day, all night if they had to.

Then Sonny said, "The upstairs window, I just saw the curtain move, he's up there, I saw him."

"We'll wait."

From where they stood, the entire street could be seen; an old neighborhood with nothing but new money here. Little Anthony's house was an American colonial restoration, a two-story, with a blue shingle roof and walls of dull gray cedar shakes. Not at all what Nick expected, not what he'd figured at all. He'd figured pink flamingos on the lawn of a tasteless house.

Nick turned to see Little Anthony in the doorway, his finger jabbing the air, a stubby finger, pointing. Nick and Sonny went back up the walk so they could hear, so they could get closer to Little Anthony, the little creep in his maroon running outfit saying what in hell do you guys want? Standing out there like a couple of assholes. Making my neighbors wonder what the hell's going on with the Italian guy on the block, making me look bad. A high squeaky voice, with that East Harlem street accent, a tough guy, dealt with cops for years.

"Beautiful," Sonny said softly to Nick, "let's go and shake him up a bit. Shit, I wish this was an arrest warrant. I'd love to drag the bum out of that joint in chains."

They eased up to the doorway, slow, no problem here.

Nick trying to sound as professional as possible, saying, "Mr. Rufino, we're from the Queens DA's office, we have a form here we want you to sign."

"Whataya nuts, I don't sign nothin'. Who you guys, ya nuts or somethin', sign what?"

Sonny said, "You want us to stand out here, or are you going to invite us in?"

"You ain't coming in my house, not without a warrant you ain't."

Nick went into his jacket pocket, took out an envelope, unfolded the notification form, and handed it to Little Anthony.

"What's this?"

"You want maybe I should read it for you?" Sonny said.

"Hey," Rufino said, "I know you. Where do I know you from?"

"My ex-partner pinched you about three years ago. I was there, remember, I drove you to the precinct."

Little Anthony sighed and took a long moment reading before saying, "The drunk Moran, yeah, I remember. Bullshit bust cost me five grand in legal fees." He paused to read some more, looked at Sonny and said, "You tapped my phone, you had the phone in this house tapped for what, two months?"

"That's right," Nick said, taking a pen, offering the pen to Rufino. "You'll see on the bottom of the form a place for you to sign. It simply means you've been notified."

"I can read. Two months, huh?"

"Yup," Sonny said. "And whatever information came across those wires is going to be turned over to the FBI. They will want to talk to you, ask you some questions."

"What, are you trying to scare me? I don't scare, and let me tell ya, you had something, you'da been here with an arrest warrant. Screw you guys and screw the FBI, twice." Little Anthony tried a smile. "For two months you heard everything that went down on this phone, is that right?"

"That's right," Sonny said, "everything."

Suddenly Rufino reached out and took the pen Nick was holding and quickly signed the form.

"C'mon," Rufino said. "C'mon in, Marie's making coffee, she can't cook worth shit, but she makes a hell of a cup of coffee."

They sat at a table in Little Anthony's kitchen, Sonny smoking a cigarette, the three of them drinking coffee, Nick and Sonny facing Rufino across the table. Ann Marie standing in the doorway, her shoulder against the doorjamb, her arms folded. Standing there amazed now, can't believe this shit she's hearing. Nick looking at Rufino, a little guy, sure, five five, maybe five six, but built like a baby bull, no neck at all, and wrists like King Kong. The running outfit seemed too big for the body, though the body seemed to be in pretty good shape, or had been before he had let himself go with too much bread, pastry, and pasta. He looked like some Las Vegas casino bouncer locked in on a troublemaker. Little Anthony squinting at them now, saying look at me, tell me what you see? Sonny shrugging, Nick saying, what are you trying to say? Anthony saying naw, you guys wouldn't understand. You couldn't know what it's like out there, what it's like being a poor kid, growing up the way I did. Going hungry sometimes, sometimes nothing to eat but polenta, you know polenta? It's like corn meal, polenta in the morning, polenta at night, cooked, fried, made every goddamn way you can imagine. Little Anthony's expression not matching his tone, he sounded angry, telling them you fight for your life every fucking day. And all you want is loyalty, that's all you ask of people, a little loyalty.

Ann Marie came to pour more coffee and Nick watched Anthony looking his wife over without looking directly at her, the guy sitting straight, his hands folded on the table. Ann Marie went back to the doorway and Little Anthony eased back in his chair, picked up his cup, starting to smile, wagging his head.

"What if I ran a little something past you guys? Off the record, no cops or nothing, just men talking?"

"Speak up," Sonny said.

"Careful," Nick said, "we're not your buddies or your priest, be careful what you say. I'm not being a hardass or anything, just telling you to think before you speak."

"You here to pinch me?"

Nick said, "No, but we're cops, remember that."

"You're cops, but you ain't here to pinch me, you're here to run some game, maybe get lucky and turn me into a rat, that's it, right?"

Sonny laughed, saying, "What'd I tell you, Nick, this is one stand-up guy. Ain't nobody turning this guy. Anthony," he said, "maybe you got something for this coffee, you know, a little something to flavor it?"

"Oh sure, sure. What do you want, a little anisette, some Irish whiskey huh? Marie, get him something, the whiskey, right?"

"That'll be fine," Sonny said.

"And you, mister hardass," Anthony said, "you want anything?"

"No," Nick said, "I'm okay."

"You're the smart one," Rufino said. "I bet you're the smart one. Went to college, ain't that right? Well, pal, if you're real smart you won't look at me the way you do." He winked at Nick and Nick couldn't help himself, he smiled.

"You know," Anthony said, "the worst mistake I ever made was to give my kid an education. Now I don't hear from him anymore, moved to California, then to Oregon, works on an Indian reservation teaching school. A bunch of red niggers, is what I told him. Nothing more than that."

Ann Marie placed a bottle of whiskey on the table and returned to her post in the doorway.

"You mind if she stays?" Anthony said. "Because if you mind she can go and do something, fix her makeup, go and make a telephone call, woman lives on the phone."

"I don't mind she stays," Sonny said.

Nick was silent. He glanced at Ann Marie, waiting for her to say something, but she didn't, just stood there, her arms folded, her eyes locked in on Little Anthony. Anthony saying, "All right, look. I'd like to see those transcripts, how can I do that?"

"You can't," Nick said.

"Can't I? Why not?"

"We should go now," Nick said.

"Twenty-five hundred, whataya say? I give you two twenty-five hundred, you'll let me read them?"

Nick watched Ann Marie's beautiful face go gray. There was a white line around her mouth, her lips were pressed tightly together, and Nick thought he could hear her moan.

"C'mon," Sonny said. "You're kidding, I know you're kidding, you don't mean that. You could get your ass busted for bribery. What're you, nuts?"

Rufino smiled politely and looked carefully at Sonny.

"Your partner, that Moran—Eddie, right? He was a good guy, I'll take a chance with you."

"No chance, forget it," Sonny said.

"Okay, okay, five grand. You get me a copy of those tapes, or transcripts, I'll give you five grand. No, fuck it, ten, I'll give you ten."

"Hey," Nick said, "cut it out. Cut the shit for Christ's sake. Mention it again and I'll lock you up. Understand me, I'll bust your ass, Anthony. I don't like you, remember that, I don't like what you do. You got a nice house here, a nice wife, you're a lucky little bastard, but don't push it."

Little Anthony kept still. He knew Nick meant it. Telling Ann Marie, if he wasn't careful he'd get himself pinched over some bullshit bribery charge. He got up from the table and moved around the room. He said, "Nice meeting you guys, see you around. I'll handle this, okay? I don't pay you, I'll pay someone else. But I'll get those transcripts, what do you wanta bet I get 'em?"

Nick standing now, putting on his jacket, motioning to Sonny. Sonny sitting still, finishing his coffee, his drink. Nick was annoyed that he had to sit and listen to this guy, share coffee and conversation with the creep. Nick said, "There isn't anything on those tapes that you don't already know. No surprises, you're on those tapes, just you."

He shot a quick glance at Ann Marie. She was staring, her eyebrows raised, pleading, staring at him.

A long pause. Nick looked at Sonny, there was a playful look in Sonny's eyes.

Rufino smiled briefly and shrugged his shoulders as if to say we'll see. He said, "Maybe, maybe that's true and if it is, what's it hurt to let me see them?" Rufino suggested that Nick should calm down. "You get too excited, too serious. Chill out a bit, buddy."

The hell she doing staring like that? Nick thought. Nutty woman still looking at him, this little loser here will notice that, the way she's looking, the fear in her eyes.

Rufino said, "Guys, I appreciate what you tried to do here today. It's your job, I understand. I hope I didn't twist anybody's nose out of joint. I can do that sometimes, say things I don't mean. You know, just bullshitting for fun, some people don't think I'm funny."

Sonny standing now, cocked his head at Little Anthony. "We understand, no big thing, forget it. You try and do what you think is right. We all try, ain't that right, Nick?"

Ann Marie had left her spot at the doorway and disappeared into another room without a murmur. Nick knew she was frightened out of her wits, standing the way she had, rigid as a stone, and he guessed that if Rufino had upped the ante another five thousand, Ann Marie would have come apart.

He could scarcely keep his mind off her. She was a knockout all right, if you went for magnificent bodies in tights, with an out-to-lunch sign flashing topside. He ached with a longing that was not lust but loneliness. He hadn't talked to Renata in weeks, months. And there was no one who was even remotely promising in his life. Then he thought about Little Anthony here, and an anger grabbed his stomach and would not let go. He nodded at Sonny and cocked his head at the door.

Nick said, "I'm leaving my card. If you have a change of heart, Anthony, give us a call. It's up to you."

Anthony's ironic smile made Nick still more angry and he turned and took Sonny by the elbow, saying, "C'mon partner, we have things to do." At the front door they waved to Rufino. He did not wave back.

Out in front of the house they heard a knocking, and they looked up to see Ann Marie in the second-floor window. Once, when he was on the youth squad, Nick had watched a sex video, and the woman in that video could have been Ann Marie's twin. The actress had seemed just as foreign and unreal as the woman that watched them now. Ann Marie smiled and put her hands together as if praying; she bent her head and smiled a thank you, not once but twice.

When they left Sonny said, "I've never been that close to the perfect body before. Christ, I've had a hard-on for about an hour, you figure it'll go away?" And they sat in the cruiser laughing for a long time, Sonny slapping the dash, while traffic built on the LIE. Nick assumed that Sonny had seen Ann Marie Rufino in the second-floor window, but he became less certain of this when after forty-five minutes into their drive back to the courthouse, Sonny had mentioned not a word about seeing the woman in the window.

"The wife was scared to death," Nick said.

Sonny insisted that Ann Marie was the dumbest woman he'd ever met and to prove this he reminded Nick of the way she stood in the kitchen, her eyes wide, listening to Little Anthony, showing Anthony that she had something to fear, it'd be obvious to anyone.

Chapter 28

When he walked into the office the following Monday afternoon, Nick found two messages in his mail slot from a Dr. Conforti, asking Nick to call him. The word *important* was underlined, twice. The messages served to remind him of the difference between working in a DA's squad and a regular police department command. Important to a cop clerical worker means *important* and you would get a call at home. To a civilian secretary, important meant we'll see ya when we see ya.

The past Wednesday, when he had handed the squad commander the notification form for Rufino, Nick had asked Leo Turner for Friday off, and he'd gone north for the weekend to give E.Z. a hand at making his boat ready for the spring fishing season. Over the years, Nick would build up lost time in one command and then when he was transferred, he would find that most of his overtime could not be transferred with him. Andre told him that the DA's office was different and Nick believed him.

To old-timers in the job, special assignments were good for only two things, you either made money or time. Nick saved time.

And so he had linked one day of lost time with the weekend and spent three great days with E.Z. and his boat. He had checked his answering machine for messages twice a day and found none.

Nick walked into the clerical staff's office through a door that divided the civilian employees from the police personnel. He gave a short wave to Leo Turner. The squad commander was going through some files, standing at the file cabinet and drinking coffee.

The secretary was a young woman named Rose who was about twenty-six, attractive, and serious-looking, and when Nick came up to her desk she didn't look up. Nick studied her a moment while Rose worked at her typewriter.

"Did you take this message?" Nick asked.

"From the doctor?" Her voice was timid and distant.

"Dr. Conforti, yeah, that's right. Did he tell you what he wanted?"

"Excuse me?"

"Rose, did he say anything to you when you talked to him?"

"Oh yes, yeah, he said that, ah . . . ah . . . I can't remember her name. Anyway, he said the woman was badly beaten."

Nick waited. "Yeah?"

"Why don't you just call the doctor?" Rose said reassuringly, thinking.

Nick tried one last time. "Rufino? Did he say her name was Ann Marie Rufino?"

"That's it, you got it." Rose plucked at the keys of her typewriter. "She's his patient, this Ann Marie, and she had been attacked, that's what he said. And she told this Dr. Conforti to call you." Rose grinned and nodded, Nick thinking, Little Anthony, the little bastard found someone he could buy.

Back in his office, Nick telephoned Long Island Jewish Hospital. After about ten minutes he reached Dr. Conforti.

"Doc, I got this message—"

"Detective Manaris, that was Friday. Two days ago."

"I was out of town."

"Don't you get your messages? It was an emergency."

"It didn't say emergency, Doctor. What happened?"

Dr. Conforti told him, in effect, that Ann Marie had been brought to the hospital by a woman who left without giving her name. Her condition was serious though not critical. She had been beaten, apparently with a club, maybe a baseball bat. Her left arm was broken, as was her nose and jaw, and she had received a severe skull fracture. Unable to speak, she scratched out a note to call Nick.

"What did the note say?"

"Please call Detective Manaris at the Queens DA's office."

"Anything else?"

"She was in a whole lot of pain. I gave her morphine."

"Did she write anything else, Doctor?"

"Uh-huh."

"What is this, twenty fucking questions? Whataya say, Doc? What else did she write?"

"Morphine is a very powerful painkiller."

"Jesus!"

"All right, all right. She wrote that I should thank you."

"What?"

"That's what she wrote, thank Detective Manaris. Hey look, she was medicated and in severe pain. God knows what she was thinking."

Nick whispered, "Forget God, I know exactly what she was thinking," and hung up.

Nick sat at his desk, his hands clasped in his lap, staring at the Rufino file, open to the picture of Little Anthony. He stared for a long time, rocking at his desk. And as Nick gazed down at the mug shot of Little Anthony, the wiseguy sneer, he understood for the first time that what was eating at him, giving him this scorching pain in the stomach, was the recognition of a certain truth. He had been taken for a fool, totally turned around.

What should he do?

He sat for a long time thinking that it was a question with too many answers. He thought about the woman in the window, Ann Marie, thanking him, thanking Sonny too. He thought about Little Anthony saying I pay you, or I pay someone else. He thought about the look in Sonny's eyes when he smiled, and about how it was the wrong time for a smile. Nick gave himself time to think it through, what he should do. He stared at Little Anthony's picture, considering, beginning to get worked up. Then something snapped in him, and he said, "Fuck it," loud enough so that a pair of investigators passing threw him a curious look. Nick made a decision, and he felt no regret about the decision he made because he had never pretended he was any other way. He knew that this gut-wrenching pain he had would not be healed by any kind of conversation, that the cure would come from this talent he had, his ability to bust someone up. It was just a matter of deciding who would be first.

Nick Manaris figured that it was time to make someone pay, get a little wave of retribution going.

Sure, assignment to a DA's office is a great detail, Leo Turner told Nick. Major investigations, clean work, none of the day-to-day chickenshit that you find in other commands. But otherwise, say you hope to get promoted, go from third- to second-grade, then first-grade detective, no chance. Say you're a captain like me. That's it for the civil service tests, now on out it's merit promotion by the PC. That's in most commands. But when you're in a DA's squad, you're out of the loop, away from the department, you can forget promotions.

Leo Turner called out to the secretary, asked Rose to bring in a couple of cups of coffee. "So," he said, "how do you like working here? I mean so far, I know it's only been a few days, but how do you like it so far?"

Nick told him it was fine. Turner said, how many detectives can you name went to work for a DA and got promoted? All Nick could come up with was Fred Burke and Ollie Anderson, both went from third- to second-grade detective up in the Bronx. If you're a detective, Turner said, and expect to get promoted in a DA's office, you got to be soft in the head, a bit of a dreamer. No promotions here, pal, none, he said.

Nick had been around long enough to know that police commissioners do not promote detectives on special assignment outside the department. Only he was a first-grade detective, top of the line, nowhere for him to go but down. Nick didn't say that to Leo Turner because the captain was trying to make some silly-ass point, and when a captain is trying to make a point, silly-ass or not, it's always best to be polite and listen and nod. What he did say was, "McCabe check in?"

Captain Leo Turner was a bit eccentric, one example of which was the stuffed owl he kept in a bird cage in his office.

"Detective McCabe," he said, "called in from court about eight this morning. Told Rose he was good for the day. Guess she forgot to mention it. Anyway, McCabe said if you needed him he'd be at Post Time, after five tonight."

"Good, that's good," Nick said, and was startled by the sharp look the captain gave him.

Leo Turner told Nick that it was a hell of a note that first-grade detectives were drawing down practically the same pay he was. And he had to bust his ass studying for three, count 'em, three civil service tests. "Nothing personal," he said, "but it's a good thing some first-graders don't have to pay taxes on what they think they're worth."

Nick smiled, checked out the bird in the cage. Weird.

"You know what else I was thinking?" The captain sat back, stretching, and sighed. "I was thinking that there are some cops and criminals that can interchange roles on a horizontal plane. Why is that, I wonder?"

"I couldn't answer that question, Captain," Nick said. "I don't know anyone who has the answer to that."

"Did you know that your partner Sonny is the nephew of a retired chief, William Regan? Man's retired maybe three, four years. Wild Bill they called him. Had the Sixth Division. Worked Harlem for years. Probably a millionaire."

"I heard of him."

"If you don't mind my saying, you seem a bit on edge."

"The coffee. And I haven't been sleeping well."

"Have you ever experimented with drugs, Nick?"

"No, can't say I have."

"Not in high school, not in college?"

"It never came my way. I was busy with other things."

"Do you know that the secrets of religion and philosophy can be found in the mercurial rush of some drugs?"

"Really?"

"That's what I understand, that's what I get from reading this article here. Where you off to? I can tell you're in a rush to go off somewhere."

"Long Island Jewish Hospital. I'm going to see a Dr. Conforti."

"All right, fine. Stay in touch."

"You know Captain," Nick said, "I think if you read a little further along, you'll find that when the drug wears off the mystical insights disappear."

"I'm glad you told me that. By the way, just make sure *you* don't disappear."

Damn, she looked like a little girl now. Asleep, curled up in the bed, layers of bandages wrapped around her head, across her face, her one good arm stretched out behind her, an IV going, tears running down her cheeks, a container with a glass straw containing her lunch on the nightstand, her eyes shut tight, swollen and black, making small sounds, like a wounded puppy. Nick thinking shit, and she's here, what, three days? What was she like a day or two ago? Nick didn't see any monitors, any machines like that, so it seemed to him that Ann Marie was not dying.

Dr. Conforti said, "Bad huh? She looks a whole lot worse than she is."

"She don't look good, I'll say that."

"She's in and out, I gave her plenty of medication. Let her sleep." He glanced around. "She's comfortable here. I could use some coffee. You want some?"

"I've had plenty, thanks."

"Who could beat on somebody like that? On a woman? What kind of man does something like that? He could have made her blind, damaged her brain. As it is it'll take months for her to heal. Probably need some plastic surgery on the chin and nose, definitely needs major dental work. And her vision, I'm worried about long-term vision impairment. Who could have done such a thing? A person like that should be locked up, people like that should not be free to walk the streets. You probably see a whole lot of this sort of thing, being a cop and all."

"Too much," Nick said. "Way too much."

"I drink too much coffee. Smoke too. Sure you don't want coffee?"

"We all have a vice or two, coffee and butts are not as bad as some others. Do you think I could wake her, maybe ask her a question?"

Conforti frowned. "I'd rather you didn't, not right now. Come back later."

"You have the note she wrote?" Nick said as a nurse appeared, a short one, Asian, in a starched white uniform. Perky, pretty, carrying a bottle of hospital lotion.

"Let her sleep," the doctor told her. "Come back in an hour or two. The famous note?" he said to Nick. "No. I threw it out. Didn't make much sense anyway. Her mind was muddled, the painkillers. Kind of drug-induced, if you know what I mean."

The nurse said, "She's a beautiful woman, and so sweet, always trying to smile. Are you a relative?"

"No, I'm not."

"This is Nick Manaris, he's a policeman."

The nurse looked at Nick for a moment, her eyes wide open in surprise, telling Nick you're a little late aren't you? Saying the police are truly never around when you need them, telling Nick it's the same old story, again and again. You won't find the man that did this. He'll never get the justice he deserves. And then Dr. Conforti saying you're leaving? Will you be back later today? Should I tell her you were here?

This is what you do, Nick thought, stand around and be polite and courteous, listen to the doctor, listen to the nurse. Go man, you know what needs to be done. Nick cranking up, tired of listening, of hearing people talk, tired of his own voice too.

"I'll call later today, see how she's getting along. Tell her I was here, tell her I got the message." He wanted to say something more to the nurse, who stood watching him, arms folded, but there was nothing more to be said.

Chapter 29

Nick pushed his seat back and opened up the car windows. He was at the corner of 115th Street and Pleasant Avenue, across from Rao's and a block from the East River. The afternoon had warmed, bringing a silken tranquility to the river. Suddenly out of the east a light breeze rose, that breeze had swept out of the Atlantic, crossed thousands of miles of open ocean, taking the cool fresh scent of the sea, bringing it right to Nick. A deep, warm feeling, something indefinable but indisputably real, came over him. For the first time in a very long time he felt alive, revved and ready.

Through his rearview mirror Nick had a clear view of the Pleasant Bar and Grill a block north, and the four phone booths out front, the phones and the corner busy in the afternoon. On a fine day at Pleasant Avenue the gathering of wiseguys, like Satan, was eternal. Drug dealers, bookmakers, and loan sharks, some of whom Nick recognized, some he knew had Mafia yellow sheets a half-mile long, mingled with small-time thieves and junkies. The pay phones in front of the bar were off limits to all but a few. Out-of-order signs dangled from all four. The wiseguys here used the telephones and the corner like it was their personal office, going in and out of the bar, carrying drinks, laughing, toying with each other. A man with chin whiskers and long sideburns, wearing a red T-shirt and blue suspenders, came out of the Pleasant Bar. He spun in a half circle, stamping his foot, and then went back inside. The windows of the tenements that lined the street were open, and Nick noticed women sitting in those windows, watching.

He glanced down on the seat, at the open file folder of the Kennedy Airport case, checking photos, surveillance reports, and mug shots, putting names with faces on the corner. Little Anthony, they said, showed here every day; it was from here he did his business. The avenue was wide, one-way traffic coming his way, cars double- and triple-parked, all of the cars new, most of them with out-of-state registration. Three young guys in undershirts, maybe mid-twenties, stood head to head in close conversation in the intersection, stopping traffic.

After he had left the hospital, Nick made a quick stop at home to pick up a pair of handball gloves and the automatic .25 Beretta. Now, he slid a loaded clip into the gun, made sure that the safety was on, and that a round hadn't worked its way up the snout. He dropped the gun into his jacket pocket, put on the gloves, and started the car.

Nick circled the block, cruising by the bar. Little Anthony's Lincoln was parked on the side street. He parked right behind it, sat and waited. A half hour later Rufino came out of the bar and went to one of the phone booths. Nick got out of the car, nodded to an old lady in black pushing a baby carriage. The old lady looked down at his gloved hands and quickly walked off.

Rufino stood in the booth with his back to the street, his back to Nick. Nick heard Little Anthony say, "I ain't gonna wait here all day." Still wearing his maroon running outfit and sneakers.

Nick nudged him in the back with stiff fingers and Rufino turned. Nick looked into his eyes and was met with a dumb, glazed look. Little Anthony stared at him, seemed about to say something.

"I'll call you later," he said into the phone.

Rufino hung up and stood with his arms folded, wary. "The fuck you doing here?"

"Came by to say hi, see how you're doing. Want to express my condolences over your wife's accident."

He looked at Nick as if this was something brand-new, something he hadn't heard before. Rufino said, "You heard about it, huh?" With surprise. "Hell of a thing. I find those guys . . ."

"Who'd you pay?"

"You crazy? I didn't pay anybody anything."

Nick liked the look on Rufino's face, liked the way the little bastard tried to push past Nick and couldn't. Those brown eyes of his showing fear, wondering what the hell do I got here?

"Ey," Little Anthony said, "you come up to the Avenue looking for trouble, you'll find a one-way ticket to the hospital." Sounding tough now, a rough street guy, used to making people quake and tremble with a look. Nick could see him swinging the bat at Ann Marie's arm, her face, her head.

Nick figuring Little Anthony was probably pretty good with his hands, came up hard, a street fighter hit you with whatever he could get his hands on, a garbage can cover, a bat, a piece of pipe. Nick put his hand on Rufino's chest and pushed him back into the booth. Little

Anthony, glancing around the street now, looking for some help, narrowing his eyes, looking at the gloves on Nick's hands.

"I'll have your fucking job, what the hell you think you're doing?" He rose up at Nick, shouting now, "You know who my fucking lawyer is, you ever watch television? I'll fix your ass!"

Nick grabbed him by the velour jacket of his running suit with his left hand and caught him with a fast right chop. Nick had been trained by his father, a professional, had been a pro himself for a while; it was a perfect straight right, picture-book, six inches, no more, but with power, from the shoulder, no wasted movement, no warning. And then again, Nick felt the guy's nose go this time, grabbed the neck of that maroon outfit, blood pouring over the front of it now, grabbed Little Anthony's hair too, and slammed him against the inside of the phone booth, letting him slide to the floor. Not a word from Nick, not a sound, hardly a grunt, this guy was easy.

Rufino making funny, retching, snoring sounds now, hurt bad and subdued, a lump on the phone-booth floor. Nick on him, all over him, on top of Little Anthony, twisting his arms now, shoving him facedown, pulling his arms behind his back, putting cuffs on him. Nick grabbed the phone, got a dial tone, and punched 911. Asked the operator for the 225, told her he was an NYPD detective, had an emergency. A moment later he told the cop on the switchboard to send a car, maybe two, he had a prisoner on Pleasant Avenue and 117th Street.

"You think Marie is gonna press charges against me, schmuck? That what you think?"

"I doubt it," Nick said.

The jacket of Little Anthony's pretty maroon velour running suit had deep pockets, the automatic .25 slid right in, no problem.

Patrol cars appeared, their sirens and whoopers going full out. Nick dragged Little Anthony caterwauling and kicking from the phone booth and into the middle of the avenue. The bar emptied out, men who had been drinking and laughing inside a moment earlier became intensely agitated and angry at the sight of Little Anthony bleeding and being dragged off in cuffs. And Anthony himself, his face a wild mask of rage, scream-shouted, choking on the blood that poured from his nose. A flock of gray pigeons rose up from the gutter and crisscrossed the sky, and from the next block church bells rang.

About twelve teenagers, half black and half Puerto Rican, had run to see the excitement from a side street; they seemed more entertained than angry.

The crowd from the bar moved toward the cops. The two groups faced each other in the center of the avenue, the uniformed cops staying close to their patrol cars, the crowd closing in. Bent over, shouting like angry dogs, the cops and crowd exchanged insults, the cops fingering their holsters.

"He's a man not an animal, don't drag him like that!" demanded the man with the chin whiskers.

Rufino was doubled over, his arms raised behind his back, as Nick dragged him to the lead patrol car.

The crowd closed in.

Four cops motioned for them to get back. One of the cops glared at Nick, saying, "What happened, whataya got here?"

"I was talking to this bum and he came at me," Nick said.

"So whataya got, an assault, that it?"

"Take him," Nick shouted and shoved Little Anthony into the arms of the cop.

"Move it," another cop said, "let's get outta here, before these fuckers eat us."

"Christ," the first cop said, "didn't you toss this guy? He's got a gun for Christ's sake. A loaded gun." And then the crowd stopped moving and gazed at the cop, who turned the .25 Beretta in the sun and held it high.

Nick drove his car behind the patrol car that carried Little Anthony to the precinct, his hand fluttering on the steering wheel, a noise like an alarm, a whistle, in his head. Thinking that he had just done something that he had sworn years ago he never would do. He'd planted a guy, dropped a gun in Little Anthony's pocket.

Phil Manaris, Nick's father, like Nick, had been born in Brooklyn. Raised in a series of tenement apartments in and around Red Hook, never far from the docks. The dreams of his young life steered him to the sea, and at seventeen he shipped out. It was in the merchant marine that Phil Manaris began prizefighting. He roamed the world for ten years and at the end of the war returned to Brooklyn. Phil Manaris would have been a priest had it not been for a young woman by the name of Linda Laprise, who lived in the same house he did, on Sackett Street. Phil and Linda married, and a year later Nick was born. The following year Linda decided to take a long vacation to Seattle to visit her sister and never returned. Linda was a shrewd, temperamental woman, tall and thin, and Nick's father liked to say that Nick had inherited his mother's brooding temperament but not her height. The luck Manaris men had with women, it seemed to Nick, had always been bad. In any event, Nick was raised by his father, and he listened to him, read the books his father gave him, books by Jack London, Joseph Conrad, Ernest Hemingway, Mark Twain. Nick's father never insisted that Nick read, it was not his way. Nick willingly embraced most things his father taught him, with great attention, not only because his father was a strong and good man, but because it seemed to Nick that he was wise. Everything his father taught and told Nick made such simple sense, all those things stayed in Nick's head like favorite films.

Phil Manaris brought Nick up in a way that made it impossible for Nick to take what wasn't his, steal another man's money or property— or woman for that matter. Nick wouldn't lie or cheat, and when he became a policeman he could not imagine sending an innocent man to jail. And any cop that did wasn't a cop at all, just an empty hole in the ground, worthless. His father's words coming fast and hot in his head now, you want to be cop, fine, just be a good cop, be an honest cop, be your own man. Remember, when you are at peace with yourself you can go to war with the world, was what his father had said.

Nick squinted at the police car ahead of him, parking now in front of the stationhouse, and he thought of Ann Marie in that hospital bed, thought of his attempt—his failed attempt—to get through twenty years in this job maybe bending but never breaking the law. "I tried, man. I gave it my best shot," he said aloud.

Nick parked about two lengths behind the patrol car. He saw the uniformed cop hovering over Little Anthony, Rufino leaning backward, blood all over his nose, lips, and chin, another cop coming up, the two cops sandwiching Little Anthony, taking him by his elbows up the stairs and into the stationhouse. Nick followed them inside.

On the desk was a Lieutenant D'Buono, who was called the Candy Kid, when he worked in narcotics, when he was a sergeant. When he was Nick's boss. Nick stood looking at him, D'Buono, great, this guy was no fan of his. Knowing D'Buono's reputation for sticky fingers, Nick figured that the lieutenant could easily be a playmate of Little Anthony's.

D'Buono seemed like he was in a good mood, almost friendly, and it made Nick paranoid, made him think that the Candy Kid knew things he could not know. But at least it all went quickly, D'Buono telling Nick to bring the prisoner up to the detectives' squad office and print him. "Hurry Nick, get it done, then bring him to me and I'll book him." D'Buono was smiling, but the smile on his face was not warm, not real. It could hardly be called a smile at all, a half-assed grin was what it was.

Nick found himself smiling back and nodding, though he had no idea why, there was nothing about this that was funny.

Rufino, still in cuffs, bent his head to his shoulder, rubbed his chin and nose against his upper arm. "You think I'm gonna sit still for this?" he said. "You're crazy if you figure I'll roll over for this one."

D'Buono said, "What are you talking about?"

"A gun, a gun, God damn it. He put a loaded gun in my pocket."

"Who did?"

"Whataya mean who? This prick, this bastard, this cop Manaris."

"Nick Manaris?"

"Him, right."

"You tell me he punched you in the face and busted your nose, I believe you, Anthony, I believe you in a heartbeat. You tell me he planted you, framed you, I got to tell you that I know this guy, he worked for me. Not a shot in a million. Not his style. Now, the punch in the kisser, well, that's Nick all right."

"Well who the fuck did it? That ain't my gun, a bullshit twenty-five. What am I gonna do with a gun like that, kill fucking birds?"

D'Buono's expression changed rapidly from a smile to annoyance. "What are you, Anthony, a three-, four-time loser? That bullshit bird-shooting gun is gonna get you a pound. That's five years, maybe more, smartass."

Nick looked closely at Anthony Rufino now, measuring him, defining the qualities that made him Little Anthony. He said, "What was that, Rufino? Speak up, sounded like you said I framed you."

"You heard me, you phony bastard. You planted me, you bum."

D'Buono said, "Keep talking, Anthony. I'll call the hospital, ask them to send someone to look at your nose. You keep mouthing off they'll be wiring your jaw too."

It went fast, the printing, the booking, the notifications. Leo Turner, and Andre too, overjoyed that he'd collared Rufino. Jaywalking would have been fine; a loaded gun, a felony, with Little Anthony's sheet chock full of priors, perfect. Sonny had checked in, said he'd wait for Nick at Post Time. Ann Marie Rufino came into his mind, a vision of her standing in that window, smiling, thanking him, thanking Sonny McCabe too.

He was driving south on the FDR. It was almost five thirty but seemed later. You believe it, he told himself, you believe how easy it is to frame a guy? He thought about it a moment longer, then got rid of it, easy, there and gone.

He would remember arriving at Post Time near six P.M. Sonny's and Eddie Moran's cars were parked out front at the curb, and inside the place seemed dark and quiet as a tomb.

As Nick opened the door the early evening air drifted in with him and mixed with the smells in the bar, tap beer, sawdust, frying food, sweat, a man's cologne, waiting garbage. Nick thinking that the smell of Post Time was the smell of the street, the smells of the city mixed into one.

He found them sitting in the back, Eddie drinking beer from a bottle, Sonny sipping from a glass of something dark with ice cubes, their faces lit by the candle in the small frosted red bowl in the center of the table. Eddie asked what took him so long, they had been waiting for two hours.

Sonny said that he had called the 225 and heard from D'Buono, good ol' Lieutenant D'Buono, that Nick had kicked the shit out of Little Anthony and then collared him. Sonny said that was good, the guy needed to be busted. Then he said that was a terrible thing to do, to flake him, flake a guy like Little Anthony. D'Buono told him that as far as he knew, Little Anthony never carried a gun. A bat yeah, a pipe, maybe even a hatchet, but not a gun. A gun could get him big time. If Little Anthony needed a gun he'd have someone else carry it. Not him, he's past that shit, carrying guns. Sonny told Nick he didn't think Nick had it in him, to flake, frame, plant a guy. If Little Anthony gets time, he'll get big time, five, maybe seven years. He could flip out, he is dangerous. Knows many cops, has done business for years with cops, all kinds. If he ever told what he knew, he could cause plenty of trouble. Embarrass a load of people.

Nick stood looking down at Sonny, and suddenly all the anger that had been waiting in his stomach, churning offstage, returned. He didn't hear what Sonny was saying, he just watched him talking, and he could see in his eyes a kind of fear he had never seen there before.

"I didn't flake him," Nick lied. "I went to the hospital and saw Ann Marie. She'd been busted up real bad. So I took the ride, went to the Avenue to talk to Rufino. The fucker went nuts, came at me, and I dropped him. I turned him over to a sector car, it was the uniform that came up with the gun. Not me. I never even saw it."

"That the way it happened?" Sonny said.

"That's right. See, I know Rufino got to somebody, somebody took his money and gave him a transcript of the wire. The little bastard then went and grabbed a bat and broke out the gym set on his wife. He gave her a hell of a workout. Beat her bad, heartless bastard."

Nick looked at Sonny a long time, watched Sonny looking at him and wondered if it was hard for the guy to hear this. "What I'd like to know," Nick said, "I'd like to know what happened to his driver. That guy Paulie, he's probably in the trunk of a car somewhere, or looking up at six feet of dirt."

"Who do you figure sold him the tapes?"

Nick just stared at him for a moment. "You, you did it. Who else? I know you did it."

Eddie Moran laughed, but Sonny did not seem amused. He looked up at Nick saying are you for real?

Nick had always thought, perhaps unwisely, that whenever he confronted a liar with the truth, he could see the lie reflected in that person's eyes. As he watched Sonny McCabe sitting there, smoking his cigarette, sipping his drink, Nick's mind was projecting scenes of Sonny and Little Anthony smiling together, an envelope passing between them, then Ann Marie screaming, covering up, Little Anthony banging away.

Sonny was quiet now, staring up, the candlelight catching his eyes.

Sonny squinted at him over the top of his glass, said, "So, you feel better now, you busted his ass?"

Nick said nothing.

"You came here with the intention of doing the same to me, isn't that right?" Sonny said smoothly, keeping his tone mild, an understanding sort of guy.

Eddie Moran stood up and got himself into a fighter's stance, bobbing and weaving, throwing rights at the air. Not bad, Nick thought, not too bad. Eddie's face was so red it looked at though his head would explode. And when he spoke his voice went high with exhaustion. "Wooooo," he said, "Nicky boy is looking to lock horns."

Sonny said, "You really came here to pick a fight with me? Are you nuts or what?"

It was, unfortunately for Nick, a reasonable question. He wondered how Sonny had figured his intent so easily.

"I'm not sure why I came here," Nick said.

"Sure you are. You figure I sold you out, turned you around, took Little Anthony's money. And you want to do something, want to take a shot at me."

For a moment Nick considered pushing aside all the bullshit light conversation that he and Sonny fell into, that they'd always fallen into, from the beginning, maybe just grab the guy, grab him and drop him, knock smiling Sonny McCabe right on his ass. But he stopped himself. Nick would find later, many years later, that Sonny's anger would cloud his memory of exactly what was said, and by whom. He would remember how McCabe got up from the table, how he stood there, how perfectly his tie accented his suit. How those blue eyes in the candlelight began to change.

"Go screw off," Sonny said in a whisper, and for a long moment he glared at Nick.

"Why don't you just take a hike," Eddie Moran said, and then looked away.

A light film of perspiration dampened Nick's forehead and neck, and he could feel fine, threadlike streams running down his back. As Sonny talked, Nick's anger grew, and a meanness too, and that was what he wanted, that feeling, the rachet turning one more time, he wanted that feeling of anger that was building.

Nick said, "You want to come with me to the hospital and maybe explain to the wife why you burnt her? Woman like her, she'd understand. Say you needed the money."

"Hey friend," Sonny said, "you don't know who Little Anthony got to. It could have been anyone."

Nick said, "Don't call me friend, we are not friends, we could never be friends, we could not be less friends if we had never met."

Sonny said, "You want to fight me? That what you want? G'head, take your best shot. Let me see how tough you are."

At times Nick saw people in terms of their fighting potential, how fast they were, how heavy their shot. Were they good with both hands? How much heart did they have, could they stand after taking one or ·two, or more? In Sonny McCabe he saw a big reputation and small potential, small hands, styled hair, not one out of place, big talk, small heart. Like his father, Nick had been blessed with big hands.

Sonny drained his glass. "C'mon," he said. "Take your shot."

Nick could see that Eddie was watching; Moran glanced at Sonny and then back at Nick. An observer, Eddie was fixated on something, his expression a little lost. Some secret drama taking place in his mind. He tried to get Sonny's attention, but Sonny was locked in on Nick.

"He'll have to go through me first," Eddie Moran said.

It was not dread or fear that made Nick hesitate, he simply was not sure what he wanted to do. Whether Eddie wanted in or not, it didn't matter, he could whip both their asses if he had to, of that he had no doubt. A couple of drunks, easy. And Nick could tell by the way Eddie Moran smiled at him that the guy had no idea how easy he would be.

Sonny McCabe lit himself another cigarette. The flame from his lighter illuminated his gold cuff links and watch and cast a bizarre glow over his face. He took a deep pull on the cigarette and blew out a smoke ring.

Nick stood and Sonny flinched; he was quiet now, as if to see where Nick was going to take this.

Nick said, "Bullshit time's over. I want you out of Robinson's office. I don't want to have to see you, hear you, smell you. I don't give a shit how you do it. Pick up the phone, with the weight you have you can go wherever you want. Just stay out of my way."

Eddie Moran came forward, for effect, for the look of it. Nick shoved him aside. Then he got up close to Sonny, put his left hand on Sonny's chest, felt him breathing in and out next to him. Look at those eyes, scared now, he felt the silk of Sonny's jacket under his hand. Nothing there, no heart at all. Nick leaned in close, eye to eye. "And, I'll tell you something else. I don't believe that kid Cienfuego had a fucking gun."

"What?"

"You heard me."

Sonny said, "You're crazy, you know that? That's what you are, a fucking nut."

When Nick thought of Sonny McCabe, he thought to himself, how do you like a guy and be repulsed by him at the same time?

"You know," Sonny said, "you think you know me. Think you can see inside me, see what's going on, what I'm thinking. But you're wrong."

"I've never been wrong about you."

"Screw him Sonny," Eddie shouted, "screw the bastard. Don't talk to him, he's nothing, he's nobody."

Nick said, "Hear me, Sonny—you paying attention? I ever find out you wasted that kid for no reason, I'll come for you, I'll come for the both of you."

**Wickham, Rhode Island
May 1990**

Chapter 30

The first week in May came in warm and gentle, and Nick decided to spend a long weekend at his cottage in Wickham.

He pulled out of the courthouse garage sometime around four on Thursday, driving two hours in unusually light traffic to New London, where he turned off the highway and had a quick dinner at the Chart House. After he had eaten he drove to the turnout before the entrance to the highway. He pulled in and sat for a moment, looking out at the sound. It was a clear evening with hardly a breeze, the slate surface of the sea was flat, peaceful. With the engine of his car idling he used his cellular to check his messages and found one from E. Z. Brochard.

"Listen, Emma is off to visit her sister, and I noticed in the paper here that an old friend of yours will be on Larry King tonight." E.Z. sounded as cheery as ever. "I thought that maybe we could have a beer together and watch a little TV. Anyway, call when you get in," he said.

Unable to guess who Larry King's guest could be, Nick slid Puccini into the tape deck, turned up the volume, and headed north.

Nick wasn't impressed with many people anymore, or many things, for that matter. He would have preferred not to be that way, but there it was, he was like that. It was not something he could explain to anyone. He hardly understood it himself, but after twenty years of doing police work, most people appeared to him to be outrageous frauds and hypocritical, empty suits full of air and oil. So whoever it was that planned to show their face to the vast television audience, little curiosity stirred in him.

He made Wickham right at dark and unloaded the car. For a moment he stood on the back porch of the cottage and watched the setting sun settle into the sea. From where he stood the bay opened eastward to the western passage into the vast Atlantic. A snow white egret swooped out of nowhere, gliding overhead and flashing on out into the bay, a dazzling splash of beauty.

Perfect, he was thinking.

He stowed his gear and switched on the power in the cottage, putting water up for tea. When it boiled he made himself a cup and called Andre at home.

"I'm up north," he told him. "Took Friday off."

"Fine. You're the commanding officer, you don't need my approval for a day off," Andre said. It had been nine years since Andre had been elected Queens County district attorney, and two years since Nick had been promoted to captain. He was now the CO of the Queens County district attorney's detectives, and as such supervised thirty city police officers and twenty civilian investigators.

"Well, I always feel the need to check in with you."

"And I appreciate it. By the way, you have a TV up there, don't you?" Andre said as he was about to hang up. His voice had a note of humor in it. "Watch Larry King tonight, Frank Kurtz and Sonny McCabe will be his guests."

Nick stood in silence and shook his head, remembering E.Z.'s message.

"Nick, did you hear me?"

"Yeah, sure. Sonny huh?"

"They do books together."

"I heard."

"Watch them, you'll probably get a charge out of it. I know I will."

A reply came to Nick's mind but he didn't like it. He could see Sonny talking now, the gold flash of his cuff links, that phony smile. He said, "Well, you know what it's like, in the country I turn in early."

"And alone."

"Sad, but true. I'll see you Monday," Nick said. He decided to give E.Z. a call, have him over for a beer, and together they could toast Sonny's TV appearance. Ten years, he thought, can you believe it?

At nine that night, in the room with the windows that opened onto the bay, Nick sat with E.Z. watching TV, listening to Sonny McCabe and Frank Kurtz spout meaningless jargon he would not remember.

E.Z. sat stretched out with his hands curled up in his sweatshirt, his feet up on the coffee table. Nick was across the room in his reading chair, under the large window.

There was Sonny's face on the TV, turned toward the camera. Nick leaned a bit forward in his chair. In his pearl gray suit and red tie, all bronzed, with newly capped teeth, Sonny appeared to have just stepped off a Hollywood stage set.

"You worked with this guy, didn't ya?" E.Z. asked.

"Sure did," Nick said. Then after a moment, "He looks better now than he did back then, and back then he was quite the guy."

E.Z. stared.

Nick found that he could not bring forth the least vestige of anger. Ten years, feelings fade. He simply watched the show, listened with E.Z. as Sonny flogged his and Frank's new book, Sonny's inimitable slick chatter silencing both of them.

Slowly and deliberately, E.Z. stretched, lacing his hands behind his head. He was close to six feet tall, went about two twenty, most of it chest and shoulders and arms. Had a handlebar mustache. Wearing jeans, work boots, and a hooded sweatshirt, he would go almost everywhere. He appeared to be getting quite a kick out of Sonny's rap.

"What a piece of work," E.Z. said. "This guy for real or what?"

Nick smiled. "You haven't seen anything."

"I haven't seen anything? I've seen guys like this all my life."

At seventeen E.Z. had enlisted to fight in President Johnson's war, served in the military police and saw action at Hue and in Saigon. Then he came home to continue his police career with the Providence police.

"These two make money selling this stuff?" E.Z. asked him.

"I guess."

"Bullshit reigns."

"As always."

E.Z. had married a Woonsocket woman of French-Canadian stock, blond, attractive, large-boned, and plenty tough. Emma was a barmaid with two children when they met, a woman who didn't like cops; nevertheless they married and settled down to the business of making a life. After much daily pressure from Emma to find other work, E.Z. quit the PD and moved to Wickham in 'eighty-one. E.Z. had been a cop in Vietnam and again in Providence, a narcotics detective, but he came from old South County stock, and his heart and soul belonged to the sea.

E.Z. said, "I have to be up at three every day and hunt the fish. These two tell stories. There's no justice."

He and Nick exchanged glances of resigned acceptance. E.Z. was an astute and deliberate charter-boat fishing captain in the truest sense. For many years he took no vacation. Spring, summer, and fall, he fished. Winters he managed Mancini's Lumber Yard on the Old Post Road. He made a reasonable living and named his boat after his wife. In 'eighty-three he built a small cottage east of Wickham harbor on four acres of family property, with a barn and a shed for his boat. Sometimes Nick gave E.Z. a hand, went to sea with him as mate. It was Nick's job to make sure the castoff and approach went smoothly, to toss off the mooring lines and drop the fenders. At sea Nick would hook and bait the lines and work the chum slick and act as handyman for the paying customers. Over the years, E.Z. had asked Nick to consider going in with him on a larger boat, but he'd recently given up trying.

There was a video of a police raid on the homeless settlement in Stuyvesant Park; as the cops moved in, a bottle flew through the air at the police line, and the police broke rank and started flailing at stragglers. Three uniformed cops beat on a bearded man. It closed with interviews with the police commander in charge, who tried to explain himself, and with one of the spokespersons for the homeless.

"I'll tell you, Larry," Sonny said to Larry King when the clip had ended, "in the middle of a battle you don't make judgments about people. When it's over and everyone is sitting around and taking notes, people should remember that."

"It's my feeling," King said, "that tacit acceptance, turning away from knowledge, can itself be a crime. I mean there were other cops in the park. They should have done something, stepped in and put a stop to that outrage."

"Larry, my old partner is sitting in the green room. I'd like him to tell you how tough it is out there in the street," Sonny said. "Eddie Moran was involved in five shootings during his police career. He's a true hero."

"I'm sure he is," Larry King said. "But—"

"Police work is a contact sport," Sonny said. "Some cops are rugged."

"What are you saying?"

"You can't have one without the other," Frank Kurtz said impatiently. "When violence is turned on the police, you're bound to get a violent reaction."

"That's about all I can take," Nick said. "Let's see if the Red Sox are playing."

Thoughts of Sonny McCabe that had disappeared years earlier boiled up in Nick's stomach again. For a moment he wanted to try to explain certain things to E.Z., but it was part of the fabric of their friendship that they never talked shop. E.Z. had been a cop, but he may as well have worked on Saturn, as far as their mutual experience went.

"New York cops," E.Z. said admiringly. "You guys have to deal with a mountain of shit. I don't know how you do it."

"It's not as bad as it seems."

"You figure those uniformed cops were off base there?"

"Some were, sure."

"You know, Captain—I'll call you Captain for this one—cops, when they make boss, are often shocked by the behavior of cops, and they are the same people." They smiled at each other.

"Do you think it was necessary for that group of cops to whale the shit out of the homeless guy?" Nick asked him.

"Somebody throws a bottle at me, I kick his ass."

"Really? Okay. Good thing it's only tuna and sharks you deal with nowadays."

"Dangerous work, but you're always in control."

"Unless you go overboard."

E.Z. laughed. "You got that right. Listen," he said, "your buddy McCabe. Man, he loves himself so much I bet he collects his own autograph."

"Sonny McCabe is no friend of mine."

"I would be surprised if he was."

Afterward, Nick sat on the back porch drinking a beer and looking out at the bay. Thoughts of Sonny McCabe, Moran, and the time he had spent with them made pictures in his head. For years he had not thought of either of those two characters at all, and now they came rushing back at him, all that craziness back then. He told himself to forget it, it was history, and then he was thinking again. After the Rufino incident he had not heard from either Sonny or Moran. Sonny transferred back to the OCCU, and a year or two later, he and Moran retired.

As for Rufino, he had gone for a hearing regarding the gun possession and lost. Nick testified that he had simply placed Little Anthony under arrest for assault, and the .25 was discovered later by the uniformed officer. Rufino's lawyer took a shot at a motion to suppress the evidence, lost that one too. Faced with a trial, which he would surely lose, and then maybe a sentence of seven-and-a-half-to-fifteen years, Rufino plea-bargained for attempted possession of a firearm. He got himself three-to-five at Greenhaven. Nick understood that what he'd done was not legal, but on the other hand what else could he do? Ann Marie, as Rufino said, would not sign an assault complaint against her husband. Still, justice, by Nick's lights, had been served.

He was wondering how that guy, Diego Cienfuego, how his kids made out, and that woman Natalia Punto. He had often thought maybe he'd reach out and find them, see how they were doing. The trouble was, there was a can of worms best left unopened. Half the time he thought Sonny and Moran had lied about the kid having a gun, and half the time he believed their account. Andre had been more than happy to see the whole Los Campos case go by the boards. Benny Matos and that Colombian, Medina, had disappeared into the Witness Protection Program. All the remaining defendants had pled out to various crimes, and most of them, Nick thought, should be back in the street by now. All the same, the case itself had produced plenty of positive publicity for Andre.

Nick shook his head and watched the single green light of a fishing trawler heading into Wickham Harbor. It was still and hushed, just night sounds, light waves along the shore and a barking dog.

Forget Sonny McCabe, he told himself, just forget about the guy.

Later, when he started thinking again, he picked up Mark Twain's
Gilded Age and began to read:

> In mid winter, an event occurred of unusual interest to the inhab-
> itants of the Montague house, and of the friends of the young
> ladies who sought their society.

Friday morning Nick and E.Z. were the first boat out to the Southeast
Light on Block Island. It had been years since Nick had seen the water
flat as it was. In no time at all they were in among all the striped bass
in the world, and birds flying. Aboard they had a cardiologist with his
two teenage sons fly-fishing for striped bass. By their third cast all three
had fish on, and the cardiologist, whose name was Trevor Hathaway,
told Nick that he had been preparing all his life for a morning like this,
a morning he thought he would never live to see.

The doctor and his boys were fly fishermen who fished freshwater
streams and lakes. They were accustomed to one- and two-pound trout
and were astounded at the fierce, unrelenting action of eight- and ten-
pound striped bass. No keepers, but the day went quickly and the action
never ceased. The boys and their father were cheerful and polite, the
three of them casting with experienced ease into the sea, their faces
warmed by the Atlantic sun.

Trevor Hathaway had done astoundingly well for himself and now
owned real estate all over Connecticut. He gave his sons the requisite
private school educations and spent as much of his off time with them
as he could. How familiar it all was, instantly recognizable, fathers who
got along well with their children and shared life's best moments with
them. Most times Nick watched families with hardly a thought, sometimes he felt a certain sensation, more than a little pain. It had been
fifteen years since his father's death, and at times it seemed to Nick as
if it were yesterday. In his heart he knew there would never be such a
life for him, that he was somehow destined to go through this life alone,
that he would never have daughters or sons, never celebrate gradua-
tions, marriages, or any of the other things that sometimes occupied
his daydreams, never have grandchildren. It was not what he wanted
but at the same time, little by little, life had passed him by.

By noon a mist began to rise, and E.Z. headed in toward Wickham
Harbor, falling in behind *Fiddlers Green* out of Newport. When *Fiddlers
Green* peeled off toward Point Judith, Nick waved to a redheaded man
in the wheelhouse, then went below and made some coffee. Mug in
hand, he returned topside, sat next to E.Z., and looked for the channel
buoys.

"I wonder why I can't seem to find a woman," Nick said.

"What?"

"I said, I'm forty-six years old and there is no woman in my life."

E.Z. looked at him blankly, then went back to steering the boat.

"What the hell," Nick said, unable to keep from saying it. "It must be me. I mean, I'm always coming up empty."

"You're not easily pleased, pal. You're pretty selective."

"No, no," he said impatiently. "I'm not hard to please. I'm just careful."

"What's going on?" E.Z. said. "What is it?"

"I'm tired of being alone."

"This the same guy that told me he's his own best company?"

"It's getting old. I'm getting older. I'm lonely."

E.Z. looked at him in surprise. He smiled and shook his head. "You need a beer, maybe a few. We get in, we'll stop at the Lighthouse; there's always a few stragglers there. I'm thinking you need a roll in the sack with some sweet thing."

"I dunno," Nick said. "What I'd like is what they have." He nodded toward the doctor and his family. The two teenage boys and Dr. Hathaway stood in the stern tossing chunks of bait fish at the circling gulls.

"Hey friend," E.Z. told him, "who knows better than you. Things are almost never what they appear to be."

"Meaning?"

"Trevor's wife skipped out on him about six months back."

"Really? Poor bastard."

"With his partner's wife."

"Say again?"

"You heard me."

When Nick turned to look at E.Z. he could see that he was grinning. "You're kidding me, right?"

"A hell of a story, the two women set up a soup kitchen in Boston. You know, for the homeless."

Nick glanced for a moment at the doctor and his sons, he looked at each in turn.

"What I'm curious about," Nick said to E.Z., "is how a decent man like yourself can lie with such a straight face. It must have taken you years of practice."

E.Z. shrugged and shook his head. "I was a cop," he said, "it came with the territory. It's like swimming, you never forget how. Like riding a bike, like making love. Understand what I mean?"

Emma's wake cut a path through the water, and a gentle breeze rose astern. Nick picked out the first of the channel buoys, feeling on edge, certain that seeing Sonny McCabe smiling on TV, his fuck-the-world look, was no small part of how he was feeling. Nick imagined Sonny's wild laugh and the way he winked when he was up to something. There was no question about it, he thought, the guy left his mark on you.

After docking and cleaning the boat, Nick and E.Z. made their way to the Lighthouse Bar and Grill in Wakefield. At the bar E.Z. engaged two fishermen from Galilee in heated conversation about the shark derby the past July. In these parts, fishermen lived and breathed by the swordfish, tuna, and shark, and where they were running was a topic of continual discussion. And it seemed to Nick that E.Z., along with everyone else, lied. Fishermen had plenty of solitude, plenty of long hours alone with fish and lines and a bloody boat. So when they went out, they broke out. Fishermen, Nick considered, were harder drinkers than cops.

A henna-haired woman from Pawtucket whose name was Shirley came his way, and not, Nick figured, by chance. E.Z. had walked off with Shirley when he and Nick had come through the door, E.Z. doing his I'll-fix-you-up deal. Shirley had the appearance of the once attractive town girl who had knocked around a bit. She was wearing a pair of faded jeans, huge dark glasses, a white sweatshirt with DON'T WORRY BE HAPPY across the front. She walked up and said, "Okay, let's me and you get wickit drunk and talk about the loves of our life," surprising the hell out of him.

Shirley went on for about fifteen minutes about men, her life, a quarter hour of sad country songs. It seemed to Nick that this woman's life had been reduced to a manhunt. She told him she wanted to learn about boats and fishing, to know as much as her ex-boyfriend, Danny, did, so that Danny would love her as much as he loved fishing. And she loved Danny, and believe it or not she couldn't come unless she was in love. Fishermen, she said, were shy and timid around women, fishermen were only brave out on the water. Men, she said, men are strange.

"And what about you," she asked, "what kind of man are you?"

"I am a man about whom almost nothing is known."

"Just like my ex, my Danny."

Shirley moved toward him; Nick felt the outside of her thigh brush against his leg. She stared at him. "What the hell happened to your nose?"

"Broke it when I was a kid. Broke it twice."

"You did? A shame, a handsome face like yours."

Shirley told him that she liked men who could read her mind. "I bet," she told him, "you can read my mind." Nick thinking right, I can, I did, and lo and behold there's nothing there.

Shirley put away a margarita and asked him was he busy that night? there was a wild-game dinner at the Exeter VFW, and everyone was going. Nick turned to watch E.Z. at the far end of the bar. E.Z. grinned, looked from Shirley to Nick, raised his hand and made a small wave.

Shirley said, "So, would you like to be my guest and eat some wild game?"

"Thanks," Nick told her. "But I'll have to take a pass. Next time maybe."

"They don't come around often, these wild-game dinners don't. Once a year and that's about it."

"Next year then."

"Christ," Shirley said, "that's a long way off. So," she said, "what is it with you and women? Hell, a man like you should be beating them off with a stick."

"Thank you," Nick said. He didn't know what else to say. What he finally said was, "I look but I don't leap."

"Personally," she said, "I'd love the chance to have a man in my arms instead of one on my hands. Do you know what I mean?"

Nick toasted her wisdom and smiled.

Shirley sighed. "What I need," she said, "is some love in my life."

And what about me, Nick thought, what do I need?

The hunt is really the kick, E.Z. told him on the way home; what happens later is no big deal.

Chapter 31

Saturday morning Nick helped E.Z. grind three hundred pounds of mackerel and some squid into chum. They put the chum in heavy plastic containers and dripped some menhaden oil on top, then stacked the containers in E.Z.'s freezer. Nick spent the afternoon buying paint and some lumber for the shed. As he drove over the Triborough Bridge late Sunday afternoon he glanced at the sign for Queens. He took this particular route once, sometimes twice a month. Most of the time he passed the sign with hardly a thought; on this day he thought of Sonny McCabe, Captain Hawks, and Sergi Monserette. Los Campos had been one hell of a case, a whole lot of bad luck, a bad business all around. He pulled into his garage on Sixty-third Street at around five o'clock, deep into the memories.

At the video store later that evening he came across a stack of the works of Martin Scorsese. Nick had seen *Mean Streets* maybe six times; *Taxi Driver* he found a bit too violent. A posted sign told him he could buy *Mean Streets* for nineteen dollars. There was a picture of Robert De Niro in a pose from *Raging Bull*, his all-time favorite. Violence, Nick thought, is relative.

"De Niro is the best American actor alive," the slender dark woman said. "Pacino is not bad either."

For a moment Nick was not sure if she was speaking to him.

"There are many terrific American actors," he said cordially.

"Name ten."

"I couldn't."

"Have you seen *Bang the Drum Slowly*?"

"Yes, I have. A bit slow, but a great film."

"Slow? Did you say slow?" The woman smiled; she touched his hand and Nick felt his insides hit a speed bump. "The average American knows so little about films," she said. "They're into video games." She was smiling at him the way a woman alone smiles at you in one of those East Side bars, the way a woman smiles at you when she wants you to talk to her, to take her home. "Americans," she said, "think *Star Wars* was a great film."

He didn't hear an accent, not one he could recognize; his first re-action was to ask where it was she was from, if not America. It passed; he lacked the courage to say too much. And so Nick did precisely what you would expect, he agreed with her. "Americans don't have very good taste in films," he said. Nick hated calling movies films, he didn't know why exactly, but it made him feel like who knows what, a feeling he didn't like at all.

"Do you know what my favorite American movie is?" she told him.

Nick shrugged, looked left, then right, searching for *Citizen Kane*, trying to be cool.

"*Death Wish*," she said. "Just the first one. The sequel lost all its originality."

"I liked that movie," Nick said. "It was good."

She walked away laughing. "Slow," she said. "*Bang the Drum Slowly* was slow."

She was wearing a red cashmere turtleneck, some sort of slim skirt, and flat shoes, and her hair was in a black bobbing ponytail. She was, in a word, sensational, and her walk was a personal statement, Nick would have followed her anywhere. He glanced at her over his shoulder and saw her talking seriously with a man half Nick's age, a young man her own age. Suddenly he felt like a tire that had just run over a steel spike.

The following morning, as was his habit, Nick rose at six thirty, put water up for coffee, threw on a pair of sweats and sneakers, a hooded sweatshirt, and went into the street to get a bagel at the Tal, and a copy of the morning *Times*.

Even though it was not yet seven A.M. the place was packed, primarily with men in suits clutching their attaché cases, waiting in line for coffee and a bagel. No one smiled. Nick stood in front of a counter that ran the length of the store and held every kind of salad you could name, along with whitefish and lox and sliced meats and cheese. Nick glanced around the place. Everyone seemed to be standing around like they were in a dentist's office, waiting for their number to be called for root canal. A tall guy in chinos and a lightweight running jacket tapped Nick on the shoulder and pointed with his thumb to the end of the line.

She stood about ten feet behind him, dressed in shorts and a T-shirt, one arm across her stomach, her hand supporting the elbow of the other arm, making these little waving motions. To the front of her and to the rear of her were well-dressed men in ties and jackets. The guy behind her looked like he was about to freak staring at her legs, her ass.

"Good morning," she said. Nick thought she was watching him suggestively.

There were about ten people in front of her waiting to be served. "Can I get you something?" he said. She shook her head and motioned to the line, indicating to him that she would wait her turn. Nick gave her a sour look implying there was nothing he could do. For a split second an invisible beam connected their eyes, and she pursed her lips. A pucker, Nick thought. That was a quick little pucker. When his turn came Nick ordered his bagel, plain, and felt a heat wave hit his stomach the likes of which he hadn't known since high school. As he walked through the door he turned and looked back at her, and she grinned. Nick's heart was racing and he felt his face turn bright pink.

Later, when he drove from the garage out into the street he thought he saw her walking with the young man from the video store. The couple turned into Sixty-eighth Street and for an instant he was sure it was her, but it was too difficult to see, the street was crowded, and a bus turned in front of him, he caught just a glimpse. Who was this

guy, this guy walking with her? And she looked different, with her hair
up, and wearing a dress.

That night he walked around the neighborhood, in and out of the
crowds along First Avenue, went into Sheridan's for a beer and sandwich. At one point he ran into a team of detectives he knew from the
local precinct, who were checking out an abandoned car. He left the
detectives to their work and wandered past a crowd waiting in line at
the foreign films theater while a black guy in dreadlocks entertained
them with his guitar and a song. After a few more minutes of cruising
he decided to head for home. He stopped at the Pakistani smoke shop
and picked up a copy of the *Post*; when he went out the door, out into
the street, she was standing there. Thank you Lord.

She stood there, arms folded, wearing another turtleneck, a brown
one this time, and a bronze miniskirt. She had amazing legs and knew
it, wasn't at all shy about showing them. With her sensual face and
lean figure she put Nick in mind of an Italian movie star whose name
he could not remember. Fact of the matter was, watching her standing
there, he was fearful he'd forget his own name. His brain was screaming
hi, hello, how are ya?

"You know," she said in a hushed voice. "We have to stop meeting
like this."

"Believe me, the pleasure is all mine." That was the gospel truth.
Her eyes were shining, green he thought, or blue, they sure looked
cheerful and full of light.

"Can I ask a favor," she said. "Would you mind walking me to the
ATM? I get nervous this time of night."

He almost danced with glee. "Sure," he said, "sure, sure. Which one
are you going to?" He didn't care if it was in Bangkok, he was going.

"On Sixty-seventh, right on the corner."

"Perfect, I live nearby."

She took his arm. "Really, where?"

"On Sixty-seventh, between First and Second."

"Oh that's great, then I'm not taking you out of your way."

"No, not at all, not at all." Along the sidewalk a steady stream of
people moved about, window-shopping, walking, couples laughing. Nick
felt himself shifting into lightweight conversation, loosening up, trying
to relax. He felt light-headed. It was foolish—no, not foolish, ridiculous—to be so self-conscious, but God, she was beautiful, people actually turned their heads as they walked by.

"Has anyone ever told you that you look like Marcello Mastroianni?"
she said.

"No."

"Marcello, I'll call you Marcello."

"Call me whatever you like."

"I love your nose, the first thing I noticed about you was that nose of yours."

"I boxed, when I was young, I used to be a fighter." Was she impressed? "I broke it so often they took the bone out. See?" He touched his nose, she touched his nose and laughed, they both laughed. She was a model . . . of course. A student at the New School studying screenwriting. Might like to act someday, maybe, didn't think she had it in her. But loved films, loved to write. Been in New York three weeks. Her name was Laura and she was twenty-four years old. Twenty-four, man, he had suits that old.

She went into the ATM, came out, and they looked in a woman's clothing store, a bookstore, silent, but it was okay; he was feeling more and more comfortable with her. He felt a glow; he believed he could ask for her telephone number.

"Can I ask for your phone number?"

"Marcello . . ."

"My name is Nick, Nick Manaris."

"You told me, but I told you I would call you Marcello. Marcello," she said, "I don't give out my phone number. I live with my brother, he doesn't like it."

"Your brother?"

"Yes, his name is Mariano, and he is very protective, sometimes too much, but it's okay."

"All right."

"Don't look so sad, Marcello, give me your phone number and I will call you. We will go to the movies, how's that?"

"You won't call me."

"Why not? Of course I'll call you. I said I would call you and I will."

"Listen, Laura, I'm sorry."

"About what?"

"You know, your phone number and all. I mean you don't know me, you just arrived in New York, and . . ."

"What? What, Marcello?"

"I'm old enough to be your father."

Not even a blink. "No you're not."

"Yes I am."

"How old are you?"

"Forty. No I'm not, I'm forty-six."

"Hmm. Well, you don't look it, you don't look forty." That sounded wonderful. He felt something that was purely physical, like the first hint of his stomach going bad. He wanted to ask her out right then, take her to the Rainbow Room or Tavern on the Green, some place nice and fancy, a New York tourist trap, who cares, a fancy joint of some kind. He started fantasizing about blowing her away with a fabulous New York night, something original, something different. But he was too tense, too nervous. His heart banging in his throat like a drum. "Forty-six," he repeated. She gave a so-what shrug.

"Give me your phone number," she said, "and I'll call you."

"You won't call."

That took her aback. She touched his arm. "I will," she said. "I like you. Of course I'll call. By the way, what do you do here in this big city?"

"I'm a policeman, a captain. I work for the Queens district attorney." He started to calm down.

"It's settled then, I'll be safe with you. A captain, boy I'm impressed. I'll call you in a day or two, you can show me a little of the city."

Nick said, "Can I ask you a question? Do you like the ocean? Fishing, boats? Do you like the country?"

She narrowed those eyes. "I'm Cuban," she said, "my blood gets warm when I'm near the sea. I'll call you," she murmured, giving him that pucker, that smile, and walked away.

Nick strode home singing, "Start spreading the news, I'm leaving today . . . da, da, dada, da, da—New York, New York."

He was feeling good, feeling like a man with something going for him. Nick believed he could levitate, rise above the sad crowds around him and fly off. His head was full of thoughts of Laura, of leaving New York, of a life in Wickham. Something was most definitely in the air. All his fantasies included life in Wickham. Having someone rest her head in your lap on a cold, snow-blown winter night. Sitting in front of a good fire, listening to Verdi and Puccini and drinking wine. Someone's arm around your waist on a long summer walk along the beach, boiling lobster and cold beer, slow sex on a rainy Sunday afternoon. And laughter, laughter was important, maybe most important of all.

Nick imagined E.Z. saying, "Man, where did you find her?" He could hear Andre, "Excuse me? Twenty-four, did you say she is twenty-four? What the hell do you talk about?"

In front of the mirror in his bathroom Nick pinched the soft skin at the corner of his eyes saying, "Okay, okay, no more bagels and coffee, tomorrow it's Special K, some lowfat milk and orange juice. A little run, a good walk for sure. Break out those weights, do the sit-ups and leg raises. He'd lost some hair after turning forty, and his gut, which had always taken serious work to keep firm, now protruded a bit over his belt. That's it, sit-ups, leg raises, get back in the swing, it's easy, you're a pro, a jock, it's nothing at all, just a matter of commitment.

Nick thought that his marriage had been a disaster from the start. Hell, he was still using the wedding-present towels when she split. His marriage had ended when Laura was what, nine years old? Thinking of Laura, the child, he was driven to silent, guilty laughter. Not that dating a younger woman was at all unusual for him. There was Renata, ten years younger, now living in Tampa with a physical education teacher. And after Renata there was the clinical psychologist who, whenever she came to see him, would always check his medicine cabinet just to be certain he hadn't come down with some sexually transmitted disease. He hadn't been able to maintain an erection with her, always talking, as she did, about the ravages of AIDS. Then there was the black-eyed Puerto Rican nurse from Park Slope with fingernails like daggers and forty kinds of shampoo in her shower. Then the lawyer from Garden City, the blonde who just loved doing a couple of lines of coke before a night out. The poet who had been married four times and had attempted suicide twice. The tall, redheaded chef who had two children and a sick father in her sprawling ranch house in Woodstock, all of them practicing Buddhists.

Nothing came of anything. Oh, there was some great sex, the Buddhist was exceptionally terrific, and the Puerto Rican, with those nails and that thick, black hair, could turn you loose. Still nothing came of it, nothing came of any of it. They still called from time to time, all of them. He would go fishing instead, hunt shark and tuna and dream about the woman he could truly love. Wherever she was. Man, he had known enough women in his life, and the ones he'd known weren't all that different. He had been married and divorced, he had been single a long time. Single was better. Would anybody get married if they knew what it really meant? When all the wonderful nonsense falls away and life turns to the day-to-day tussle, when you realize that you have to spend the rest of your life with someone you can hardly talk to; that's when it all goes into the toilet. Still, there was a woman out there for him, but she kept escaping him. All he knew was that he had been searching for years. What were the odds it was Laura? A remote possibility at best.

He lay in bed too happy to sleep. Laura. He said the name to himself, and then out loud. What the hell are you thinking? She didn't even give you her phone number. Nice try, Marcello. Right before Nick fell through the surface of sleep he was thinking, when you go to sleep hungry don't you dream of food?

When two days passed without any call from Laura, Nick began to brood. He had gone to the Tal every morning and had not seen her. He walked the nighttime streets and she was nowhere to be found. He passed the days in his office catching up on paperwork and avoiding Andre for no reason he could name. One day he spent twelve straight hours working a bank fraud case with a team of detectives and a team of FBI agents. He could only wonder what had possessed him to imagine that Laura would call him. What had he been thinking? The woman was barely more than half his age. By Wednesday he had an urge to head north. He telephoned E.Z. to ask about his plans for the coming weekend.

Chapter 32

For Chino and Manny Vasserman, Wednesday night surpassed all other nights of the week. On Wednesday nights the brothers got high on aguardiente and tropical snow, on Wednesday nights they packaged ounces and eighth-kilos of cocaine and then went to Sleepy's whorehouse, where they tried to fuck women and failed hopelessly because they were too stoned, too high, the coke turning their pricks to worms.

Manny was sitting at a Formica kitchen table, wearing a green long-sleeved shirt, counting money. Chino was testing a sample from a new package of cream-colored cocaine base. It was one o'clock in the morning, and Chino sucked his teeth and sniffed, saying, "I have to kill somebody to teach somebody, I mean that's the way you have to be out here."

"Is that package stretched like the last one?" Manny asked.

"Sure, just like the last one. These people think we're stupid. They must be crazy to think we're stupid. Because you know, man, I'll kill somebody, I'll take somebody out."

After his release from prison, Manny Vasserman moved to Union City, New Jersey, opened a bodega called Dos Hermanos, and waited for his brother, Chino, to come home and join him in freedom and the cocaine business. Chino had been home a year, and now the brothers were waist deep into drugs and sinking in oceans of cash.

"Did you tell him? You got to tell him his product is shit," Manny said. He was hunched in his chair, his massive arms folded on the table. Chino sat across from him, rubbing some cocaine between his thumb and forefinger. The pure cocaine would be absorbed into his skin, the mix, which was not supposed to be there, shone and glimmered between his fingers. Chino's Asian eyes narrowed, his face grew red with anger and his mouth held a cold firm smile. "You know this fucking guy keeps bringing us this shit that has been stretched. It's supposed to be pure and look here, man, the mix is right here, you can see it."

"We'll tell him. C'mon, man, hurry up, finish up, the women are waiting at Sleepy's."

Dos Hermanos was at the end of a street that ran past tenements and two-family houses to the interstate. The neighborhood was in serious decline, still the bodega stayed open late, sometimes until one or two in the morning. In the rear of Dos Hermanos was a three-room apartment, a bare, evil-smelling place where the brothers kept Kiki, their pit bull, where they kept their coca, where they were sitting when they heard the knock on the bodega's front door.

Chino looked down at the tabletop. "Now who the hell can that be?"

Manny was silent.

The knock came again, louder this time.

Manny reached across the table for the bottle of aguardiente and poured some into his glass.

Chino said, "Are you going to see who is there or what?"

"The store is locked, the lights are out. It can't be anyone we know."

Manny tried to will his brother up from the table; as for himself, he felt no desire to leave his drink. When the knock came again Chino said, "Will you get up and see who is there?"

"They'll go away."

"Go, go and see who it is."

Manny got up quickly and went inside the bodega. The store was dark, he switched on the lights. Outside in the doorway two people were waiting, two women, and from where he was standing Manny could not believe his luck. The sound of Manny's laughter covered his soft steps as he went through the store to the front door.

"Who is it?" Chino called out.

"You won't believe it, man."

The two women wore red dresses, both of them carrying what appeared to be shoulder bags of fine leather. Manny unlocked the door to open it, taking a good look at them, realizing how attractive they actually were. Had he not been so thrown off balance by their beauty he might have considered why here? Why now? Why me? But he was shaken for a moment. He could not remember a time in his life when such fantastic women had stood before him smiling.

"Yes, ladies, yes, what can I do for you?"

They stood side by side looking at him, smiling at him, and they gave off a scent, a woman's scent that was somewhere between jasmine and sea air. The older of the two, and she was older, and not quite as breathtaking as the younger, still she was fantastic, with large breasts that seemed to be pushed up and out of her dress. She said, "We came here to buy some cigarettes. We were told we could buy cigarettes in this bodega."

Well, well, thought Manny. Fate at last is smiling at me.

"As you can see we are closed, but for you, for you two, anything, whatever you like."

"Who is it?" Chino called.

"Come see brother, come see what God has sent us."

The young one had a nice body, really a thin woman with small breasts, but man was she beautiful. Manny thinking he would love to suck her small tits and play a game with the both of them. But the young one looked serious, too serious, and there was a sadness in her eyes. She stood as if she was posing, one of those thin models, tall and firm-looking, good, man, looking so good.

"Hey brother," Chino said, "who are your friends? Where are your manners? Ask them to come in."

"They want to buy cigarettes," Manny said.

"Good, cigarettes, yes, we have cigarettes. What kind would you like? We have all kinds," Chino said.

The young one spoke for the first time, with her thumb and forefinger she made a circle. "Fat ones," she said, "about this fat, the kind we can take tobacco out of and put something in. You know, something worth smoking." She spoke softly, quietly, like an angel.

"*Coño*," Manny said, "I'll give you something to smoke, something good and fat to smoke."

"You know what we want," the older one said. "We're ready to pay a fair price. People tell us—"

"What people?" Chino said. "Who told you to come here?"

"Names," the older one said, "are not important to us. We don't use people's names."

"Aha," said Chino, "you are not only beautiful, you are funny too." He motioned for the two women to come into the store. "I am Chino, this one here is Manny, we are brothers."

The older one spoke first. "I am Natalia and she is Maria, my daughter. Well, not really my daughter, I only think of her that way, like she is my daughter."

"Chica," Manny said, "c'mon, you are lying. This is your sister, she can't be your daughter."

The women were looking around the bodega, turning away from
Chino as he spoke, and it seemed to Manny that they were checking
the place out.

"Yes, yes, she is my mother," Maria said. "Do you have some of what
we want?"

"Woman," Chino said, "maybe we have what you want, maybe. For
sure I have what you need, believe me."

Chino took a deep breath and glanced at his brother, then he
grabbed his crotch, tugging upward. He looked very macho. When he
turned back to the young one, the one called Maria, he noticed the
pistol in her hand.

"I won't ask what you're doing," Chino said. "I am going to tell you
to take my advice and put that away and leave while you can."

"Just turn around and go into the apartment," Natalia said. "Just do
what you're told and everything will be okay."

Manny said, "What do you want? Coca? Money? What?"

"We want you to go into the apartment now," Maria told him.

"Okay, okay," Chino said, "we'll go." He turned away from the sight
of the gun, took Manny by the elbow, and the brothers went through
the bodega into the kitchen of the apartment.

"Sit down," Maria told them.

Manny turned and looked with disgust into the beautiful young
woman's cold green eyes. He could not stand to be the object of a
woman's games, and his cocaine-flooded brain told him that that was
exactly what was happening. He was being toyed with by a young
woman. They were alone in the kitchen now, the older woman, Natalia,
had remained in the bodega, but after a moment she appeared at the
kitchen door, and standing with her was a young man with a smile on
his face and a machine pistol in his hand. The young man pointed to
the bottle of aguardiente on the kitchen table, saying, "Colombians
drink that shit, not Cubans."

Manny shrugged his massive shoulders, smiled, and said, "Ey, compadre, do you know who you're fooling with here?"

"Compadre, compadre, compadre," the young man said, and that's
all he said.

Bewildered and frightened, Manny smiled and tried to shrug. The
young man seemed like one of those crazy *pistolocos*, a Marielito, a
shooter, one of those fucking nutty kids from the boats. He was thin,
with a light complexion, maybe twenty-four or -five, and he carried
himself like a man of authority, a dangerous man, with his machine
gun and crazy smile.

Chino sat still at the table and looked at his captors without expression.

The young woman started talking, and as she talked, the older one said yes, yes. Manny could not believe what the fuck he was hearing.

"Please," Manny said, "you people are wrong, you have the wrong brothers here. What you say has nothing to do with us."

Chino sat in silence, he understood what was happening and was too frightened to speak.

"We are Cienfuegos, I am Mariaclara and this is my brother, Miguel," the young woman said. "Do you know that name, Manny? Do you remember Diego Cienfuego? Do you remember our father?"

Manny slowly shook his head.

Maria smiled coldly. "There were many people in that room, Manny. Many people in that jail. They saw what you did, they watched you cut our father's throat, you pig. They told me you danced when you were through."

Manny could only sit and stare, taking each breath as it came. She spoke for a long time about her father, about her uncle Benny, how Benny and Cano had killed her stepmother's husband, Rodrigo. How they tortured him, how Manny killed Diego as if he were a chicken or a lamb or a rabbit. Manny listened to all this and more with great attention, and when the young woman was through he held out his hand and said, "Please, you know it was a long time ago."

He knew it was a stupid thing to say. He wanted to get up and run but he was too terrified to move.

"I won't ask you for a break," Chino said finally.

Manny's mouth fell open.

"*Hijodeputa*," Miguel Cienfuego said, "you can ask for whatever you like. It never hurts to ask."

"Fuck you," said Chino, and he stood up from the table.

"Sit," Maria ordered him.

"Fuck you too lady. Fuck you."

"No," Natalia said. "Fuck you." She took the gun from Miguel's hand and cocked it.

"What are you doing?" Manny said.

Chino stepped back.

Natalia looked down at Manny. Nothing but hatred in those black eyes. She raised the gun with both hands and pointed it at Manny's massive chest; Chino turned to follow the gun with his gaze and angrily she turned the pistol on him and fired.

The explosion filled the small room as Chino pitched over backward and lay dead.

"Please," Manny said. "Listen, I don't blame you—" Natalia's smile stopped him, he froze in his chair. When Maria cocked her gun he turned, hearing the explosion. A hole the size of a quarter erupted from the front of his head in a great flash of red.

Maria took two hoods from her shoulder bag and handed them to Miguel, who went to where Manny and Chino lay, lifting their heads and pulling the hoods over their faces. From his pocket he took two pieces of paper, on each was written the words FOR TORTURE AND MURDER YOU PAY THE PRICE. He pinned one to each of the hoods.

The three of them went back out through the bodega, careful to make no noise, as if they might awaken the two corpses left behind.

Chapter 33

On the night Laura telephoned him Nick had already come to terms with the fact that he would never hear from her again. Yet there she was on the phone, her voice soft and sweet, as if she were talking to him in a confessional.

It was Thursday night, around eight o'clock. Nick was sitting in his apartment at the kitchen table writing checks, paying the bills, thirty-one dollars for the cable TV, when the telephone rang. Laura told him that she was sorry it had taken her so long to call. It had only been what, three days going on a century? Laura, sweet Laura, sounding so sympathetic and kindhearted on the phone, her voice like an angel's. I'm sorry, she told him, I've been busy, real busy, with school and looking for work and all. He held his hand against his chest, feeling it rise and fall. Her voice was deeply sexual, and he wondered if she knew that.

"Well," Nick said, "to be honest, I didn't think you'd call."

"Marcello," she said softly, "I said I would call you, and here I am."

That voice of hers was giving his nerves a real workout. Still, he was not so sure he liked this Marcello business.

"Any luck?" he said. "You know, with a job?"

"Some, we'll see. Listen, do you have any plans for the weekend?"

"Sort of. I have a place in the country. I go there most weekends."

"Oh, all right. I was thinking that maybe we could have had dinner

Saturday, go to a movie, something like that. But if you have plans, there's always next week."

Somewhat to his surprise, Nick asked her if she would like to come along. Said it's a small cottage, no big deal, but with a guest room, and after all he was trustworthy, a police officer, one of the good guys, no problem.

"Are you always good, Marcello?"

Nick thinking enough already with the Marcello. Also thinking, her voice, a trace of an accent, softening all that she says. "Yes," he told her. "I'm always good." Nick felt himself blushing.

"We'll see," she told him, speaking even more softly.

"So?"

"What?"

"Would you like to come to the country with me? You'll have your own room, you can relax, inhale some good sea air."

"I don't think so."

There was silence, a long moment of silence. Nick was sure that his next words would be that he would stay in the city for the weekend. And they were.

"How early can I call you in the morning?" she asked him.

"Why?"

"I should have known better," she said. "Policemen always answer a question with a question, don't they?" Like shrinks.

"You can call me as early as you like, six, six thirty. Do you mind if I ask why?"

"Because I don't want you to change your plans for me. I'd love to go to the country with you, but I'll have to let you know tomorrow."

"Okay, call me, let me know. Anyway, I'd be glad to spend a weekend in the city for a change."

"You love your place in the country, don't you?"

"Yes I do."

"You know," she said, "my father once told me that it's easier to be in love with a place than a person."

"A smart man, your father."

"Yes, he was."

"He's dead?"

"Yes. For quite some time."

"Mine too. I'm sorry."

"I'll call you in the morning."

It occurred to Nick that they talked as if they were already lovers. Later, getting into bed, Nick was suddenly very happy. It was something he never confessed about himself, the fact that he thought he had gone

by the possibility of ever feeling truly happy. Thinking of Laura reminded him of days in college, the sensation of it, a new woman in his
life and great expectations. When he would stay for a long time in the
shower, shave just right, dress just right, walk with a certain sureness
to his step, a confidence that he had something going. The intense
experience of feeling good about himself, and now Laura was bringing
him back.

She called him at six thirty in the morning. What time should she
be ready for him to come and fetch her?

Fetch her? He smiled. No one he knew used such a word.

"Would three be too early? I like to beat the traffic."

She'd wait for him on the corner of First Avenue and Sixty-seventh
Street. "I'll be packed, waiting, and ready."

"I'll be there." Beaming. "Laura," he said, "I can't wait."

She laughed.

Not then, but later, Nick compared that call from Laura to the
only other time in his life when he thought he had hit love's jackpot.
Spring when he was seventeen, the night of his senior prom. The girl
who accompanied him for a night on the town was Jeanne Latori;
she was small and thin and wore long drop earrings and had a great
head of curly hair and a hippy's style, and on whom he had a terrible
crush. They were both high school seniors, he at Saint Frances Prep
and she at Dominican Commercial. When she attended class Jeanne
wore a school uniform, brown and dull, with these clunky shoes. Under the uniform she wore a G-string, one hell of a girl that Jeanne.
The night of his prom was beautiful and warm; they found themselves alone on the Staten Island ferry, watching the sun rise. Beneath the dawn sky, in the salt spray, Jeanne made love to him on a
deck chair. Taking him from his tuxedo trousers, she lifted her prom
dress and straddled him, and sweet Jesus, he watched the sun rise
and knew he had found love.

As it turned out it was the last time he saw her. Jeanne ran off to
San Francisco with some older guy who had a beard and waist-length
hair. He suffered that summer, his heart broken, his father telling him
over and over, don't confuse loneliness and lust with love—but then
again, why should you be different? Everyone else does.

The next morning Nick went into the office early. Andre was already
at his desk and Nick told him he would be leaving sometime after
lunch, he wanted to break out of the city before the weekend rush.

They spent twenty minutes over coffee discussing current cases.
Andre was interested in the bank fraud case, liked the idea that his

investigators could work easily with the FBI. Nick explained his concerns about working with the feds, nothing new, the same old stuff; Andre was patient, he'd heard it all before. They spent a few minutes talking about Sonny McCabe's TV appearance. Andre was a Larry King fan, the guy was his favorite among the current crop of talk show hosts.

"You know," Andre said, "Sonny embodies everything the old-time wanna-bes aspired to but only a rare few ever achieved."

Nick folded his arms and looked at the floor. "Sometimes," he told Andre, "you sound like a fan of his."

"I'm no fan. But now that you mention it, Sonny understood how it was done. The guy needed no lessons, there's no one around like him anymore."

"Sure there is, you read about them in the paper all the time."

"By the way," Andre said, "did you get that message from Bill Kenney, the DEA agent?"

On Tuesday Nick had found a message from Andre telling him to call a DEA agent in Miami. He tried, twice, but was unable to connect with the guy. "I did, but I wasn't able to reach him. Who is he?"

"You don't remember him?"

"I'm afraid not," Nick said. He rose. "I'd better get back to my office. I've got to work out these summer vacation schedules."

"You do remember the Los Campos case?"

"Sure . . . oh, the DEA guy that adopted the Matos and Medina case. He worked with an FBI agent—what was his name?"

"Cosgrove, Jim Cosgrove. He left the Bureau, took a huge job with IBM. Heads up their security in Tempe, I think."   ·

"So do you know what Kenney wanted?"

"I only spoke to him for a minute. He caught Sonny's act on the King show and wanted to speak to you."

"I'll call him."

"What are your plans for the weekend?"

"Going north."

"What else is new."

"I've got company this time."

Andre's eyes twinkled and a smile crept across his face. "A woman?" he said.

"Uh-huh."

"Something special?"

"Very. And very young."

"Good for you. How young?"

"Very."

"Fifteen, sixteen? How young?"

"Twenty-four." Nick began to explain how he met Laura, had to stop and start over. Andre interrupted him.

"Hey listen," Andre said, "I understand the fun of jumping from bed to bed and having meaningless affairs with lots of people. But somehow I never think of you that way."

Nick nodded quickly.

"What's her name?"

"Laura."

"Laura what?"

Nick was embarrassed. "To tell you the truth, I don't know."

"Sounds exciting," Andre said.

"We'll see."

"Give Kenney a call. He liked you. It's good to be friends with some feds."

It turned out that Agent Kenney had been waiting to hear from him. He had called Nick twice himself and left messages with Nick's secretary. Nick had not received them.

Nick told him it was these civilian workers, you know the type, come-in-late-leave-early, that type. Then Kenney asked him if he'd caught Sonny on the King show the other night. Nick said yeah, well he'd sat through most of it.

"He looked good," Kenney said. "The guy's still me-deep in conversation after all these years. Actually, when I saw him I thought of the Los Campos case, and I had to give you guys in New York a call."

Nick said, "I'm glad you did, it's nice hearing from you. Been busy, I bet. Miami and all. So, what's new in the drug wars?"

"I do some work down here with Dade County and the Miami police. Anyway, about two weeks back they found two Cubanos alongside a canal, Miami Metro did, killed execution style, one bullet apiece, in the head. Now, things being how they are down here that's no big deal, except there was something a bit strange."

Nick waited.

"Somebody covered their heads with hoods. Attached a little note to them. Something about betrayal, and torture. Different, you don't see that everyday."

"No you don't," Nick told him. By then Nick regretted giving Kenney a call, he had things to do, a busy schedule, a ton of paperwork. And he had to get himself a haircut, a big weekend coming up.

"Anyway, these two guys, the Cubanos in the hoods, one was a small-time dealer named Felix Caban. He was a coconspirator in the Los Campos case, and he was that guy Diego Cienfuego's cellmate at Rikers. The other guy was Luis Ruiz, a.k.a. Cubano. A shooter out of the Bronx, a buddy of the Vasserman brothers. You remember them, right?"

"Sure. Look, these cowboys pop each other for exercise. No great loss."

"So you don't think it's anything?"

"Yeah, it's something. We're minus two drug dealers."

Agent Kenney finally understood that Nick wasn't into any of this, and Nick wasn't sure if the guy was relieved or disappointed. They went on discussing drugs and their relationship to American politics for about five minutes.

"I hope you don't take this wrong," Nick told him, "but the less I have to do with Cubans, Colombians, drugs, and guns, the better I like it. It's bank frauds and hijackings for me. Not as messy, if you know what I mean."

Kenney favored him with a quick, uncomfortable laugh and told him to stay in touch, said if Nick ever came down to Miami they'd eat some stone crab and have some beers.

"By the way," Nick asked him, "whatever happened to your two stars? You know, Medina and Matos?"

"Look, those guys did great by us. They testified down here and in New Orleans, put together some major drug cases. As a matter of fact, they testified at a closed session of Congress, about drug money and corruption in the Bahamas. Nick, they knew people that rented islands down there, cays they call them. Some of these cays, these little islands, had landing strips. The Bahamas cops helped them unload the coke planes. You believe that?"

"To tell you the truth, it doesn't surprise me at all. So what happened to Matos and Medina?"

Kenney said, "They were in the program for about five years, relocated, you know, the whole bit. The last I heard, they flunked out."

"What do you mean flunked out?"

"The U.S. Marshall Service runs a tight ship. Once you're in the program you have responsibilities. You don't live up to them, they cut you loose."

Nick laughed. "Responsibilities? You mean you can't kill anybody, or sell drugs, you have to find a job? Who you kidding? None of the characters you guys drop into that program work out. What you're doing is relocating crime around the country and that's about it."

"I don't know why you say that," Kenney said. "The program works. In fact it's about the best thing we have going."

Nick said, "So there you have it. They're back in the street. Medina and Matos are out and about."

"Last I heard they were."

Nick shook his head, laughing. "Fucking great."

Chapter 34

Well," Natalia Punto said, "I do not see a word of it in any of the newspapers."

She and Mariaclara were sitting at a window table in Victor's Café on Amsterdam Avenue drinking coffee. It was lunchtime and the avenue was busy with people; Maria frowned at the passing crowds. "Maybe no one found them yet," she said.

"Please, the bodega was left open, people come and go."

In the years since her father's murder, Maria and her brother Miguel had lived with Natalia Punto in a pleasant house in Southern Florida, in a town call Hollywood, north of Miami. It was a community mostly of retired people who had fled the crime, the cold, and the taxes of the north. Most of their neighbors were American, but a few were Cuban; it was in the Cuban section of town that Natalia had opened a small restaurant and coffee shop.

The family of three had lived a simple life among kind and friendly people, free from the cruelty and brutality that characterized so much of their lives in New York City. The brother and sister had grown up Cuban-American and deeply indebted to Natalia who, they were convinced, had saved them from being separated, from becoming wards of the state.

Natalia was still as strikingly beautiful as the day she turned Diego Cienfuego's head. She was also completely obsessed by thoughts of revenge; other than Maria and Miguel, little else in her life had any meaning to her. She was a deeply angry woman, filled with hatred and fury and images of the vengeance she would exact for the murders of Diego, the man she considered her one true love, his poor son Justo, and Rodrigo, a man who had married and cared for her since her arrival in the United States. Natalia had read the accounts of Rodrigo's brutal torture and death, had read every painful detail. For years she hated Benny and Cano with such unbridled fury that when their names were mentioned the odor of that hatred came through her skin. Natalia's relentless rage was fostered in Maria and her brother; there had been many late nights of planning, much spinning of schemes, the three of them devising ways they would find retribution.

"You won't find any mention of it in the New York newspapers," Maria said. "You have to look in the New Jersey papers."

Maria had come across town to convince Natalia that her trip to the country with Nick Manaris was a good idea, but Natalia was totally opposed to it and didn't want her spending any more time then she absolutely had to with the cop.

"Nothing in the papers, nothing on the TV, it seems strange to me," Natalia told Maria.

She called the waiter over and ordered another coffee. "We agreed that none of us would do anything on our own, we decided that long ago. What will you accomplish by going off with this man?"

Maria put her elbow on the table and rested her chin on her fist.

"I want to know more about him," she said.

"What for? All we need to know is where to find him and his two friends."

Miguel came through the door holding a newspaper absently in his hand.

"Good morning *niño*," Natalia said, looking into Miguel's face, smiling at him, tapping the seat alongside her.

"Sweet sister, you look good, your usual dazzling self." Miguel called the waiter over and gave Natalia his nice-boy smile. "Four down, four to go," he said. "We're batting a thousand."

Around them the restaurant was beginning to fill now with the lunch crowd. A young black couple sat at the table just behind them.

"Your sister has made some plans of her own," Natalia said. "I want you to speak to her."

"What plans?" Miguel said. His smile faded and he turned his head to look around the restaurant. "What are you up to now?"

"Don't worry about me, let's talk about you. Any word from your friend about Benny and Cano?" Maria said.

"We'll hear, we'll know soon. They are both in Miami, we know that. In a few days, I bet no more than a week, we'll have them."

Natalia sipped her coffee, her eyes locked in on Maria over the rim of her cup. "Tell your brother what your plans are. Go on, tell him."

"Yes, well, this cop, this Nick, I am going to go with him to his country house."

"Shit on that idea, what are you, crazy?" Miguel said. "Because if you're going crazy, I'm through with this. I'll leave tomorrow for Spain and forget all about it."

"Miguel, I want to know more about this man, that's all." She put her cup down. "I don't think that is strange, to want to know a bit more about the man you're going to kill."

"What do you mean, know more about him? Know what? And what will you do, sleep with him, make love to a man we have marked for death?"

"Tell her," Natalia said. "You are her brother. I don't think it is right to make love to a man who is responsible for the death of your father."

"Who said anything about sleeping with him? My God, I'm only going for a ride with him. He has a guest room, I'll sleep there."

"He is a handsome man," Natalia said. "Handsome men have ways about them."

"I am not you, Natalia; I don't sleep with a man because he is handsome."

"Don't be disrespectful," Miguel said. "And don't give me a big headache. We are going to kill this man. You know that."

"Of course I do."

"Who?" Natalia said. "Who did I sleep with just because he was handsome? Tell me, who?"

"I'm sorry," Maria said. "God bless you, Natalia, I'm sorry. I'm nervous, you know, a little upset, that's all."

"I understand," Natalia told her. "After all, that pig Manny, I understand. It must be hard for you. I understand."

"Please, no, no, no, it's not that. I don't care about that pig. I waited ten years for that moment."

"All right, as long as you understand that I'm going to kill the son-ofabitch cop." Miguel said it simply matter-of-factly.

"You know," Maria said carefully, fighting a sense of alarm, "this cop Nick, he is not the one that killed Justo, it was McCabe."

"Speak softly," Miguel said, lifting his chin toward the black couple.

"They are Americans," Natalia said softly. "I heard them talk to the waiter, they don't understand a word of Spanish."

"Look," Miguel said, "we've talked this through a million times. Day in day out my entire fucking life, that's all we talked about."

"Miguel," Natalia said, "please watch your language, there are ladies present, be nice, be a gentleman."

"I'm sorry, excuse me, but you know we talked about this, this cop, this Nick, he took our father and threw him in prison with all that scum, when he knew our father was an innocent man. Put poor Papi in a hellhole where he was murdered by animals."

Mariaclara ran her hands through her hair. "Yes, yes, yes," she said. "Okay."

"You know," Natalia said, "maybe we should have taken Rodrigo's money and paid some people to do this for us. We should have gone to some Marielitos, some people who know what they are doing."

"Marielitos," Miguel said savagely. "A bunch of drug addicts and crazy people, sons of bitches are worthless."

In spite of herself Maria smiled. "Okay," she said, "okay. I have made a decision. I'm going to go for a ride with this Nick. By the way, did I tell you he is a captain now? Manaris is a police captain. When we kill him it will be big news, you won't have to look far in the newspaper for that story, Natalia."

They sat in silence. Maria finished her coffee. If the time had been right, she thought, she would have said then and there that maybe they had done enough, that she was not sleeping well, tormented as she was by nightmares, afraid all the time, that she was feeling more and more like a woman condemned to live out an ancient curse. But the time was not right.

"Look, Maria," Natalia said, "this McCabe is the one we truly want. He murdered your brother, killed poor Justo. This Nick will lead us to him. That is your job, that has always been your job, to find this McCabe, this Sonny McCabe."

Maria put her hands across her eyes.

"They are friends," Miguel said. "Good buddies, you know the American way. Pat each other on the back and laugh and drink beer and make jokes about blacks and Hispanics."

Maria had turned her face away and was biting her lip, trying to calm herself down. Miguel watched his sister, frightened for her; he felt a terrible pain in his stomach.

Like his father, Miguel was the picture of a *gallego*, a descendant of those soldiers from the north of Spain who were sent to Cuba to put down revolts. They were light-skinned and blue-eyed like Celts. Fidel himself was a *gallego*.

"You know," Miguel said. "We can wait awhile, *Díos*, we have waited ten years."

Maria only shook her head.

She was truly beautiful, Miguel thought, a real Cienfuego. His sister could have this wonderful tenderness, this kindhearted radiance, she'd just turn those extraordinary green eyes on you and you would feel like you were under a big hot sun. Mariaclara could make you feel warm. She was a little too good to be true.

"Yes," Miguel said, "we can wait awhile. But we are going to see this through. It's too late to turn back now."

"I know," Maria said.

Natalia said, "Do you really think we can do this? I mean, do all that we planned?"

Maria sat stiffly for a moment and then her tension dissolved and she gave a great smile. "It's crazy you know, really crazy. But it is certainly not impossible."

"So far it has been easy," Miguel said. "Far easier than I could have hoped." Miguel thought of himself as an intellectual, and inspired by the writings of Che and Marx; in his own mind he had given Natalia's plans of bloody revenge a political twist. His political leanings had made him no friends in the Cuban community. In fact he had few friends anywhere, of any kind.

"It was too bad that Manny died so quickly," he said. "I would liked to have seen him suffer more. Sad that you are such a good shot, Maria."

Natalia said, "I thank God that he let me live to see the man who killed my Diego die. When we put hoods on Benny and Cano my mourning will end."

Maria nodded. "I know how you feel. Now that the pig Manny is gone, I live for the day when I can look into the face of the man that murdered my poor brother." She sounded uncertain even to herself.

They sat without speaking for a moment.

Miguel said, "Does anyone think about the fact that we have violated a law of God and taken lives ourselves? Does anyone even care?" He smiled. "As for me, I don't." He looked at Maria.

"You know what I feel like?" Maria told them. "I feel like one of those Israelis that go to Argentina and kill old Nazis. I feel good, like I've done God's work."

"Yes," Natalia said, "God's work."

Miguel smiled in agreement, nodding, saying, "Someone once said, I have fought many battles, traveled long distances and at last I looked into the face of my enemy and he is me."

"What do you mean?" Natalia said. "What does he mean by that, Maria? Sometimes you are strange, Miguel, with these thoughts of yours. Just like your father. Just like Diego."

Maria hastened to answer that of course she understood Miguel. He was a Marxist, a man of the people, a man with a conscience. Miguel said yes I am. But someday I would like to own a beautiful house in Málaga and drive a big black Mercedes with dark windows, roam the streets and blow my horn at beautiful women. A Communist, said Maria, a Communist with a Mercedes, that's our Miguel.

"You two are too smart for me," Natalia told them. "It's only half the time that I understand what you are saying."

Miguel said, "It's the intelligentsia that plan revolutions, Natalia. But it is people like you, people with courage, soul, and passion that carry them out."

Maria gazed at Miguel's face. She felt then that all the affection, all the love she had ever required in this life was in her dear brother's eyes. And Natalia looked at him too, lovingly, as lovingly as any mother could look at her own child. Miguel's green eyes shone like her father's, those eyes Maria remembered so vividly. She could not stop looking at her brother.

Maria had always been haunted by a photograph of her father in a suit and tie, his long black hair sleek, looking at her mother holding the baby Justo with that wide smile of his, as though those two were the most important people in the world. Her family had been ripped from her, stolen from her, murdered by strangers in a foreign land.

Miguel had been born chubby and smiling; it was a relief to Maria that at the end of his sixteenth year Miguel had grown tall and slender. A quiet boy, a daydreamer, like his father, with few friends. He spent much time alone reading and practicing his guitar, a gift from Natalia on his sixteenth birthday. There was a sense of peacefulness about him now, something firm and orderly, it was as though he had control over his young life. Occasionally he would play and sing for Maria and Natalia or at a birthday party, and all the applause pleased Maria, made her feel proud of her brother, so much a reflection of her father.

Maria was much more her mother's child; she had a temper, and her mother's expansive personality, loads of friends, followers really. Maria was a born leader. Still, people wondered where all the anger came from. What was it exactly? And why didn't she smile more often, like other children? Mariaclara, the angry one, they called her. Everyone has secrets, even the sixteen-year-old Mariaclara. One day she told Natalia her terrible secret, she was in tears; I want God to die, she told her, I want him to die because he killed my father, and my brother. My poor child, Natalia had told her, God didn't kill your father and brother, the outlaws did. And someday, we will make them pay.

Chapter 35

On his way to the courthouse garage Nick bumped into Mark Malone, Andre's assistant and private secretary. Andre was the public face of the office, he left the day-to-day business to Mark and his staff. It would be possible, Nick thought, to describe Mark as effeminate, yet there was something assured and confident about the guy.

"Nick," Mark said. "You're off to your country house?"

"I thought I'd head out early, beat the traffic."

"Andre wanted me to tell you that you should speak to Kenney. You know, the DEA agent in Florida." Mark absently brushed the front of his suit jacket and straightened his tie.

"I spoke to him this morning."

"He called back, spoke to the man. Andre would like for you to give him a call."

Mark often referred to Andre as "the man," a habit Nick found affected and annoying.

"Kenney?"

"Right."

Nick felt his insides swell with apprehension; he wanted to get going, Laura would be waiting. "I'll call him from the car," Nick told him.

"Good, that's good. The man thinks it's important."

Nick had known Andre Robinson for what, twenty years now, and in the last he had been privy to a few of Andre's personal secrets. One was that for fifteen years Andre and Mark had been lovers, which was the reason Andre's political career had stalled in the DA's office.

Andre was certain that his well-kept secret had not been such a secret for quite some time. Sonny McCabe had known and if Sonny knew there were others, journalists, the TV guy Steve Stern, who was not a friend. It was true that times had changed; all the same, a man that wants to be mayor needs to be a straight citizen. Andre once told him that dying was easy, New York City politics is tough.

"Listen," Mark said, "did you straighten out the summer schedules? Some of the newer investigators are not at all happy."

"They're on your desk. We could use more people. It won't be easy to come up with full coverage this summer. Some of the detectives and investigators will have to work double shifts."

Mark flashed a false smile. "They are not going to like that. They'll get on my case."

"Of course, you're easy," Nick said. "They know better than to come to me."

Nick never did things simply to be liked, to be loved, it was not his way; and sometimes he did things just to let subordinates know that he didn't care if they liked him or not. He was a fair boss, but he was tough; he'd heard the stories, Captain Nick Manaris is a ballbreaker.

"We should go over it," Mark told him.

Nick glanced at his watch. It was two thirty, he was to meet Laura at three. He felt as though he was having hot flashes and wondered if men got hot flashes, his skin was heating up and his heart was racing, the skin on his neck felt like a thousand tiny pins were attacking it.

"Can't it wait?" Nick said.

"Sure, Monday is soon enough. You'll call Kenney, okay?"

"First chance I get. Sorry," he said. "I'm late. A bit at loose ends, if you know what I mean."

"It's an adventure you're off to," Mark said.

"Who told you?"

"Andre."

"What did Andre tell you?"

"Love's trumpet calls."

"Andre said that?"

Mark smiled without humor. He said, "We all need some love in our life."

In his car, Nick turned on the radio, punched in the stations one after another, then turned it off. Staring out the windshield, watching the streets go by. Jesus Christ, traffic was already building.

On the FDR he found himself in wall-to-wall traffic. How long would she wait? If he didn't show on time, how long would Laura stand on a corner? A half hour, he figured, no more than that. She'll be there, of course, she wants to get out of the city on a weekend. Who wouldn't want to be out of the city? No phone number. What if there were an emergency? No way to reach her. As the traffic got heavier, Nick felt as though he were standing on a trap door and bang! it opened. He was late, he was always late. Why was he late so often?

Nick looked in the rearview mirror, the wrinkles in the corners of his eyes were still there. And Christ, gray hair, more today then he had ever seen before.

He was getting desperate, making up a list in his head now of things they would do over the weekend. A boat ride, some fishing, a picnic at Beavertail, wine and sandwiches. A long walk on the beach, searching for rocks and shells and driftwood. Breakfast on the porch, shopping for antiques, a fire—it was too warm for a fire. Not at night, Wickham nights, even at the end of May, are cold. Did he have enough wood cut? A fire, a little wine, maybe he'd get lucky. Get lucky, get lucky, oh man, it had been a while. He hated meeting her in a suit, in a suit he looked older. He should have changed at the office. Put on a pair of jeans, work boots, and his blue sweater. In his navy blue sweater he looked younger. Traffic was impossible, he felt a crushed feeling in his stomach and wondered if she could tell, waiting there, how heavy the traffic was. He thought about that face, that smile, which made him want to get there all the more. For a moment he was positive Laura would be standing there waiting, would greet him warmly, happy he had made it; the next moment he was sure she would grow tired and leave, go off with that young guy, whoever the hell he was.

Nick Manaris turned into Sixty-seventh Street at the corner of First Avenue and there she stood in jeans and boots, a red sweater, carrying an overnight bag, a picnic basket at her feet.

She spotted him and shifted her shoulders, waved.

He pulled in at the corner and she got in, tossing her bag onto the backseat and carefully placing the picnic basket on the floor behind them. She gave him a wide, brave smile, saying, "Okay, I'm ready. Listen," she said, "I stopped at Herman's; I wanted to buy a fishing rod, then I figured you must have an extra. I want to go fishing, can we do that?"

"We can do whatever you like. If I can't deliver fishing in Wickham, I can't deliver anything."

She bent her head and put her hands over her eyes. "*Dios,*" she said, "I can't believe I'm going to be out of this city. You don't know how happy I am."

"Relax," he told her. "It's a long drive."

"How long?"

"Two and a half, three hours. Depends on traffic."

"I brought sandwiches and some wine; we can have a picnic on the way. Do you know Cuban sandwiches? Have you ever had one?"

"Sure, roast pork and cheese and ham and—"

"You know Cuban sandwiches, *bueno*. These are good ones; I went to the West Side and bought them just for you."

"Shouldn't they be eaten hot?"

"I have to admit that they won't be perfect. I wrapped them in aluminum foil; they'll be warm."

A few blocks from the First Avenue bridge they stopped at a red light and were approached by a black Hispanic teenager. The young man offered to clean their windows. Laura leaned across Nick, pressing her chest against his shoulder, giving Nick's stomach another ride through the speed bumps. She looked more angry than frightened, Nick could tell the difference. She spoke to the young man, softly and quickly in Spanish. The young man put his hands up and backed away. The light changed and they drove off. "What did you say to that kid?" Nick asked her.

"First of all, he was not a kid. Second of all, I told him that he looked young and strong and he should go and find himself a job."

"You did not."

She smiled. "You speak Spanish?"

"No. C'mon, what did you say to him?"

She gave him a troubled look and then smiled. "I just told him that you're a cop with a big gun and if he touched the car you would shoot him in the knee."

"You did not."

"You speakee the Spanish?"

"No, I do not."

"Drive, Nick," she told him. "Drive fast and far, get me out of here. C'mon, go, go. I am very excited." Then she gleefully pinched his cheek.

Very Latin, Nick thought. Her playful grin had a rowdy, slightly menacing quality that was as seductive and as sexy as anything. He stepped on the gas pedal and drove past the decayed and burnt-out streets of the South Bronx, heading for the Bruckner Expressway and I-95 North.

He thought that maybe she was on something, so animated and cheerful, so full of stories and descriptions of her favorite films and books. And she made lists of things, things she hoped to do, of people she'd met and of who among them had been kind to her. People she would one day repay. And when he gave her the short version of the story of his life her eyes grew wide with wonder. When he told her the tale of his father, of his death at a young age from cancer, she stroked his cheek. He wanted to hold her hand, he wanted just to touch her. But of course he didn't. Nick simply looked at her, smiled and shook his head, thinking Christ she's young. So young.

"To be alone in this life without family is terrible," she said at one point.

He drove very fast, speeding them out of New York and across Connecticut. Just north of Mystic they pulled off the highway, went down a curving road to a spot that overlooked the sound. They sat looking out at the sea and sailboats and each had a glass of wine and half a Cuban sandwich.

"Have you ever been afraid? I mean as a policeman, were you ever frightened?"

"Sure," Nick said.

"The big city sometimes scares me," she said. "Sometimes I'm frightened too."

"The city is no more dangerous than anyplace else," he told her. "As long as you don't put yourself in harm's way and you pay attention to what you're doing. In the city, you don't go where you don't belong."

She looked out at the water without answering.

"Tell me about your brother," Nick said.

"Mariano. He's different. You'll meet him." She looked him in the eye and smiled. "He's a good guy."

"Any other family, brothers or sisters? You told me your father died; what about your mother?"

"Gone," Laura said. "Except for Mariano, I have no other family here. I have cousins in Cuba. Who knows if I'll ever see them again."

"You were young when you left the island?"

"Very. I can barely remember what it was like."

"It must be beautiful. Cuba must be a beautiful place."

"Yes," she told him. "It is, it is also a sad place. I mean the people suffer there, you know, the embargo and all. Let's not talk politics, politics bums me out. And I want to be happy, I want to see this town you call Wickham. A place that is surrounded by water."

"It's not Cuba," he told her.

"What, no palm trees, señor? No long white beaches, no coconuts, no mangoes?"

"No," he said, "only *yanquis*, lobster, and clam chowder."

"You lied to me," she said. "You do speak Spanish, *yanquis*, that is very good."

When they were back on the highway heading north he told her, "I've arranged a fishing trip for us in the morning."

"I have no fishing pole."

"You won't need one, we have plenty. You don't get seasick, do you?"

Laura gave him a sidelong glance, amused. "No, I don't think so. So what will we fish for?"

"Sharks."

"*Un momentico*," she said. "Did you say sharks?"

"Yes, sharks. We will fish for sharks."

"The ones with teeth like this?" Laura opened her mouth and showed him her teeth.

Nick laughed. "That's right."

"Shit man, you crazy? I'm not going to go and bother any shark. How big?" she asked him. "How big are these sharks?"

"All sizes."

"Like this?" Laura spread her arms.

"Hard to say, they get big."

"Nick, how big? How big is big?"

"About the size of the car."

"Really? Well my friend, I'll be waiting for you when you return. The size of the car . . ."

"If you prefer we won't go."

"No," she said. "I said I wanted to go fishing and I will."

"For sharks."

"*Claro,*" she said. "If you go, I am with you."

It was still light when they got to Wickham, and there was a strong breeze that brought some whitecaps to the bay. As they crossed the bridge over Ryan's Inlet Nick said, "I love the water."

"Yes," she said, "I see that you do."

Chapter 36

Great house," Laura said. They parked in the driveway near the stand of white pine. It was quiet, the only sound was the hum of the wind as it blew through the trees along the driveway. They carried their bags to the front porch, and Nick took his key and opened the door.

The cottage was not large and it was old, seventy-five years old; he had recently painted the wood trim green. The years and salt air had turned the cedar shakes more white than gray. Inside it was light and airy, with extra-large windows that faced east. It was a three-minute walk to the bay, and from all the rooms of the house you could hear the sounds of a bell buoy. There were two huge bedrooms, a living room with a stone fireplace, and a kitchen large enough to eat in. The cottage had a front and rear porch; the rear porch was screened and overlooked Wickham Harbor and Narragansett Bay.

Leaving her bag at the foot of the stairway, Laura walked down the hall, to the rear porch. Nick watched her for a time as she stood gazing at the bay and the early evening sky. "The water is right here," she called out.

"A three-minute walk, five tops," he said. It was a little before seven.

Within a few minutes Nick joined her with a bottle of wine and two glasses. He poured himself some wine. "How about you, Laura?"

She took the glass from him and drank it down, then poured herself another.

Nick looked at the treeline, then at the bay, then up at the sky. The wind had increased, clouds moving quickly out of the east. "It might be a bit too rough to go out tomorrow."

Laura was silent for a moment, as if figuring things.

"Of course it's up to you," she said, "but if you go out, I'll be there."

"Okay, we'll see how it is in the morning. I'd better give E.Z. a call. It's his boat we'll be going out on, the *Emma*."

"Tell him he will have a passenger who expects to catch a big fish."

Nick turned and went into the cottage. In the living room he found two messages on his telephone answering machine, both from Andre, both asking Nick to call him at home. As he picked up the telephone he remembered the DEA agent, Kenney. He glanced at his watch and hoped that Kenney hadn't been sitting around waiting for his call.

"Where you been?" Andre asked him.

"On my way to the country. Listen, I totally blew off Kenney; Mark told me you wanted me to call him. I picked up Laura and—"

"He called twice, I spoke to him. Listen to this. The Vasserman brothers, you remember them, right?"

"Yeah."

"Sometime last night somebody took them out. Both killed execution style in Union City. Hoods on their heads, the whole bit."

"Same as the two others in Florida. How'd you hear about it?"

"Kenney. There were notes attached to the hoods," Andre said. "This is some strange stuff, all these people were involved in the Los Campos case."

"I know, I know," Nick told him. "It is strange."

"I don't think anyone is going to lose too much sleep over these guys," Andre said cheerfully.

"You got that right," Nick told him. "Still, it's weird. He tell you what was written on the hoods?"

"There were hoods over their heads with notes on them, that's all he told me. Call him, will you?"

"He's probably gone for the weekend, but I'll leave a message for him to call me here."

Andre said, "You sound chipper."

"Do I?"

"Sure do. How things going?"

"Fine . . . Oh, you mean with Laura?"

"Has she told you her last name or is it a secret?"

"We just got in. We're having some wine and watching the sun set on Narragansett Bay," Nick said. "She hasn't told me her last name."

"Are you sure she's old enough to drink?"

"Don't be funny."

"What the hell do you talk about?"

"All right," Nick said. "I'll call Kenney."

"So what do you talk about?"

"Life."

"Whose life? She hasn't had one yet."

"She's terrific."

"Whatever you say."

"I'm impressed; she impresses me."

"Really, are you feeling okay?"

"Better than I've felt in years. And we just got here."

"That's great. I'm jealous."

He had asked Andre if he was gay about ten years ago. It was a week or two after his last conversation with Sonny McCabe. He just came out and asked him. Andre had looked at him with a silly-ass grin on his face. It's a reasonable question. I guess so, he'd finally said. Nick said what am I, deaf, dumb, and blind? He remembered Andre laughing, remembered how disconcerting his laughter was. Nick didn't know what to say, finding the right thing to say was not easy.

So he had said, "I guess as long as you're happy."

"Yes, well, happy about being gay, you could say that. Now, can we still be friends and get on with our lives?"

"Ey, I've always been proud to be your friend. And anyone that has a problem with that, I'll knock on his ass."

"My hero," Andre said.

Nick telephoned the Miami office of the DEA, left a message for Agent Kenney, gave the woman who answered his number in Wickham. Then he called E.Z., E.Z. telling him the trip was set for the morning, he had picked up a new Loran and the water had warmed over the last couple of weeks. It was a little early in the season, but there might be some sharks around.

"I'm going to bring someone along," Nick said then.

"Who's that?"

"A woman, a woman I met. Her name is Laura."

"I'm glad to hear it."

"She's young." Nick could not shake this awkward feeling he had about being with someone so young. Sometimes thinking about it, he found it hard to look at her. Inwardly he couldn't be more pleased. The way she raised her eyes to him, Christ he'd never seen eyes like that. And she was fun, funny and sweet. And she wanted to go fishing.

"Never mind young, what does she look like?"

"You would say a knockout. That's what you would say."

"I'll see you at the dock at four thirty."

"What?"

"Okay, I'll let you sleep. Make it five."

Nick hung up the phone and went out onto the porch and sat with Laura watching the sunset. At around eight, Kenney returned his call. They talked about the two murders in Union City and how similar they were to the killings in Miami.

"Union City is going to send me whatever they have," Kenney said. "When I get it I'll give you a call."

"Well, to tell you the truth," Nick said, "as long as they don't kill anyone in Queens, we're not involved."

"Andre seems interested. He thinks there is a connection to the Los Campos case here."

"He hasn't told me that. But I suppose you're right."

"Sonny McCabe was here last night, flogging his book on local TV. I wanted to give him a call but decided against it."

"He's everywhere, like crabgrass."

"My wife liked his last one."

"I'm sure it was pretty good, the guy knows how to tell a story."

"Well," Kenney said, "McCabe's an asshole. Sorry," he added, "I know he was your partner. I don't mean that. He's a smartass, I'll never forget how he popped my tires."

"Do you really think these killings are connected to Los Campos?"

"Drug dealers killing drug dealers is more like it. You were right when you said these jerkoffs kill each other for the exercise."

"Yeah," Nick told him. "But the hoods, the notes. It almost sounds political."

Nick succeeded in getting Laura off the porch, and after he helped her put her things away, they drove to Jamestown and had dinner at the Blue Oyster. The restaurant was crowded. Summer people up for the weekend, a world of yuppies and Volvos, and Nick and Laura had to wait in line. After dinner they had ice cream cones and walked along the seawall with the gulls crying around them.

"We were in New York City today," she told him, "with crowds and noise and people rushing about. This is so much better."

"It's peaceful here, something different."

She stood sucking on an ice cream cone as if she were sucking on him. He smiled at her, and for a moment their eyes seemed to connect, then she turned away. Maybe she wasn't looking at him at all. Laura bent to pick up a shell, studied it a moment, then tossed it out into the water. He looked at her in a discerning sort of way; what a body, her skin, her eyes with their curious child's stare, and her hair, drawn back tonight tightly from her high forehead. She did this trick with her lips, pursing them before she spoke. None of it seemed real, it was like watching some other man's woman standing at the end of the dock, a dim light on a pole above her. For a few minutes they stood quietly in the dark, letting their eyes adjust.

Laura gave an indifferent shrug. "I sometimes wonder," she said, "what life would have been like for me had my family stayed in Cuba."

"Not so terrific," he said. "It is not easy there."

"That's true." She gave him that quiet look, the little cute smile. "It hasn't been a great big party here either."

Nick went and took her arm. "It seems to me," he told her, "that you're more American than Cuban."

"Don't kid yourself," she said. "I'm a Cuban."

"We should get going, we have to be up early."

They drove back to Wickham, talking very little. When they got inside the cottage, Nick snapped on the kitchen light. Laura yawned, stretching her arms above her head, showing him those pear-size breasts of hers. Instantly he felt a shyness, an excitement. Nick felt as though the bones in his legs had turned to liquid; he was slowly dissolving, he felt anxious and unstrung.

"Time for bed," he said. He felt vaguely hopeful. What are you thinking? he thought. You'll never be that lucky.

Laura smiled at him. She seemed to be computing something in her head. "If I'm not up, you'll wake me, right? Don't leave me here."

"Not a chance," he told her.

She glanced at her watch. "It's almost midnight. We have to be up in five hours."

Nick blinked and nodded.

Chapter 37

Nick woke to the aroma of coffee and recalled that the smell was the best part of certain experiences. Rolling out of bed, he struggled with his jeans, sweatshirt, and sneakers, and glanced at the clock on the dresser. It was four A.M., he hadn't had much sleep.

Nick regarded himself in the bathroom mirror. He looked pale and worn; his hair was a mess. Using both hands he brushed it back.

He walked into the kitchen and found Laura at the stove. She looked fresh and wide awake, her hair was up in some sort of bun. She turned to him, folding her arms.

"Good morning," she said brightly. "I made coffee. Brought my own, my own pot too."

All Nick could say was, "I need some coffee."

"I looked around for things, things to make us lunch. There is nothing here. No bread, no—"

"Laura," he said. "Let me finish my coffee."

"Do your *compañeros* know what a grouch you are in the morning?"

"I can be a grouch all day; some people say I'm a bastard."

"I believe it," she told him.

A half hour later they pulled into the marina and then walked around about four dry-docked boats looking for E.Z.'s pickup. He and Laura got halfway to the tackle shop before Nick saw the truck parked with its nose toward the water. They went up the steps to the dock, then out along the slips until Nick spotted E.Z. in *Emma*'s stern, packing ice into a four-foot cooler.

The *Emma* was a thirty-one-foot Bertram Bahia Mar, powered by a pair of diesels. She had full electronics and a flying bridge, and she was fast. E.Z. kept her spotlessly clean; she was a comfortable boat.

"So," E.Z. said, "I get to meet the famous Laura."

Laura cocked her head. "E.Z.," she said. "Are you?"

"Some say. Let's go, get aboard. Morning, Nick. You look like shit."

"Thanks," Nick said with a wide toothy grin.

It took less time to cast off and set out than usual, Nick thought, but it all went smoothly. Throttles reverberated in the early morning stillness, and boats maneuvered their way through the harbor. E.Z. fell in line behind the *Intruder* and the *Double Hoodoo*. "Danny Golden," Nick told Laura, "the captain of the *Intruder*, last summer he caught an eleven-hundred-pound bluefin tuna."

"*How* big?"

"Eleven hundred pounds."

"That's a whole lot of fish, a whole lot of sandwiches."

"A whole lot of money," Nick told her. "If the fish has the right fat content, the Japanese will pay thousands of dollars for it."

"That reminds me," she told him. "I didn't pack any lunch. You men are going to get hungry."

It crossed his mind that sure Laura was young, very young, but this was a man's woman, someone trained her well. A good woman, a Latin lady. Sensual, smart, erotic, and kind. What else is there?

"E.Z. brings the food," Nick said. He pointed to the cooler he had carried aboard. "I bring the beer."

When they were in the channel maybe two, three hundred yards from the slip, *Emma*'s lights caught a heron out for a stroll in the salt marsh. There were no stars or moon, still, E.Z. was never confused by the dark. E.Z. took the channel around the sandbar right to the breakwater, then motored on at about half speed, running out with the tide.

E.Z. was checking out the loran, lining Emma up with Block Island, when Laura joined him and Nick in the wheelhouse. She came up with a thermos of coffee and three mugs. E.Z. let Nick take the wheel, told him the bearings. The sun ran a narrow line across the horizon, a glow of pink with tinges of red. It was just past five thirty.

They ran as fast as the sea would allow. Just past Block Island they turned south toward the Gully. No one spoke.

The radio was busy with calls from the captains of other boats, Mariaclara supposed. E.Z. had many friends, it seemed he was constantly on the radio. To her ears the boat's engine was powerful, loud and variable, rising and falling. Between the sound of the radio and the exertion of *Emma*'s engines the ride was anything but calm.

Nick said, "How you doing, Laura?"

"Fine," she said. "This is great."

"I've got good news and bad news for you," E.Z. said. "What do you want first?"

"You're going to strip me naked, rape me, then tie me to the front of the boat," she told them.

"Whew," E.Z. said. "That's the best idea I've heard in weeks. Whataya think, Nick, how'd you like to strip her naked?"

Nick struggled to get over the effect her words had on him as Laura laughed. "What's the news?" she said.

"When the sun comes up the sea will flatten out," E.Z. told her. "We have about two, two and half hours of this bumpy ride before we get to where we're headed."

"Sounds great," Laura said, showing those teeth of hers, her eyes glowing.

"You'll be okay," Nick told her. "And you'll get the best tan you ever had."

"You like dark women, Nick, huh?" she said.

A long moment of silence.

"Well, Nick?" E.Z. said.

"I like kind women," he told them.

After a while E.Z. left the wheelhouse to visit the head. Nick drank his coffee and ate an egg sandwich E.Z.'s wife, Emma, had packed. He checked the loran and the RDF, glanced at the chart.

Nick said, "What are you looking at?"

"Your nose."

She brought her coffee cup to her mouth and spoke over the rim. "You are very handsome, Marcello. *Guapo.*"

"Thank you. In case you forgot, my name is Nick."

"Marcello, Marcello." She pinched his nose.

"You know, Laura," Nick said, "you have never told me your last name."

"Of course I did. I didn't? I'm sorry, my God we slept in the same house and you don't know my last name?"

"That's right."

"Diaz," she told him. "My name is Laura Diaz."

"You grew up in Miami?"

"Hollywood. That's Hollywood, Florida."

E.Z. returned and took the wheel. "Are we having fun yet, children?"

She nodded at him. "I love this," she said, her eyes suddenly opening wide as *Emma* took them for a sleigh ride down a long rolling wave into a smooth trough.

Maria would remember the little details, how Nick sat there in his green sweatshirt, how the shirt clung to the curve of his shoulders, how he let his eyes glide across her face, how he smiled; she could feel the way he looked at her, the way no man had ever looked at her before. There was so much more there than pure, dumb want. She liked him. And like matters, like isn't love but like matters. A glance at his profile never failed to delight her, that nose of his. The smell of coffee, the sea, Nick's smiling face, it was all intoxicating. She looked at him for a long time, thinking, considering—and then instantly regretted it, regretted all those thoughts of like and love and all the confused feelings in between.

Dawn broke glorious and bright with a fresh light wind and calming seas. An hour later, E.Z. pulled back on the throttle and announced, "We're here."

Nick began working the chum ladle. Maria watched as he slowly poured the obnoxious-looking souplike substance into the sea. "What is that stuff?" she asked him. "It smells awful."

Nick said, "Ground-up fish that we mix with an oil. In the water it produces a slick behind the boat that draws fish. And that's what we want to do, isn't it? Draw fish."

It looked to her like a bloody Rorschach spreading behind the boat. Nick and E.Z. worked together wordlessly, as if the two of them had rehearsed together for many years. Maria was impressed; they were a pair, and all that they did seemed to be second nature to them.

E.Z. set out three rods baited with mackerel and chunks of bluefish. They were just south of Block Island, south of the Gully. E.Z. fed the first line out off *Emma*'s aft quarter, about a hundred and fifty feet from the boat and a hundred feet down. He handed a red balloon to Maria, told her to blow it up and tie it to the line. Then he fed out the second line, halfway between the first and the boat and down about fifty feet. To the second line he tied a yellow balloon. The third line, with its green balloon, was twenty-five feet from the boat and about twenty-five feet down.

"Sharks cruise the sea at different levels," Nick told her. "So we got bait moving at twenty-five, fifty, and a hundred feet down."

About thirty feet off the stern a school of bait fish broke the surface. Then gulls came in, and terns and some tuna birds.

"How deep is it here?" she asked them.

"Deep," E.Z. said. "It's the ocean."

More birds, more bait fish, the birds diving into the chum slick. Suddenly the yellow balloon ripped through the water and disappeared beneath the surface.

The reel clicker whirred, stopped, then went off again, and the balloon shot to the surface. "There you go," Nick said. He smiled and handed her the rod. "You got one, go ahead, jerk it, jerk it, set that hook."

"Got what?" she screamed. "A shark? Are you kidding? Take this thing!"

"It's all yours, baby, you got it. Go to it."

Maria felt as though a beast beneath the surface of the sea had snagged itself on her line and was trying to jerk itself loose. Her heart was racing, her breath coming fast and hard. Terror and excitement becoming one in her stomach.

"Don't horse it," E.Z. said, "reel, honey, reel."

"Is this a shark?"

"I doubt it," Nick said. "Keep reeling. C'mon, c'mon."

Twenty feet astern the fish broke the water. "I got it, I got it," Maria shouted.

"Reel," Nick shouted, "just keep reeling, Laura."

E.Z. set the gaff and lifted a ten-pound bluefish into the boat.

Laura had hit the lottery, or so it seemed. "I got it, I got it, I got—"

"Okay, calm down, Laura, you'll go right off the boat," Nick said.

Silver-blue and glistening in the morning sun, the bluefish bounced across the deck. E.Z. gaffed it again through its gill and dropped it in the cooler.

Laura said, "What is it? He's pretty; can I cook him?"

Nick laughed and E.Z. said, "Some people eat 'em. Some people like them a whole lot."

"What do you call it?"

"It's a bluefish," Nick said. "A good-size one. You got dinner."

"Better as bait," E.Z. said.

"Bait? Bait?" Laura said. "A fish that big?"

"Yup," E.Z. said, and that's all he said.

"I'm exhausted," Laura said. "He put up a hell of a fight."

Nick smiled and E.Z. wagged his head.

"He did, he put up one hell of a fight," Laura said. "For a minute I thought I'd lost him, then boy—"

"Fins in the slick," E.Z. said. "We got shark here."

A pair of blue shark eased their way through the chum slick in a steady glide, heading for the boat. "*Dios,*" Laura said, "they're sharks, real sharks."

E.Z. helped Nick slip into a heavy-duty vest with a rod holder, a gimbal in its center. "Laura," Nick said, "these are blue sharks. What we do is bring them in if we can. Then we tag them and set them loose."

The reel clicker on the rod with the red balloon went off for a second, then stopped. "A fish on?" Nick asked.

"I don't think so," E.Z. told him. "Hold still a minute."

"Are they dangerous?" Laura said.

"All sharks are dangerous," Nick told her. "Blues are the least dangerous. But they are big and heavy and strong and can pull you right off the boat if you're not careful."

E.Z. smiled at him and climbed to the flying bridge. He stood for a moment looking down into the water. "The balloon's not moving," he said. "Whoa . . . Nick, bring in the green and yellow lines. Quick Nick, bring them in."

Laura reeled in the line with the yellow balloon, and Nick brought in the green. "What's going on?" she said.

"Just do it, Laura, do it quickly," Nick told her.

"A mako, Nick, I saw a mako," E.Z. shouted. "He was in the slick and then he sounded."

The clicker on the rod with the red balloon went off again. Coming down from the bridge, E.Z. gently took the rod from its holder and handed it to Nick. Then he scooted back up the ladder. Laura was watching Nick. Nick glanced at E.Z., then out at the balloon. E.Z. was staring at the water. "Set the drag as high as it will go, Nick," E.Z. said. "Okay," E.Z. shouted, "hit it, hit it hard, Nick, set that hook."

Within a second Nick was hit with an arm-jolting smash. A two-hundred-pound mako shark came out of the water like a Polaris missile and skyrocketed about ten feet into the air, shaking its head side to side in a sawing motion, the bait between its teeth. Laura let loose a scream that could easily have been heard in Havana.

The mako plunged down into the sea in a geyser of foam and spray; he jumped again and again. Yard after yard of Nick's line sped out into the sea.

"C'mon," E.Z. yelled. "You got him, buddy, don't let him run off and hide!"

For twenty minutes Nick played the fish, the mako jumping, doing cartwheels, running line out, then coming right at the boat like a freight train, coming right at Nick. Finally it seemed to Nick that the fish had given up the ghost. Nick had him reeled in close to the boat now. E.Z. was over the gunnel with his gloves on, trying to grab the wire lead with the gaff, when in desperation, the mako made a final jump. E.Z. threw his hands in the air as the fish splashed back into the water and shot directly under the boat, popping the line.

"He's off," Nick said.

"Son of a bitch," said E.Z.

"He was beautiful," Laura said. "Majestic, a fighter. I'm glad he got away."

"How would you like to walk back to the dock?" E.Z. said.

"A hell of a fish," Nick said. He put the rod back into its holder. His hands felt numb, his arms were numb. It had been over a year since he had a mako on, he was out of shape. E.Z. made his way up to the wheelhouse, saying, "I knew it was too early in the season to get a mako. You can't get makos this early. This one must have been a loony, lost his way."

Laura went over to the cooler and took out a beer. She unscrewed the cap and handed the beer to Nick, her hand touching his. "I'm sorry you lost the fish," she told him.

"So am I."

"Be honest now," she said. "You feel better that you didn't have to kill that beautiful creature. You don't have a violent nature. Isn't that true? Come on, say it, you're happy you didn't have to kill him. Say, I'm happy—"

"That was one hell of a fish and I wanted him," Nick said. "Sorry, but the way I see it, it's me and him, nose to nose. This time he won, but there's always tomorrow, and the day after that."

She said "Oh," and was silent.

Nick could understand the justice of what she was saying. He felt it more looking into that face of hers. But he doubted she understood how he felt, how E.Z. felt. She was a sweet woman, a good woman. Some women, Nick considered, have a hard time understanding fishermen and sharks. But she liked being out on the water, knew when to open a beer, and didn't get seasick. Can't have everything, he told himself. Look at her.

Chapter 38

At the Spain Restaurant in Narragansett that evening, Nick was impressed with the way Laura ordered their meal. Speaking in both Spanish and English, flattering the waiter, making him smile. Ordering both of them steaks, asking Nick if it was okay, because, you know, I've seen enough fish for a while. Laughing when she said it, making Nick laugh as well. Laura could have been created just for him. Smiling and gay and a bit timid, he didn't care for hard-faced women, frowning, and not the other way, loud and painted, haughty, or aspiring to be. And what he really liked, and what he would remember, was the way she had earlier showered quickly and had combed out her hair, letting it fall to her shoulders.

The waiter mixed them a special sangria, chopped up the fresh fruit in front of them, the fruit dripping with juice, and mixed the fruit and juice with the wine. Laura gracefully lifting her glass in a toast to Nick and his shark. The way she looked at him over the table, briefly at first, then after another pitcher of the wine and juice, with a long and piercing gaze, sending Nick some message, what he was not sure, but he sure was hopeful. The steak was wonderful, spiced unlike any Nick had ever tasted before, but he knew there was garlic, plenty of it.

After dinner they walked along the seawall, and the waiting was almost too much. They walked holding hands, then her arm around his waist, his arm across her shoulders. They kissed and embraced among people walking and kids on bikes, belly to belly, they kissed mouth to mouth, for a long time. Once he tried to say something but then thought better of it, figuring that whatever he said was bound to come out lame. Standing on the steps that led to the beach he kissed her again and flashed on the women he had touched, smelled, and kissed, all the women he'd known, some great with their mouths and experienced lovemakers, none of those women could kiss like Laura. Kissing, Nick considered, was intimacy, kissing was perfect sex.

Back to the cottage, a nightcap on the back porch. A ridge of clouds was building above the horizon over the bay. A thunderstorm broke, and together they stood on the covered porch while the rain poured down. The air was heavy with sea smells from the bay and pine from the stand of wood alongside the cottage. They stood for a long time, staring blindly into the sky, looking for the next lightning bolt.

After a while Laura took his hand and they went inside, through the cottage, up the stairs, and Nick would remember creamy soft skin, warm to the touch, a flash of thigh, and dark thick hair. Legs close together, then spread wide, and small sounds almost impossible to hear in the middle of a thunderstorm on a summer night.

"Oh," said Laura, after what Nick thought had to be an hour, lying dazed and spent in his arms. "Tomorrow, I will cook you the bluefish."

All Sunday morning and early into the afternoon they played in bed. Around one, E.Z. telephoned and left a message on Nick's machine, his voice sounding loud in Nick's bedroom. E.Z. wondering what he was up to, if Nick needed a hand with anything. After the thunderstorm that had raged the night before a soft but steady rain had settled in. Nick refused to go down the stairs; he would not leave the bedroom. Lying in bed with Laura was so good he felt like cheering. He wanted to lock her in the room, strap her to the bedposts, handcuff himself to her leg. I love her, he thought. She lights me up.

"Man," he said, after he had come for the third time, a record for him, "I feel . . . I don't know how I feel. But I feel good—no, great, it's great how I feel. I mean it," he said, when she laughed. "I don't think

I've ever been this happy. I can die now, the sky pilot can take me. I'm ready."

They lay in bed covered with a light quilt. A stiff breeze had come up on top of the steady rain. Sometime around two in the afternoon, Laura went naked to the rain-streaked window and looked out at the bay.

She said, "I remember once waking up in bed with a man and wishing I were a wolf."

"No confessions," Nick told her. "Please, I don't want to hear the story of your sex life, it would not make me happy."

"I was thinking about you actually. How different you are."

"I'm not all that different from anyone else."

He watched her as she toyed with the thin golden chain around her neck. On the chain was a tiny medallion imprinted with the smiling face of one of the saints. "Oh yes you are," she said. "Anyway, I met this guy, this character who called himself a virgin surgeon. Whatever that meant."

"We both know what it means. You are going to go on with this story, aren't you?" Nick sat up, laced his hands behind his head.

"I had never in my life drunk so much, been so out of control. When I woke up in the morning I had my arm around this guy's neck. I felt as though I were in a trap, one of those steel things with teeth that slam down on a wolf or a coyote. He was asleep in the crook of my arm. I couldn't move, I was stuck, caught. The slightest movement of my arm would have wakened him, and then I would have to talk with him, deal with him. It was horrible."

Nick kept looking at her and didn't reply. It would be necessary, he thought, to grow accustomed to confessions. Unlike Laura's, his generation was not into sharing. "Why a wolf?" he asked her.

"So I could chew my arm off. That's what they do, you know. Wolves and coyotes, when they screw up and step in a trap, they chew off a paw or a leg. So they won't be caught and taken, they chew themselves apart."

Nick laughed.

"It's not funny," she said.

"No, it's not," he managed to say. "I do think you were a bit hard on yourself. We all make mistakes. We all play the fool."

Laura looked thoughtful. She shrugged. "Uh-huh," she said. "Have you ever made a truly terrible mistake?"

"Me? Sure. That's what we do, that's how we get through this life."

Laura looked at him in a way that made him feel cold, tilting her head, saying, "But you forgive yourself, you find a way to forgive yourself."

Nick only laughed. "Don't be so serious. This is not the time for serious conversation. C'mere," he told her and slapped the bed.

"Is that all you want from me?" she said. "Is that it?"

He had to admit that every single smell and sensation he experienced with her was new to him. She was different all right. He did want her back in bed, push the record.

"C'mon," he said. "Lighten up."

"There are things people do," she said, "that there is no forgiveness for. There are some tears that never dry." Then she laughed a little, and he was glad she did because he was beginning to feel that he had just found her, had his hands on that great ass of hers, and now he was losing her a little. He wanted to ask her what? What in her short life could she have experienced that she would not forgive?

"I guess you're right," he told her.

"You agree with me?"

"About what? That there are human beings who can do appalling things, things that are beyond forgiveness? Fucking right, there are, there was a guy named Hitler, a bit before your time."

"I'm sorry," she said. "I'm feeling a little strange. You know I didn't expect this."

"Expect what? That we would sleep together?"

"Yes, and that I would like you so much. Isn't that silly?" She smiled, showing those teeth of hers, in that face of hers, puckering those lips.

"C'mere," he said. "Come on back to bed."

"First," she said, "I'll make some coffee. I need coffee, and I'm getting hungry."

"You'll pardon my saying this, but sweetie, you have one hell of an appetite."

"The salt air and fucking, it'll do it every time."

That word bothered him a bit, more than a bit, making him feel, as it did, a bitter form of envy. "Funny," he said, "I don't like hearing that out of your mouth."

"What, fucking? Fucking, fucking, fuck—"

"Sorry I mentioned it."

"What do you want me to do, promise you you're the first? I'm twenty-four years old, Nick, I'm not a kid."

"There are people who used to think of that as pretty young. Still do, I guess."

Presently she went down to the kitchen and made them coffee and some scrambled eggs and toast. She had three eggs and four slices of toast. It was amazing, really, how much this woman ate.

They sat in bed eating and drinking coffee, the rain out of the southeast, serious now. Before they made love again, she told him, "I'm happy."

"Same here," Nick told her.

Later, when they finally got out of bed, she walked around the cottage in one of his T-shirts, the black bush between her legs exposed. For some unknown reason she had brought with her a pair of highheeled red shoes, and she wore those shoes along with his T-shirt and nothing more. Nick had to admit he was thrown some by the way she moved about. Once she went out the back door to the porch and sat there in the hard-backed chair. Nick had always been shy, he never undressed fully in front of a woman. He was, in any case, delighted to watch her, smiling, her ponytail bobbing, as she gaily walked around the cottage, her tush bared, her legs long and brown as a berry.

She did dress for the ride back to Manhattan. In jeans, a light sweater, and tennis shoes.

"I hate to have to leave this place," she told him.

"There is always next weekend. I live for the weekends," he said.

"Maybe," she said. "Maybe."

"Come with me next weekend. Next weekend we'll find lobsters and boil them and drink beer. You like lobsters, don't you?"

"Love 'em."

"Then come, come back with me."

"We'll see," she said.

He thought she was avoiding his eyes.

He drove the car and played a tape she had brought with her; it was classical, Spanish, a guitar. The artist, she told him, was from her hometown in Cuba. Nick did not ask his name. By the time they had crossed into Connecticut, she was sound asleep on the seat next to him. He woke her slightly when he stretched out his arm and with the tips of his fingers gently touched the curve of her head. She smiled at him, half asleep. When they had crossed from Connecticut into New York State he glanced again at her beautiful, innocent, sleeping face. He felt a compatibility with her, a perfect harmony.

They were somewhere in the north Bronx, city traffic starting to build, when he had a momentary, gut-wrenching sinking feeling, as though this gift he had found would surely be taken from him. That easy-come-easy-go business. In spite of everything that had happened over the weekend, Nick was consumed with the thought that he would lose her.

I should be careful, he said to himself, I shouldn't push so hard. If she wants to come up next weekend, great. If not, that too should be okay. Careful, he told himself, don't act needy. She has seen that before with other guys. Other guys sure, but not with him. How about her phone number, how about that? So she hasn't given you her phone number. You should understand that it might be complicated. The brother, Latin families, that sort of thing.

As was his way, he picked apart the story of her life, the bits and pieces. She had told him about one lover, there had to be more. Someone that she liked keeping her arm around, someone that didn't make her wish she were a wolf. And yet . . . there had been no confessions, no stories of loves found and then lost. Perhaps there were none, she was only twenty-four. Perhaps sex for her was nothing more than a game. That would account for the way she seemed so free, walking around as she did, half naked. Sex, she was very good, too good. Someone taught her, someone had to teach her, for her to be this young and that good she had to have instruction. What about that? Yet she was from a different generation. A generation that thought less about love than it did about lovemaking. He'd seen the videos, he'd watched MTV. What did he have in common with someone from a generation that listened to music called "rap"? A bunch of numbnuts, going brudda' this, brudda' that. During the week-end they had talked about every damn thing under the sun. She loved music, all kinds of music—some rap, she insisted, was pretty good. Songs of the street, she said. On the Bruckner Expressway he thought, what the hell you thinking? It was all so complicated and made him feel old, very old, made him feel half fucking dead.

At the toll plaza for the Triborough Bridge, Laura made a small moan and put her head on his shoulder, like someone who wanted him to defend her from the world outside. In her sleep—or maybe she was just pretending sleep—Laura let her hand slide across the top of his thigh. And it was evident that there was a part of him that was far from dead, a part of him that had an impressive life of its own, making its presence felt under the zipper of his jeans. No way was he going to lose this woman, no way.

He pulled over on Sixty-seventh Street, and she took off her seat belt, unlocked the door, and got out. He got out too, helping her with her bags.

"It was great," she said warmly. "The best time I've had in years."

But when he bent to kiss her cheek she seemed to freeze, stepping back, turning her chin into her shoulder. As though she was afraid someone would see.

"I'll call you," she said after a moment.

"You don't want to give me your telephone number?"

"Soon," she told him.

He could see her glancing around the street, looking, watching. For who? Her brother? C'mon.

She took his hand and held it tightly. "I'll call you later. I'll call you tomorrow," she said gently.

"You have your reasons for keeping your phone number private. I respect that, I do." Don't push, he told himself, accept it.

"I never got to cook you the bluefish," she told him.

"It's frozen, the fish is not going anywhere. And neither am I, Laura. Call me, will ya?"

"Sure," she said. "I'll call. I'll call."

She was standing on the corner as he drove off. He glanced in his rearview, she stood smiling, waving, she blew him a kiss.

In his apartment, undressing to take a shower, he thought about the music they had played in the car, he thought about Laura and found himself getting hard. It was embarrassing, it was as though he only had to think about her. Christ, he thought, am I in love? Maybe I'm just tired of living alone, inside my own head. He stood under the hot water for a long time thinking that this woman, this Laura, was nothing short of marvelous, rarer than a mermaid.

Chapter 39

Mariaclara found Tio's bustling with people. The people and the noise they produced surprised her; she glanced at her watch. It was near midnight.

For a while she stood just past the entrance, near the bar, looking around. Miguel called her name, and she turned to see her brother and Natalia smiling at her. They were seated in a booth opposite the kitchen, a sombrero and a Mexican blanket hanging on the wall above them.

Maria stood staring at them for a moment. They were smiling, both of them sitting there with huge grins. For some reason they found her amusing.

"Come sit," Miguel said as she approached. "Tell us how things went with the cop."

Gripping the edge of the table, Maria slowly lowered herself into the booth, across from Natalia and next to Miguel.

"Tired eh?" Miguel said.

"Exhausted."

"*Claro*," Natalia said, "a weekend with a handsome man, a captain. My sweet child, you are bound to be exhausted."

Arriving at her apartment she had found a note from Miguel telling her to come to Tio's. For a long time she sat in the apartment, drinking coffee, thinking, considering. She was confused, searching for clarity, and she found it was not to be had. How much of a villain was this Nick, this cop? How evil? Could she actually take part in a plan to kill him; this outwardly decent, gentle man with his collapsed nose and funny smile? If it came to it, could she kill him herself, shoot Nick the way she had shot Manny Vasserman? Maria was divided, torn in two. One of the two selves hated Nick for what he had done to her father; the other self loved to be with him, loved to make love to him. When she was with him she had almost come to the point of forgetting who he was.

Mariaclara had never been in love before. All her experiences with boys and men had little to do with love. But from what she had seen, this man, this Nick was special. She did not want to let him go now. And what about Natalia and Miguel? They were her family, her only family. They needed her, they counted on her. Could she betray them? She would die before she broke faith with her own blood.

Natalia said, "So? What happened? Did you find out if he knows where McCabe is? The man who murdered your brother; did you find out where he is?"

Maria shrugged.

"She'll tell us later," Miguel said. "Come, have a drink, sister, we are celebrating."

To her own surprise and relief, Maria found them both in a good mood. They had been drinking, probably for quite some time, both of them were lit up, eyes glistening, big silly grins on their faces.

"Miguel came through for us," Natalia said. "Tell your sister what you told me."

Miguel put down his drink and said to Maria, "Uncle Benny and the Colombian are living in Miami, kind of hiding out."

"We know that; your friend George told you that a month ago," Maria said. "We paid him five thousand dollars, this friend of yours."

Miguel stared at his hands. "Nothing valuable in this life comes cheap," he told her.

"Go on," Natalia said, "tell her the rest."

"They are in the coke business," Miguel said.

"Who isn't?" Maria said.

Natalia Punto leaned across the table and put her lips next to Maria's ear. "He spoke to them," she whispered. "Your bother spoke to Benny tonight." Natalia patted her cheek. This irritated Maria. She stared at her hands.

Natalia said, "What's the matter with you? For years we have been searching for these two animals. Now we have them, you should be happy."

Maria said, "What do you mean, we have them? What are you talking about?"

"George," Miguel said, "knows a man who was sleeping with a woman whose brother has been doing business with Cano. Drug business in Miami."

"Yes, we know all this," Maria said.

"George was trying to meet with Cano. It took time, it took money," Miguel told her.

"He met with him?"

"No, Cano is very careful. It was Benny he met; George told our dear uncle that he had a friend in New York with plenty of money to buy drugs."

"And Benny believed him, huh?"

"You know he is a greedy bastard. Money blinds people like him," her brother said.

Maria only half-listened as Miguel went on, glancing at him from time to time, her mind filled with thoughts of Nick, of a cottage by the bay, of her father. Jumbled thoughts, and half-forgotten visions of the man she called Papi and her poor brother Justo.

Miguel described his phone conversation with Benny; it was Benny who was out front, it was Benny who did the business of Cano's business, the drug business. Miguel went on and Maria looked at Natalia, trying not to let her catch her at it. She seemed to be enthralled by each word Miguel uttered; Natalia sat erect and rigid, the expression of pure hatred on her face never changed. Natalia sat like a witch passing judgment, a beautiful witch to be sure, but a witch nonetheless, a witch that wanted vengeance.

"He wants me to come to Miami," Miguel said, "wants me to meet him there."

"You're not going to Miami to meet Benny. Are you crazy?" Maria said.

Natalia said, "Listen to him, Maria, listen to your brother; he is smart, he has a plan."

"You are not going to Miami," Maria said again.

"I know, I know. I am not stupid, sister. I will send him money through George. Good faith, you know. I will send him twenty-five thousand."

"That's a lot of money."

"We have it," Natalia said. "And more. Not much more, but we have enough."

"When he gets this money his mouth will water," Miguel said. "He will give George a kilo of cocaine."

"George is doing very well, huh?" Maria said.

"If not for George, we have nothing."

"Okay."

"Anyway, in a week, maybe two, I will tell Benny I want five kilos. And I want them delivered to New York. I'll tell him I can sell five kilos a month, but he must come here to talk to me."

"This is too complicated," Maria said. "This is crazy."

"It will work," Natalia told her. "I know these people, how they think. It will work. They will come here, both of them, Cano will come here to talk business. He is the boss, he has always been the boss. He will not let anyone else speak for him."

"How can you be so sure?" Maria said.

"I know these Colombians, how they think. He will come, believe me he will be here. He will bring your uncle, but Cano will be here too."

My uncle and Cano. Yes indeed, she thought. The men who ordered my father's murder. Finally.

"How will you send the money?" Maria asked Miguel.

"Overnight mail," Miguel said. "It couldn't be easier."

Maria nodded enthusiastic agreement.

"It's happening," Natalia said. "I can feel it happening." She sipped her drink, staring at Maria. "They will pay for killing my Diego, and Rodrigo too. God will have his justice. You know," Natalia said, "you look a little strange, Maria. Are you all right?"

"Yes, well." She tried to laugh. "Listen," she said, "this cop, this Nick, he wants my phone number. I can't see how I can keep saying no."

"It's easy," Miguel said. "Tell him I don't want men calling you."

"That's silly."

"The phone, Maria, is listed in my name," he said. "He's a cop. He could check it."

"He has no reason to check the number."

"Maybe not to you, but he is a cop," Miguel said. "Did he mention McCabe?"

"No. Not yet."

"So how was it, huh?" Miguel said. "How was your weekend?"

"To tell you the truth, brother, I had a nice time. He . . . he is different."

Natalia said, "Did you sleep with him?"

"Of course not."

"Maria," Miguel said, "are you okay with this, with what we planned? Can you do it?"

"I don't know."

They seemed neither surprised nor alarmed.

"Dear daughter, that is the difference between you and me." Natalia tapped herself on the chest with the tips of her fingers. "I know," she said sharply. "There are no doubts here in this heart. To make them pay gives my life meaning, it is what I live for."

"I love you, Natalia," Maria said. "You know I love you, you are the only mother I have ever known. But we are different people."

Natalia said, "You couldn't understand the pain they gave me. At night when I am alone I swear to all the saints I will make them pay."

"You don't have a monopoly on pain, Natalia," Maria said.

"We all have pain," Miguel told her. "Maria, we need you to know, sister. We need you to be sure."

"She will be fine," Natalia said. "She is strong, and Maria knows we need her to be strong for us." She smiled a thin, nervous smile.

Maria checked the impulse to tell them she was not strong, she was anything but strong.

"Are you?" Miguel said. "Are you strong enough?"

"I think so," she told him. "And you brother, how are you?"

"I do what I do for my family, for all of us," he said. "What we do, we do for justice and for family; it is the only honorable thing to do."

"It is not justice, Miguel, it is revenge. There is no other word for it." She avoided meeting their eyes.

"Should we forget it?" Natalia asked, watching her. "Should we forget them, should we allow killers, animals that murdered the people we love, to live free? Allow them to walk around as if nothing happened? You must pay for what you do in this life."

Miguel seemed to smile as he sipped his drink.

"I want them to pay," Maria told them. "I just wonder sometimes if this is the right way."

"Sister, I wonder if there is a right way, if there can be such a thing as the right way."

"You are confused, Miguel," Maria said. "Like all of us."

Natalia Punto finished her drink and stared at the two of them in wonder. She was not in the least confused.

Nick sat in his office with the telephone to his ear, his hand over the mouthpiece, waiting to be connected with Agent Kenney. Andre stood in front of Nick's desk reading a report from the Union City police. He read each page quickly and when he got to the last one, he started over again.

"This is an assassination," Andre said, "a liquidation. Have you looked at these photos? They look like something out of El Salvador. The hit squads put hoods on their victims' heads, just like this."

Kenney came on the line and said, "Nick, how you doing?"

"Bill, we're looking at the Union City murder file of the Vasserman brothers. What we'd appreciate is the file folder from Dade County on the other two. Can you get them for us?"

That morning Andre had told Nick that he wanted him to look into the killings. Just out of curiosity, don't make a big thing out of it, I'm nosy, he told him.

"Sure," Kenney said, "I think I can get that for you."

"Ask him," Andre said, "ask him about Matos and Medina, ask him if they are around."

"Hold on a minute, Bill," Nick said into the phone. "Why?" he asked Andre.

Andre shrugged. "Curious," he said.

Into the phone Nick said, "The district attorney, who is standing in front of my desk trying to make me nuts with this three-way conversation, just asked me if you know anything about Matos and Medina."

"Tell Andre," Kenney said, "that as far as I know they have both been cut loose by the Marshall Service quite some time ago."

"They're out of the program," Nick told Andre.

"Nick," Kenney said. "You can bet those two are back in the game."

"As long as they stay out of Queens," Nick told him, "I don't care what game they're playing."

On their way to lunch, Andre said, "We'll see what Kenney gets for us."

"It could be interesting," Nick said.

"What would you say, Nick, if I told you that I have a strong feeling that these murders are connected to the Los Campos case? The names all fit."

"Then I'd ask you why it is any of our business."

"It's interesting, don't you think?"

"We have our share of interesting cases going on right in this office. I'm up to here in interesting cases."

A smile played on Andre's face. "I admire the way you're able to handle them all."

"We could use more investigators. Good ones, enough already with friends asking for friends to be assigned here."

Inside Part One Andre waved his hellos to the gathering of the Queens defense bar, a generally smiling, but fiercely competitive group. The racket was considerable. A waiter escorted them to Andre's reserved table in the back of the restaurant.

"Talk to Mark," Andre said as they took seats. "Tell him you need more people—so what else is new?"

"Let's see, we're thinking about putting a wire in that real estate office across from Aqueduct," Nick said. "It's a connected operation, the Bucci family stretching their legs into Queens."

Andre didn't say anything.

"They got a loan shark and two bookmakers working out of that office. We'll put a bug in, see what we get."

More silence. Then Andre, staring at him, said, "Matos and Medina both out in the street. Man, is that asinine or what?"

"Kenney will tell you that the Witness Protection Program is the best thing the government has going," Nick said. "I suppose it works in some cases, so why get upset? Anybody you talk to about it who knows anything says it's the best way to beat organized crime. You know why? Because nobody today can do big time—and the government is giving centuries. You tell me about a guy, a made guy in a Mafia family, who is willing to do a hundred and fifty years in Atlanta. I don't know of any. You promise them protection, you promise them a new life with a new name in a new city; we've seen it happen I don't know how many times, big-time tough guys, killers, jump aboard. You've been talking the Witness Protection Program up for years."

Andre took his time; he nodded.

"Matos and Medina, Kenney told me, gave them huge cases. Solid information about people in the Bahamas and in Colombia. They testified in front of Congress, for chrissake."

Andre nodded again.

Over the appetizer Andre said, "So tell me, how was the weekend?"

"Great. It was great. I think I'm in love."

"You're kidding me."

"I'm not. I think I've found something here, something special."

"She tell you her last name?"

The question provoked a tight bitter smile. "Yes she did," Nick told him. "This is a good woman. What's the matter, don't you believe me?"

"Sure."

"So she's young. I know she's young, but she's bright, beautiful, sexy, and full of fun."

"You only live once," Andre said.

"That's true, and if you do it right, once is more than enough."

"So they say."

Sitting across from him, watching him glance around the room, Nick thought Andre looked good, a handsome man. He was dark-skinned, with fine features, and his suit, as always, was perfect. His striking good looks caught people's attention, and his easygoing style brought him a measure of respect.

"When do I get to meet this woman?"

"We'll see."

"Is she a New Yorker?"

"No, she's not. Listen, I hardly know her, but what I do know about her makes me feel good. You know, makes me feel something I haven't felt in a very long time."

"A beautiful woman shows up out of nowhere, bumps into you, becomes your newest best friend. You're lucky."

"She came from somewhere."

"Everybody comes from somewhere."

"She came from Florida."

"You're such a compulsive good guy," Andre told him. "I hope you take a long look before you leap."

"You know I've never trusted women that make me feel too good, but Laura, Laura is a different sort."

"Really?"

"We were talking about music, just talking, I mean she's twenty-four years old. We don't listen to the same music. Anyway, she tells me that a piece of music is a part of life, a manifestation of life, just as much as a flower, a bird, or a deep forest. Music is poetry and poetry is made by all living things. Every living thing has a rhythm of its own. That's what she told me, out of nowhere she came up with that."

"Right off the top of her head."

"No, that's the point. It was something her father said."

"Now he sounds like someone worth meeting."

"I agree, I would have loved to have met him."

"Maybe you will."

"He's dead."

"That's sad. You know, buddy, you and the father are probably about the same age." Andre looked at Nick as if he were amused.

"How's Mark?" Nick said.

Andre said, "Let's change the subject."

During the afternoon Nick kept himself busy returning phone calls, cleaning his desk, reading investigators' reports. Nothing held his attention; he ended up walking the halls, talking over cases with detectives, talking with anyone unlucky enough to cross his path. He checked his machine at home about two dozen times.

Laura hadn't called.

What if she turned into a phantom, someone he never heard from again? How could he find her?

He was a cop, he'd find her.

What if she didn't want him to find her? Suddenly he was full of panic. What if the brother wasn't a brother at all, but the guy she lived with? He fantasized about walking into a restaurant and Laura would be sitting there at some dark table with some skinny mook from France.

A little before five, his secretary told him he had a call from a Miss Laura Diaz. "Listen," Laura said when he managed to pick it up. She started again. "Listen, do you like Mexican food?"

"Mexican food, I love Mexican food, chicken and rice, those fried crazy green bananas. I love it."

"That's Puerto Rican."

"I love it all. You know a good Mexican restaurant? Let's have dinner, we'll drink margaritas, get drunk and sing love songs."

"Sounds like my kind of night. Do you know Tio's?"

"On Seventy-second." He felt something coming loose in him, an explosion of joy.

"I'll meet you there, around eight."

"I'm glad you called me, I was going batty." Thinking he sounded forlorn and pathetic. "I think I'm going crazy."

"I don't think so."

"You don't?"

"No. I miss you too."

Her voice was so full of feeling that it made him dizzy.

He got to the restaurant at seven thirty, took a quick look around, had a drink at the bar, then went out to stand on the street in front of the place. After what seemed like a thousand years, he saw her crossing the avenue, she skipped once, then she was running, running up to him, kissing him, once on each cheek, taking his hands in hers, saying, "Marcello, I missed you."

She was wearing a pale green beaded Indian sweater and a red silk skirt and sandals. "You are beautiful," he told her. "Don't you know how beautiful you are?"

"No." She shook her head, then gazed up at him with those eyes. "You really think I'm beautiful?"

"Are you ever."

"C'mon."

"The place is crowded," he told her. "We'll have to wait a bit."

And Laura said to him, softly, in that voice of hers, "Let's get a cab, let's go, let's go to your place. But maybe you're really hungry, you've worked all day."

"Are you kidding? C'mon."

He took her back to his apartment and made love to her on the sofa. The minute he locked the door she hiked up her skirt, put her arms around his neck and jumped up, wrapping her legs around his waist. Very athletic. They went from the sofa to the floor to the bedroom, where they stayed until nearly midnight. Afterward he called out for Chinese food. Suddenly Nick loved New York; try calling out at midnight for Hunan beef and sesame noodles in Wickham. They watched some Leno in bed, saw Letterman harass a New York cabdriver. Nick clicked to a local cable porn channel, a blonde going at this overweight guy with a vengeance, sucking him. Laura stared at him coldly as if he were her sworn enemy. Get that off, she said, you don't watch that, do you? Never, I never do, Nick told her. C'mere, come on, why would you have to watch that when you have me here? And, I do it better, she said. Much better, he told her. By then he was capable again, and when she leaned over him, he knew he'd found paradise.

Laura woke him twice before the sun rose over Manhattan. Nick found himself begging and pleading, asking where in the hell she found the energy. Telling Laura that what she needed to do was to find herself a pacifier, a good one, strong, something sturdy, something plastic. He was forty-six, over the hill. And it was an unwritten law of medical science that once you reach forty-six, to come more than three times a night is toying with brain damage. Coming four times is so radical he couldn't even consider it. It was too terrifying to contemplate, he told her.

"Marcello," she told him, "shut up and relax."

And if the sex hadn't been magnificent, it would not even have mattered. The way she woke him in the morning, with coffee and a bagel and a copy of the *Times*. The way she came at that pacifier of his, his wakeup call.

Chapter 40

In the days that followed Nick found himself increasingly weak and tired at the office. He was half comatose by noon. He started taking naps at his desk. At the end of the day, he would meet Laura and they would walk and walk and walk and walk, through Central Park to the West Side, to Lincoln Center, along Amsterdam Avenue. She loved the city. They ate dinner in Cuban restaurants, not in silence, as he had seen so many couples do—she never stopped talking, and laughing and eating, man could she put it away. The long evenings and nights together were a series of athletic events for him. Nymphomania, Nick decided, was not a disease but a gift from God. By Friday the thought of the drive to Wickham was like salve for his soul.

It was late Friday morning, sometime around eleven, when the call came in on his private line. Nick listened, couldn't believe what he was hearing. "Who is this?" he said.

"It's me, Sonny. C'mon, you remember me, your old partner. Sonny McCabe."

"Sonny."

"Captain. Well I'll be a son of a bitch. You're a captain."

"You are a son of a bitch. What the hell do you want?"

" 'Scuse me, I expected a little better reception. It has been ten years."

"Fuckin' Sonny."

"Are you going to hang up on me or can we talk a minute?"

"Go on."

"Listen, Captain, if I'm imposing on your valuable time, I'll call back. I know how busy you must be, standing on the barricades keeping the shitheads off the wall and all."

Nick smiled, he couldn't help himself.

"Whataya want, Sonny? I know you want something, you wouldn't be calling me if there wasn't something you wanted."

"Nice of you to ask. I'm fine, been well, getting a little gray around the edges, but otherwise, I'm good. Good. Yourself?"

"Great man, great. Ten years, you asshole."

"Ah yes, a decade. A long time. I want to talk to you, Nick."

Nick took his pad, started drawing circles inside circles. "We're talking," he said.

"In person."

"What for?"

"Eddie Moran is dying. His liver is the size of a football and as hard as your heart, brother. He's got a week, maybe two at the most."

"I'm sorry to hear that. I am."

"Well, I was going to wait until he passed away before I reached out to you. But the guy's going real fast and I've got to be in L.A. next week."

"Call me when you get back, why don't ya?"

"I'm not coming back for a while. I'll be out there for a couple of months."

"Look, Sonny—"

"I'm going to be in Boston over the weekend, doing a little local TV and radio. I've got a new book."

"I heard."

"Well anyway, I'm going to be there. I understand you have a place in Rhode Island?"

"That's right."

"What's that, an hour or two from Boston?"

"About an hour, a little more."

"Whataya say I take the ride and meet you somewhere?"

"I don't know."

"I got things I want to tell you. Things you should know." He sounded sad, depressed. In a bizarre way it made Nick feel pleased. "Whataya say? I really want to talk to you, Nick."

There was a long moment of silence. Nick wondered if Laura had decided on coming with him for the weekend. She'd told him she wasn't sure.

"Sure. Call me over the weekend. I'll give you my number."

"I have it."

"You have it? It's unlisted."

"Big deal."

"Sonny the wizard."

"That's me."

Nick stood at his apartment window having a beer, watching the sunset colors over Sixty-seventh Street. Laura was in the kitchen putting together her third pot of coffee of the day. Nick thought how colors were different in the city, the orange and pinks sickly compared to the colors above the bay in Wickham. He was tired, his back ached, and he felt this cramping in the back of his legs. He thought of Sonny, wondered just what it was Sonny wanted to tell him. He doubted it was something he didn't already know. Nick supposed it was about Eddie Moran, the Los Campos case maybe. Eddie dying of cancer, poor bastard. Decades of hard drinking and smoking, what, three, four packs of butts a day, a diet of chili dogs and fatty french fries, living here, sleeping there. Eddie was a fucking mess, always had been.

Nick took several deep breaths. The apartment smelled of brewing coffee and a woman's scent, Laura's perfume, Fendi from Bloomingdale's, not the most expensive but not cheap. On his kitchen table there was a vase of fresh flowers. Patsy Cline's "That's My Desire" came from his tape deck.

"Are you sure you don't want coffee?" Laura asked. "It's made."

Nick smiled bravely, telling her she should cool it with the coffee. "You know," he said, "you drink way too much coffee."

"I would someday love to drink coffee with you," she said, "while we watch the sun set on the Costa Verde."

"Where?"

"In Spain. There is this little town, near Puerto de Vega, called Navia. We could drink this wonderful wine, eat the most wonderful food, and listen to marvelous music. There are beautiful beaches there, with cliffs and wooded hills. It is peaceful, so peaceful, a place locked into a time when people were kind."

"It sounds wonderful."

"Ah yes, it is. But you have your Wickham, don't you? And Wickham is real and Navia only a dream."

"Who knows," Nick told her. "We play our cards right, who knows?"

She smiled and turned and went back into the kitchen, leaving him to wonder about New York and Wickham and a place called Navia. He considered Laura, the difference in their ages. Thinking, how many years, really, lay ahead for the two of them? Enough, he thought, more than enough to find their share of happiness.

He put his beer on the windowsill and stretched his arms, clenched his fists, did a quick bare-fisted curl. Pleased with his muscle tone, the thickness of his shoulders. Sure he was out of shape, way out of shape, but the muscle was still there, round and firm, the skin still tight. And he didn't smoke, man he was glad he never started.

"Yes, I do drink too much coffee," she said from the kitchen doorway. "Would you like some?"

Nick laughed.

"C'mon, finish that beer and have a cup of coffee," Laura said.

"No thanks." She took her cup and came to stand beside him. "We'll leave after the traffic dies," he told her.

"Fine, I'm all packed and ready. Brought my red high heels. I hope you're rested."

"It could turn out to be an interesting weekend," he said.

"I'll do my part," she said with a quick smile. He half-listened as she talked about the unemployed and job interviews and employment agencies. She went to two or three a day, nothing doing; the job market was running at two speeds, slow and stop. After the summer, she told Nick, things should pick up.

"Government employees, bureaucrats, never have to concern themselves with unemployment," she told him.

Whenever she talked about government or politics she always seemed so angry and tough, her humor gone. A rage would build in her eyes, she looked like some sixties radical. He'd known his share of those, and her passion intrigued him, although he had a hard time following her meaning.

"Civil servants never have to worry about how they will care for their families, they don't worry about a paycheck," she said. It took Nick a moment to understand she was talking about him.

"At one time that was true," he told her. "It's no longer the case. Even the police department has had its share of layoffs." He saw that she was waiting for more, so he said, "In my case, I've been lucky, things have generally gone my way."

She forced a laugh. "Cops," she said. "Tell me, Marcello, is it true that you are all corrupt?"

"What?"

"That's what I've heard, that's what I've been told."

Where the hell had that come from? "C'mon," he said.

"No, it's a fact that cops are racist. And I've heard that sometimes they kill innocent people."

"Okay, enough coffee for you. And do me a favor, stop reading *The Village Voice* and listening to BLI."

"Common knowledge, it's common knowledge."

"I've been in the police department twenty years and I've never seen anything like that."

"And you would tell me if you did? C'mon yourself, who you kidding? You cops protect each other. Be serious."

"Seriously? Okay. I've no reason to lie. I'm telling you, I've never seen a cop put an innocent person in jail or God forbid, kill someone who didn't need killing. That's what I know seriously."

Then she was off on stories she had heard about the Miami police, how they'd drowned some drug dealers and stolen their dope. And about Los Angeles, and the stories she'd heard about New York City cops. She drank her coffee, nodding.

Finally she said, "So what are you telling me? If you're telling me that in all the years you've been a cop, you've never seen police do brutal things, criminal things, then I'm telling you—"

"Whoa," he said. "Hold it. Listen, I know *I've* never done them, and the people I've worked with have been pretty straight, that's all I'm saying."

She kept staring at him as though poised to attack, but the attack didn't come. "So what do we have planned for the weekend?" she asked suddenly.

He felt an impulse to tell her about Sonny McCabe, then thought better of it. The idea of Laura's meeting Sonny made him a bit anxious—more than a bit anxious.

"I've got a little work to do around the cottage, and I promised you lobsters. If the weather stays clear we'll have a nice weekend."

"The rain last weekend was beautiful," she said. "I wouldn't mind some rain."

"It was nice, wasn't it?"

She nodded her head, did a suggestive little trick with her eyebrows.

It was flattering that she thought well of him in that department. It made him blush. Well, he'd never really had any complaints—then again, he couldn't remember anyone exactly jumping for joy either.

"There is a small chance," he told her, "that an old friend of mine— not a friend really . . ." His stomach tightened up, he found himself thinking of Sonny's way with words. "There's a chance that an old partner of mine might stop by for an hour or two."

Laura watched him, nodding as though deep in thought. "Maybe it's best I stay in the city. You have business, things to talk about."

"No, no business. You know, an old partner wanting to see me. Actually the guy's pretty famous, wrote a book. More than one."

"I don't want to be in the way," Laura said. "Don't worry, I can stay in the city this weekend."

"No way. I'll give Sonny his hour and then I'll chase him."

Laura went into the kitchen and poured her coffee into a thermos.

No milk, a little sugar. From the bedroom phone Nick tried Andre. Still the machine. He thought of trying the office or Mark's apartment; Andre had given him Mark's home number, but he'd never used it. It was getting late, he could call from the car.

On the drive north Laura was extremely quiet. After an hour or so he glanced at her and found her staring out the passenger window, her arms wrapped around herself. He asked if she was okay and when she turned there was a strange smile on her face. He thought that she had been crying. When she spoke her voice was soft and small, she didn't sound at all like the Laura he knew.

"I'm fine," she told him. "Tired, that's all."

"You've had a hell of a week. Running around the city can get pretty damn exhausting. Then at night, when you should be getting your sleep, you're keeping me up, keeping us both up." He tried a smile.

She turned back to the window. "Nothing ever seems to go the way I've planned."

"You're not the only one; life has a way of throwing plans in the air. Look," he said, "why don't you put your head on my shoulder, get a little sleep. I'll wake you when we get there. Better yet, I have a blanket in the trunk. Why don't I pull over and get it? You can stretch out in the backseat."

"I can't sleep, I've tried. Too much coffee, I guess."

"Okay then, just try and relax. Do you want to listen to some music? Did you bring your tape? That guitar piece is beautiful; it will relax you."

"I like the silence," she said. "Quiet unwinds me."

He had no way of knowing how she truly felt about him. As for himself, he believed the feelings he had were some kind of love. Laura was dazzling, exciting, the feelings he had were too good, far too good to be love. Love, he had always thought, was solemn and sedate. And the way he felt about Laura was anything but. Anyway, words were not important, emotions were, and what he felt was something brand new. He knew his history with women was abominable, and maybe it had all been his fault. In most cases, he was at a loss as to what had happened or what he should have done differently. Things just led to things—and then nothing. Finis. You've led a cautious life, he told himself, avoiding risks. Now that's over. He'd go all out for this woman. He would do all that he could to keep her; still, ultimately the decision would be hers. There were things he wanted, things she must want. Christ, they'd practically just met, how the hell could he know what she wanted?

Don't forget, he told himself, no matter what you think, she is twenty-four. There was no denying the way she looked at him, touched him. The way she laughed, it was real, you couldn't fake a laugh like that. Still, whenever he thought about how young Laura was it gave him the heebie-jeebies. Forget it, he told himself, don't think about it. The thing about love, he decided, was that it came around once, twice in a lifetime. Three times if you were really, really lucky.

He hit the high beams, stepped on the gas, shut out all thought of everything other than getting there, getting to Wickham.

E.Z. had been to the cottage and had left a bucket and a note on the porch. *Picked up five bugs today, thought I'd leave you a couple.* E.Z. called lobsters bugs, a strange guy, that E.Z. Strange, but the best, a class act.

Saturday afternoon Nick was working in the shed, emptying it, trying to figure out if he should scrape and paint the old wood inside or forget it and stay with the exterior siding. He'd started working on the shed, what was it, a month ago? No, the month before. He'd replaced some two-by-fours and a pair of two-by-sixes, then reshingled the roof.

Nick felt anxious, his mind unable to focus. What was the point of meeting with Sonny? Then again, he could talk to the guy, hear him out, then send him on his way. Nick nodded, thinking, ten years, like nothing, *zip*, just like that.

The sun was bright coming off the bay. It was a pretty warm day, by no means hot, still Nick felt himself sweating, and he had this peculiar feeling in his stomach. Sonny McCabe, goddamn Sonny. He sat himself in a chair on the lawn in front of the shed. It was a beat-up chair he had bought for five dollars at Rocco's on Boston Neck Road. When Rocco sold it to him, Nick had intended to strip it down to the bare wood. It was a good chair, a work of art, Rocco told him, oak. Nick hadn't got to it. Laura was on the back porch, reading Jack Finney's *Time and Again*, one of Nick's all-time favorites.

What the hell did Sonny want? He'd told him to stop by. Why did that feel so wrong? Over the years he had listened to plenty of people he had no use for, jerks he *had* to listen to. Nothing Sonny might say should take him by surprise. The difference was that he hadn't warned any of those people to stay clear of him. They hadn't screwed with him, turned him around and taken advantage. None of them had pretended to be his friend, his partner. None of them had betrayed him.

He could leave. Take Laura for a ride to Jamestown, go over to Beavertail, bring a lunch or something. Maybe write a note to Sonny and tell him he'd changed his mind. He didn't want to talk to the guy.

Didn't want to see him. He felt anxious again, as though something was building, a bad storm kicking up waves. He wondered if this was what Andre felt all the time, the fear that someone was going to embarrass you, force you to deal with things best left private. Andre was scared to death of a newspaper story, some tabloid bullshit about him and Mark.

That was a little of how Nick felt now, paranoid that Sonny would be able read his mind. The smart bastard, laughing about how Nick framed that wife-beating creep Rufino. Like he knew, which of course he could not. At least not for sure. For the first time in all the years since the Rufino case, he found himself thinking about it. Sending the guy to the can for five years for a gun that wasn't his.

But that was not why Sonny wanted to see him. He wanted to talk about Eddie Moran. Sly bastard wanted to tell him something, but what could it be? The guy had called early that morning, said he'd be there sometime in the afternoon. It was afternoon, where the hell was he?

Laura had been in a strange mood last night and again this morning. Subdued and quiet, different. A side of her he hadn't seen before. They hadn't made love. This morning she had made breakfast and then they had walked to the water, and there, among marsh grass, bleached beer cans, and horseshoe crab shells, Nick had told her that he thought he was in love. He thought, he wasn't sure, no commitment, but he had the feeling. She just smiled at him.

When they turned to walk back toward the cottage they discovered three whitetail does in the field. One ran off, her head and tail held high, one stood still watching them, the third turned her head away. As they came closer the deer turned back to look at them, standing still as a statue. Suddenly she disappeared into the woods.

"I think deer, when they see you," Laura said, "know instinctively who it is that you are. She wasn't afraid, was she?"

"No," Nick said. "She was young, she'll learn."

"Nick, do you believe in God?"

"It doesn't work in my head," Nick told her. "I've never been able to get it, the thought of an all-seeing benevolent God. There is simply too much pain in world, too many innocent people suffer, for me not to wonder where is he? Where is this all-seeing all-knowing compassionate spirit?"

"Me neither," she told him. "But sometimes when I think of Jesus, I cry. So innocent, so sweet, and made to suffer so."

Nick would remember that it was at that precise moment that his heart was seized with love.

Chapter 41

Nick had just finished emptying the shed when Sonny McCabe drove down the driveway, smiling behind the wheel of a rented black Lincoln Town Car. A car just like Little Anthony Rufino's, a curious coincidence there. Nick felt a little blast of panic. He should walk up to the car, meet him halfway maybe? He shook his head. Better just to wait here.

Sonny got out of the car, his movements seeming stiff and mechanical. He stretched and yawned, saying, "Where in the hell am I? And what in the hell are you doing here among all these Episcopalians? Christ, doesn't anyone smile around here? I had to ask directions three times, and all I got was yup and nope and that way. Not a single smile, looks to me like the whole county is constipated. How the hell are ya, Nick? How the hell you been buddy?"

There was a short quiet moment before Nick acknowledged him. The shine in those blue eyes was still there; the mischievousness that was all Sonny. Nick waved, a vague gesture of hello. Sonny put his hands on his hips and turned in a circle, wagging his head, playing to some secret audience.

"It's nice, I guess, if you like isolation and seagulls," he said.

Nick found himself grinning. "How was the trip down? You had some problems with my directions, huh?"

"No problem, no. I was double-checking, asking some of these white-skinned square heads where the hell this road of yours was. It was fine, it went okay. Don't you get lonely here?"

They shook hands and Sonny put his arm around Nick's shoulders, and as was his way he gave him a little hug, and they went up onto the porch.

In all the years Nick had known E.Z., and he felt as close to him as he did to any other man, E.Z. had never hugged him. Tolerance and distance, E.Z.'s way. A kind of New England ethos, don't crowd people, don't come around unannounced or uninvited, most important, don't touch. Sonny was a whole other package, a New York neighborhood guy, into pinching cheeks and hugging. Sonny hugged everybody.

Sonny sat in a chair on the front porch, while Nick went into the kitchen to get two beers. Looking around at the fields and woods, Laura had left the back porch; she'd put the book down and walked off to the water's edge. Nick watched her for a moment, saw her throwing stones into the sea. He didn't call out to her, Sonny by himself was enough to deal with for the time being. He went back out and handed a beer to Sonny, sitting down next to him.

Sonny seemed genuinely glad to see him, smiling, leaning forward to pat his shoulder, as though there had never been anything bad between them.

"You haven't changed a bit," Nick told him. And he hadn't. Sure, there was a hint of gray, but look at him. With his dark tan and those blue eyes of his, the guy looked like a million bucks. Nick felt strange sitting there watching Sonny. He was surprised to find that there was still some anger, surprised to feel his stomach twisting the way it had at Post Time when he confronted Sonny and Eddie. He was still convinced the slick bastard had sold him out to Little Anthony, and just as hurt as he'd been back then.

They sat drinking their beer, neither saying a word. Then Sonny told Nick very quietly, hesitantly, that he'd forgotten how much he liked Nick, how much he respected him for going his own way, not taking crap from anyone. It was a nice thing to say, but it didn't move Nick, he was still pissed at the guy.

"I haven't been inside," Sonny told him. "But I like your house. It's different, like you."

"I like it. Been here for a while."

"A place like this expensive? Yeah, sure it probably is. Bet you have a hell of a nut?"

"It's not cheap. I knew the family that owned this cottage. They're holding the mortgage." Nick didn't like talking to Sonny about money. It irritated him.

"I remember you always talking about fishing and the ocean," Sonny said. "You once promised to take me on a fishing trip."

"Yeah, I remember that. And Andre and Eddie too. I'm sorry to hear that he's so sick."

"About as sick as you can get. He's at Memorial, they'd send him home if he had a home."

Nick nodded. "I remember the way the man abused himself. But I guess it was the way he wanted to live."

"I guess."

Sonny stood up. He took a swallow of beer and put the bottle down on the arm of the chair. "Do you know how many times Eddie Moran has been married?" he asked Nick.

Nick shrugged. "How would I know?"

"Three times. Do you have any idea what his take-home pay was? I mean after the alimony, liens against his check, and so on? Two hundred and ten dollars every two weeks. Can you believe that, Nick? They expected the guy to live on a hundred and five a week, fucking judges."

"C'mon. That's not possible."

"It's not, but it's true. Eddie took home two hundred and ten dollars a paycheck. And that was it."

"That's not even his bar tab at Post Time."

"Yeah, that's right."

"Some people," Nick said, "have nothing but bad luck."

"That's the truth."

Nick looked around, wondering if Laura was still by the water. "Some people," he said, "you can't tell them anything."

Sonny said, "I know what you think. You think I put you on and lie to you. You think I'm a phony bastard."

It surprised him. "No, not really. I think your values are twisted. But within your own frame of values you're sincere. At least, I think you try to be."

Sonny let a long silence fill the space between them. He smiled and nodded.

"You know, Eddie and I were partners for almost ten years." Sonny's eyes held Nick's for a moment. "I know the guy abused the shit out of himself. Still, I can't believe he's dying. You never really got to know him. The guy was a hell of a cop, hard as nails and smart as a whip. Before the booze turned his brain to oatmeal, that is."

"You're right, I didn't get to know him." In fact he had had little interest in getting to know Eddie Moran. The guy, Nick thought, was a whack job. But maybe before, before the booze? Who knew?

Sonny turned to Nick with a confident smile. "You didn't get to know me either," he said.

Nick said, "Wrong. You I worked with for six months. You I got to know."

"You have an answer for everything, haven't you?"

"You want to go for a walk?" Nick said. "Stretch your legs a bit?"

"Not me. Where the hell you gonna walk around here? You see these shoes, you know what they cost? If it's okay, I'd rather just sit for a while and finish this chitchat."

"Fine. You want another beer?"

"You got one?"

"Got a case."

Nick went off with two empties and came back with two fresh ones. "So what did you want to talk to me about? I know it's not Eddie Moran."

"I'd like to straighten you out on what happened with Rufino. The wire and so on."

He'd guessed that it might be that. He waited.

Sonny hesitated, shrugged his shoulders, nodded. Said, "I think it's about time we straighten this out."

"It was a long time ago, Sonny. For me it's a dead issue. Besides, I can figure out what happened."

"You can?"

"Of course. It's not as complicated as all that."

Sonny kept his eyes on his beer.

"There's two sides to every story, Nick," he said.

"No Sonny, there's always more than two. In this case, for example, there's my side, there's your side, there's Ann Marie Rufino's side, and Little Anthony's. Everybody's got a story. There's truth and there's fiction, there's right and there's wrong."

"You know, Nick, you've got as much give as a steel rod. You got this real happy-to-be-a-bastard attitude."

"All right," Nick said slowly, "let's see if I can guess what happened." He drank some beer, sat silent for a minute. "After we left Rufino's house and went back to the office, you split. Right?"

Sonny nodded.

"You went down to Post Time, ran into Eddie, told him the story about the wife getting laid on tape. Then ol' Eddie went and sold us out. Him being as broke as he was, who could blame him? That about right?"

"You got it."

"Really? Good. And you don't see that you have any responsibility there? He beat her with a bat, Sonny. Beat the living shit out of her, damn near killed her. Today she's deaf in one ear and she's lost the vision in her left eye.

Look at the guy blink. Like nothing is registering. "What I'm saying is, it doesn't matter that you didn't go to Rufino yourself. You went to Eddie, knew the guy was hard up, knew the guy was out to lunch. Still, you gave him sensitive information that put an innocent woman's life in the jackpot. Now that's the truth, it's not complicated, that's the story." Nick watched Sonny's eyes. "Am I right?"

"Sort of."

"Sort of?"

"Yeah. Look, I was going to wait until Eddie was gone. I gave him my word, but I figure what the hell? I mean, I hate to break my word to a dying man, but the guy's gonna go, there's no hope for him. And this has been eating at me for years and maybe I'll never again get the chance to sit with you. Or maybe I just wanted an excuse to see you." Sonny laughed. "A fucking captain, I can't get over it."

Nick kept quiet, let him talk.

"You know I've always been jealous of you. How you got through the job in a straight way, with your honor intact. And still, you were a tough guy, a good street cop. The respect you got from everyone, the kind of respect that I was denied."

"Sonny, cut the shit. No one's ever even heard of me. You, on the other hand. Mr. PD big-time detective. Everybody's buddy."

"You're right, it was said that I was the best detective in the city. So what if it was me that said it."

Nick shook his head. "So Eddie sold the tapes to Rufino?"

"Never said a word to me about it until you came down on me, threatened to punch me out. Remember? You were serious, weren't you?"

"It was on my mind."

"It wouldn't have been so easy, you know."

"Easy, hard, what's the difference." Nick looked straight at him, smiled. "It would have got done."

"Look at you, you're still pissed."

"Sonny, what do you expect, a box of candy? You fucked me over, screwed me. Lied to me."

"Eddie Moran was my partner for ten years. No one knew him better than I did. When I told him the story about Ann Marie Rufino, I told him he couldn't do anything with it. It had to stay with him."

Nick said, "You're serious."

"You bet I am. I knew he was broke, but still, if he really needed money he could have asked me. And he did, he had, plenty of times he came to me for a hand."

Nick kept silent.

"I misjudged him a little."

"I'd say you did."

"Look," Sonny said, "let me tell you a little bit about me. I came to this job when I was twenty-one years old."

Nick started to laugh. "Sonny," he said, "I've heard this story before. You're going to tell me about being a football player, all that other crap. Save it, pal. I heard it."

"Can I get a word in?"

"Go on. Jesus, you haven't changed a bit."

"See, you see? You think you know everything." Sonny finished his second beer. "What I wanted to tell you was that when I came on the job, I was like most guys. You know, do the job, get it done, do the right thing."

"And somehow you got lost along the way. Sonny," Nick said, "I really don't have to hear this. To tell you the truth, I don't care."

"Fine, fine. But hear me out. What I was trying to get to, my partner was the most important person in my life. I—"

"All right Sonny, it's all right. Enough now."

Sonny gave Nick a long, steady look. "You know," he said. "You piss me off."

"Excuse me? Did you just say, *I* piss *you* off?"

For a moment Sonny looked annoyed that Nick had distracted him. "There was never a question in your mind that it was me that sold those tapes to Rufino. Am I right?"

"That's right. But you came after me, came up with a story to convince me I was wrong."

"See, you see, if I really did sell you out, then I wouldn't care what you thought, would I?"

"Sure you would. You're Sonny, Sonny McCabe, you want everybody to love you. You need your fans like those gulls up there need the air to fly in."

"Oh man, fuck you. That's not true."

"Maybe you've grown up, maybe you've changed. I don't know."

"Yeah, maybe I have. What about you?"

"What about me?"

"You ever think that maybe you're not as smart as you think you are? You ever think that maybe, just maybe, you see only what you expect to see, nothing more?"

"What the hell does that mean?"

"Look, Nick, I don't judge people. You do. Always have."

A bubble of acid broke in Nick's stomach; he'd had this guy right up to here—again. Still. "That's right, I judge people, it's my job to judge people." Nick breathed in and out through his nose and shook his head at himself. He said, "Yeah. I judge people."

Sonny said he didn't blame poor blacks for being street criminals. He didn't blame hard-pressed Puerto Ricans or members of the Mafia either. Had he been forced to grow up in their world, who knows how things would have gone for him. He'd work them, arrest them, take their liberty and put them in jail, but he wouldn't judge them. He didn't judge anybody. No one, he told Nick, has the right to judge anyone else unless they've been there, you know, walked in their shoes, carried their load. I'm here trying to tell you something, trying to explain something, you make me feel like a schmuck. For what? Do I need this shit? Finally saying Nick, you got to heal that attitude, you have to stop judging people. It's not a healthy thing to do.

Nick laced his fingers together behind his head, worked his neck a little, stretched. He believed Sonny in a way, understood him in a way, and if someone tossed Sonny McCabe's ass in the can, he wouldn't lose any sleep over it. Still, there was something about the guy that you couldn't help but like. But watching Sonny as he sat back down, leaned back in the chair, his hands folded in his lap, his eyes closed, Nick tensed up again, thinking, wondering, remembering.

He got up and went into the kitchen for two more beers. Looking out the window, he did not see Laura. That's going to be tricky, he thought, introducing Laura.

"Sonny, let me ask you a question," Nick said as he sat down again on the porch.

Sonny took a beer from Nick. His expression was bland, open, like he was listening but his mind was off somewhere. He seemed relieved.

"Go on," he said. "Ask."

"You popped that kid—the kid in Los Campos, Cienfuego's kid—you popped him by mistake, right?" Nick saw Sonny thinking a moment, considering his answer.

Sonny actually shrugged. He leaned toward Nick. "What do mean by mistake? It was no mistake. I saw him come out of the kitchen, I saw him come at Eddie, and I took him out." He put his hands on the arms of the chair. "You want me to believe that you found a gun in Little Anthony's pocket. Some guy, okay, a creep bastard, but a guy who is not known to carry a gun. A guy who they say hasn't carried a gun in years. You want me to believe that you found a gun on him in the middle of the day?"

Nick didn't say anything.

"All right," Sonny said. "I believe you. So why don't you believe me when I tell you that the fucking kid had a gun? He had a gun, Nick, and that's why he's history."

Behind them in the cottage, something fell. Not a big crash, but something hit the floor.

When they went inside they found Laura in the kitchen on her hands and knees, a sponge in one hand, a baking pan in the other. "Sorry," she said, "I made a mess, I'm sorry."

"Sonny, this is Laura Diaz, a friend of mine."

"Well, hello Laura," Sonny said with thinly veiled surprise.

Laura nodded, looked up at Sonny and turned on a glittering smile. "Hi," she told him. "I hope I didn't disturb you. I was trying to be quiet. I dropped the saltshaker and a baking pan." She began explaining it all to them in a careful way, telling Nick she planned to make them dinner, the bluefish; she was going to bake it Cuban style, with lots of spices, but she needed some fresh tomato and basil. "Sonny," she said. "I caught this fish myself. Didn't I, Nick?"

"Yes, you did."

She said, "Fresh from the ocean, Sonny. I'm going to bake you the best fish and lobster you ever tasted, Cuban style. I even brought my own spices."

Sonny turned to Nick. "Is she kidding?"

"I don't think so."

"You'll stay for dinner?" Nick said.

"That would be nice," Sonny said.

Nick was surprised to find himself pleased that Sonny would stay for a while. He and Sonny went out on the back porch. Nick took the old wicker lounge chair and Sonny the Cap Cod rocker, and they sat together in silence, looking out at the bay, watching the sun disappear behind the hills of Jamestown.

Chapter 42

From his table near the window, Miguel spotted the massively fat man dressed all in white as he came through Tio's front door. You could hardly miss him. Miguel called out and waved his hand. Benny nodded and waddled toward him, taking these little steps. When Miguel glanced across the room he noticed Natalia seated at a table, waiting and watching. Natalia looking hot in a blond wig and heavy eye shadow.

Earlier that day they had gone out looking for a costume, a disguise or something. Natalia pointing out that Benny had been in her coffee shop on Roosevelt Avenue many times. She had served him herself, more than once. True, it was ten years ago; still, she told Miguel, the elephant has a long memory. Natalia chose the blond wig; it made her feel dangerous and sexy. Even though it had been a clear and sunlit day, the thought of Miguel meeting with Benny made her shake.

Although Miguel had been a young boy when his brother and father had been killed, he remembered them clearly, Justo and his father, they were always around him. But he wasn't certain now what he actually remembered and what he had been told by Natalia and Maria. They were handsome, both of them, and gentle. People loved them, everyone loved Diego. Thinking of his father and brother, Miguel would flash on their smiling faces, how they had laughed and played with him and brought him little presents. Then a feeling of terrible loss would seize at his heart, and his blood would turn to ice.

When he and Natalia had returned from shopping, Miguel lay down on the bed in Natalia's apartment, his arms tucked behind his head, and fell asleep and dreamt of his father. He considered the dream a sign, an omen from God.

As he watched Benny's smiling face, clear even in the restaurant's dim light, he wondered if Cano too would show. The red-headed Colombian satan, Natalia called him.

Miguel shook his head, feeling a little desperate and lost. Maria should be here, he thought. Things did not feel right without his sister. When he was alone he found it hard to hold onto his anger, much less his confidence, and then the image of his father came back to him like a piercing agony, bringing with it the calming thought of vengeance.

The meeting with Benny had been arranged quickly, with a telephone call. There would be only conversation, no money to pass, no drugs to move.

Miguel watched Benny come nearer. His obese body drew attention to itself, and his eyes were black and large in his round soft face, set under thick eyebrows and bright with the light of cocaine. Miguel's father and uncle had been about the same age; he guessed Benny to be near fifty. He glanced again across the dining room at Natalia, whose face was distorted with a revulsion beyond hatred.

Benny stood over him, looking around the restaurant, smiling, saying, "So you are Miguel, huh? A kid, I knew you would be a kid."

"Sit," Miguel told him, "take a seat."

"There's a lot of people here," Benny said. "A lot of strange fucking people."

"It's New York," Miguel said.

Miguel felt his confidence return, and he was angry at himself for having doubted himself. Look at him, look at this fat bastard, dumb as a rock, standing there thinking he is smooth and slick. You killed my father, a man of value, he wanted to say. You piece of shit.

"Too many people, you know," Benny said.

"Sit. Make yourself comfortable. Where there are many people there is safety," Miguel told him. "And we are here only for the conversation."

Benny pulled out a chair and lowered himself into it, no easy task. He said, "Your friend George in Miami sends you his regards. I saw him before we left. We had a nice talk."

"We? You said you would come alone?"

"Yes, well, I am alone, am I not?"

"Would you like something to eat, something to drink maybe?"

"No. You look familiar, you know that? I've seen you before, where have I seen you?"

Miguel took a moment to answer him. "We've never met," he said.

"You sure?"

"I don't think I would forget."

Benny said again, "You sure? You know, I don't forget anything, man. I remember faces, and your face is familiar."

"One face, one race, one people. I am Cuban, of course I am familiar to you."

Benny seemed to smile then, almost. "You have some money to invest, hah?" he said. "You want to buy some suits, I sell suits. Not shirts. You want shirts, you are talking to the wrong guy. You want shirts you go to Harlem, talk to some street bum. I only talk about suits. Good suits, imported suits, but not cheap."

"I understand," Miguel said. He looked around, imagining for an instant that he saw Cano at another table. Then he actually did see someone seated at the bar that could be the Colombian. "I can take five suits a month, no problem," Miguel told him. "I'm ready to take five suits now."

"Just like that. You make it sound easy."

"Easy for me, you know. Easy for me."

Benny took from his jacket pocket a small white pad and a pen. He wrote a number and showed the paper to Miguel. The number was one hundred twenty-five. Miguel shook his head and wrote his own number. One hundred.

"These are the best suits you can buy," Benny told him. "I said they are not cheap."

"Yes, yes," Miguel said. "I saw the suit that you gave to my friend George. It is very good. But this is all I can spend right now. And I need five suits."

"You have the cash here? Well, I don't mean right here, but you could get it quick, huh?"

"Sure."

"The world is full of villains, frauds, and fakes," Benny said, turning his head slowly, looking around the restaurant. "You too, you could be a fake."

"Have I done anything to make you believe that?"

"Not yet," Benny said softly. "But we shall see."

"When?"

"Tomorrow night should be good. Let's say I meet you here around ten o'clock. Is that all right?"

"Fine by me."

"You'll have the money? No bullshit, please, huh?"

"Of course not."

"Then we'll go someplace safe, someplace private and quiet."

Miguel nodded. "What do you have in mind?"

"The Holiday Inn, maybe?" Benny said, peering around the restaurant.

Miguel smiled at him, a small wave of apprehension rising up. He was nervous, more than a little frightened; he knew that with or without Maria this was going to happen.

Benny suddenly gave out a little screech of a yawn and said, "I'm tired, man. I need some sleep. I'll see you tomorrow. Here, ten o'clock. Be ready, and don't fuck me around." He stood, stretching his arms, and turned and walked out of the restaurant.

Miguel looked at Natalia and saw her smiling, arms folded across her chest. She winked at him and then puckered her lips and blew him a kiss.

After dinner they all sat on the back porch. Sonny said right off, "Laura, to tell you the truth, I'm not a big fish eater. I'll eat lobsters, some shrimp once in a while, but not much fish. But that fish, that bluefish, was terrific. How'd you do it?"

"Glad you liked it." A little of a snappish tone to her voice. No one other than Nick would have noticed, but it was there, some anger. There was a wineglass in her hand, and an half-empty bottle of white wine on the floor beside her. "So you're a writer, a regular Gabriel Garcia Marquez," she said.

Sonny said, "I don't know him, he must be one of those Mexican guys that write for Hollywood. I basically know the New York people. People that write hard-boiled stuff."

Laura said, "Cops killing people you mean. The world of the flat-foot."

Nick felt himself tighten up at that. He got up and went to the back door, putting his hand on the door handle. "Another beer, Sonny?"

"No, thanks, none for me. I've had plenty. Laura," he said, "I write about what I know. What else am I going to write about?"

Nick thought that Sonny sounded self-conscious; he'd never seen Sonny McCabe embarrassed before. It was something to see, his tight little-boy smile.

Nick said, "Well I need one."

He went into the kitchen, opened the refrigerator, and took out another beer. "So you were a cop, a detective, like Nick, huh?" he could hear Laura say as he poured it into a glass. Nick wondered if Laura had heard his and Sonny's conversation earlier. Sure she had, she'd have to be deaf not to have heard it.

Sonny saying, "Well, not like Nick, nobody is like Nick."

"Ever kill anybody? I mean, when you were working as a policeman," she said, "did you have to kill someone?"

There was a long moment of silence. Nick stood still in the kitchen, curious, wanting to hear how Sonny would handle this one.

"Sonny?" Laura said.

"Yeah?"

"Nothing. Forget it."

"Nick," Sonny called out, "I changed my mind. I think I'd like a beer. Laura," he said, "I did what I had to do. I didn't like it, it didn't give me pleasure, if that's what you're thinking. But I did what I had to do, no questions asked."

" 'What I had to do'—that's a polite way of saying you killed people."

"Nick," Sonny said, "where in the hell did you find this lady? Don't tell me, let me guess, she came to your door selling tickets for a fundraiser for the ACLU."

When Nick came back out onto the porch, Laura swung around and looked at him hard. "You know," she said, "earlier, when I was in the kitchen, I couldn't help but hear you two. The things you said, how you said them." She was drunk, slurring her words; she seemed furious and yet pleased with herself.

"What are you talking about?" Nick said.

Laura said, "I don't want to argue, but the things I heard you say were offensive. More than that, they were—"

"Laura," Sonny said quickly, "I don't see that there is anything to argue about. I don't know what you think you heard, but try and understand, we were cops a long time. Twenty years. Things happen, some good and some bad. Believe me, the good far outweighed the bad."

"Look," she said, "don't fake it. You killed people, admit it. You made a bad decision and took someone's life."

Sonny getting a little edgy now, glancing up at Nick, his jaw tightening. "What is this," he said, "some little parlor game you two worked out?"

"No," Nick said. "I don't know where this is coming from." Nick thought he heard someone walking along the driveway; he heard footsteps, but when he looked no one was there.

Laura said, "I was standing right there, I heard you, Nick. I heard you say he killed a boy. The Cienfuego kid, you said. You said he did it by mistake. By mistake?"

Sonny rolled his eyes at Nick. "So," he said, "how'd you two meet?"

Nick patted Sonny's shoulder. He said to Laura, "You heard me say that?"

"I'm not deaf, Nick. I was ten feet away from you, for chrissake."

Nick said, "If you heard that, then you also heard Sonny say it was no mistake, the boy had a gun and he was going to—"

"So what, he had a gun!" Laura got up angrily and began pacing. The look on her face put Nick on guard. For a moment he had the sense that she was about to lose it. He watched her, thinking why? What in the hell is going on here?

"He was living in New York!" she screamed. "A place full of predator animals. Maybe he carried that beat-up old gun to protect himself, or someone else. Maybe he carried the gun to protect his family." Laura was shouting, shouting pretty damn loud. "Does that mean you had to kill him, a sixteen-year-old boy?"

"I was saying," Nick said carefully, "that the boy had a gun and he was going to shoot another policeman. Our partner."

"Who?" she said. "Who was he going to shoot? You mean this Eddie you talked about, this miserable bastard that did business with some gangster? It was because of him, wasn't it, that an innocent woman was beaten almost to death? That was him, right? I heard you say that, I'm not making any of this up. It's what you said. Eddie, right? The one that has cancer—the one that I am so glad to hear has cancer. God is just. You know—"

"Laura," Nick said, "you should try and calm down." He finished his beer and sat back in his chair.

"Calm down? I don't want to calm down."

"Look," Nick said, "policemen go out and do things, they put their lives on the line. Sometimes people get hurt, sometimes people die, but it's not premeditated. It's not murder. You can't call it murder."

"I call it murder," she said, "because murder is what it is."

"Hey," Sonny said. "Hey, hey Laura, can I ask you a question?"

"What?"

"No one said the Cienfuego kid was sixteen. How'd you know that? And tell me, how'd you know the gun was old, and beat-up? Nick," Sonny said, "it was, it was an old thirty-two Colt revolver, practically an antique. A real piece of garbage. But it would kill you as dead as anything else."

"Heartless killers, murderers," Laura said drunkenly.

Sonny watched her with what seemed to be some mindless pleasure. He was smiling. "So Laura," he said, "you want to tell me where you heard that the Cienfuego kid was sixteen and that he owned an old gun? Did you tell her, Nick?"

Nick closed his eyes and shook his head. "I don't remember telling you that, Laura, but maybe I did. Except I didn't know that the gun was old. I couldn't have told you that."

Laura was silent for a moment, then she opened her mouth to speak.

But Nick said, "We never talked about any of this, Laura, not the Cienfuego kid, not the gun. I never discussed any of this with you."

"I read about the case in a Spanish-language newspaper," Laura said. "I know the whole story."

Nick looked at her for a moment and said, "I see." He'd leave it alone for the time being. She was drunk and hot-eyed, there was no use in discussing this with her now.

"I don't know who you people are," she said morbidly, "but I can see you can be evil and do evil things."

She smiled at Nick, and for a moment he was positive that she had slipped away, that she had cured herself of him and he had lost her. It had happened before with other women, the look on her face was not new to him.

"I don't feel too well," she said, going to the back door. "I'm going to bed." Laura turned in the doorway, her face a mask of regret. "I just wanted to be happy, you know. Find a little joy in my life. I just wanted to be like everyone else."

"Listen," Nick said, and swallowed. "It's the wine, you drank too much wine. You'll feel better in the morning."

Laura closed her eyes and shook her head.

A great sadness had settled over Nick. It had to do with loss and Laura, and not a little to do with curiosity. He didn't buy the bit about the Spanish newspaper. Not that it wasn't conceivable the story had appeared somehow, it was possible. But if it had, it had run ten years ago. When Laura was what, fourteen?

Sonny laughed good-naturedly. He turned to Nick with a confident smile and made a short whistling sound, saying, "I bet you're happy as hell I stopped by."

Nick shrugged. "It's not your fault," he said. "Then again, you always bring with you some bad news."

"I'm sorry. I am. I feel responsible. It's not at all what I had planned."

"I know."

Nick wondered how on earth could things that were so good go so wrong so quickly? Now he was irritated at Sonny for being sorry. He was embarrassed and didn't know why. And he was fearful that there was more to this than he could see. Sonny had said maybe you're not so smart. Maybe you just see what you expect to see. Something like that. Possibly Sonny was right, although he doubted that Sonny McCabe could be right about anything.

"Nick," Sonny said, "for chrissake, are you thinking about some of the things she said? Who is she? Where in the hell did you meet her? This is not someone off the street." Sonny whispered, "Laura knows things she has no right to know. You think about that?"

Nick closed his eyes and considered the incomprehensible. He told Sonny, not looking at him. He started with the video store and how they had bumped into each other. How he ran into her the next day, and the day after that. About the brother, and how she wouldn't give Nick her phone number—that made Sonny shift restlessly and get to his feet. Nick told it step by step, how they got together, trying to make it funny, right down to the shark-fishing trip the past weekend.

"Laura! What in the hell?" Sonny said suddenly, interrupting him.

Nick turned to see Laura standing in the doorway. On her face was a smile that was bright and full of contempt, and in her hand was an automatic, an automatic with a silencer on its muzzle. A goddamn silencer, Nick didn't know whether to be scared or angry. Twenty years a cop, seen a silencer maybe three times, if that.

"That better not be loaded," Nick said, standing.

"It's loaded all right, a fifteen-shot clip," she said, watching Sonny, her face hard and bitter.

Nick said, "What the hell do you think you're doing? Put the gun down, Laura, you could hurt someone."

"Vengeance," Maria said in a fake heroic manner. "Retribution. I'm going to shoot that son of a bitch, I'm going to kill him."

Sonny said, "Nick, who is this wacky broad?"

Nick took a step toward her.

"Don't," Maria said. She held up one finger and said, "Don't push me. Don't. Sonny," she said, "tell me something? How do you learn to live with yourself after you've killed an innocent boy?"

"Hey lady," Sonny said, "I'm not going to take this shit from you. You think I should feel guilty for doing my job? If you're talking about that Cienfuego kid, I'm telling you he had a gun, and he was pointing that gun at my partner. If you think shooting him keeps me up nights, you're dead wrong."

"He wasn't that Cienfuego kid!" Maria shouted. "He had a name, his name was Justo and he was my brother! My brother! You killed my brother!" She closed her eyes for a second, and a shudder ran through her. "Man," she said in a low voice, "he was only a boy."

Then it came to Nick, it came in a rush—she was Diego Cienfuego's daughter. The pretty child he'd seen in a courtroom and in Andre's office ten years ago. Diego's daughter, so enraged, so furious, so full of hate. Her, that kid, that young girl looking at him back then as if she wanted to stick a knife in him, would have if she'd had one. That kid.

"Sweet fucking Christ!" Nick yelled. "Give me that goddamn gun."

"I'm going to shoot him! He murdered my brother!" Maria shouted back.

Nick held out his hand and took a step toward her, overwhelmed by what was happening, embarrassed for her, pissed at her too, wanting to help her, wanting to help Sonny. She was going to shoot, he could see it in her face, she could shoot Sonny, she could kill him. Her eyes going back and forth between Sonny and Nick, considering.

"Ey," Sonny said. "You want to even up? I'm the one, I shot your brother. I wish I could take those bullets back, but I can't, it's done, it's history. It was me, look at me, I'm the one, not Nick. Hey Laura, or whatever the hell your name is," he said. "You with us?"

Maria was making an odd face, as if she could barely keep from crying—as if she was unbearably sad and desperate and frightened. She glanced at Sonny, then back at Nick, turned the gun on him. Nick stepped back, feeling the porch railing behind him. Maria's eyes were open wide, wider than any eyes he'd ever seen before.

"What are you going to do, Laura, shoot me? Shoot Sonny and me? You can't do it, you could never do it."

Maria gave a short, harsh laugh. "No?" she said, screwing up her face at him. "You don't think I can do it? You don't think I can shoot him? Oh yes I can—I've done it. I've killed killers, it's easy. You want to see how easy it is?"

It was clear she meant just what she was saying. Laura—Maria—his Laura was a killer, a murderer. She had killed people, she said she had done it before, and he believed her. Nick was feeling sick to his stomach, but there was an anger building too, coming together with a searing pain, a hurt so real he thought he would vomit. Nick thinking she had used him, turned him around and used him. At that moment, as far as Nick was concerned, these past weeks, the glorious time they had shared together became phony, unreal and fake, and it made him heart-sick, it made him furious, and so woozy that he felt as though the floor was tilting.

Suddenly he was thinking about her on E.Z.'s boat fighting that bluefish. Drinking sangria and finding a mild warm buzz. A walk along the seawall. The night and entire day in bed, so much better than he'd ever had it before. It had been all real to him, the real thing. He watched her staring at Sonny, saw her raise the gun.

"Laura!" he shouted.

She brought the gun down. "I can't do it," she said. "I can't shoot him. Ah shit, what am I doing? Nick, I don't want to do this. I'm so sorry, I'm sorry."

Helpless, Nick stared at her.

"I couldn't shoot you, Marcello. You don't believe that I could hurt you, do you?"

"Look," he told her, "I'm no hot-shit hero or anything, but I want you to give me that gun, or I'm going to come and take it."

She handed him the gun, barrel first, saying she was sorry, so sorry, over and over and over again. But no matter how much he wanted to, and he wanted to badly, he couldn't quite believe her.

"Laura, you don't know how glad I am that you didn't shoot anyone," said a voice from behind them.

E.Z.'s eyes were mild and worried in the light from the cottage. "I know Nick a long time. And hell, man, I only have but two or three friends, can't afford to lose any."

Nick felt his heart thumping. Maria said, "E.Z., what are you doing here?"

"Just walking by, came over to say hello. I could hear you from up the road. This is the country, Laura. Voices carry."

"This guy here, this Sonny," she said, "this guy, he killed my brother. What would you do? What would you do to someone that murdered your brother?"

E.Z. shook his head as if to clear it. "Sometimes," he said, "we all have to do the impossible, Laura. Sometimes we have to forgive and move on."

Maria turned away from E.Z., away from Nick and Sonny, pressing her fists against her temples. "You want me to forget them, my father and my brother?" she said, her voice shaking.

For an awkward moment there was absolute silence, then Sonny McCabe muttered, "No one would ask you to forget your family, Laura. I . . ." He looked at her, but she didn't say a word. Then Sonny turned away and walked off the porch.

Nick told E.Z. to go with him, make sure the guy didn't get lost in the woods. Nick called out, "Sonny, hey Sonny, don't go too far. It's wet out there, you'll ruin your shoes." And Nick saw, or thought he saw, Sonny glance nervously over his shoulder. He kept walking, his hands in his pockets, his head down, E.Z. right on his tail.

Chapter 43

Nick turned and said to her, "You know, Maria, I think I probably do love you, but I'm going to tell you, if everything that has happened between you and me over the past three weeks has been some sort of setup, some sort of game, then you may as well have shot me." He tried a smile but couldn't manage it. "If it was a game, you'd better shoot me."

"I'm lucky to have you, Nick," she said. "You've changed my life. And let me tell you, it needed changing."

For a moment Nick just stared at her. "So why did you point a gun at me?" he finally said.

"I was afraid."

"You weren't the only one."

Maria said, "And now what?" She looked at Nick with a terrible fear in her eyes. "I've lost you, right? I've lost you too."

"You haven't lost me. I'll help you," Nick said. "I'll do all I can to help you. I will. I love you, I do."

At this Maria burst into tears like a child. She just stood there crying, sobbing out of control, her breath coming in gasps. Nick was overwhelmed, perplexed. It had been so long since he had seen someone cry like that, must have been ten years, more maybe. He had forgotten just how sad it was to watch someone cry like that. Nick went to her, grabbed her, held her tight, fearful that he himself just might start in, seeing her in such pain. Maria tried to get herself together. Between sobs she said that she was sorry, so sorry, that she had done terrible things, things no one would forgive, not even him, especially not him. He found a tissue and handed it to her, saying those guys in Miami, and Union City? Maria nodding, Nick saying oh shit, trying not to think about what she was telling him now, what she had said earlier, about having done it before, killing someone before, knowing now for sure, she was in some deep shit. Surrendering for a moment to the terror, the knowing beyond any doubt that this woman, this woman he loved could be taken away, dragged off and put in chains. Coming together himself finally, telling himself no way, I won't let it happen.

"I'm not going to let anything happen to you," he told her. "I won't."

"I know you, Nick," she said. "You're not going to forgive me, you'll never forgive me. It's not your fault, it's just who you are. I love you for who you are, but you're not the forgiving type."

"You're wrong. You don't know me; if you knew me, you'd know I'd forgive you almost anything."

"How I want that to be true."

"Laura," he said, "I've forgiven you already. Let's forget this forgiveness jazz and try to figure out how to get you out of this hole you've jumped into. There's got to be a way. I'll think of a way."

"You know," she told him, "my father and my brother were good people who never harmed a soul."

"I know," he told her. "I know."

Nick and Maria sat alone on the back porch, E.Z. and Sonny still off on their walk. It was sometime around midnight. Nick said, "Life is one surprise after another, isn't it?"

For an hour Maria had told him what happened, how it happened. Her life in Florida with Natalia Punto and her brother, Miguel. How they had sworn revenge on all the people that had killed Justo and her father, and Rodrigo too. How they were planning to get to Benny and Cano. How Miguel was close, real close, setting up a meet with Benny; it could happen anytime now. Nick knew right off that he would have to put a stop to that. He understood the law, recognized that the law, unlike Nick himself, did not forgive. He wanted to believe that she loved him; he understood that she was frightened; he knew she was not stupid and hoped she understood that she was in way over her head.

Nick said, "You'll have to call your brother and Natalia."

"I can't do that," she said, tough now. Another side of her.

Nick said, "Yes, you can. And you will. I'll help you. I can get you through this, but you'll have to trust me. You'll have to trust me totally without question. I know I'm asking a whole lot, but you've done a whole lot."

"I'll do all that you ask, anything you want—except that. Ask me to betray my blood and it's over."

"I am not asking you to betray them. There is no reason to, you haven't told me anything that puts them in jeopardy. At least not yet you haven't. You just watch what you say, not only to me, but to anyone."

"What are we going to do, Marcello?" she said.

"Let me think about it. But first, you're going to stop calling me Marcello and I'll stop calling you Laura. You're Mariaclara Cienfuego. I'll call you Maria. You call me Nick, okay?"

She nodded.

He went to the porch railing and stood looking out at the Jamestown Bridge.

Maria said, "So tell me, have I lost you?"

He didn't answer.

Maria tried again. "Nick," she said, "what are you thinking about?"

"Questions I don't want to hear the answer to, I suppose. You just remember that you admit nothing, and I mean nothing."

"I asked you a question. Have I lost you? Right now that's all I'm thinking about. You know what I'm doing? I'm telling you I'm sorry. I've never been more sorry in my life."

"That's good," Nick said. "You should be."

"Look," she said, "tell me, don't lie to me, will we be all right?"

He turned and looked at her. "Sure," he said. "Sure." Nick had a sudden compulsion to tell her what life would be like for her in prison, and he would have if he thought it would do any good.

"I could ask you," he said, "about a couple of dead people in Miami, and a pair of drug-dealing brothers in Union City. I could ask you about hoods, and notes."

Maria gave Nick a little nod. "But you won't?"

"No, not now."

"Does that mean you will?"

He looked at her and shrugged. "I don't see any reason why I would have to," he told her. "So when was the last time you spoke to your brother?"

"I called him from the apartment before you came home."

"From my apartment?"

"Yes."

"And what did he say?"

"He wasn't happy that I was spending another weekend with you."

"Better with me then Matos and Medina."

"He was waiting to hear from them."

"Matos and Medina are pros, real pros. They'd have the three of you for lunch. What the hell were you thinking?" Nick gave Maria a long, steady look. She seemed impassive, not worried at all. He said, "I want you to call Miguel right now. I want you to call and find out what's going on."

"I'll call him."

"You can use the phone in the kitchen. And Maria," Nick said, "speak in English."

She looked at him. "I talk to my brother in Spanish," she said evenly. "I'm not going to speak to him in English. Please," she said, "don't ask me to play games with my brother, Nick. I won't do that. You ask me to trust you, you'll have to trust me too."

"I'm asking you to let me help you. That's what you want, right?"

Maria began to fidget. She took a deep breath and said, "Yes, yes, Nick, I do."

"No more games, I'm not good at game playing." Nick drifted off for a moment, beginning to imagine himself explaining himself to Andre. Forget Andre, he'd have to explain himself to the police department, to the media. He could see it all, a shitstorm waiting in the wings.

"What do you want me to say to Miguel?"

"Find out if he has heard from your uncle. Is Benny your uncle? I seem to remember your father saying—"

"No, he's not my uncle. We called him uncle. He is my mother's cousin. You remember my father, huh?"

"Sure I do. He was quite a guy, he impressed me."

"He was an innocent. A gentle man."

"That's how I remember him."

She held out her hand and he pulled her up. Maria folded her arms and looked out at the bay.

"You know," she said, "my father saw this country as alien and hostile. Nothing like the homeland he left behind." She smiled at Nick. "He never had a chance to see much, just Miami and New York. He would have loved it here. It's a shame he never had a chance to see Wickham."

"I'm sorry I didn't get to know him," Nick said.

"There is a whole lot of Diego in you," she told him. "I know what a shrink would say, I don't care, it's true. From the day I met you, there was something in you that reminded me of my father. He was like you, a real straight shooter. An honorable man."

"Truly honorable men are rare. Take it from me, I'm not one."

She reached over and put her fingers against his lips. "More honorable than any man I've ever known. You're far more honest than I am. But I guess that's clear."

Nick took her hand away from his mouth. "I know you a short time," he told her. "The time we spent here and in the city. I know what you're like. A little wild, but with a good heart. You give me more joy than any woman ever has. I don't plan on losing you."

She just looked at him for a moment. Then she walked off and looked at her watch. "You don't know me," she said finally, "not really."

Nick went to her, took her face in his hands, saying, "I know your eyes and throat and the sweet smell of your hair. I know you can catch a bluefish and cook it too. What else is there? Maria, I knew we were right for each other. From day one, I knew it."

"You knew it and I knew it," she told him. "It was strange how I knew."

"Now go and call your brother. We have to put an end to this."

"Can we?" she said. "Is it possible?"

Nick nodded. "Through everything that's happened, all that went on, we—me and you—we found each other. Now if that is possible, I'd say anything is."

Maria breathed out, tossing her head. "Oh God," she said, "I hope so."

Nick still hadn't decided what he would do about four murders. When those thoughts closed in on him, he was stabbed with a sharp sense of panic, but then they would recede, and he was more worried about Maria than the law. When the panic passed he worked on what he would do about Natalia Punto and Miguel, Benny Matos and Medina. A plan was forming in his head, nothing solid, just some thoughts.

Nick didn't want Maria to talk to her brother in the state she was in, but he had to find out exactly what was up. He'd move from there. He was anxious, getting more so by the moment. Killings he'd known nothing about were one thing. Murders he could prevent were a whole other game.

Maria went inside. A cold breeze slapped the screen door, startling Nick. Maria sat down with her back to him and studied the telephone; she lifted the receiver and punched out some numbers.

It was twelve thirty.

Nick hadn't noticed Sonny and E.Z. standing in the darkness near the porch, but they had been watching and listening, and when Maria went into the cottage they came to join him.

"So," Sonny said. "What now?"

"You can stay the night," Nick told him. "There's a guest room. You can leave in the morning."

"Uh-huh," Sonny said.

"What are you going to do?" E.Z. asked.

Nick shrugged. "I'm not sure. Something, I'll do something."

"You're not going to burn her?" Sonny said. "I mean, what are you going to do?"

"I don't know. But you can bet your ass I'm not going to burn her. I'll work this out; there's got to be a way."

"Look," E.Z. said. "Me and Sonny were talking."

"Shit," Nick said. "Now that's a combo for ya."

E.Z. said, "We were talking, me and Sonny. We want to hang in with you. You know, go along for the ride."

"What ride?" Nick said.

"Whatever you're planning, Nick," Sonny said. "And I know you got something going round in that head of yours. You're going to need some help."

"I appreciate your offer," Nick said. "It means a lot to me. But I don't think you two know just what is involved here. The trick bag this woman has gotten herself into could be bad. I mean real bad." Nick paused, chewing his lip, thinking. "Anyway, you've both been through enough for one night, don't you think? You damn near got shot."

Sonny glanced at E.Z. "This guy looks like he can take care of himself. He survived Vietnam, and I endured sixteen years in the NYPD. He's alive and well, and in all my years in the job, I didn't get hurt or go to jail. We're survivors. Some would say we're winners. You could use a pair of winners with you."

"It's not like we're amateurs," E.Z. said.

Maria came out through the porch door. "My brother met with Benny tonight," she said. "He ordered five kilos of cocaine. Benny told him he'd have it tomorrow night. They're going to meet at Tio's around ten o'clock."

Nick nodded at the bay and said, "Good for Miguel."

Maria said, "Cano was there. Natalia saw him; he was at the bar, didn't speak to Miguel, but he was there."

"Double trouble," Nick said.

"I told Miguel that I would be back sometime tomorrow afternoon. Early enough to go with him." She raised her eyebrows. "What do you think?"

"I think we got a date," Nick said.

"All of us," said Sonny.

E.Z. grinned at him. "I'm there, you need me. I'm gonna be there," he said.

Nick felt himself flush. "I can't allow you two to get involved," he said. "Too many ways things could go wrong here."

"Look," E.Z. told him. "Fishing is great, it's how I make my living, but it's fishing. I'd like to do something to get the blood flowing, you know what I mean? And it's not like I haven't done it before."

"As far as I'm concerned," Sonny said, "I'm going. I don't care what you say, I'm there too."

Nick gave Sonny a dirty look. "What are you up to?"

"*Moi?* What could I be up to? I'm here to help is all."

Nick watched Maria straighten up, glancing at the three of them. Her gaze showed a faint gleam of hope. Nick looked at Sonny and E.Z., the two of them as different as they were alike. He didn't know what to say. He wanted to turn them down, try and do this on his own. But there was no way.

"Okay, we'd better get some sleep," Nick said softly, mostly to himself. "Tomorrow is gonna be a hell of a day. One for the books."

McCabe was smiling, Sonny's silly-ass grin in full force. He picked up a half-full bottle of wine and pulled out the cork. "Here's to us," he said. "All of us."

Chapter 44

In the morning they set out for New York City, Nick and Maria in his car, Sonny in the rented Lincoln, and E.Z. in his pickup. They stopped at the Middlebridge Crossing for breakfast. Nick had coffee, wheat toast, and some juice. Sonny, E.Z., and Maria each had eggs and ham and a blueberry pancake. Maria had four cups of coffee.

All during breakfast Maria stared at Sonny, and when he caught her at it she'd smile at him, a small tight smile, hardly a smile at all. Nick had already outlined some of his plan, and the others seemed to be reassured that he had thought this through. Which was not true. E.Z. and Sonny finished first and went outside to smoke and look at the river and watch two men fishing the bottom for spring flounder.

"Maria," Nick said, "didn't you see how crazy this was? I mean for you?"

"C'mon, Nick," she said. "I'm doing what you asked. My mind was a mess, I've got it straight now."

"I hope so. You figure out how you'll explain all this to your brother and Natalia? You think about that yet?"

Maria looked down at her lap and then up at the ceiling. She smiled at him, a warm and familiar smile. Nick sat still, waiting until she was ready.

"I mean," Nick said, "there is no room or time for debate here."

Maria nodded.

Nick paid, and he and Maria went out. In the parking lot, Maria tried the passenger door of Nick's car but Nick had locked it. She turned her back and stood with folded arms looking at the river. Sonny McCabe was walking and talking with E.Z.; they were laughing, horsing around.

Nick called to E.Z. and Sonny as he got into the car and opened the door for Maria. They came up to the passenger window, still smiling.

"All right," Sonny said. "We'll follow you; you're going straight to the office, right?"

"What is it now, ten?" Nick said. "We should be there sometime around one."

"Don't drive too fast, Nick," E.Z. said. "This old pickup of mine has more heart than talent. Not unlike your pal the writer here."

"I'll take it easy," Nick said, thinking E.Z. and Sonny, buddies now. That's Sonny for you, the charmer.

Nick started up the car feeling a bit peculiar. He glanced at Maria; there was something about the way she was staring at Sonny, the way she looked at him, cold, nothing there, eerie. There is no forgiveness in her, Nick thought. Forget understanding.

Nick realized that Maria was someone Sonny would never charm. His humor was lost on her. He hoped it wasn't more than that. The notion came to him that maybe Maria had her own plans. Maybe Sonny was still her target. Something more to worry about, something else to consider.

Maria sat rigid in the passenger seat, her face turned away from Nick. He could feel these chilly vibes coming off her body. He watched her rub her temples in slow circles with the heels of her hands. "Hey c'mon," he said, "you're going to be all right. Natalia and Miguel too, you're all going to be fine. We just need a little luck."

He watched her chest and stomach rise and fall. She turned to him, saying, "How can you be so sure?"

"I'm not sure, I never said I was sure. I said if you keep your head and listen to me, this should work out. But you can't be sure, you can never be sure."

She stared at him from across the seat. "I'd like a normal life," she told him. "That's all. I keep asking myself, what will it take? How will it happen?"

Nick drove the car, keeping them ahead of Sonny and E.Z. until he got on the highway. All the way to the Connecticut state line Maria sat silent, staring out the window. He wanted to talk, to tell her things, but at that moment the words were out of his reach. Look at her, Nick thought, it's not every day you find a woman like this. And it's not every day she escapes you. He could see that happening as he thought about it. Losing Maria after he'd finally found her. It wouldn't happen, he wouldn't let it happen; that was it, end of story. Whatever it took, it took. Shoot the moon. He hoped for some help, prayed that he would find some real justice in this world. He'd like to believe he had earned it.

They were practically in New York State before she spoke again.

"I think of my father, of all the trouble he found in the States," she said. "And all he ever wanted was to belong here. My dad wanted to be a citizen of Cuba, a citizen of America, and a citizen of the world. Maybe he didn't know how to express that, but he believed that there should be a place for him somewhere."

Nick drove the car, keeping silent.

"We weren't in the country a month when we were mugged in Miami," she said. "They stole my mother's necklace from me, tore it right off my neck. My father begged them not to hurt me. They were bad kids, real street toughs; they had guns. You know, I don't remember being afraid. I remember being angry, but not frightened. I was furious. I was so young and so angry. Not about the necklace. Sure it was a terrible thing to lose, my mother's necklace. It was important to me. But I was more disturbed for my father. How they had humiliated him, how he begged them not to hurt me."

Nick let her talk, let her get it out.

"In my nightmares, and I had plenty when I was younger, I'd see him begging for my life on that Miami street corner. Then I'd see him begging for his own life in that jail, that prison. They cut his throat, you know. That's how they killed him."

Nick could feel her building up to something, and it made him nervous. Made him think that maybe he didn't know her. Maybe she was a bit twisted and crazy, and a damn good actress. He thought of that and told himself, ey, what are you thinking, stop thinking like that, you'll make yourself batty.

Maria said, "I grew up believing blood for blood, it's the only way to end my nightmares."

"Listen," Nick said carefully, taking his time, "the only way to end your nightmares is to start fresh and put all that wild shit behind you. Maria," he said, "you don't need that in your life anymore."

Maria sat slumped in her seat, her head down, her chin on her chest. She seemed to be looking into herself, or perhaps not, maybe just considering, deciding what to do. Nick hoped that in the end she'd have some choice in the matter.

He shook his head, looking straight ahead through the windshield at the highway. "It's not too late, you know," he said. "We can pull this off, we just might make it. But you have to convince Natalia and Miguel to come along. Without them, we can't do anything."

"They trust me, they'll listen," she said.

"I hope you're right."

She looked at him sharply. "What are you saying? Be careful what you say to me, Nick. My family comes first, before everything, before even you."

He knew that. He hadn't thought about it a whole lot, but he knew that was true.

"I hope you're not thinking of pulling something clever here, Nick," she said. He could feel her eyes on him. She was looking at him the way she had looked at Sonny McCabe the night before.

Nick said, "I've known you what, three weeks? And I'm shooting crap with my life for you. Maria, I'm not being clever, I'm being anything but clever."

"I know who you are and what you're risking," she told him. "I love you for it. I'm crazy about you. Then again, maybe I'm just crazy for letting you talk me into this."

"I told you last night that it is all a question of faith," he said. "My way or Natalia's and Miguel's. You've done it their way, that doesn't make it right."

"We've had this conversation," she said. And they had, into the night, then into the early morning hours. "If I didn't love you," she told him, "I'd never do this, I'd let it be, take my chances."

Nick thinking take your chances on what? Killing four, six people maybe? How crazy is that, how nuts? But he couldn't say that.

Nick considered that love was an overused word in an old game. When you got right down to it, what did it mean? Certainly the way she said it touched him. And what did he feel? Love? Lust? The need not to be lonely? So what's wrong with all three, what's wrong with that? Look around you, smart guy, he told himself, check it out. You're being drawn into things you should want no part of. Tricks of the heart, Nick thought, tricky tricks.

Checking to be sure that Sonny and E.Z. were close behind him, Nick picked up speed. He made his way through light Sunday afternoon traffic toward the Whitestone Bridge and Queens. He pulled into the courthouse garage sometime after three, and Sonny and E.Z. pulled in alongside him.

Nick and Maria looked at each other for a long moment.

"Are you ready?" he said. "No change of heart?"

She shook her head.

He leaned toward her, whispering, "It'll be as though I'm with you, as though I'm right there. And I will be, like a ghost, you just won't be able to see me."

Maria said, "My guardian angel."

"Anyone else I'd say no, but you can do this, I know you can," Nick said. "If there was any question in my mind, I wouldn't let you even try."

She nodded.

"I've thought this through," Nick told her. "I've looked at every angle. This can work; the way I see it, it's the only way to go. Okay? So what we have to do here is, we get out of this car, me and you, we go into my office, and I set you up. Once you're ready you arrange to meet with Miguel and Natalia and make your pitch. Pull this off and you're free of this for the rest of your life. Pull this off and you've saved your family too. That sound good to you?"

She nodded again. "You know," she said, "I could have killed him. You understand that, right? I could have killed Sonny. I came very close. Then I said, no, no, it's not right, and there's Nick, my Nick."

"You believe that? Is that what you think?"

"What, that I could have killed him? Are you kidding?"

"No, that it's not right. Forget Nick, forget me. The killing, you believe it's not right?"

Maria said nothing; she reached up with her hand and stroked his cheek, touched the tip of his nose. "I love you," she told him.

"Jesus," he said.

It was quiet in the building, no one but the security guard around. Nick took them up to his office. He turned on the lights and let them look around for a moment.

Nick said, "First things first. I have a gun, Sonny you have a gun. You have a carry permit, right?"

Sonny said, "It's like my foot, I'd go nuts trying to get around without it."

Maria shot him a quick look. Just a look, but that look sent a chill through Nick. "E.Z., I don't know what to do about you. In case of anything I want you to be able to protect yourself, but Jesus, if something were to go wrong . . ."

"I have a gun," E.Z. said, "this one." He lifted his sweatshirt and drew a Glock automatic from his belt. "If you think I'm gonna come to New York City, play tag with you guys without a gun, you're out of your mind."

Nick opened his mouth to argue but all he could do was sigh. "Just be careful," he said.

He went to the cabinet behind his desk. Opening the door with a key, he took out three portable radios. He gave one to E.Z. and one to Sonny, keeping one for himself. Then he took out a leather attaché case and brought it to his desk. Inside were several body transmitters. He chose a Kel, the best wire he had. It was "line-of-sight"—if you could see the person wearing it you could hear them. It was powered by a ten-volt battery and could bang out of most closed rooms. Under normal conditions, you could lose sight of the subject and still get something, not much, but something.

"Okay," Nick said, "how about you two give Maria and me a minute here. Take a radio and an earpiece, tune the radio to F-three, go down the hall, I'll let you know when we're ready."

Sonny glanced at Maria. He looked at Nick and then at Maria again. He said, "You remember the last time you were here? I do."

"So do I," said Maria.

"You stuck out your tongue at me," Sonny said.

"Not at you Sonny, at Nick. And it wasn't the last time either." She smiled at him, gave a quick nod.

"You have your father's eyes," Sonny said. "Anyone ever tell you that?"

"Everybody. You remember my father?"

"Of course. Listen, I want to tell you something," he said. Sonny McCabe lit up a cigarette and inhaled to his toes.

Nick held his breath.

Sonny said, "The women I've known—and believe me I've known a few—compared to you they all had about as much spirit as cement. You're quite a lady. However this goes, whatever happens from here on out, I'm glad to have met you. I needed to tell you that."

"And you haven't seen her fish," said E.Z.

"Right, and I'll tell you something," Sonny said, "I never will. Out in the middle of the ocean, grabbing sharks, you guys are nuts. Maybe the next time you go I'll tag along, but I'll be waiting for you on shore in some gin mill having a butt and a beer and a bimbo. Heaven."

Nick laughed and E.Z. did too. When Nick looked at Maria she was smiling. Nick thinking Irish charm, try and top it. He reached into the attaché case and removed the Kel, and the laughter died. E.Z. turned and started for the door.

"E.Z.?" Sonny said.

"He's gonna open her jeans and take off her blouse. I'd like to stay, but Nick got no sense of humor."

"Oh. Right," Sonny said, "wait for me."

When E.Z. and Sonny had closed the door behind them, Nick locked it. Maria unbuttoned her blouse and took it off, laying it on Nick's desk. "The bra too?" she said.

"It's a good idea."

The bra went on top of the blouse.

"The jeans?" she said.

"Just open them."

She did, she opened them, her eyes never leaving Nick's face. Maria hesitated for a moment, smiled, then quickly peeled off her jeans. Kicking them aside, she took off her panties; he could hear her breathing now, his own breathing too.

"Christ, you're beautiful," Nick said.

"The door's locked," she told him, "and we have the time."

Nick cleared his desk, threw everything onto the floor. He kicked off his shoes and unhooked his trousers. Nick took her hand, went to the desk where he worked every day. He lay flat on his back. She stood alongside him; he closed his eyes but he could feel her watching him. He reached out and found her hand and pulled her to him. He held her there until he felt her climb up onto the desk and straddle him. Without one kiss he felt himself inside her, felt her hands on his head, touching his forehead, his eyes, his nose. Maria was moving now, a Latin dancer, a Cuban dancer, a slow bolero. Her hands held tight to his, real tight, and soon, too soon, she was moving faster, and in a moment he could feel it happening, the energy of it, through her hands into her arms, all over her body. She pulled his hands to her breasts and bent her head until it touched his. And then she reared back gasping for breath, squeezing his hands, holding tight, spreading her arms wide. "Marcello," she said. Nick thinking why not?

Twenty minutes later she stood naked in front of him, her head back, her eyes closed. Nick had cinched the Kel transmitter belt around her waist, now he was taping the wire and tiny microphone between her breasts.

"The waistband of your jeans," he told her, "will cover the transmitter belt. This is the best tape job I've ever done, it's good and tight. No one could find it unless they strip-searched you."

There was a rap on the door, then another.

"In a second," Nick said.

Maria went up on tiptoes to kiss Nick's cheek. "Am I ready?" she asked.

"About as ready as you're ever gonna be."

She dressed quickly, and when she was through, Nick opened his office door.

"Works great," Sonny said with a huge grin.

"What?" said Nick.

"There's an on-off switch on that thing," E.Z. said. "Clearly you had it on."

Nick said again, "What?"

"Marcello?" asked Sonny. "Captain," he said, "you make me proud."

In spite of herself, in spite of everything, Maria covered her mouth with her hand and laughed. It was a good laugh, infectious, causing everyone to join in.

A short distance from the apartment building where Natalia and Miguel were waiting, Nick found himself a place to park beside a newsstand. He could see the building entrance. He stayed where he was for a moment, then backed up a bit. E.Z. and Sonny were parked on the avenue behind him.

When he turned to Maria he saw that she was biting her lip. He looked back out at the street.

"A couple of things I want to go over again, make sure you understand," he said.

"Nick, we've gone over this for hours. I know what I'm doing."

"First of all," he said, ignoring her, "remember, I don't speak Spanish. Neither does Sonny or E.Z. You'll have to throw in enough English so that we won't get lost."

"I know."

"Don't carry any ID. Make sure Miguel doesn't either. Benny and Medina will ask to see some ID. If we had more time I could have arranged to get you some."

"Okay, I know, you told me."

He was silent for a moment.

"Listen to me. Benny mentioned the Holiday Inn, it doesn't mean he has any intention of really going there."

"Nick, we've gone over—"

"Listen. He will most probably use a hotel, and that's okay. I can get to every single one, they all have a retired detective as a security chief."

Maria sighed.

"They could be registered under any name," he told her. "You have to get me the room number. Make sure you get it to me. I can just see myself kicking in the doors of a hundred rooms."

Maria was looking straight ahead through the windshield. She shrugged. "You'll know," she said. "I'll make sure you know."

"Look, you're going to be dealing with a pair of real bad guys, real pros. Cano and Benny, those two guys, as everybody knows, they can spoil your entire day. Be smart, be patient."

"Sure, sure," she said. "You know, your friend Sonny takes some getting used to."

"So maybe you were wrong about him?"

"Growing up, I was shown the faces of evil, Sonny was one of those faces. It's kind of a shock to the system to discover, after you've met him, that the enemy is but an average guy. No better, no worse."

He shook his head. "People are people, some good, some bad, most just trying to get by. Sonny's not evil. That half-a-hump Cano, and your uncle, we're talking evil there, we're talking blackhearted bastards."

"I told you, Benny's not my uncle. But there are others, plenty of other evil people."

"I know that."

"Do you?"

"Sure."

They sat in silence for a moment.

"Miguel and Natalia are waiting for me. I'd better go," she told him.

"All right, all right. Is your transmitter on?"

"No, should I switch it on now? You said you were worried about the battery. It's three hours before we're to meet them."

He put his hand on the nape of her neck and looked into her face. "You have that little piece of tape I gave you, right?"

"Calm down, will you? It's in my bag."

"Before you go out, turn the switch to on and tape it down. I don't want you moving around and turning the transmitter off."

"You told me, Nick, you told me all this."

"Yeah, well, I got something new to tell you. You ready, you listening?"

She smiled at him. "Go on, you're making me nervous."

"Make sure you bring the guns and the hoods. Put them in the bag with the money. It's very important you don't forget. Bring that stuff, don't screw around, bring it all. You understand what I'm saying?"

She smiled and shrugged and raised upturned palms.

Nick said, "All right, okay. Fine, we'll all be fine."

She put her arms around his neck and kissed his forehead, his nose. Then he heard her say, "Oh shit, they're here."

She released him and opened the door and got out of the car. He watched her walk to the apartment house, saw her hug and kiss a young man standing out front. The same young man he'd seen in the video store. Then she turned to Natalia Punto and threw her arms around her neck. His heart rose as he watched her. He could see her vanishing beyond him, getting out of his reach, moving into her other life. Nick remembered Natalia Punto. Rodrigo's wife. She hadn't changed at all. Maybe just a bit older, from where he was sitting. Nick thinking, I didn't wish her good luck. Damn, I should have wished her luck. Not a good sign, not a good sign at all.

Maria understood the chance she was taking. He'd spent half the night convincing her that these were risks she must be willing to take if she hoped to walk away from this. It would take courage, more than a little. What it came to, what he had to face, was that soon he would go with her, hand in hand, so far outside the law that there would be no turning back. This, all of this, was so foreign to his nature it made him nuts. In the name of love? C'mon. But what else? He was about to put everything he valued right on the line. Nick imagined that it was a form of justice he was seeking, assumed that what he was doing was just and right and had to get done. His arguments were strong, and he almost managed to convince himself.

When he started the car she turned to look at him, she seemed to raise her hand, she seemed to smile, then she turned away. He thought of her father, Diego, and the kid Justo. For a second he flashed on Natalia, her husband, Rodrigo, the basement in Los Campos, the men hanging there. At that moment, Nick Manaris was as frightened as he'd ever been.

Nick learned that the chief of security of the Holiday Inn was a retired homicide detective, a guy named Reinhart. Sonny knew him, of course he did. The weather report said it would be warm that night, clear and warm, a full moon. Just what we need, E.Z. told him.

Nick let Sonny handle it. When Nick told him he'd found a spot to park on Sixty-ninth, about a half a block from Tio's, Sonny said I'll go to Seventieth, right off the corner, there's a hydrant there. I'll sit in the car, squat right there. I told E.Z. to pull right up in front of the joint. Him there, me and you on the side streets, we got it covered.

It was nine thirty.

Chapter 45

The streets were Sunday night early summer quiet. The weekenders were taking their time getting back to the city. He walked along the avenue and every so often he'd catch a peculiar look. It was the earplug and the way he talked into the top pocket of his jacket every ten minutes or so. People moved out of the way when he walked by, a homeless couple winked at him reassuringly.

He was expecting to hear Maria's voice any time now. If only these two jokers would cool it, he could hear her. But what a pair, Sonny and E.Z., and they were on the same frequency as Maria's transmitter. Now Nick was getting hot, listening to these two guys screw around. Finally having to tell the both of them to stop the chatter and stay off the air.

It was near 9:45 when Nick spotted Benny and Cano getting out of a black Mercedes. He watched them walk into Tio's. The car turned the corner and drove into the street where Sonny was parked. Nick stepped into the doorway of a Korean grocery, pushed the send button. "Sonny," he said. Nick turned and smiled at the grocery clerk, who gave him a look like what the fuck? "Sonny, a black Mercedes with Florida plates."

"Yeah, I see him, he's pulling into a parking garage."

Nick said, "Our two guys just left that car and went into the restaurant."

"The big fat dude in white and the little guy with red hair?" E.Z. said.

"That's them. Benny and Cano, our boys," Nick said. "Sit tight."

At that precise moment he heard Maria, making it plain in a soft voice that she could see him, clear as day, and E.Z. too. She wondered if that was smart, E.Z. parking right in front of the place.

Nick spotted them standing on the corner a block from the restaurant, all three standing with arms crossed, looking at him as if he were someone they'd rather not see. He raised his hand, did a quick little wave. They shook their heads, he saw them, the three of them shook their heads and then turned around. A nightclub act.

Nick could hear Natalia's voice, then Maria and Miguel said something. What? Man, he wished he understood Spanish.

Maria said, "Can you walk toward us?" in a soothing tone. "Somebody wants to talk to you."

As he drew near, Natalia moved away from Maria and Miguel, took

Nick's arm, and together they turned the corner. "Natalia Punto," Nick said. "Nice to see you again, how have you been? You look the same, you haven't changed at all."

"Me, you want to talk about me? I don't want to talk about me," she told him. "I want to talk about you." She was grinning at him now.

"Sure, what do you want to know? But make it quick, Benny and Cano aren't going to wait forever."

"They'll wait. For money, they'll wait until the sun burns out."

"So what do you want to know?" Nick discovered that Natalia made him nervous, the way she held on to his arm, squeezing it, trying to tell him something with her hand. "Maria said you wanted to ask me something."

"You love my baby, right?" Squeeze. "I know you love her, you want to know how I know?" Squeeze.

Talking right up close to his face, making Nick ask, "How?"

"If you didn't love her you would have arrested her already. You would have had a hundred cops over here. Am I right?" Squeeze.

Nick pulled his arm free, he didn't care for her tone at all, going from soft and friendly to tough, sharp.

She said, "We are going to do what you ask, all of us. But we have some demands, things that must be done. You want us to help, no?"

"Wait now," Nick said, "I have to hear this, what are you talking about?"

"How can we trust you, you know? I can't trust the police, you want to know why?"

Right up in his face again, forcing him to ask, "Why not?"

"Rodrigo trusted you, and look what happened to that poor man."

"All right, all right, you made your point. So what else? What do you want me to do?"

"I come along with you. Go for the ride, I want to be there. I don't come, we all go home. And you know, fuck it, do what you got to do."

This was a new one. Something he hadn't considered. Nick said, "Uh-huh."

"I am not a stupid woman, you know. Maybe you think I'm stupid, but I'm not dumb."

"I don't think you're stupid."

"Okay, let me tell you, you can't go to jail for what you think about doing. At least not in this country. At least not yet in this country. What Maria told you—"

"Okay, fine, you can come along, you'll ride with me."

"Yes?"

"Absolutely."

"You're smart," she said. "I told Maria you love her and you are smart. When a man loves a woman there is nothing he won't do for her. I know that. And Nick, I think she loves you too, maybe. I think so. She is a beautiful woman, no?"

"She is a beautiful woman, yes."

"And smart, the smartest one in her class. I keep all her report cards, A, A, A, everything A. Everything one hundred percent. Maybe she is even smarter than you."

"Maybe she is."

"You get A, A, A?"

"Never."

"You see that?"

Nick eased back in the seat of his car, not wanting to say anything, not yet. He listened to Miguel on the wire, the kid talking fast, he seemed nervous, unsure of himself. Nick thinking an amateur, this kid is an amateur, he's going to get himself killed, they're both going to get themselves killed.

Natalia said, "They're talking, just talking, nothing going on, saying hello, how you like the city, you know, that kind of thing."

Nick said, "I can't believe Benny doesn't recognize them." Moving around in his seat, feeling for his gun, holding the radio, wondering how in the hell he talked Maria into this. Thinking who you kidding? This woman took out four bad guys, she's nobody's victim.

Natalia said, "Benny only saw them once in a while, he hardly saw them at all. And it was ten years ago, and the man was always high, you know, smoking reefer, drinking—wait a minute."

"What?"

She didn't say anything. Her eyes held Nick's in the dim light inside the car.

Nick was parked just off the corner, less than a half a block from Tio's. The restaurant was practically empty, hardly any background noise, and transmission was perfect. A little luck there, it was always a crapshoot with these wires.

"What?" Nick said.

"Shh, Cano's talking. That's him, that fucking murdering Colombian bastard. You're going to kill him for me, huh, Nick? Please. You're going to kill him for me."

"What's going on?" he said. The voices were coming fast and jumbled; he couldn't catch word one.

"Cano asked Miguel if he brought the money. Maria said she had it;

she is so cool. My baby, she is so brave. Like her father, just like Diego. He would be proud."

Nick wanted to say he doubted it, doubted that Diego would be proud of Maria, of either of his kids, the man was probably spinning in his grave, but he kept quiet. What a mess.

"It's Benny," Natalia said, "he said he wants to see the money. He is stoned, I can tell, that man is loaded. I hear he does so much coke now that the bone in his nose is gone. Like you, you know, no bone at all."

"What are they saying, what the hell are they saying now?" And after a moment, "That doesn't sound good—what's going on?"

"Shh. This thing works, huh? You can hear everything, just like the radio."

"Natalia."

"They're just talking."

"About what? Jesus Christ."

"Miami, food, you know. Maria told them they will see the money when she sees the coke. Wait a minute, Cano said he is ready for them. He said they got everything waiting for them. But not here, not in Manhattan. They are going to Queens. They are leaving." Natalia looked at Nick, who stared at her in return.

"Where?" he said. "Where in Queens?"

Natalia shrugged.

"Okay, listen up," Nick said. "You guys with me? Sonny, E.Z., you there?"

E.Z. said, "I'm here, I hear you."

Sonny said, "What's up?"

E.Z. said, "Hold it, yep, that's them, they're leaving, just walked out of the place. Going along the avenue now, heading for Seventieth."

"They're on their way to Queens," Nick said. "Watch them, Sonny."

"I got them, can't miss that fat bastard in white. They're going for the car, Nick."

Nick said, "Don't lose them. Stay right with them, don't mess this up."

He could never understand how people carrying a hundred thousand dollars in cash and who knows how many guns could drive like they're out for a Sunday cruise and never look around. They followed the Mercedes over the Fifty-ninth Street Bridge to Broadway, then over to Roosevelt Avenue. Like following your grandmother to church, it was a snap. The Mercedes turned onto Corona Avenue.

"Are they going where I think they are?" Sonny said.

Nick said, "Can you believe this?"

The Mercedes parked and everyone got out. Sonny said, "Jesus Christ, they're going to Los Campos."

Nick said, "The place is closed down. E.Z.," he said, "how you doing?"

"I'm here. I've never seen so many Latin restaurants and clubs. What the hell did we do, make a left turn into Bogotá?"

"Back down the street, back down, let's not get too close," Nick told him.

"You know," Natalia said, "I'm starting to worry. What happens now? They're taking my babies into that club. That club where—"

"What are they saying?" Nick said.

"Same thing, nothing much, they'd be stupid to pass up this deal. Something like that."

"Who said it?"

"Maria, she said it."

They set up across the street about half a block from Los Campos, close enough to see the front door and get there pretty quick if they had to. When Maria and Miguel went inside Los Campos with Benny and Cano, Nick got out of the car, telling Natalia to flash the lights if anything serious was happening. He told her don't touch the radio, just leave it on the seat and listen. Then he walked back to Sonny's Lincoln, and E.Z. got out of his pickup and followed.

"So what now?" Sonny said.

"We wait," Nick said. "But not too long. If this is legit they should only be a minute. If this is legit they got five keys of coke in that place. Knowing these two creeps they most probably got a whole lot more."

"Why Los Campos?" Sonny said. "Why put your stash here? I mean, it's not like the place is cool, you know what I mean? Cops were killed here."

"And other people," Nick said.

"So this is the place Maria's brother was killed," E.Z. said.

"That it is," said Sonny. "That it is."

Sonny was facing Nick, backlit by a streetlight. Nick couldn't see his eyes, but in his voice there was sadness. The guy was a regular toy box of surprises.

"You know, Sonny," Nick said, "the kid had a gun."

"I know, I know, man you don't have to tell me. Still . . ."

E.Z. said, "The driver of the Mercedes just came out of the club. He's standing by the door. A little guard duty, huh?"

"I don't like this," Nick said.

Sonny said, "Let's go in, c'mon. They're not going to do this to me again. Let's go right the fuck through that door."

The lights of Nick's car flashed.

Los Campos stood at the end of a string of woodframe row houses and walkups. It was a residential street. A couple of dozen sycamores lined the curb. The trees kept the street in shadow, and even with the full moon it was dark. Eleven thirty at night, no one around.

"Hey, Nick, I'm going," Sonny said.

"Wait a minute, will ya? E.Z.," Nick said, "me and Sonny are going to take a walk down this street. We're gonna go nice and easy. When you see that we're about twenty yards or so from the front door, you pull that pickup right in front of the place. Ask the guy for directions or something. We take him out and go in."

"I've been through this before," Sonny said. "What if the door's locked?"

Nick didn't answer.

E.Z. went back to his truck, started it up.

Nick felt a terrible weight bearing down on him suddenly, not because of his decision to do this but because he was putting E.Z. and Sonny out front with him.

Walking quickly beneath the shadows of the trees, he started to tell Sonny that he'd told Maria to bring the hoods and guns, but Sonny cut him off.

"The door better not be locked; if there is a God that door is open," Sonny said.

"Say it's locked," Nick said, "we don't wait, we go through it, me and you we take it down."

"You kidding me, you remember that door? It was reinforced oak, it'd be a bitch to take that down. What we need is a little luck now, a hand from the sky pilot."

E.Z. pulled up in front of the club, got out, and walked around the front of the pickup to the sidewalk. The guy standing guard duty didn't move. A young guy wearing a red shirt, a whole lot of bushy hair, gold chains and teeth to match. "I'm looking for I-Ninety-five North," E.Z. said. He didn't know what else to say.

"¿Qué?"

"I-Ninety-five. You know, the highway?"

Red Shirt leaned his back against the door and slowly lit a cigarette. "No English, man. I no understand."

Nick and Sonny were coming fast, moving quietly, maybe twenty feet away when E.Z. said, "You understand hole in your fucking head?" In the time it took him to tag a blue shark, E.Z.'s left hand went around the back of Red Shirt's head; in his other hand was the Glock. He pushed that pistol right up against Red Shirt's front gold teeth.

Nick and Sonny were there now, right at the door. Nick tried it and smiled.

The guard, whose name was Alberto Jesus Rios, would have liked to have gotten out a yell, a shout, some kind of warning. But the guy with the gun looked like some kind of crazy. And Rios wasn't getting paid enough to take a bullet in the teeth. Anyway, the man acted like a cop, he sure hoped he was a cop.

When Nick tried to hand E.Z. a pair of handcuffs, E.Z. said, "Keep 'em, you might need 'em. I got my own."

Nick was surprised at how calm he was, like he did this every day, no big deal.

They went in, closing the door behind them. The interior was in semidarkness; some moonlight seeped in, and the glow of the street-light, not bad, they could see fairly well.

"The basement," Sonny said.

They made their way quickly and quietly through the club into the hallway. Nick could hear voices coming from below. Nick moved Sonny aside and stood listening at the basement door. The conversation was in Spanish, voices at a normal pitch. Then suddenly a shout, and Nick snapped to attention. What struck him as odd was that he knew the voice was Benny's, deep and full, a big man's voice. Nick poked Sonny with his elbow, saying you ready? And although he had no idea what was happening down there, he put his hand on the doorknob and tried it. The door was unlocked.

Sonny pushed him aside, threw open the door, and flew down the stairs, shouting, "Police! Police!"

Nick said, "Goddamn," but he followed Sonny down the stairs. Running, not thinking at all, down into that basement. The birthplace of so many of his nightmares.

When Nick's feet hit the basement floor he glanced around the room, and the first thing he saw was Sonny standing in a shooters crouch, both his hands around his pistol, saying, "Police! Police! Police!"

The Colombian and Benny were sitting at a table in the center of the room facing Nick. On the table were stacks of money and half-kilo packages of cocaine, at least ten, maybe more. Maria and Miguel stood with their backs to the wall, arms folded, watching wide-eyed. There was a small grin on Maria's face; she seemed so out of place here that Nick, in the first few seconds, didn't notice the guns at her feet. Miguel appeared bewildered, a little lost and angry.

Cano turned toward Benny and it seemed he was about to say something, but then he turned back to Nick and stared at him, just stared and said nothing. His stare was intense. As far as Nick knew he'd never met this guy, never even seen him before, but the look Cano shot at him was one of recognition. It was an untroubled stare, Nick thought, eerie. Benny sat with his thick hands clasped in front of him, his head down, his chin on his chest, rocking, swaying, squeezing his eyes shut, then opening them again.

The basement itself appeared to be the same as Nick remembered, and he found himself checking the damp whitewashed cement block walls for hooks. Ten years earlier, he'd seen two men strung up on these same walls. He inspected the floor for old bloodstains. Nick stood very still, not thinking at all about the gun in his hand, his pistol, the old-timer, the .38 S&W detective special, the old standby. It didn't appear that he would have to shoot anyone. So far, so good.

Maria was smiling broadly now. She appeared almost happy.

Cano looked over at Sonny, frowning. "Police, huh? City police? I hoped you were DEA, better if you're DEA. Me and the DEA are friendly. You should know that. Friends take care of friends, you know. It's the way of the world. I have a card here," he said. "It's from a congressman."

"Cops," Benny said. "They're just cops."

Cano grunted unhappily.

Sonny took out a pair of handcuffs.

Nick went to Maria, put his hand on her shoulder. "Are you all right?"

"*Claro*," she said. "I'm fine."

Miguel came forward to stand in front of him. "My sister is fine," he told him. "What now, huh? What the hell are you going to do now?"

It was a good question, and for a moment Nick tried to come up with a good answer. Then he thought better of it and told Miguel to shut up and stand there.

"Go on," Miguel said, "arrest these two. Then your government can cut them loose again, is that your plan?"

"What's the matter with you?" Nick said.

"Sister?" Cano shouted. "She's your sister? You told me she is your girlfriend, your lover. You lied to me, you liar."

"Liar, liar, pants on fire," Benny said.

Natalia had been right about this guy, this guy Benny had done up a whole lot of something; he was very stoned.

"I am the son of Diego Cienfuego!" Miguel shouted. "I am Miguel and she is my sister, Mariaclara Cienfuego. I am my father's living ghost and your fucking nightmare."

"Diego Cienfuego, I never heard of him," Cano said. "How about you, Benny, you ever hear of Diego Cienfuego?"

Benny smiled; he glanced at Miguel and Maria and smiled.

"The DEA," Cano said, "know something about what we are doing here tonight. You should know that we are covered."

"Captain Nick, you want to know what is the matter with me? He is the matter with me," Miguel said. "You hear him? He is working for the DEA; Cano is an agent of the government, your government. He was trying to trap us. Everywhere a trap, the whole world nothing but trap, trap, trap. What a joke, what a fucking joke."

Benny Matos pointed a big fat finger at Miguel. "Liar," he said. "Diego Cienfuego is dead."

"Jesus!" Nick heard himself shout. "Jesus, Jesus, Jesus!"

Sonny was cuffing Cano and Benny together; he said, "Not for nothing, buddy. But this went down real easy. Way too easy, if you know what I mean. It does look like a reverse, a sting. Maybe these guys really are working for somebody."

"*Seguro,*" Cano said. "We are working for the DEA, I told you that. I'm not lying. Me and Benny, we work for the U.S.A."

"It's not possible," Nick said. "My luck could never be that bad."

"Now what?" Miguel said. "What will you do now, Mr. Captain of Police Nick Manaris?"

"Give me a minute," Nick told him. "The hell's wrong with you anyway?"

"Damn it," Miguel said. "I don't know why I let Maria talk me into this."

Nick looked into the young man's face, a whole lot of Diego there. "So you wouldn't have to spend the next hundred years in jail. Maybe that's why, huh?"

Miguel said, "Bullshit, man."

"No," Nick said, "no bullshit. They got the death penalty in Florida, the electric chair. The electric chair is no bullshit, pal."

"Nick! Nick!" E.Z.'s voice shouted from upstairs. "Ey, Nick, I'm coming down! We're coming down!" Then the sound of footsteps on the stairs.

Cano was laughing silently, in the way of someone with a secret.

Chapter 46

The way E.Z. remembered it, as he testified in answer to Andre's questions in front of the Queens grand jury, he followed Agent Rios down the basement steps.

"And it was strange. You know in retrospect, when I look back on it, I couldn't believe that this guy Rios was a federal agent. I mean the man had gold teeth, and his English was terrible. Anyway, if I'd have believed him, I would have taken off the handcuffs. So that when the shooting started, the poor guy would have had a better chance to protect himself."

"Mr. Brochard," Andre said, "I want you to describe to the grand jury just what the scene was like in that basement at twenty-six hundred Corona Avenue. Tell the jury what you saw and what you did."

"I followed Rios down the stairs," E.Z. said, "and Natalia Punto, who was pointing a Browning at my back, a fifteen-shot automatic outfitted with a silencer, followed me. She was shouting, really screaming, 'I shoot this guy! I shoot him quick! Put your guns on the floor! Quick, more quick, I shoot this guy, I mean it! I don't care, I shoot him!' She kept on shouting like that, over and over. In my opinion it was her yelling and carrying on that started things."

"When Natalia Punto said she would shoot this guy, the guy she was referring to was you. Am I right?" Andre asked.

"Yes, that's right."

"Is that a guess? Or do you know that for sure?"

"It was my back she was poking with the gun. And every time she poked my back I jumped through my skin. I know those guns, those automatics; it doesn't take a whole lot to set one off."

"And, when you say Natalia Punto's yelling and screaming and carrying on started things, you mean the shooting?"

"Yes."

"We'll get to the shooting in a minute. For now, if you can, please tell the grand jury what you saw when you came down the basement stairs. What did you see?"

"There was a table in the center of the room. Everyone that had a gun put their gun on the table. First it was Detective McCabe, he put his gun on the table."

Andre said, "Excuse me, Mr. Brochard, when you say Detective McCabe, you mean Robert McCabe, known as Sonny McCabe?"

"Yes."

Andre said, "The foreman should take note; at the time of the incident Robert McCabe was no longer a New York City police officer. As a matter of fact, Robert McCabe had not been a police officer for close to ten years. So when the witness refers to Detective McCabe, what he means is former detective McCabe, or retired detective McCabe. Am I right, Mr. Brochard?"

"Yes."

"Go on, please go on," Andre said.

"Natalia Punto made us stand in a sort of semicircle around the table, Nick, Sonny, Agent Rios, and me. Rios kept saying he was an agent, a DEA undercover agent, and he had the credentials to prove it. He told Captain Manaris that he was working with Matos and Medina. That's when Mrs. Punto really began to shout and scream, and then everyone joined in."

Andre asked, "Do you remember, can you tell us, who said what?"

"It was mostly in Spanish," E.Z. said.

Andre said, "Captain Manaris spoke in English."

"That's true."

"What did he say?"

"He kept trying to get everyone to calm down. He was speaking to Mrs. Punto, trying to calm her down, when Rios, Agent Rios said, 'A stupid mistake. That's all this is, a mistake.' That did it. Benny Matos, who was sitting at the table alongside Medina, shouted, 'Oh fuck this.' He came up with a gun, I don't know where he got it from, but the next thing I know, Matos had this gun in his hand. There was a shot and everyone was jumping around, diving for cover, grabbing guns."

Andre said, "Benny Matos started the shooting?"

Sitting up straighter in the witness chair, E.Z. rubbed his eyes. The members of the grand jury waited.

"Benny Matos, he yelled, 'Liar, liar, pants on fire.' That thing kids say. It was so weird. And because it was so weird, what he said—liar, liar, pants on fire—I remember it. The next thing I knew he had a gun in one hand, his other hand was handcuffed to Medina. He fired the first shot, Matos did."

Andre said, "That's when everyone that could grabbed a gun and started shooting?"

"Yes. I can't stress enough how crazy things got. Shooting, shooting, everyone shooting."

"And you shot too? You picked up a gun and you began to shoot?"

"That's right."

"Was it your gun? Did you have a gun when you went down into the basement?"

"Me, no. I didn't have a gun. I know it's illegal to carry a gun in New York City."

"Okay, you grabbed a gun and shot it. Do you know how many times you fired?"

"No."

"Would it surprise you if I told you that Mr. Matos was shot sixteen times, Mr. Medina twelve times, and Agent Rios once."

"No, not at all. There was a whole lot of shooting. Reminded me of Vietnam. Down and dirty, we'd say, do it, we'd say, get it done, pop their asses."

Some members of the grand jury laughed. Others shook their heads.

E.Z. said, "Excuse me, I didn't mean to say 'asses.' I'm sorry."

Andre said, "That's a good analogy, the Vietnam parallel. Would you say Agent Rios was killed by friendly fire?"

"An accident, you could say a mistake, I suppose. But it was Matos that shot him. I think he intended to," E.Z. told him.

Andre said, "You saw Benny Matos shot Agent Rios?"

"Yes, I did."

Andre said, "One final question, regarding the hoods." Andre went to the evidence table, where guns were marked and labeled and sealed in plastic bags, and half-kilo packages of drugs. One bag contained several brown cloth hoods. He brought it to the witness chair and showed it to E.Z. "Have you ever seen these before?" Andre inquired.

"Yes," E.Z. told him. E.Z. looked at the faces of the grand jury and said, "I saw Captain Manaris remove those hoods from the pockets of Mr. Matos and Mr. Medina."

"Do you have any idea what these hoods were to be used for? Disregard that. Did anyone tell you what the hoods were to be used for?"

E.Z. said simply, "No. All I know is what I saw, and I saw those hoods removed from those two men's pockets. They were in their pockets, they were going to use them for something. I don't know what."

"And when you say those two men, you mean the men in these photos?" Andre handed E.Z. a pair of photographs. "Matos and Medina, is that right?"

"Yes," E.Z. said, "that's them, those two guys."

Andre stood in front of the podium as Sonny McCabe was sworn in. Two women grand jurors in the front row actually smiled at him as he took his seat.

Grand juries not only seem to be but are in fact rubber stamps for the prosecutor's office. And this witness, like E.Z. before him, was clearly a friend. Sonny was impressive, tall and well dressed, calm and orderly; he was the image of competence and honesty, a man to be believed. Andre's questions were direct and well presented.

Sonny described what he heard, what he saw, and what he did in the basement of Los Campos. He identified the sealed plastic package containing the brown hoods that were lifted from the bodies of Matos and Medina, and a larger package containing the guns the two had used. The same guns, it turned out, that were used to kill the Vasserman brothers and the two Miami men. "Matos shot first," he told them, "it was Benny Matos."

When Sonny finished and was preparing to leave the stand, Andre said, "I would like the record to reflect that Robert McCabe, when he was a member of the NYPD, was one of the most decorated police officers in the department's history.

Sonny left the grand jury room with the smiling faces and soft applause of the grand jurors warming his heart. Andre followed him to the door, went with him into the hallway, Sonny saying, "This case should pump some quarters into your political machine. It's time for you to go round the next bend in your career. What will it be? Congressman?"

"You're a tough guy," Andre said.

Sonny said, "Nick once told me that toughness without brains is like string without a kite, a hook without bait."

"A smart guy," Andre said.

"He certainly is. He taught me a whole lot."

"You know," Andre told him, "what Nick taught me was that outside the military, the police department is the greatest institution devised by man to spread the epidemic of male bonding."

"Is that a bad thing?"

"No," Andre said, "it's just not always good. I once told Nick that he had everything in the world except common sense. I was wrong."

"You're right, you were wrong."

"And you, have I been wrong about you?"

"I don't know. You tell me. I've always been just a cop doing my job. Maybe you didn't like the way I did it. Can't please everyone."

Chapter 47

Six months later Nick met E.Z. for breakfast at the Middlebridge Crossing. E.Z. suggested that Nick have Thanksgiving with him and Emma. They'd have a nice day, Emma'd ordered a twenty-pound turkey from Ryan's. Nick told him he'd let him know. E.Z. asked the obligatory questions about the job, about Andre, whether Sonny had called him from California, and he talked about the upcoming fishing season. He asked about Maria.

"I haven't heard a thing," Nick said.

"Strange."

"Not so strange. The grand jury brought back no true bill. She was free and clear, her brother and Natalia, they all wanted to put this behind them."

"Can you?"

"Me? Sure."

"I'm done giving you advice about women," E.Z. said.

"That's good. It looks like rain."

"Maybe snow. It'd be nice, a little snow. Got enough wood? 'Cause if you don't, Ken has some trees down on his place, hardwood, some oak."

"I could use a couple of cords."

"So why don't we do that? I'll oil the chain saw, sharpen the blade, then I'll pick you up later. We'll load the pickup."

"Sounds good."

"You okay?"

"Me? I'm fine."

After breakfast Nick drove E.Z. home. Then he went over to James-town, out to Beavertail. He parked the car and walked around to the front of the lighthouse. The sea was up, four- and five-foot breakers; there was the tide, the wind, and the currents. Rocks, ocean, lobster traps, and nothing more. The wind was cold, some snow in the air. He could feel it happening, the air growing gray and heavy around him.

He returned to his car, got in, and sat looking out through the wind-shield at the sea. The ocean, the great cleanser; everything, it seemed to him, would dissolve in the sea. Lately he had been traveling to these sad and unknown worlds inside his own head. He'd been making him-self nuts, and he knew that the business of feeling sorry for himself had to end. But that was how it had gone these last months. A few weeks back he thought he'd hit bottom and found that it was not possible to hit bottom. There was no bottom. No matter how bad things got, how miserable he felt, rest assured, he had told himself, you can always feel worse.

It remained to be seen.

C'mon, consider the human condition. Some things are possible, some things are not. This too shall pass and fade away; all things are survivable.

Some months ago Andre thought Nick had lost it, and right before Nick testified to the grand jury Andre tried to talk about it with him. He wanted to point out to Nick just how much danger he had put himself in. As if he had to be told. Nick was not surprised; he had been expecting something of the sort, he was ready, was amazed that it had taken Andre so long to come at him.

"You'd better think about what you're doing," Andre told him. "A man as smart as you, you should think twice, three times, before you do this. Letting your little head overrule your big head—it's just not you."

They were in the hallway, the grand jurors were on break. One or two smiled when they passed by.

"What are you trying to say?" Nick asked him.

"You're a friend," Andre said. "A real friend, a very good friend."

"I hope so, it has been twenty years."

Andre had looked around nervously. "There are people that would describe the shooting in Los Campos basement as an execution. My God, Nick, that many shots fired and the only people hit are Matos and Medina and their covering agent."

"Benny Matos shot the agent. He and Medina were shot by me, Brochard, and Sonny. That's a whole lot of bullets flying. As for me, I lost count."

"C'mon?"

"Excuse me?"

"Putting you in front of the grand jury, feeling as I do, is not exactly ethical you know. Some would say, there is a real legal question."

He was tense. Nick had never seen him so tense. "If you want," Andre told him, "I can adjourn this. You could think about it and come back tomorrow."

"What for?"

"I'm serious."

"So am I."

"Nick, listen, I know you think that you are in love with this woman, this Maria. But you're going way out there, way, way out, and that limb is mighty thin, pal."

"It doesn't matter. I'll be testifying to the facts, to what I know of those facts."

"It does matter—you'll be under oath. It's no joke."

They were quiet for a moment. Nick looked at him. Andre stared back.

"Maria," Nick told Andre, "was brought to that basement along with her brother by Matos and Medina. They intended to kill them, just as they had murdered the Vasserman brothers and the two guys in Miami. Don't ask me why. I don't pretend to know the mind of killers."

"But—?"

"Natalia Punto will testify that she followed them. She will swear under oath that what she did, she did because she truly believed Maria and Miguel's lives were in danger."

"But—?"

"You know what I'm talking about," Andre said. "I know fucking well you do."

"You're wrong, Andre," Nick had said. "I don't know what you're talking about."

"You just happened to be passing by, a coincidence, you and Sonny wanting to show your friend from Rhode Island the famous Los Campos basement? That's your story?"

"The door was open," Nick said. "We just went in."

"And I should believe this?" Andre said calmly. "Convince the grand jury that what you're saying is true?"

"If you'd been there, you would understand. Things happen. Of course if you don't believe me . . ."

"Can you live with it?"

"The truth? Of course. What is easier to live with than the truth? Isn't that what justice is all about, the search for truth and fairness? It's the American way."

Andre had held his sober expression steadily, then broke and he smiled. "Truth and justice?" Andre said.

"That's right," Nick told him. "Like the ocean, like the sea, you see it your way, I see it mine. What matters is that it's real and it's there for the both of us."

After a half hour or so Nick left the island of Jamestown and drove to the Old Post Road. He stopped in at the Aunt's Attic and bought a handpainted teapot and two cups. You amaze yourself, he thought, you are amazing. What did you expect? Marriage, kids? Amazing. Schmuck. Incredible, he thought, what love can do. Worse yet, the loss of love.

He drove down to Bonnet Shores and pulled in in front of the video store. It was snowing harder now; his thoughts were mostly on firewood, tea, and Hennessy, a video maybe, or a good book.

He was in the foreign film section, deciding if he really wanted to watch *La Strada* for the tenth time, when there was a voice at his shoulder.

"Ever try *Bang the Drum Slowly*? Someone once told me it's a little slow but a great American film."

"I hate when people say 'film,' it sounds so, so . . . I don't know, so New York. What's wrong with 'movie'?"

"It's a film," she told him.

"You look wonderful."

"Please don't hate me because I'm beautiful."

"You didn't say that. You didn't just say that."

She bit her lip and looked away. When she met his eyes again she was smiling. "You know," she said, "I found a place on the Costa del Sol, right in the foothills of the Sierra Bermeja and Sierra do Tolox. It is called San Pedro de Alcantara. It was almost heaven, it would have been perfect if you'd have been there."

He watched her for a moment, then shrugged. "It can't be better than Wickham in the spring, summer, and fall."

"Excuse me?"

"And my buddy E.Z. needs me, can't get along without me."

"The Costa del Sol, Nick. The Costa del Sol."

He put his arms around her and pulled her in close, held tight to her, nuzzled her ear, whispering, "Maybe in the winter, things kinda get slow here in the winter. In the winter we can go to Spain."

He rented *Bang the Drum Slowly*. She carried it in one hand and took his arm with the other.

"How'd you find me?" he asked her.

"Miguel drove and I looked. This is not exactly the big city."

"How is your brother?"

"Fine, fine, he sends you his regards."

Nick nodded. "And Natalia the beautiful, how is she?"

"She went to live in Barcelona, met a retired bullfighter. They're talking about opening a restaurant. It's a long story. We have many things to talk about, it's been six months, one week, two days, and nine hours. We'll need to spend some time catching up."

"It's going to snow," he said. "We have a movie, I have a new teapot, there's Hennessy at the cottage, and soon I'll have enough firewood to last till spring."

"I brought your T-shirt and my red heels. I'm rested and ready and packed to stay around awhile."

"See that," he said. "Perfect."